DETOUR NOWHERE

BY THOMAS LOONE

ISBN:-13: 979-8-6026-8100-0

FOR SOPHIE AND FOR MY FAMILY

CONTENTS

1   Chapter One   1

2   Chapter Two   25

3   Chapter Three   58

4   Chapter Four   93

5   Chapter Five   120

6   Chapter Six   151

7   Chapter Seven   175

8   Chapter Eight   198

9   Chapter Nine   222

10 Chapter Ten   246

11 Chapter Eleven   270

12 Chapter Twelve   287

13 Chapter Thirteen   325

CHAPTER ONE

Let us begin...

Just like the stern eyes of drunk, angry men, that meet across half downed pint glasses and torn-up coasters, the clouds that had hung in the skies that night had threatened to burst into violence at any moment. They had seemed to teeter on the precipice of pouring rain and purple lightning bolts, but instead, had chosen to remain silent and still. Somehow their inaction, had made them seem more frightening.

And just like the furious fist of a drunk, angry man, sucker-punching another, causing stars to revolve around the recipient's skull, tiny silver dots were speckled across that same night sky. Although they had seemed so bright, that at any moment they might've exploded into a supernova, much like those dreary, ominous clouds, they too had remained still. Watching, waiting, presiding over the country roads that had run below them. We find ourselves in danger of roaming into the territory of cliché, but we do indeed begin this story, on a cold, dark...*almost* stormy night.

In fact, it was a night of '*almosts*'. The steep, towering pine trees that lined either side of the twisting country road, had meant that you could *almost* see around the bend ahead and behind of you, but not quite. The whispering of the early spring winds, that had jostled branches in the dark, had meant that you could *almost* hear ghostly voices coming from the forest, but not quite. And Mr. Steve M. Brooks, who had been driving home tipsy along that lonely, secluded woodland road, had *almost* decided to leave *Joe's Bar* before he'd surpassed the legal limit, meaning that he'd have taken the main highway home, but not quite. Instead, in order to avoid the Middleborough police patrols, he'd taken, quite literally, the road less travelled. It had forced him straight through an as of yet unnamed forest, somewhere deep in the Northeast of the Yorkshire Moors, and straight towards the waiting stranger in the dark.

One could hardly blame Steve for his decision to stay at *Joe's* that night, or for turning to the bottle at all for that matter. At forty-eight, Steve's hair had all but vanished. With the front receding and the crown balding, it had seemed only a matter of time before what had been left of his grey strands had caught up with each other in the middle. He'd also resigned himself to the fact that he'd never have been able shift his middle-aged gut, which drooped over his belt, or that his yellowing teeth and wrinkled skin would ever again revert to their youthful glory. But these were all superficial things, cherries on the top of Steve's double choc-chip cake of misery. What had *really* sealed the deal and made him sell his soul to the Whiskey Church, had been his job.

Years of working for a merciless property law firm, where the name of the game had been sorting through contracts and answering telephone calls, under the reign of a manager half his age, had left Steve dead inside and wading through the boggy marshlands of depression. What had happened? Steve had often asked himself that very question, as he'd attended yet another soulless corporate meeting, or as he'd poured himself another wretched coffee from the machine in the hallway.

Steve was supposed to have been an Olympic swimmer, *that* had been his destiny, not suits and filing cabinets. From as early as his pre-teen years, everyone had always told him that he was going to be a rockstar, and that he'd paddle with the best of them. So convinced of this mantra were his parents, that they would often take him out of school, contrary to the heads permission, in order for him to take part in competitions. They'd lived and breathed their faith in their son, paying for private coaching, and making sure that he'd always had the latest and greatest in water sports gear, and so it hadn't taken long before young Steven had started to believe in it himself. His parent's belief had been well-placed. Steve cruised through the youth tournaments, jetting past the others with a slim lined precision and velocity that couldn't be rivalled. He'd dive-blast straight into first place nearly every time, leaving everybody else in his bubbly wake. The envy of all, the other swimmers would tremble in their teeny, tiny trunks when '*Shark Brooks*' strutted his stuff on the pool side. Steve had a gift, he'd made it look easy, but the truth is, to him, it was.

'He'll go all the way' tipped the words of his coaches.

The planets seemed aligned for Steve to live the life of an aquatic champion. With handsome brown eyes and a sculpted Atlas-esque physique, the internationals had almost been within his fingertips. Steve had had 'everything going for him', the commiserating trainers would later say.

So what had happened? What had happened to the gold medals and the chlorine soaked glory? What had happened to the locker-room girls? Life. Reality. A career destroying leg injury. Steve wasn't made for a normal job, those things were supposed to be for the other people, the boring people. For Steve, all he'd ever known was the water, the bobbing weights of the lane dividers, the re-runs of Michael Phelps races alone in his bedroom. His planetary purpose was clear from the very first day that he'd dipped his toe into the local Malton Swimming Baths. But one morning he'd woken up and found that the pools, with their stunning neon lights and sponsorship banners and their bright blue reflections, had all but dried up, leaving him sat alone at the bottom, the stands empty, and his youth and his glory left behind in a coffin of porcelain tiling.

And it had been this culmination of tragic events, coupled with his new, less than ideal career choice, which had acted as a matchmaker, a Cupid, between Steve and his new best friend.

'I can make you feel better.'
'I can wash the pain away.'

...the drink would say. And wash it away it did, along with whatever hope or semblance of himself that Steve had had left.
Just like the water had blurred the screen of his goggles after he'd been

submerged, the whiskey had smudged Steve's vision as he'd driven his Mustang that night. But it had been a long time since he'd stepped foot between the four stone corners of a proper pool, and to save himself from swerving off-road and into a ditch had required every ounce of his concentration. He'd been lucky so far, no other cars had passed his way. Very few took the woodland road at all anymore. But it would only take one. One sighting. One crash. One breathalyzer test, and what had been left of his life would've come crashing down around him. He may have hated his career choice, but it was all he'd had left, that, and his drink. And so for Steve, it was too, an *almost* night. He drove his Mustang on the left-hand side of that lonesome country road, upon a tightrope, balancing between destruction and deliverance.

'Are you home soon xxx?'

The text had read on his *iPhone* screen, which was held into place on his dashboard for easy access to *Google Maps*. The text came courtesy of his wife, his boring, plain, prudish wife. Well, she could go to hell for all he cared. And while she was at it, she could take his annoying kids along with her, and his receding, balding hair, and his podgy belly, and his wrinkling eyes, and his disappointed Father, and that fucking Law firm, and the fucking biker that crashed into his leg, and-

Steve re-focussed. His mind was wandering. And a wandering mind wasn't what he'd needed that night. In his loathing, the Mustang had veered ever so slightly onto the other side of the roads yellow lines. Panicked, Steve glanced furiously into his wing mirror, but thankfully hadn't been greeted by any headlights, nor any blue or red ones. He was safe. For now. He carefully readjusted the wheel like a compass axis so that he was back on course, took a deep breath, and then continued on into the darkness.

The road ahead was pitch black. Without the Mustangs full beam headlights, driving through the night would've been impossible for Steve. Even cranked up to their maximum wattage, vision had been limited to strictly the immediate vicinity. Whatever had lay ahead of the avenue of light cast by the lamps, whoever had lay ahead, Steve wouldn't have been able to see. But they'd have seen him.

The crowded pine trees stood so closely and tightly next to each other, that no moonlight stood a chance of penetrating their fortified bulk. Only via the night sky overhead could it have found its way onto the road. But if one were to have looked upwards they'd have seen that the jagged edges of the pine leaves, bunched together on either side of the road, had looked not unlike the shutting jaw of some gigantic, nightmarish monster. The black teeth seemed to slowly close the night sky away, leaving the on-looker trapped in the darkness of its belly, forever. Steve found the trees presence unsettling, like a cult line-up of faceless wooden men, with sharp, splintered, meshing branch arms. A sleeping army, waiting to be awoken by a drifting traveller. There was no escaping the road. Not now.

It wasn't long before Steve noticed something up ahead, waiting, on the right side of the road. It was the dim figure of a man, stood just in front of the pine tree's as if he'd emerged from inside of the forest. He was holding his thumb out in the air. Very few amongst us would be unaffected by the approaching of two distant headlights in the pitch black; the creeping ghostly light of them, as they peak around the bend, like the prelude of fire before the coming of the Four Horsemen's hooves. But not this man. No. In fact, those headlights were exactly what he'd been waiting for. One could say, that he'd been waiting for them, for a very, very long time.

Once the mysterious stranger had seen the artificial sunrise of Steve's headlights over the ridge, and once Steve had locked his eyes upon the poised thumb and the jet-black silhouette of the stranger, panic began to set in for the driver. Just like his Mustangs headlights, Steve's inebriated defects had become amplified to the maximum upon seeing the unexpected figure. The incoherence of his jumbled thoughts, the blurriness of his vision, the salty sweat on his temples from where his hair had once grown, all of them succumb to a free-falling frenzy of alarm.

'Shit shit shit shit fucking shit fuck shit' Steve repeated to himself, clinging to the words like some incantation that might've brought him absolution. It didn't.

The obvious answer was to keep on driving, to maintain his current speed of 53mph and to not look back until he'd pulled up onto his chalk-stoned drive in Pickering. But what if he'd been swerving? He'd felt as though he'd been driving straight, but God knows whether that had been the truth or not. For all he'd known, the Whisky, the worst of all the back-seat drivers, might've had him zigging and zagging across the lane dividers ever since he'd left *Joe's*. What if the passer-by could see that?

What if he'd had a phone? Let's say, for one hypothetical moment, that Steve were to have whizzed on by and were to have continued along that gloomy road until he'd his reached home. Perhaps he'd have been okay for a mile or two, but Steve couldn't quite shake the brain-gnawing feeling that after that he'd have been surrounded by a haze of flashing blue and red lights, thanks to a tip-off from a local do-gooder who'd been looking to save innocent lives. Next stop a breathalyser. And once again, though Steve had despised his job, he'd known enough about the UK's legal system to have known that the courts were never kind to drink drivers, a strict liability crime. *Goodbye Job. Goodbye House. Goodbye family. Goodbye what's left of your pathetic life Shark Brooks.*

That settled it. Steve carefully slowed down the Mustang. The stranger lowered his thumb, and smiled. The vehicle rolled gently and then came to a standstill alongside him, the engine still running. Steve wound down his window, and thanks to the headlights, could now get a better look at the man. But there wasn't much to see. A dark, olive green trucker cap had been pulled down low over the guy's face, shielding his eyes and features. A huge grey and black beard, mainly grey, had done the rest of the disguising. It was wild and unkempt, just like the straggled hair that had ruffled its way under the edges of his hat, and at the back. He wasn't a young chap that was for sure, if Steven had hazarded a guess, he'd have tried for late 50's. But this geeza weren't no age old pensioner, in fact, as he'd slowly approached the car with his cap drawn down, Steven had felt the hairs on his neck begin stand on end, and had wondered whether or not he might've been better off with the Middlesbrough cops.

'Good evening' said an anxious Steve through the open window. The night air was cold and prickly.

'Is it?' replied the man. 'Because my idea of a good night isn't waiting in the cold on the side of a dark road'. He laughed, but it wasn't the comforting northern chuckle that never fails to put even the most restless of minds at ease. Steve found it unnerving.

'Are you here to save me?' the stranger continued slowly. His voice was deep, low and gravelly, like each phrase that he mumbled was a cluster of falling stones in a quarry, paving the way for a boulder.

'Looks like it. Where you headed?'

The man looked around at the desolate country road.

'Anywhere but here would be good.' He grinned. Like his laugh, it wasn't warm nor comforting.

'Well I'm heading as far as Pickering if that suits ya? We're only about ten miles out. I'm sorry I can't go much further than that. The wife's got tea on' Steve proposed, scared of the response.

'The old ball and chain. Gotcha. And like I said...anywhere but here. I'd say Pickering falls under that category. As nice as this forest is...' replied the stranger, kicking a mound of dirt that he'd been standing on with his left foot and laughing behind a closed mouth. It was at this point that the figure in the dark had lifted the rim of his cap, revealing a pair of weathered, bright blue eyes. They were piercing and striking, not so much 'Cornish Ocean Blue', but more a pair of frozen-over lakes, with secrets and bodies hidden beneath their icy surfaces.

'So, I'm thinking I'll take you up on that offer my friend' he said, his eyes never leaving Steve's. Steve paused and then gazed at the man, fingers locked, tightly wound around the black rubber of the steering wheel.

'Are you just gonna sit there? Or are you gonna' give an old man a ride? I'm freezing out here' joked the shadowy loner, jolting Steve.

'Oh. It's just been a long day. I'm sorry, I didn't catch your name?'

The man seemed thrown by the question. He hesitated a moment, and a flicker of panic replaced the icy-coolness of his deep, arctic eyes. But it was only for a moment, before he rediscovered his composure and then said;

'That's because I didn't give you it. The names Jim' he said, reaching through the open window of the Mustang for a shake. His hands were huge and his knuckles were hairy like a bears paws, there was dirt underneath his fingernails. He didn't look like a Jim. Steve pried free his fingers from the wheel, like an anaconda uncoiling itself after strangling a rodent to death, and then shook Jim's hand back. His grip had been tight and hard.

'Steve.'

'I've been hiking over the Moors all evenin'. Not one of my smartest ideas I know. Not at this time of year anyway. Before I knew it the sun had set and I hadn't the foggiest where I was. I've been waiting here for the better half of two hours hoping that someone like yourself would show up. My bloody phones only gone and died too, hasn't it. People don't drive down this way much, do they? The one or two that did just let me be. I guess people just want to get back home to their cosy beds and their warm dinners much more than they want to help a poor old man in distress, huh? Thank God a Good Samaritan like yourself crossed my path or I could've been here until mornin'' explained Jim, cold clouds of breath leaving his mouth, which had been barely visible through his bushy, sea-salt beard.

'Not exactly dressed for moor hiking, are ya?' asked Steve, somewhere between banter and accusation. In Jeans, a t-shirt, flat black trainers and a thin grey fleece, Jim had indeed hardly seemed prepared for the harsh expanse that was the North Yorkshire Moors during April showers season.

Jim smiled at this. It was a crooked smile, revealing a row of twisted, mottled smoker's teeth. It resembled the false grimace of a Halloween pumpkin. Through his hollowed eyes and mouth you could see into the unending pit of his soul.

'Well I never said I was a good hiker...
Now are you gonna let me in that warm looking Mustang of yours? Or should I settle myself in for the long haul?'

Steve had no longer cared whether or not Jim had thought he was drunk, the entire encounter had had a rather sobering effect on him. Instead, all he could think about was what might happen if he were to say no. For no matter how many jokes Jim made, or how many smiles he'd thrown Steve's way, Steve couldn't help but feel as though he'd been one wrong move away from having his throat cut wide open. With this in mind, our driver reluctantly nodded. Like most middle-aged Yorkshire men, he was a man of few words, but on this occasion his lack of conversation had stemmed not from a grumpy stubbornness, but from a deeply rooted fear, a fear for his life.

'I thought that'd be your answer' replied a pleased Jim, walking around the back of the boot to climb in next to Steve. The road was silent and empty. The rumble of the car's engine was the only sound that could be heard for miles around, like the buzz of an abandoned chainsaw.

Steve watched back over his shoulder, across the cream leather seats, as Jim circled the rust bucket Mustang (*a mid-life crisis gift he had given to himself*). He'd stared as the man had passed the rear windows, and then the backseat ones, before finally he'd arrived at the passenger side. He'd walked with a very prominent limp. Jim swung open the door with a confidence that Steve had found disturbing, it was as though it had been *his* car and Steve had been the guest. As Jim opened the side-door the cars overhead bulb automatically turned on. It was dim and yellow and hadn't cast much light, but it had been enough for Steve to get a better look at his new friend. This time, he'd noticed details that had escaped him on first instance. For one, Jim was big, real big, and even through his grey fleece Steve could still see huge laterals and biceps bulging beneath the sheep wool. He mentally added two broken legs to the 'cut throat' shopping list that he'd predicted earlier. He gulped. Even in his swimming hay-day Steve had never been *that* big, he'd always fallen into the 'slim and toned' bracket.

He cleared old cigarette packets and fast-food wrappers from off the seat.

'Mmmm now that's more like it' sighed Jim as he sunk himself into the leather passenger chair. He bore resemblance to a boxer climbing into a hot-tub after a fight, to soothe his wounds and bruises. He closed his eyes and rubbed his huge, muscular back into the chair before sitting still, as if all of his bones had fallen into alignment and had settled into their rightful sockets. Steve had thought that the man looked not just tired, but world weary, like he'd crossed the breadth of the country, battling earth, wind and fire and destroying anyone who'd gotten in his way, all to get that chair, on that night, in that car, on that lonely country road on the Yorkshire Moors.

'What happened to your leg?' braved Steve.

'Huh?'

'Your leg. I saw you had a limp.'

Jim laughed, 'Oh, this? Let's just say one of those huge rocks out on the Moors and I had a slight disagreement. Just a sprain from fallin', nothing to fret about dear Steven. I may be old but I ain't over the hill just yet. I'll suffer through. Now are we gonna hit the road or what?'

Jim hoisted the injured ankle in question, along with his non-injured one, onto the glove compartment in front of him. Steve's eyes lingered for a moment. Usually he'd have lost his rag over anyone who'd have been rude enough to put their scruffy, muddy shoes all over his baby, but not him. As far as Steve was concerned, Jim could do whatever the fuck he wanted to. If he'd have lit a cigarette and started singing Motown show tunes right there and then, Steve would've granted him a free-pass. He followed his instructions like a good little boy and released the clutch, took the gear out of neutral and then rolled back onto the left-side of the road. He'd cautiously checked over his left shoulder before he'd set off, although it had been a pointless exercise, no one was coming.

Steve re-sealed the driver's window, the only windshield between him and the cold night air, which had hushed and silently blown like the dying breath of a poor young woman. On and on went the road, Steve had felt as though it would never end. And as he drove that sunless drive, and had wondered whether or not he'd ever see his wife and kids again, Jim spoke.

'Ain't it crazy Steve?'

'What now?'

'This. You, me, here in this rickety old car of yours. It's crazy how out here in the middle of nowhere, probably the only two people within a forty mile radius, we just happened to meet. I'd say those are some pretty darn insane odds, wouldn't you?' Jim leant his elbow onto the sideboard as he spoke.

'Well, you *were* standing on the edge of a main road' replied Steve dryly, counting down the miles left to go in his head.

'Yeah but c'mon. You and I both know hardly anyone comes down this way. Hardly anyone. Nope, there was some serious fate-work at hand here if you ask me. It's like we were meant to meet Steve', Jim smiled a sickly smile. His gritty voice showed no signs of smoothing over, even in the textures of his phrases that had been whispered it was rough and gravelly, a word, that come to think of it, stands remarkably close to 'grave'.

'I guess so' staggered Steven, he was getting scared now. Oh, he'd been scared before, but sitting no more than one foot from the guy, and hearing him talk in the way that he did, it had given him a leg-up into a whole new league of fear.

'Wanna know a secret Steven?' Jim leant in close. 'Even if you hadn't come. Even if I'd been left alone all night on that lonesome, spooky road out in the arse-end of nowhere, I wouldn't have been scared. That's right. The whole time I was waiting there in the dark, I weren't scared of nothing. You see Steve, to me, these Moors are home. And I know there's nothing to be afraid of. Maybe for some folks. But not for me.'

Steve would rather have ditched his car and his keys under an overpass and have taken his chances out on the Moors if it had been a choice between that and his current circumstances. Why, oh why hadn't he just taken the main road home? He promised never to drink again, never to set foot in *Joe's* nor to grace his throat with whiskey for as long as he'd lived, if only Jim would leave.

'You must be a walking man too? Am I right? Living in Pickering you've got the Moors right on ya doorstep.' Steve prayed for lights, for houses, for other cars, heck, he even prayed for the Middlesbrough police. Now '*Shark Brooks*' was the prey.

'Actually I ain't much one for walkin.''

'What?! Ain't much one for walkin'? Out here? Steve. Oh Steve, I must say I am disappointed. Fancy that, a man like you, lucky enough to have all this beautiful land around him. Well I'd say that's a real shame, a real crying shame Steve. These Moors are wasted on you my friend'. Jim toyed with him. After he finished speaking, he placed his gigantic bear hand around the back of Steve's headrest and then leant in closer. Steve could smell the wet and the soil of the earth on Jim's clothes, like he'd climbed straight out of the ground, a solitary hand bursting out of the countryside, and then the rest of his body, dragging itself out slowly.

'I truly am shocked by that response Steve I must say. Why, this is the heart of Gods own country. And I believe, walking through it is one of the single-greatest gifts we've got in this life'. Jim became more and more animated as he spoke, gesturing with his free hand and gripping the back of Steve's head-rest tighter and tighter with the other. Steve could feel the tips of Jim's fingers touching the edges of his skull.

'I know, I get it I just-'

'No Steve. I don't think you do "get it" quite frankly. To be honest with you, I really don't think you do. Then again, who does these days? No one appreciates the great outdoors anymore.'

The road continued, still.

'You wanna know why I like it out here so much Steven? Do ya? It ain't gonna be the answer you expect either. I ain't gonna tell you it's the miles of green, or the birds singin', or any of that bullshit. No....

...it's the quiet. That's right, the silence. Ain't nobody out in these hills for miles. And it's just the way I like it. Away from all the noise. I often find myself thinking on my walks, do you ever do that Steven? Get lost thinking? In your thoughts like? Coz I sure do. Sometimes I think, when I'm out there, alone on the Moors in the mist with the stones, I think "if someone were to kill me right now, to smack me over the head with a great big axe and leave me for dead, well, nobody would even know. I'd bleed out alone in these hills on the cold, hard grass and then that would be that"'.

Steve had taken his eyes off the road by now. He had been more terrified of dying by the hands of his passenger, if he were to have broken the gaze of his piercing blue eyes, than he had been of colliding into the solid bark of a pine tree.

Jim let go of Steve's headrest, sat back in his chair, and then took a deep breath.

'To be honest with you though Steve, I feel a bit of a phoney. Here I've been, jabbering on about these Moors and about how much I love them like I'm some PhD holdin' botanist. But to tell the truth, I ain't walked on these hills in a long time...a very, very long time.'

He took a long pause before he spoke again.

'But as of tonight I'm going to change that.'

He looked at Steve, and Steve looked back, and the bright blue of Jim's eyes had seemed magnified to what some might've called, an unnatural level. But it wasn't by pure chance that Jim's eyes had lit up. Like a stain-glass window of the Virgin Mary in an old cathedral catching the sunlight, the retina of Jim's Iris had reflected a stronger force. And that force, had been the spiralling blue of a police car lamp just ahead. The Mustang slowed to a halt.

Steve and Jim found themselves at the back of a seven car-long queue, at the front of which were two parked police vehicles, one on either side of the road. Four officers, two per car, had been gathered around the mouth of the queue. Wearing high-visibility jackets, radios and hats, one had remained stood at the foot of the traffic, whilst the other three had been collected around the pedestrian's car at the front. One officer questioned the driver, crouched down, through their open window, whilst the other two officers had appeared to be searching the car itself, the boot, and the backseats. They were looking for something, or someone. Once the task-force were satisfied that whatever it was that they had been searching for hadn't been in the vehicle, then they'd sent it on its way along the road, and then the officer assigned to the traffic control duty had beckoned the next car to be recon'd.

The red and blue lights painted the figures of the pine trees, the former smearing them like fresh blood and the latter giving them the frosty UV glare of an evidence lab. The abundance of torches and glowing headlights had meant that the once terrifying portrait of the lonely, dark road was now flooded with an artificial luminescence. But for the passengers of the 1970's Mustang, a new fear had taken hold.

The panic that had set into Jim's eyes when Steve had asked him for his name had returned, but this time it was here to stay. And Steven, who only minutes before had prayed for the presence of police to rescue him from the clutches of his villainous guest, had now wished that he could've taken all it back, and while he was at it, the cruel comments that he'd thought up about his wife and kids. He just wanted to hold them and to never let go. All his agonising frets had suddenly returned with a vengeance, once he was confronted with the reality of a breathalyser test. These officers wouldn't have been rookies, they'd have been able to spot a drunk a mile off, they'd have seen straight through Steve with his slurred speech and his dizzy eyes. Hell, the smell of whisky on his breath alone would've been enough to give the game away. Both men were in trouble, the driver, for the crime of drink-driving, the passenger, for something far, far worse.

'What's goin' on here then?' asked a rhetorical Steve, trying and failing miserably to keep his cool.

Jim ignored him, he was busy preoccupied with the contents of his fleece's left-hand pocket. He'd hoped that he hadn't had to use the thing, but that had been wishful thinking. He supposed that he had been lucky to have gotten as far as he had without having to stab someone. But he'd do it, if these police had thought for one second that they were taking him back, he wouldn't have hesitated in doing whatever he'd had to in order to reach where it was that he was going. Nothing would get in his way, not the police, and certainly not this gutless Steve fella. Now only five cars stood between them and the security checkpoint, they had to think fast.

'What do you think they're looking for?' asked Steve, again, a waste of breath. Jim didn't reply, instead, he continued to grip the stone handle of the six-inched knife that he'd been keeping in his pocket. It was poorly made, but it would've had no trouble in piercing the flesh of one of the police officers. Jim, without Steve noticing, had already discretely undone his seatbelt, he'd performed the action with the ease of detective lifting up a yellow roll of tape cordoning off a crime scene.

But for the whole time that Jim had been preparing himself to fight, Steve had been preparing himself for flight. With four cars now lying between him and his inevitable breathalyser test, the police having just sent a nuclear family of four and their German shepherd on their merry way back home to Malton, Steve had managed sweat out a plan of action. Luckily for him, no other cars had parked up behind the rear of his Mustang and had joined the queue of waiting, and so the road had been clear for a getaway. The police officers being busy preoccupied with the searching of a large Range Rover, and the traffic controller radioing HQ, had meant that Steve had had the perfect window of opportunity that he'd needed. The prospect of it burning to ash before his very eyes had meant that he'd suddenly found himself discovering a new-found appreciation for his existence, and it was this appreciation that had inspired the swift left turn of his steering wheel and the reverse of his gear stick, that would mean saving both men from prison.

'What are ya doing?' asked a dumbfounded Jim, caught somewhere between shock and relief. He hadn't thought that old Stevey boy had had it in him.

'I'm not waiting here, whatever they want it'll take ages. I'm tired' replied Steve defiantly. He felt a buzz in his blood and an adrenaline that he hadn't experienced for years, it had reminded him of the youthful electricity and the excitement of his swimming days.

Without any of the cops taking notice, Steve reversed into a small grassy alcove on the road, spun the wheel, and then began driving down a smaller forked passage, one equally murky and gothic, but welcomed in comparison to the waiting patrol. The two men left the checkpoint in the dust, the white and the blue of Her Majesty's cars washed away in a screen of exhaust smoke and petrol fumes. Gone was the twisted turnpike, where the toll for crossing would've been the invaluable price of the two men's freedom. The Yorkshire lads had escaped.

Back on the road again, both men sighed a private sigh of relief to have evaded the boys in blue, unbeknownst to the other that each had had their own very different reasons for wanting to avoid them. Jim relinquished his grasp on the knife in his pocket. It was to remain silver and clean of crimson then, for now. Away from the radiating brightness of the blockades lamps, the path ahead descended once again into the familiar shadowiness of the Moors, but Steve had been too pumped on his body's natural caffeine's to notice nor to care. He'd almost made it home.

'Woooooohoooo' yelled Jim. Even in his head-voice he managed to sound butch. Both men laughed hysterically at their getaway, as the passenger patted Steve on the shoulder. It was considerably smaller than his own.

'It'll add a few extra miles onto our journey, you don't mind do you?'

'Steve, right now I'm just enjoying the ride buddy....' replied Jim cornily. Then, he reached over to the vintage built-in car radio and fiddled with the dial until he came across something that tickled his ear drums.

'You like "*The Boss?*"' asked an enthusiastic Steve, in response to Jim's choice of channel. Bruce sang about being *born to run* over country guitar chords as the wheels of the Mustang spun under the open road, arguably the way that *Springsteen* was *meant* to be heard.

'Does a bear shit in the woods?' winked Jim, interlocking his hands behind his head as if falling asleep in a hammock. His stocky feet were perched up on the dashboard and his huge tortoiseshell back was massaged into the leather chair.

Steve smiled, and then turned his eyes back towards the road, feeling at ease for the very first time that night since he'd left behind the frothy beer heads and warm log fire of *Joe's Bar*. What a fool he'd been. Jim wasn't a murderer, he wasn't a deadly serial killer who was going chop him up into tiny pieces and bury his dismembered limbs beneath the Moors. He was just a kooky old man with a stubborn patriotism for his county. Steve had let his sombre surroundings get the better of him. The towering black pine trees, the deafening screaming silence of the lonely winding road, the blood red drench of his tail lights. Steve had let all of those horror movie tropes construct his reality for him, so that when he'd finally stumbled upon the stranger on the road, his foolish mind had already made itself up that the man *must've* been a harbinger of harm. Boy, did Steve feel silly now.

'Baby I was born to run.'

He sang under his breath, just low enough for himself to keep in tune. Like most middle-aged Yorkshire-men, he wasn't one for singing, but what the heck, the ridiculousness of the occasion had called for a little reckless abandon. Soon he'd be warm in bed, holding his wife close to his hairy chest, and the events of the night would've been nothing more than a distant dream. He'd drop weird old Jim off on a cobbled Pickering street corner and then all would be well again.

But let us not forget, that this was not a night of *'all being well agains'*, this was a night of *'almosts'*. And if Steven really had believed that the bulky, mysterious, grey bearded old man that had been sat next to him, with his hypnotic sapphire eyes, had been nothing more than just that, then he had been sorely, sorely mistaken.

Jim unwound the window next to him, impervious to the rush of cold blustery wind, and inhaled the robust scent of the Moors around him. The scent of hundreds of miles worth of rainy grassland, wet oily bark, sludgy moss and limestone all snorted up into his lungs like a line of bright white cocaine. He was home again.

'It's going to be one hell of a night Steven....' he smiled.

'....one hell of a night', he laughed as the car vanished into the black. Beady-eyed crows watched it disappear from above, suspended on swaying branches, like silent observers.

CHAPTER TWO

The version of the sea that he saw in his dream wasn't the bright-blue holiday catalogue iteration, Ted never liked that one. No, the picture of the ocean that he saw was the cast iron sheet that roared and folded in on itself, its waves crashing and splashing against the jagged cliff rocks. They were salty splashes that would chill you to the bone if they were to touch your skin, like Mother Nature's warning to those mulling over swimming in her raucous riptides.

It was the freezing cold ocean, the cruel ocean, the untamable, wild, '*force of nature*' ocean that had the power to both captivate with its beauty, and to violently sink with its steely grip. It was exactly the kind of North Sea that would make holiday go-ers and sun seekers return to their cottages, but it was exactly the kind of North Sea that coaxed Ted out. He loved having the beach to himself. Seagulls cawed over the young boy's head. Some rotated in the sky above, whilst others perched on shallow seabed rocks that jutted just above the surface. Both sets kept an eager eye on the look-out for fish, ready to scoop up wiggling gills but using slightly differing tactical positions. *Airborne vs Close-Range*. They were Teds friends, they'd grown accustom to him, and he could remember many a time that he'd sat by the pier eating chips, and the birds, notorious for scavenging, had left him and his battered potatoes alone. The air smelt of cod. Greeny-black seaweed with lumpy leaves littered the sandy walkway where the boy sat, soft footprints following him from where he'd came.

Ted was sat on a small limestone ramp that dove diagonally down onto the shore, it allowed easy access to the beach when the tide was out, but in his dream, it had been in in for the morning. His little boy shorts were rolled up at their hems and his bare-feet were muddied with powdery brown sand, his nails were wetted by the edges of the sea's closest wave. It lapped at the base of the ramp, beginning as a thunderous, curled wall of girth from a distance, but diminishing in size and power as it approached, until it was reduced to nothing more than a thin layer of watery foam at Ted's tiny toes. A small, empty, wooden row-boat, tied to a pier-pole, bobbed up and down on the waterfront. The weather was flat and cold and dull, and the sea seemed to mimic the unfeeling setting.

The young lad, no older than ten years old, suddenly felt in his minds periphery that he was no longer alone. He turned to see a tall figure descending the stairs by the quaint seaside houses, to meet him at the water's edge. The dream refused to allow Ted the ability to make out the strangers face, his mind withholding his features from him. It only granted him the ability to see him from the neck downwards. He could see his navy blue heritage fisherman's jumper, stitched with wool into a criss-cross pattern that was unique to the Bay. He could see his thick workman's trousers and black wellington boots, perfect for staying dry whilst fishing out on the sea trawlers. But perhaps most importantly, when the man approached and placed his hairy, aged hand on the young boys shoulder, he could see the small, black ink of an anchor tattoo on the man's right wrist. It was this that had told Ted in an instant who it had been, without having the need to see his face.

'Hello Ted'.

Ted woke up. Now aged 21.

A moment passed as Ted recounted where he was. The Megabus. That's right, he was on the 1:45am bus from Birmingham to Middleborough. It had passed through Manchester, Sheffield, Leeds, and Newcastle, a whistle-top tour of the North, and now the final leg of its journey would take it to Middleborough, due to arrive at approximately 10:55pm.

He'd been on the bus for a total of seven hours, but Ted didn't mind. As long as he was moving, in between places, and not settled for too long, Ted could feel as though he'd had a purpose. The knowledge of having a destination to reach, something to aim for, it gave him meaning, which was more than he could say that he'd had before he'd decided to get aboard. The night before, Ted had categorically concluded that enough had been enough. He was tired of being stuck, and that had been the catalyst by which his brain had concocted the idea of buying the last-minute bus ticket. He'd quietly packed a bag and disappeared without anybody noticing, and now he was five hundred miles away from his troubles, and counting. Nothing could've been worse than where he came from, and each minute that went by, each signpost that the bus passed, acted as a reassuring reminder to him that an extra measurement of distance had been added to the space between him and....there.

Hotel rooms. He liked those too, they weren't permanent nor fixed. They were in-between places as well, drop off points on the way to something greater, something better than the present. As far as Ted was concerned, staying in one place for too long, for any given time, could never have been a good thing. Speaking of Hotels, he hadn't yet booked one. By the time he'd arrived in Middleborough that night it would've been far too late to catch public transport to where he'd needed to go, a little shy over an hour from the city, and so he'd needed to find somewhere to rest his head for the night. He was sure that with the little money he'd had left that he'd have been able to secure a room above a pub, a tavern, or in a cheap hotel maybe. As long *they* hadn't cancelled his VISA card yet.

The Megabus lights were dimmed to a dark, sci-if, laser blue so that the passengers could sleep. Ted had been lucky. Whenever he'd boarded before, the bus had been packed to the rafters with crying babies and complaining teens, and he'd almost always been assured a seat next to an overweight, or smelly, or phone-talking, or just plain weird companion. However, that day had been different. Not only had Ted managed to secure a seat alone, having the full spread of the chair next to him to settle in for the journey and to make a cozy nest for himself, complete with snacks. But he'd also managed to nab the golden spot, the seat right next to the toilet at the front. Everybody knew that that was the seat with the most leg-room, which meant that Ted really did have the space to kick back, stretch his legs and to avoid the notorious muscle cramping that the transport was ill-renowned for. It made the stench of the cubicle piss somewhat bearable.

He couldn't see much outside of the bus window on account of the late hour, but he could make out a few things. The luminous orange jackets of repairmen stood around open-hood cars that had broken down along the sides of the highway. Wrapped bales of circular hay-stacks, covered to protect farmers crops from the coming rain storms. The still outlines of docile sheep, long-maned horses and some cows, either staring out into space, sleeping or munching on grass. Through the windows on the other side of the aisle, those that weren't blocked by weary passenger heads, Ted could see floating headlights. Like lost souls, or the ghosts of crash victims, they'd endlessly search the motorway for bodies to reunite with, without any luck. High reaching wind turbines silently spun their propellers, the tips of their blades seemed to scrape the underbelly of the black clouds that hung over them, but made no damage.

It was then that Ted had noticed that he'd had another missed call on his phone, it was from her. He put his ear to the speaker.

'Hey Teddy, it's me...again....
Look, I wish you'd just call me. It doesn't have to be long, just something, anything to let me know that you're alright. I'm worried sick here. I'm going out of my mind. I haven't called the police yet but if you don't get back to me by the morning I'll have to. I'm not angry I promise, just please, I'm begging you to call me. God, I love you so much. Please be okay' the message ended there.

It broke Ted's heart to hear his mother in so much pain, to hear her holding back tears. It broke his heart in exactly the same way that it had broken when he'd listened to the previous voice mail, and the five preceding ones before that, each one becoming increasingly more anxiety riddled and worrisome. Those seven rips in his heart were adding up, and he didn't know how much more his little ticker could take. But no, he knew that he'd done the right thing by leaving, there was nothing left for him there anymore. His mother's sentimentality hurt like hell, but there was no way he was going back, not ever. He put the phone down and sought to solder the wounds in his feelings with sugar and fat.

He rummaged through his brown leather backpack on the free seat beside him for sustenance but came back with nought. He was out of food and drink, and his sea faring-dreams had made him hungry. Just then though, like the voice of his guardian angel, with the virtuoso timing of an escape-route excuse on a bad date, the drivers Geordie voice spoke over the PA.

'Okay guys so...we're running pretty ahead of schedule to Middleborough. And when I say "pretty ahead", I mean fifty minutes ahead. And since there's no room for me at the station to park in just yet, I figured now would be a great to time to make a pit stop for food. So feel free to grab any drinks or snacks because we'll be pulling up outside any minute. I will inform you however, that we will only be staying here for twenty-five minutes. So please ensure you're back and seated on the bus by then, or we may leave without you. Thank you very much'.

The static-filled voice had awoken many a passenger, much to their annoyance, but for Ted his prayers had been answered. He'd grab a snack and a drink and stretch his legs. The golden spot was good n' all for space, but nothing could've compared to taking his feet for a spin in the great outdoors. The bus took a left turn, the first divergence it had steered in for over two hours, having been travelling in a straight line along the motorway since Leeds. It approached the lamps of the rest-stop. The lights guided the mammoth vehicle towards it, like a lighthouse warding a shipping vessel to shore in the dead of night. It pulled into the carpark of the service station, which was moderately full of traveler's cars, either going to or leaving their destinations, and then ground to a halt.

The interior lamps of the bus switched back on with a cruel suddenness. It was a rude awakening for all of the sleeping. The light exposed all of their crusty eyes and chin dribbles, a pretty sight it was not. Here, Ted also took note of the abundance of irritating vegan-hipsters that the coach had been carrying.

'Leeds', he thought to himself. 'They'd definitely gotten on at Leeds'.

After a bus-wide stretch and groan had been shared, people began to pull down bags and luggage from the overhead storage areas.

Ted wisely waited as the passengers all eagerly scrambled to get out through the open doors, pushing and shoving their way to the front of the line. Once the path was clear, he vaulted down the stairs beside the foul smelling toilet and into the liberation of the outside. Boy, did it feel good after being cooped up inside of that sweat box for most of the day. But that wasn't the only reason that Ted had had a smile on his face. Once he'd planted his feet firmly on the ground and greased the gears of his tired, piston legs, Ted had taken one look around himself and known exactly where he was. He'd returned home. He was in the North. Sure, the bus had crossed into the Yorkshire county hours ago, but it was one thing gazing at an identical motorway through a window, indistinguishable from that of one anywhere else in England, to actually standing on the turf of the province itself. He was one step closer to where he'd needed to be and it felt magnificent. Birmingham was long gone behind him.

While to Steve M. Brooks, the stars had been threatening and chilling, like unknown bogies on a black radar converging in on his location, to Ted, they were quite beautiful. They twinkled peacefully like fireflies in a grotto, and reminded him, in their clean beauty, of the white Yorkshire Rose, the insignia that he'd come to love so much, one that he associated with freedom and hope. If he'd had any doubts before, they were now null and void thanks the glittering assurance of those stars. Buying the last-minute bus ticket and escaping Birmingham had been one of the best decisions he'd made in a long time. Ted was excited, excited like a young lad on a snow day who's school had just been announced 'closed' by a breakfast radio broadcast.

He took a deep intake of the cold North. The breath was damp and full of moisture, as though some untraceable, leaky pipe had let rain water leak into the landscape around him. It pleased Ted, and quenched a thirst in his lungs that the oxygen back in the Midlands cities, tainted by spewing factory fumes, could never have satisfied. The air just felt so much cleaner and purer in Yorkshire. Even in its cities, its great cities, like York, Liverpool and Sheffield, the air stayed natural and unaffected, their streets decorated by stunning architectures, instead of towering offices and apartment complexes that seemed to poison the supply.

York's Minster, the golden barricades of Clifford's Tower, the cities Roman walls, even the KitKat factory that sprinkled the air with sweet chocolate wafer smells on windy days. Ted flipped through images of these buildings in his mental picture pad, truly staple remnants of English Heritage if he'd ever seen them. And how could he forget the topsy-turvy cobblestones, old bay windows and the timbre framed rooftops of the infamous Shambles Street? Home to the finest confectionary, crusty pork pies and Magic stores that the county had to offer. Walking its narrow channels, a deliberate 14th century design to allow the smooth flow of blood wastage to reach the Fossgate, was like stepping back in time, and re-treading the steps of Anglo-Saxons, as they'd perused fresh meat selections that hung dripping from iron hooks outside of the butchers. To Ted, York was a never ending nest of historical nooks and rustic crannies just waiting to be explored. It was overflowing with friendly faces, steeped in kind voices. And all of it, every steak and onion pie and every Japanese tourist-filled Museum, was based around the bountiful free-flowing body of sparkling water that was the River Ouse.

The name was apt, it had oozed its way into his blood had Yorkshire, it would forever be a part of him and him a part of it, well, to be genetically precise, exactly fifty percent of him. The roots that were from the Northern half of his family tree felt nourished and fed once again. He could feel its weak branches growing stronger in familiarity and proximity to his birthplace, away from the Midlands, whose side had begun to wither. He hadn't been to York for a long time, eleven years in fact, and now that he'd returned to the North, he yearned for the chance to soon go back there. He'd hoped in his heart that it would live up to the high expectations envisioned in his vivid childhood memories. They'd been getting stronger and stronger as of late, back in Birmingham, like he was being drawn back to Yorkshire by some ancestral force that had been awoken inside of him.

Boy, was he glad to be back, to have crossed the border into Gods own country. He felt at home, where he belonged. And as so often happened when he'd think of the state, childhood memories and highlights and adorations came tumbling into his brain like forgotten treasures down a flight of wooden attic ladders on a day of spring cleaning. He could've spent hours musing over its majesty, the thoughts were like miniature mascots, cheering him on in his tenacity to be there. But although he was in Yorkshire, he wasn't quite where he'd needed to be, not just yet. York would have to wait for now. He'd have a while to go before his journey was complete, and so he yanked himself out of his daydream, which still qualified as one despite the set sun, and moved towards the service station entrance to grab some much needed food.

Before he could though, another piece of scenery caught his eyes, which sought to soak up anything and everything that the North had had to offer. Across the quiet motorway lanes, off the service station car park, dimly lit by street lamps (*some of which were flickering and malfunctioning*), Ted saw something that peaked his imagination. It was a large soil ridge that scaled up high above him. And though a thick cloak of pitch-black night time prevented him from seeing beyond its foremost peak, with its scattered bushes and random shrubbery, Ted had known exactly what had lay beyond it. The Moors.

To Ted, the Moors seemed to him to be the English equivalent of the barren wasteland of the Texan desert. So full of life, yet so empty of it at the same time. Ted knew that just past that hilltop would be a vast and empty stretch of grassy territory, the lush green of which would be deadened, suppressed by hovering clouds of moisture. The grey mists would give the fields the impression of an other-worldly realm, one coated in a perpetual dew. Endless belts of solitary tree's, grown alone, away from forests, would extend as far as the eye could see and further, over the snowy horizon. He thought of the cold ponds dotted across the heath, bitter and numbing to the touch from the high altitude. These Moors were far from the tame, prim and proper hedges, and man-planted beeches of the London countryside. The two lands bore nothing in common, bar the impenetrable grey fog that the Moors had borrowed from the capitals dusky streets. This was a nightmarish botanical. Its muscular hills, which rose and fell in the distance like the wavering careers of artists who might've painted them, encompassed an innumerable amount of pathways. For when a weary traveller were to happen upon an arrowed signpost, and the road had forked to the left and to the right, the path that they'd chose would lead to another split in direction to choose from, and then another, and then another. So deep would they be in the web of the Moors by then, that the way that they'd first come from would be buried in vague memory, when the time to retrace their steps home had come. *Was it a left I'd taken here? Or was it a right?* It would be a dangerous and uncultivated place, it's dominion over mankind signified by the stone ruins of old crumbling walls and houses and barns, long left behind. It was a graveyard for failed civilisation and a playground for the elements, a place meant for nature and nature alone, an unforgiving climate where mankind could never thrive. Ted thought of the famous Bronte landmark of Haworth's *Topwithens*, and from there, the tortured romance of Heathcliff, of the humble Hareton Earnshaw and his love, dearest Catherine.

The thought of the Moors that night, existing in the darkness, of uncharted spreads, of pitfalls and gullies and trenches, it unnerved him, like an unexpected creak on a flight of stairs, or a gust of wind blowing beneath a taper, giving it a human shape. It reversed his good spirits and gripped him by the spine. Come to think of it, as he gazed around the car park where he stood, he came to the ghoulish realisation that the Moors surrounded the entirety of the service station, from every possible direction. He supposed it had been what he'd wanted, to escape the busy metropolis of Birmingham, in favour of the wide-open Yorkshire countryside. But why was it then, that he'd found himself musing over how the legions of purple lavender plants up there, would've provided the perfect perfume to mask the scent of a dead body? Ted suddenly felt as though he were an unfortunate adventurer and the starry sky a descending ceiling. The four moss-topped faces of the Moors around him, too, closed in like walls in a booby-trapped crypt, doomed to crush poor Ted's bones to dust.

He gulped.

Just then, amidst that chilling feeling, atop the ridge, Ted could've sworn he'd seen the profile of a human, a man, watching him from afar. The faceless shape remained still, simply, standing there. Could it have been a trick of his mind? A tree stump perhaps? Or a small monument? But Ted knew deep down that that peculiar shape hadn't been there before. A dog walker maybe? Taking in the view? He was sure from high up on the mound that the dazzling lights of the highway must've been a sight to see. No. That was no dog walker. Whoever he was, whatever it was, it's motionless glare wanted to make Ted sprint and to never look back, into the safety of the warm service station behind him.

'Stop that! Zip your coat back up or you'll catch a cold! How many times do I have to tell you?!' yelled a Father to his child.

It distracted Ted and caused him to look away for a moment, to a young lad in his custard-coloured coat and his stern, frowned parent. He quickly returned his eyes to the spot on the ridge, in fear that the dark stranger might've seized the moment of his head turn, and might've been sliding down towards him at full speed with a bloody axe in his hand. But to his surprise, there was no longer anybody there, just, an empty space in the dead of night. An illusion, a trick of the mind. Yes, that's right, it must've been. He *was* tired after all, and hungry. That's all it had been. He was sure of it. He turned to go inside, not out fear, he told himself, but because the bus would be leaving soon and he didn't want to miss out on the chance of grabbing a bite to eat and a drink.

As he went inside, the sleepless Moor watched him go.

Ted shrugged off his worries as easily as the Megabus had dealt with pot holes in its way. He followed the crowd of passengers through the car park towards the entrance of the service station. Giant ornamental granite stones lined the pathway leading up to it. Outside the pit stop were wooden benches and picnic tables, meant to encourage the customers of its many eateries to enjoy the sunshine with their meals, however at this late hour they were empty and sullen. Even if it *had* been the day-time though, they would've been just as vacant, and the soggy blue parasols impaled through them, which had shook in the wind, equally redundant. The grassy spaces offered to travellers bringing their own packed lunches would too be unused, for the cold April weather was hardly the most hospitable of hosts. It had been wishful thinking of the establishment's manager at all to have ordered the unfolding of the tables copper hinges from their storage lockers. His hopes for a warm, sunny springtime had been dashed by the prolonged winter completely, like its corpse white fingers weren't quite ready to let go of England just yet. Ted couldn't ever really imagine a place surrounded by the Moors ever being warm, they seemed to emanate a constant icy energy, like anything they touched would freeze along with them. Midas's evil twin brother.

Ted strolled up a ramp towards a set of automatic doors. Above them, a red neon sign spelt '*O'Nowhere Service Station*'. 'Cute name', he chuckled to himself.

Below it to the right, nailed to the wall, was a commercial signboard that featured the individual logos of the food parlours and shops inside. Each brand's logo seemed more ostentatious than the next, as if they were competing with each other to capture the curiosity and attention of a hungry stomach. They weren't all just places to eat though. There was a book shop, a small clothes store, a camping supply shop and a place for Coffee. Ted licked his lips and then stepped inside, oblivious to fact that he wouldn't be leaving with the bus that night. None of the passengers would be.

Inside, the pit stop was humble and pleasant. It wasn't particularly remarkable nor was it memorable, but that was okay. The station seemed to do exactly what it had said on the proverbial tin, to nurse the yawning mouths and weary eyes of passing drivers, before they were to go into the night at 70mph once again. They'd untangle like cluttered wires after crossing paths, and head out onto the roads in their separate directions, like a search party spreading its numbers to find a missing child.

From the entrance where Ted stood, the station began narrowly before branching out into its various shops, all of which were windowless to offer customers a full view of their wares. The slanted magazine stands, the luminous overhead burger and coffee menus. Some drivers were sat with trays at littered wooden tables, already settled on their food of choice, whilst others stood, still deliberating on how best to fill their stomachs. Both were glad to have finally stretched their legs after hours of sitting scrunched and hunchbacked behind the wheel though. Their bodies had needed the rest, '*Sleep Kill's*' after all, as the many signs along the motorway were eager to remind them of. The tiling of the floors were in an uninspired beige, dark-leaved artificial plants tried in vain to liven the area. Lit up vending and toy-claw machines took up space against the walls, as well as a seldom used model red car. It would vibrate and produce cheap horn sounds if a parent were to have dropped two pound coins into its slot. The smells of the food courts mingled in the air and a dated *Tomfoolery* record from the early 2000's played quietly over the intercom.

After a momentary scan from left to right, a road-lagged visitor would've sussed out and taken in all that there was to see of the *O'Nowhere* service station, which was exactly how the owners had liked it. Small, simple, and to the point. There was no reason for anyone to have stayed there any longer than they'd had to. Anything that would happen at the station, would stay at the station. It was an in-between place, and as we know, Ted loved places liked that. Places that were purgatories, mid-points, ones that required no commitment nor the person visiting them to settle there for too long at any given time. He'd spend as long as he'd have to inside its red-brick walls, and then move on, onwards towards his true destination, his business there done and dusted and his body free to leave at his will. If there was one thing that had been guaranteed to make young Teds skin itch, one thing that was bound to unsettle his temperament and to jettison any sense of comfort from his mind, it was feeling like he was trapped somewhere. He'd hated it. And it was exactly why he'd left Birmingham behind. Entrapment.

His first order of business: pee. He followed the stick figure gender signs to the men's toilet. Next to it, were tiny shower cubicles, often frequented by large, bearded truckers, whose twenty-four hour trips across the country delivering parcels had left them sweaty and in need of a good soap-scrub. Ted had thought that they'd looked gross. The lavatories weren't much better, they were greasy and smelt of the select truckers who'd dodged the showers and had been festering in a den of BO and cheesy crisp wrappers. While Ted relieved his full bladder in the urinal, he laughed to himself over a poster framed advert in front of him on the grey panelled wall. It was for a paternity test company, depicting a sweating cartoon gentleman sat in a waiting room next to a whistling milk-man, reading the newspaper. It made Ted chuckle.

He washed his hands with a run of the tap (labelled '*Do Not Drink*') and a squeeze of the silver hand pump, and then caught sight of himself in the dirty mirror. His hazelnut hair was askew and scruffy and his whiskey brown eyes were waned and tired, the hoods of his lids barely open. He needed rest badly, he'd barely slept the night before, spending most of the time stressing over his decision to leave and then the remainder of it carrying out his plan before the dawn; coordinating his journey, buying the ticket and then packing. Even once all of that had been done though, his nerves and excitement had kept his dreams at bay. Running on no more than three hours of shut-eye in his tank, he could've quite happily curled up into a ball on the greasy toilet floor, crawled under the sinks, and then caught up on his forty lost winks. But he knew that there were plenty of freshly made and cleaned feather-down beds waiting for him in Middlesbrough, he could wait until then, and boy would that white linen be worth it.

Ted left the toilet. His next order of business: food. Though the hairy truckers and business suit commuters had had to deliberate over their choice of meal once they'd stepped foot in the station, for Ted, the nights dish had been decided long ago. In fact, it had been decided whilst staring at the ugly, blue, patterned headrest of the seat in front of him on the bus, somewhere between Manchester and Sheffield, somewhere between his mom's fourth and fifth voicemail. A piping hot pesto and ham toasty was at the forefront of Ted's head, and so, he completely by-passed the burger bar and chicken joint to his right in the promenade, and made a bee-line for the coffee house on the other side.

A wiry janitor cleaned the beige tiles on the floor, a yellow '*wet*' sign was placed by his side. Ted conscientiously side stepped around the mop-shined surface and continued towards the delicious smell of toasty.

Many of the passengers from his bus were already sat at dark wooden tables in front of the counter; families, the father and his young son in the custard-coloured coat, a muscular tanned man in full sports gear. His toasted sandwich looked comically small in his huge manly hands. He'd wolfed down the meal with the class of a silverback gorilla.

Ted joined the queue of the gentleman in front of him and licked his lips in anticipation. Maybe he'd even treat himself to an iced strawberry coffee to wash down the crusts. Running away from home sure was thirsty work, and the waft of the grounded beans smelt damn good. He waited. And waited. And waited. But no one came to serve. The seated passengers were finishing their meals by now and getting ready to return to the coach. Ten minutes had elapsed and still, no sign of any barista. The man ahead of Ted uttered an audible tut and then left, leaving Ted as a one-man queue. He really couldn't afford to miss the bus to Middlesbrough, that would mean being trapped at the station, and Ted didn't like that one bit. He'd had to keep moving. Always moving. It wasn't that he'd had to be where he was going for a specific time, no, it was that patience was a virtue that young Ted did not possess. He was happy to stay at *O'Nowhere* temporarily but no longer then he'd had to. He'd have no choice but to resort to hitchhiking in the instance that the bus departed without him. And Ted knew that that would most likely end with his molestation and dismemberment, if the true crime documentaries that he frequently watched had been anything to go by. His remains buried, forgotten on the lonely Moors, the grainy CCTV footage of him leaving *O'Nowhere* the last that anyone would seen of him.

He turned to leave the empty counter, and then stopped in his tracks. Was that a noise he could hear coming from the kitchen? He listened, and heard nothing. He must've been mistaken, just like he'd been when he'd thought that he'd seen the figure of a man standing atop the ridge. The tiredness was really getting to him now. But no, there it was again, and there was no doubting it this time. There was a strange sound emitting from the open kitchen door on the other side of the counter, past the whipped cream dispensers and plastic straw-filled boxes. There was something not quite right about it to Ted, it sounded distressed, it sounded in pain, it sounded like a human cry. And so, not one to often weigh the pros and cons of a situation, as one might expect from a young man who'd run away from home, Ted stepped past the counter and through the kitchen door marked 'Staff ONLY' to investigate.

Behind him passengers returned to the bus.

Ted edged cautiously into the kitchen, the wails were louder past the door. Spare paper coffee cups and label-less cartons of milk for the beverages covered the chrome work surfaces. Some of the cupboards were ajar revealing sauces. The silver was spotless, a blood splatter would've shown up against its gleaming fixtures like a rose laid upon a jet-black coffin. Cutlery was submerged in a white tub of cleaning liquid. A single freezer stood in the right hand corner, filled with pastries and likely the ingredients required to make Ted's order-not made. A defective coffee machine lay by the doorway, its pumps jammed and clogged with gloopy chocolate powder, along with a green bucket and mop.

The kitchen was silent, except for the messy sobbing that seemed to be coming from the far corner around the central island, and an ominous ventilation hum from the whir of the ceiling fan. Ted gulped, and then crept slowly towards the corner where the tears were coming from. It was a grizzly and a rough sound, like the horrendous howls were tearing the folds of the crier's throat. Carefully Ted navigated around the metal corner of the kitchen island, and saw that the source of the misery had been coming from a girl, from a red haired young lady who was crouched in a slump on the floor with her back to him, facing away towards bags of brown sugar. She was visibly distraught, Ted didn't have to see her face, which he imagined to be cherry red and puffy eyed, to know that. Unsure of what to do, whether it was his place or not to interfere, and conscious of the time and his bus leaving, Ted grappled with his judgment. But it didn't take long for the 'do-gooder', the 'boy wonder', the 'hero' inside of him to decide that he should check up on the poor girl. Something truly tragic must've happened to her to have left her in such a state, and his mother hadn't raised him to ignore a damsel in need. He walked silently up behind her, and then reached a hand out towards her shuddering shoulder. Just as she drew another dramatically sharp in-take of breath, to fill her lungs for the next vicious bout of sobbing, contact was made. The red haired girl turned around with a jolt, looked up at the strange young man standing over her with his hand outstretched, and then screamed.

'Get away from me!' the girl shouted, forcefully shoving Ted back towards the island. Her eyes, as predicted, were swollen and smudged with liner. Confused, and eager to establish as quickly as possible that he wasn't a sexual deviant, Ted replied.

'No no no no! I'm not a weirdo!' Something he later realised was definitely something a weirdo would say.

'Back off you freak. I'm warning you! I've got a pan and I'm not afraid to use it' screamed the girl, climbing to her feet and wielding a black iron frying pan from off the kitchen side, the circular metal underside of which looked like it'd leave a mark in the morning.

'I swear! I'm not a weirdo! Let me explain! I was just checking you were okay! I heard crying from the counter back there and came to see if you'd needed help that's all!'
Her grip on the utensils handle loosened.

'To...check I was okay?'

'Yes! Now can you just put the pan down please?' Ted held an elbow across his face to block an oncoming attack. The girl's look dropped suddenly, like a dangling grand piano plunging from the thin rope that hoisted it.

'Oh my God' she gasped, letting the pan fall to the floor with a clatter.

'...you're a...'

'...customer yes...a rapist, no.'

Ted was astounded with how quickly the tears on the girl's face had dried. The redness of her eyes had faded back to the normal, pale cream complexion of the rest of her face, no longer matching her hair.

'...I almost smacked a customer in the face with a frying pan.' A look of dismay dawned on the girl's features, before hysterics ensued.

'Please, please, please don't tell my boss. I'd be fired. Oh my God I'm so, so sorry.' She darted up to Ted, her fighting stance gone.

'Are you okay? Did I hurt you?' she asked, frantically grabbing Ted's arms and torso, examining him for contusions

'Erm...no...You actually have to hit someone to hurt them...' Ted smiled, quietly finding the girl's mania amusing, milking her apologetic state for all that it was worth.

'Oh right, yeah of course. I'm so, so, so sorry. You just...if a creepy looking guy sneaks up on you in a kitchen alone, you tend to assume the worst, don't you?'

'Oh, so I'm creepy now?'

'No! I didn't mean that! God, that was dumb. Why did I say that? I meant...'

'I know what you meant' Ted laughed, 'not all guys are bad you know. We're not all Dicks'.

'Most of the ones I've met are...' the girl regained her composure and straightened her skirt. 'Now, let me make it up to you. What'll it be?'

'Huh?'

'Your order...you must've been waiting for something at the counter right? When you'd heard me crying. So what can I get you Sir? It's on me!'

Ted was beyond confused. The girl didn't appear distraught in the slightest. It didn't seem feasible to him for her to have gone from wailing in misery to professional barista, providing service with a smile as if nothing had happened, within the space of a few short minutes. She was Europe, and him, England, running one hour behind her and struggling to catch up.

'Don't be shy now, what were you going for?' she encouraged.

'A pesto, ham toasty?' posed Ted, defiantly unsure of what his answer should've been.

'An excellent choice! One Pesto Ham coming right up sir! On the house!' the girl declared, getting to work and busying herself around the chrome space. She collected the various ingredients from their cupboards and then flicked the switching on the grill with her right hand without even having to look, as if she'd done it a million times before and that this had been her millionth and first 'pesto on brown'. She must have been put off the green stuff for life. He watched her scurry from station to station at what must have been an employee record speed.

'Wow wow wow. Slow down a second...I've got so many questions' demanded a dazed Ted. The tiredness can't have helped, he'd felt as though he'd gorged on a cheeseboard before sleeping and was now reaping the nocturnal consequences, stuck in the midst of a crazy dream he couldn't wake up from.

'Sure ask away!' the girl replied, buttering the bread, the knife gliding from crust to crust with a skillful ease.

'Well your name would be nice...erm...' Ted looked to the identity badge just above the girl's right breast, pinned in silver onto the mustard polo shirt she was wearing as uniform.

'....Mohamed...' he finished, reading the name.

'Oh this? I lost my badge so I had to borrow a spare one from the office. This belonged to an Indian dude who used to work here. My name, believe it or not, is not, Mohamed' the red haired stranger joked back sarcastically, finally slamming the lid of the grill down onto the sandwich to cook.

'Oh okay, so what is your nam-'

-'Here you go!' The girl, not hearing Ted's question, handed him a complimentary iced coffee complete with straw, foam, and chocolate sauce. She'd made it somewhere in the mess of movement. He took the drink and thanked her.

'Okay, well now that I've got your attention, can you at least tell me what's wrong? Why were you crying?' he asked the girl, finally stood still.

He could get a proper look at her now. She was pretty that was for sure. Her long, wine shaded locks were certainly a sight to behold, they gripped you by the eyes, like the scarlet-coat girl in the closing moments of *Spielberg's* Opus. Her eyes were a bright crystal blue, and looked like water to the fire of her hair and the snow of her milky skin. The only element she was missing was wind, or maybe she wasn't. She'd certainly caused a mini-hurricane in the kitchen and had swept Ted off of his feet.

He'd been adamant about not wanting to stay at the service station for long, but there was something about this girl, something alluring that he couldn't put quite his finger on, something that drew him in and made him, in a small way, wish that maybe he could've stayed a little bit longer to get to know her. She was as crazy as a box of frogs, and he liked that. But he knew that the brief encounter would be all there was to their story, like strangers exchanging a passing glance-too long on a subway train. All meetings at the *O'Nowhere* were temporary, finite moments in fleeting time that would always stay there. Perhaps recalled and smiled over on the drive out, but the smiles lifespan lasting no more than the memories of the meetings in the passers heads. No, this was it for them. But boy, did he wish he could stay a little longer.

'Crying? Oh yeah. Was it good?' she replied hopefully, arms crossed, the smell of grilled pork filling the air.

'Was it good?'

'Yeah. The crying. Like, was it convincing?' the girl probed, requesting critique.

'Erm...well it sounded like crying to me so...'

'YES' the unnamed redhead leapt into the air and power fisted the ceiling, which she almost hit given its low height. 'Killed it.' Ted accepted that he would remain dosed in a permanent state of confusion throughout their entire conversation.

'I hope you don't mind me saying, but I have honestly no fucking idea what is going on right now.' The girl giggled and turned to Ted, once again rooted to the ground after her jubilant moment.

'Oh, let me explain. I'm really sorry I alarmed you earlier, I really am. I didn't mean to worry you and I can totally see why you'd be concerned and want to make sure I was okay. But, see, the thing is, I wasn't actually crying. I was *practicing* crying'. The insides of Ted's brain resembled that of a crashed computer screen, infected with a Trojan virus and filled with random numerical digits. He was so lost.

'I'm sorry, but what kind of nut job practises crying?'

'A girl who happens to want to be an actor, that's who. And who happens to have a major audition tomorrow which requires, said crying. Clearly I'm pretty damn bloody good at it too if I managed to convince you, I hope the panel are as impressed as you are. I figured since everyone off your bus had been served, I'd have a free five minutes to go over it before anyone else turned up. Then you got hungry for ham and threw a spanner in the works of my rehearsal session'.

Out of all of the explanations that he'd expected to hear when he'd found the girl crying on the floor that night, this had perhaps been the least likely of them all. 'You're an actor?'

'I guess I should thank you in a way, you've given me a real confidence boost. I was nervous about tomorrow but now I feel a little better. I was only giving you this toasty so that you didn't complain to my manager about me, but really, this ones from the heart now'. She spoke with a general Yorkshire accent, at least, to Ted it was general, to a born and bred Northerner they'd have been able to place a pin on a map for that voice in a heartbeat. True Northerners can distinguish the subtle variations between the Hull, Lincoln, Bolton, and Sheffield voices, but to Ted, it fell under the umbrella of just being, Northern. The way Southerners, when referring to a rival, may say 'they're from the North', neglecting to bear in mind the vastness of the country's largest county, as if all North dwellers are on a first-name basis with each other and all live within ten cubic feet of the village wishing well.

DING.

The sudden stop-timer of the grill sounded. To Ted it was the wakeup call he'd needed. 'Shit! My Bus! I'm so sorry, I've gotta rush!' He panicked, placing his untouched frozen beverage on the work surface and starting out the door.

'But what about your-'

'you have It! Call it your lunch hour! Good luck with that audition, I'm glad you're okay miss!' he yelled over his shoulder as he bounded like a greyhound out of the kitchen, leaving the girl behind and forgetting his sentimental 'what if?' moment. He *had* to get to Middlesbrough at all costs. She stood in silence for a moment, and then took him up on his offer, taking a whopper of a bite out of the cooked sandwich's top left corner.

'Oh yeah' she gagged, cringing and begrudgingly swallowing the sarnie. 'I hate Pesto'. She dropped the wasted snack into the bin.

Where Ted had entered the kitchen with stealth and hesitation, he'd left it in full speed, leaving the bizarre red-haired girl behind and bolting out the door. He vaulted over the coffee shop counter like a cop across the bonnet of a car in a crime drama and sprinted past the wooden tables, now deserted of its passengers; the young boy in the custard coat, the rough looking brickhouse in the full tracksuit. The sliding automatic doors in his crosshairs, Ted ran with all the speed that he could muster, a rude awakening for his tired legs and feet, which were still stiff from hours of immobility on the bus.

'OI!'

A gravelly shout forced Ted to stop in his tracks, mere yards in front of the doors. A common preconception of the northern accent, is that it's a voice of warmth, a welcoming and kind voice who's foggy tones best suit phrases such as 'would you like a cup of Tea love?' Or 'my, look how much you've grown'. A lesser known perception is perhaps just how aggressive and threatening it can sound in the mouths of the hostile, of the dangerous. Ted reluctantly turned back. The headlights and the engine of the Megabus had fired up, he could see them through the glass of the sliding doors. Passengers were reclaiming their seats on board. He had conscientiously stepped around the cleaned tiling's, that the stations janitor had been mopping, on his route to the coffee shop, but on his way back Ted had ran straight across them, trailing mud from his boots all over the floor. It was this that had promoted the violent 'OI!'.

'Oh man, I'm really sorry about that, I'm in such a rush. My bus is about to leave, I didn't think' Ted explained frantically to the cleaner, gesturing a thumb back over his shoulder towards the bus.

'Well you're not the one who has to clear it up now, are you? Prick'
hissed the Janitor back, tightly wrangling the wooden neck of his mop
with his right hand.

'I said I'm sorry man...it was just an accident. I-'

'-I was about to get off. The boss'll make me stay now to clear it up. So
thanks a lot. Twat.'

Ted had wanted to reply with a quick quip about how his boss probably
wouldn't have approved of him cursing at his customers either. But he
knew he'd done wrong, and quite frankly he knew that he'd never have
to see the unpleasant insect of a man standing in front of him ever again,
so saw no need to cause more aggro.

'I don't know what to say to you brother. I'd stay and help you clean it
up, honestly I would, but if my bus leaves without me I'm totally
screwed. I gotta run' said a genuinely guilty Ted, starting towards the
exit.

'You ain't my brother. That's right, you just fuck off and leave me to
clean it like everybody else does.'

Ted hadn't taken much notice of the guy the first time round, but up
close he'd been forced to take in his features. He'd wished he hadn't.
The cleaner was a thin and wiry man, his navy boiler suit even at a size S

seemed too big for him. His hands were bony and his face taut and sunken like a skull. His jagged jaw jut out from under his oily skin, as though if he were to have smiled it would've cut open his cheeks. His eyes were black and beady like a weasels and his hair was a dark brown, slicked back and greasy, shinning like the floors he cleaned. His appearance seemed an appropriate vessel for the venomous, slimy words he spat at Ted.

'Like I said man, I really gotta go. I am sorry mate', shouted the muddy culprit as he picked up his sprint again, towards the bus.

'Fucking prick.' The Janitor muttered under his breath, watching the young man leave with his menacing, beady eyes. He took up his mop again, and scrubbed the dirt violently, thinking about all the things he'd wished he could've done to that cocky little shit. He wrung the mops ropes, squeezing it so tightly that his knuckles turned white.

Ted emerged once again into the cold Northern air. The bus hadn't left. Thank God. He quickly walked up to the open door of the beast on wheels, but then stopped on the spot. All of the passengers of the bus, all forty six of them, were instead congregated in front of the vehicle, along with the high-vis wearing driver. 'That's odd' thought Ted, he was sure that everyone would've been on board by now, *he* was the late one. They all appeared to be staring at something, or rather, someone, gathered together in a large bulk, blocking the glare of the headlights. He could see the boy in the custard-coloured coat, this time in his Father's arms, and could hear the dull hum of agitated, confused voices. Ted slowly made his way over to the back of the crowd and side stepped through the masses, working his way through the horde of parents, and hipsters to the front. As he overtook water-proof coat covered shoulders, rain-hoods and full, bulky backpacks, Ted was able to make out the flash of a blue and red police car light ahead of the rabble. What the hell was going on? The orders of the Inspector stood at the head of the multitude quickly answered that, he held the palms of his hands in the air, gesturing the mob to back up.

'Right folks. I want everybody back inside now. The bus isn't going anywhere. None of you are. We've had to temporarily shut down all the roads in the area and so for the time being we need you to stay put at the station. So, could please just go back in?'

'What's going on?' asked someone, it was hard to tell who, or maybe it had been a few people at once, allocating themselves the role of spokesperson for the flock.

'I don't have time to explain right now. But I promise, once you all get inside, all of your questions will be answered. Now can you please just head back? Its cold out here so let's get you all warmed up shall we? There is absolutely nothing to worry about but we really do need you to cooperate' said the bearded Yorkshire officer in a professional manner. But one didn't have to be an expert in criminal profiling to detect the thin panic underneath his professionalism. He'd deliberately omitted phrases like 'it's for your own safety' from his speech.

A few passengers stayed behind to grill the Inspector, but were met with the same non-answers. The majority of the herd began to slowly trickle with apprehension back into *O'Nowhere*, including the driver. If there's one thing the English are good at, it's following the crowd, we are a nation of queue-makers after all. They spoke amongst themselves and exchanged concerned looks, all of sudden finding themselves wishing that they were back on the safety of the blue patterned coach seats. But for the most part the tone of the group was of a collective irritation, annoyance that their already tiresome journey had been delayed even further. The weight of the sagging clouds overhead finally became too much to bare and began to leak tiny rain drops. The water dribbling out of them like a spilled drink through yarn.

Ted followed at the rear of the crowd. This wasn't part of the plan. He should've been on his way to Middleborough by now, not going back into the station. *O'Nowhere* was supposed to have been a rest stop, nothing more. But although frustrated, he was sure that whatever the issue was that it would soon be resolved. The bus would be on its way once again and he'd be perusing the Middleborough pubs for the cheapest overnight deal that included a complimentary 'Full English'. It'd be a little later then he'd hoped, but he'd be there. He walked slowly and lagged behind the others to regain his breath from running, the officer ushered everybody inside. In all the hustle and bustle, Ted hadn't noticed the seventh voicemail that his Mother had left on his phone. Maybe if he'd had, he'd have been far more worried about the police lockdown than he was. He should've been.

As he lingered at the back of the crowd, and as the clouds continued to drain, he took one last glance up onto the ridge of the Moors across the road, where he'd thought he'd seen a figure in the night. But there was no one there, just a murky space in the darkness, like the nothingness of a black hole in the vacuum of space, swallowing stars and planets and lonely astronauts.

'We won't be long. I'm sure of it' he calmly told himself as he passed the sliding glass rain-speckled doors, already itching at the thought of being trapped at the station and not reaching his secret destination on the other side of Middlesbrough. Ted hated being stuck. The police followed. And once the last of them had entered, a constable locked the doors behind them, leaving the cold, rainy carpark, empty and silent, except for the hush of the stormy country wind. Everyone was safely inside now. Well, almost everyone….

Across the road, hidden from sight, a man lay prone on his belly, against the slippery ramp of the lowland hilltop that Ted had been fixated with. He slithered through the sticky mud and then emerged as if birthed by the soil, crouching down into a sitting position on the grassy dune. He watched in silence as another throng of police cars travelled along the empty highway and disappeared onto the horizon. Searching pointlessly. The flashes of their sirens momentarily lit up the figure, revealing splashes of blood on his hands and face, and making the fiendish whites of his eyes glow like fire, but only for a moment. Once they had passed he was at one with the night once again, at one with the haunting trees and abandoned barns, and the winding paths that led to nowhere and the bats and the owls and the caves and the swampy hideouts. And it was there, on the doorstep of the Moors, at the advent of the Northern wilderness, that the figure, this emissary of terror, watched, and waited, and very carefully, planned his next move.

CHAPTER THREE

Things always seem so much worse at dusk, don't you find? Troubles, stresses, loss, the burning fever on the brow of a sick man, all of them are magnified and heightened by the falling of the night's black cover. With the morning comes a relief, sweet birdsong and warm sunshine diminishing the wrath of the night before them and making one realise that things '*aren't so bad*'. But the police lockdown at the *O'Nowhere*, much to the misfortune of the guests that were trapped there, hadn't taken place during the kind mercy of an afternoon, where the brightness of the sun would've laid bare the miles of moorland surrounding them. No, the lockdown had begun in the youth of the night, 10pm to be precise, leaving plenty of scope for its darkness to intensify, as the clock hands turned and the hours went by. The guests couldn't see more than a few feet past the glass pane windows of the service station, anything further was simply hidden in darkness. It belonged to the night now. Perhaps if they had squinted up close to the glass, they'd have been able to make out the headlights and tyres of their stranded cars, parked side by side in the lot, or the empty wooden benches on the verge, but nothing more. And it was for this reason perhaps, true to form, that the panic and paranoia that had started to set in amongst the guests had begun to escalate to a degree far higher than it ever would've during the blue sky day time. For is it not true, that the unseen enemy is far more horrifying than the one in plain sight? The desolate Moors watched the passengers in the station silently from above. *They* were in control now, the game was afoot.

The rabble of bus passengers had joined the hive of the other visitors that had graced the station that night. There were families, aunts, uncles, youngsters, old fogies, people from all walks of life. The mood was ripe with neurosis, you could smell the panic in the air. Shop workers had emerged from behind their counters and were stood at their open doorways, part glad to have had their long shifts interrupted, but at the same time very much aware of the fact that this wasn't your average, '*run of the mill*' fire drill hiatus. On a standard day the gas station would've felt airy and spacious, just the way the manager had liked it, but with the usually scattered travellers all converging at its core, the pit stop had adopted an uncharacteristic quality of claustrophobia and confinement. Amongst themselves, the homespun Yorkshire folks discussed the present situation in taxed voices, theorising and rationalising the reasons behind it. Strangers became debaters, parents comforted crying children, the worried phoned loved ones. All of them, Ted included, stood in the centre of the service station promenade, whilst police officers lined the sides, speaking into their radios and whispering behind each other's black-rimmed hats. They knew something that the civilians didn't. The army of folk looked like a gathering of frightened cattle at an auction, awaiting the slaughter. But who was the auctioneer? Well, Inspector Henry J. Simmons of course! Who else?

'Make way! Make way!' the officer said, the man who'd ordered everyone inside.

The crowd parted like the great Red Sea into two halves, allowing for the black bearded boy in blue to move towards the front. Ted watched him walk past in his bright green high-visibility gilet. He'd been segregated into the left hand bracket of the crowd. The scrawny janitor that Ted had had a run in with earlier, was on the opposite side, he too was watching the policeman walk, with soulless eyes. He clenched his fists tightly in the pockets of his navy jumpsuit so that no one else would see, channelling his frustration into the digging of his unkempt nails into his palms, leaving tiny red marks. Was is too much to ask that he could finish his fucking shift on time?

Finally, Inspector Simmons, whose wife had always found the formality of his title boyishly cute, turned to face the people. Every eye met his as the room fell silent with baited breath. He felt as though he were seated behind a long, wide desk at a press conference, hounded by journalists and about to kick start a murder investigation by way of an official statement. Henry gulped. Public speaking had never been his forte. One wrong word, one wrong turn of phrase, and he knew that he'd have a serious problem on his hands. People didn't take too kindly to being told that their lives were in grave danger.

He spoke.

'There has been an incident.'

Four words that gripped the crowd. Ted's ears pricked up and his hair stood on end at the back of his neck. The janitor too stared, it distracted him from the infuriating fact that not one, but dozens upon dozens of filthy feet were now muddying the cream tiles that he'd spent hours cleaning.

'I'm sure a lot of you are wondering just exactly what is going on. You have a right to be confused and I'm sure you all have a lot of questions' spoke Simmons calmly. He'd decided to climb onto the top of an artificial plants wooden casing to be better seen, he wasn't a particularly tall man.

'Damn straight!' cried an unknown mouth.
It was quickly *shhhh'd* by the other lips around it.

He continued. 'The West Yorkshire Police have unfortunately, due to circumstances beyond our control, been forced to close off all the roads within a fifteen miles radius. There are armed blockades at every entrance and exit between here and Haworth. And that, I'm afraid to say, includes the A1 running right past this station. So, for the time being, no one here will be allowed to drive anywhere, you'll all have to stay put at *O'Nowhere*. It's hardly ideal, but believe me when I say that this will only be for a short period of time and I'm sure you'll all be back on your way very soon'.

This prompted a small response from the crowd, but the mumble was quickly quelled by Henry's raised voice. He could sense that he was losing the room, like a washed up stand-up in a comedy club whose gags weren't landing.

'My name is Inspector Simmons but you can all call me Henry. I've been stationed here to oversee the blockade at *O'Nowhere* and I can assure you, if any of you have any questions, I'll be more than welcome to-

'what the hell is going on?!' yelled an unsettled voice from the people. This time no one *shhhh'd* them.

It was seconded by another. 'Yeah, why are the roads blocked?'

And a third.
'My children are terrified here!'

Simmons's composure faltered, even the faces of his officers seemed unnerved. You could see the worried boys behind the uniforms now. He spoke in his finest *'professional voice'*. 'I assure you, there is nothing to be concerned about. Everything that we are doing, all the procedures we are taking, they are all for your own safety'.

That did it. The crowd erupted into a boisterous outrage. Screaming and yelling and questioning, all on top of each other. The officers on the side-lines readied their batons by their hips and looked nervously for a *'go ahead'* head nod from their commander and chief. Children cried in their mother's arms and fingers began pointing, demanding answers.

'Please, just-can everyone please-'

Simmons tried in vain to calm the temper of the crowd, he'd feared this would happen. The dreaded 'S' word had done it, *safety. Everyone is so obsessed with it these days. Health and safety codes here, rules and regulations there, so much so that one mention of the blasted thing being jeopardised and everyone begins to lose their collective shit.*

The crowd roared, order and reason seemed to have all but gone, paving the way for bedlam. It reminded Simmons of those post-apocalyptic network TV Shows. When the law was abandoned, it seemed to strip away the characters of their morals, just like the rust that would eat away at the derelict cars that littered the sets. It reduced men to primal brutes who'd revert to looting and raping and pillaging, everybody fending for themselves. It always stunned Simmons at how little it took to dismantle the societal goodness in people, the compassion. In fact, it had made him question the whole thing entirely, just how much of it was an act? Just how much did one neighbor, smiling across their fence as they collected their morning milk, want to take a butchers knife to the flesh of the other, and finally slash them to death over that hideous fuck of a campervan that they'd kept parked on their drive all year round? Henry had been on the front lines of one too many murder investigations to take people at face value, he knew that things weren't always as they seemed. Behind the smiles, the '*good* mornings', the menial disputes, there was a whole world of bloody fury begging to be let out. Oh, some people could control it that's for sure, go for years and years suppressing it until it had faded away. But others would succumb, taking the blade, the gun, the chainsaw and letting all hell break loose. Simmons had, over recent years, begun to adopt the bleak philosophy that at some point or another, there is a tiny evil killer inside each and every one of us. Yes, it always stunned him, the depravity to which humans could sink, but mostly, it just disappointed him.

'There's been a prison break!' he yelled at the top of his voice. That did the trick. The crowd simmered, but he'd had a feeling that they'd recommence their riot, tenfold, after he'd finished his explanation. 'I'm not at liberty to discuss the ins and outs of the situation, in fact I've been instructed to tell you as little possible. But I'm doing this because I know this is a stressful situation for a lot of you, and quite frankly, I'd want to know too if I were in your shoes'

Muddy shoes, thought the Janitor bitterly, but only for a moment, he wanted answers too. Simmons sighed, and then continued. The cheap dated pop music wasn't playing over the speakers anymore, only the sound of his gruff northern voice filled the passage.

'At approximately 6:32pm this evening, an inmate, whose name I'm not at liberty to discuss at this present time, managed to somehow escape from *Her Majesty's Maximum Security Prison*, in Full Sutton'. As he spoke the name of the location his voice sounded particularly Northern.

'Now like I said, at this present time I'm under strict orders not to reveal the name of the escapee. However, I can tell you it is of extremely high importance to the police force that we recapture and incarcerate the offender as quickly as possible.'

There was a notable unit change in his voice then. Simmons seemed to slip from his professional, head of the department for five years-persona, and into a more personal, colloquial tone, the way he might've spoken to a friend. 'I should be honest and upfront with you. This man, he's dangerous, and we have reason to believe he's capable of doing harm to anyone he comes into contact with. And it's for this reason, we want to keep you all here. Believe me when I say it's far safer for you in here than it is out there, on the Moors, and as long as you stay in the *O'Nowhere*, you're at no risk at all. My men and I will be remaining here and in the vicinity of the building throughout the night to protect you until the assailant is caught. Please understand, this may seem extreme, but it's just a precaution. The next twelve hours are crucial if we want to catch this man. He's boxed in and there's nowhere for him to go, so it's only a matter of time before he's back in his cell and you can all carry on your merry way.'

The crowd, though still worried, seemed to respond better to this line of thought. Henry was making sense, as long as they stayed in the station they'd be safe. Ted on the other hand, didn't like it one bit. His plans of reaching Middlesbrough were instantly dashed. He should've been forcing his way through a hearty high-street pub by now, where the smell of sizzling sausages and the clinking of blonde ales in tankards had ruled the day, inquiring about the price of their cheapest single-bedroom. Instead, here he was, trapped, stuck, quite literally, in the middle *O'Nowhere*, and he hated it. He felt as though he were trying to make his way out of a thick, dense woodland without a map nor a compass, only to find himself down a path that he'd already been down before. Just when he'd begun to think that he'd figured his way out, he'd notice familiar tree stumps and patterns of vegetation and realise that he'd been hiking in circles the entire time. This was exactly the kind of entrapment that he'd run away from Birmingham to leave behind. He could wait, he supposed. Where he was headed certainly wouldn't be going anywhere. But just thinking of it, carrying on without him, of him not being there, of being so close yet so far, it made his skin itch.

It made the janitors skin itch too, really crawl, the prospect of him being forced to stay at the Goddamned pit stop, way after he'd been due to sign off. Simply punching his clock just wouldn't have cut the mustard now, no, he wanted to pulverise the thing into smithereens. It was bad enough that he'd had to work there in the first place.

'I better be fucking paid over-time for this' he muttered to himself. But somehow he'd doubted it, if his prick of a manager had been anything to go by. And these two weren't the only one's upset by the police ruling...

'Fuck this. You can't keep me here, man. I know my rights!'

The large tanned gypsy whom Ted had noticed earlier outside the coffee shop, stood up and shouted profanities aggressively at the officers. His bulky, burly figure ran towards the locked double doors of the station. He was surprisingly quick given his built, stocky frame. All eyes turned to him as he assertively shoved passengers out of his way, sending a frail elderly man tumbling to the floor with a thud. With both hands firmly gripped on its two front legs, the gypsy grabbed a nearby wooden chair and moved to swing it at the glass doors. His biceps and triceps bulged beneath his tracksuit hoody and his massive traps tensed. He looked like an orange *Incredible Hulk*. The full force of the chair came into contact with the doors with a threatening crunch, sending a sudden web of cracks across the glass. The people gasped. Luckily though, before he could deal a second blow, an officer had been on hand to make a swing of his own, colliding the edge of his black baton to the man's shin and collapsing him onto the floor along with the chair. The gypsy let out a roar of pain as he'd hit the deck.

'Fuck you. You can't keep me here! If I wanna go, I can go. Bastards!' the traveller cursed, struggling and riving as another two officers arrived to drag him away by his arms and collar, no easy task. Ted and the crow-eyed janitor watched as they heaved the colossal scoundrel around the corner, like Alaskan hunters wrestling with a wild grizzly caught in their snare. Then he was gone. The scene had disturbed the people and Simmons could sense this. He cleared his throat. Not that he'd needed to vacate any phlegm, it was just something he'd always done to make himself sound more authoritative.

'I apologise. Clearly tensions are running...a little high. But that's no reason for panic or for us to lose ourselves. I think the most important thing we can all do in this situation is to remain calm.' He'd lowered the palms of his hands as he'd said this, like pushing feelings of agitation and stress back into the *Pandora's Box* they'd come from, and then patting down the corners of the lid. 'Now as I said, I need you all to stay put for now. This could be for an hour, or it could be all night, it all depends on how quickly we apprehend the convict. But make no mistake, we *will* catch him'. This appealed to the proud Yorkshire folk's sense of patriotism, nodding their heads and affirming that *their* police force were the best in the UK. Of course they'd catch him, they'd be trained in God's Own Country after all.

'I'm aware that these are less than ideal surroundings, but myself and

Manager Perkins here...' Henry pointed behind himself to a portly man in his mid-fifties, who for the first time now, stepped forward into view. He was wearing a charcoal suit and was sweating profusely, tiny clear driblets discharging from his forehead. He had a ratty appearance. '...have come to an arrangement. He'll be very kindly providing refreshments for the entirety of your stay. Food, drink, anything else you need. If you have loved ones please do feel free to call them and let them know that you're okay. We want your stay here to be as comfortable as possible.'

'That's right. There's no need to worry' said the chirpy-voiced manager, who, unlike Simmons, filled no one with any confidence. He smiled a greasy off-putting smile at his guests, but behind it had been secretly grinding his yellowing teeth, at the thought of all of the money that he'd be forking over in order to provide them nourishment. *Vampires*. He had a non-chin that disappeared into the collar of his shirt and seemed to spill over its crisp white edges. Ted didn't trust him. The janitor knew and hated the slimeball.

To round off his speech, and because it had gone down so well before, Simmons, like a politician repeating the mantra '*Make America Great Again*', said this. 'I know this is scary. But make no mistake. We *will* catch this man. It's just a matter of time. Thank you for your time and patience. If there are any updates you'll be the first to hear them. For now, sit tight, and Godspeed'. He then stepped down from the plant stand that he'd been preaching from, and left the promenade with three of his officers, to continue the manhunt.

There was a moment of awkward silence after the Inspector had departed, as if each one of the visitors had been waiting for the other to act first, to show them how to behave. But slowly and surely they began to break off, and to accept and acclimatise to their new surroundings. Many weren't happy about it, including one friendly-neighbourhood janitor.

He couldn't believe it. Stuck in that fucking station for what might've been all night. He wasn't scared of no prisoner, he wasn't scared of anything. Whatever he'd done it couldn't have been *that* bad, in fact, the creepy caretaker was pretty sure that *he'd* done far worse, within the hidden confides of his minds darkest corners. He had shit to do, he had a home to go to. But no, no one cared that he'd been up since 6:30am, no one cared that he'd been working flat-out cleaning dirty toilets and polishing tables and mopping the Goddamned floors for ten hours. They'd just gone ahead and trampled all over them with their filthy, dirty, rich-city shoes. Well he wasn't standing for it. The gaunt man gathered his lean legs and began striding purposefully towards the manager's office, shoving passengers as he went. He planned on having some very stern words with his tubby boss, and the outcome of his confrontation had better have been '*sure thing, head on home Billy*'. On his way out from the promenade, amidst the crowd, he noticed the no-good pretty boy who'd been the first to step all over his nice, cream, soap-scrubbed tiles. Oh, he hadn't liked that kid one bit. Maybe it had been his arrogant smirk, maybe it was the blasé' way that he'd run off and left Billy to clean up after him, like he'd thought that he was better than him. Maybe Billy just didn't like the cut of his jib. Whatever the reason, Billy had shoved him with the edge of his right shoulder as he'd passed, extra hard, just to remind him not to cross him whilst he was

69

stuck in *his* station.

Ted was launched back by the push. 'Hey!' he snapped. But before he could identify the culprit of the attack, Billy had shape-shifted into the crowd. Behind Ted, police officers cordoned off the partially smashed web of glass on the doors that the gypsy had caused. What the hell was he supposed to do now?

It was then that Ted had felt a slight triple prod on the back of his jacket, and the smell of coffee beans and flapjack had come to him. 'If you want to know more, follow me to the lockers' said a northern voice, with the air of a gestapo informant. Ted knew immediately who it had been. He turned to reply, but she'd already started walking. Whilst the marooned Yorkshire tribe settled in for the long haul and awaited further news regarding the prison break, Ted followed the flow of red hair towards a back corridor behind the shops. Billy had stormed in the opposite direction. Before long the pair had arrived at a set of metal storage lockers away from everybody else, shared by staff and rarely, by paying customers. The red-head stopped outside one marked 291, and then turned to face Ted.

'This is a disaster, I can't believe we're trapped here for the night. I mean, how the hell am I supposed to get to my audition tomorrow?' she stressed, before Ted interrupted her. He'd fallen for her quirky games once before and wasn't about to let it happen again.

'Okay. If you want this conversation to go any further you're going to have to tell me your name' he insisted. She looked at him then, with her striking blue eyes, and conceded.

'Rose' she admitted. 'My names Rose.'

Ted leaned on the lockers triumphantly with an arrogant, boyish smirk across his face, perhaps the very same smirk that had pissed off Billy the Janitor so damn much. It would've been easy to misconstrue as smug, but Ted was just being Ted, there was no ego behind that smile.

'I'm Ted. See. That wasn't so hard, huh? Rose. That's pretty funny.'

She looked at him, puzzled.

'Rose. As In, the colour. It's the same colour as your hair. That's a pretty cool coincidence' he said, disappointed that he'd had to explain his joke out loud. He'd found it pretty clever, especially for 10:30pm and given the gloomy predicament that they were in. Those things had a habit of sucking out all the humour from people.

'If only. But life isn't that smart. This isn't even actually my real hair colour. Nope. I'm a blonde. Through and through. My agent suggested that I dyed it so that I'd, and I quote "stand out more". Have you got any idea just how many blonde haired, blue eyed actresses there are out there? And believe me there are ones that are way prettier than me'. Rose said this sadly, but it seemed to Ted that it was something that she'd lived with and learned to accept a long time ago. He didn't think it was true at all, he thought she was really pretty.

'Agent? Oh right yeah…the acting thing. I forgot.'

'Hold up, I don't know anything about you. Where are you from? What brings you to our humble *O'Nowhere*?' asked Rose.

Ted became cagey. 'That's none of your business' he snapped, instantly regretting it.

'Wow, okay, sorry I asked, big guy' she replied. An awkward silence followed which felt particularly uncomfortable given the pleasant rate at which their conversation had been ping-ponging before it.

'I'm sorry, I just don't really want to talk about it that much' Ted admitted, sounding like himself again. He then quickly tried to change the subject.

'That's pretty naff about your audition, I'm sorry' he said sincerely, he could tell that it had meant a lot to her. 'You're not the only one who's got somewhere to be though...that's all I'll say for now. Didn't you say you knew more about what was going on?' Ted followed the lead, if this girl could give him an insight into how long he might've been staying at *O'Nowhere* that night, then he'd needed the information big time. Middlesbrough was waiting.

The now-named Rose, who was still in her mustard yellow coffee house uniform, sensed that she'd struck a sensitive subject, and so chose to forgive his outburst. As an actor, and thus, an observer of people, she knew that humans, being the messy things they are, had an ugly tendency to say and to do things that they didn't mean, when forced to confront painful truths. So, she moved on as if nothing had happened. Whatever it was that had brought Ted to the *O'Nowhere*, it can't have been good. It could wait, for now. She glanced over her shoulder, then behind Ted's, and then over her own again to make sure that the coast was clear, it was.

Everybody was still in the promenade digesting the Inspectors bombshell announcement. She leaned in close so that Ted could smell her flowery perfume. He didn't allow himself to be distracted by the fact that an attractive girl was inside his personal space. It was a welcome invasion, but he'd needed the truth. She spoke in a whisper, the scene resembled a High school after-hours gossip.

'The prisoner, the guys who's on the run. I know who it is...' she sharply muttered. Ted paused to signal her to continue. 'His name is "Marcus Geller"', she said the name with reverence, as though it were a curse to speak it.

'I've never heard of him...'

'...well you wouldn't have. When he committed his crimes it was all the way back in the late 70's. He must be ancient by now, easily pushing sixty-six, he still scares the hell out of me though. But yeah, what *he* did, happened a way back. Thirty-odd years is basically a hundred to the news channels, it's been buried, forgotten now'.

'Wait...did you say..."Crimes"? As in, plural? How much did this Marcus Geller guy do exactly?'

Rose had indeed used a plural. She swallowed and prepared herself to tell the heart-breaking story. She always found something sickeningly pleasurable in revealing its gory details, and she knew that people always found a morbid curiosity in hearing them. It is after all, in our nature as humans to want to hear what we shouldn't, the wrong, the depraved, the inhumane. And yet, the tale took on a whole new context knowing that the perpetrator behind the crimes was at large, this time, she couldn't shake the fear in her bones. She began the account.

'I forget his name, I'm sure he went by William Blythe, or maybe it was Brown, we'll stick to Blythe, it's cooler. Anyways, so way back when, in a late 70's summer, good old Will Blythe was driving back home to Sleights from Grosmont. He'd taken the long route through Dalby Forest to pick up some supplies on the way. See, Blythe was an independent contractor who'd been hired to do some renovation work on a bridge in the town near the old railway station, you know the one, the one that the heritage steam train passes through for tourists. It had needed the repairs for weeks and finally the council had gotten around to organising the job. A stray brick had fallen from one of its pillars and almost taken out some kids playing at the river bank, that'd been the thing to finally force their grubby hands to a cheque book. It was midday, around 1:30pm or so the story goes. Will was nearly home, driving through a bend in the woods, when suddenly he'd had to stop. Now, you may think that running into a herd of sheep across the road ain't such a strange occurrence up North, especially around these parts, it's actually pretty irritating when you've got somewhere to be, but Will could tell that something wasn't quite right.'

Ted remained silent the whole time that she spoke, not wanting to disrupt the flow of her tale. She sure could spin a good narrative, if her acting was half as good as her campfire storytelling it perplexed him as to why she wasn't more successful than she was. He'd bet she'd deliver a mean monologue.

....Will didn't have to be a man of the land to know that something was
amiss. The sheep were static and scared, disbanded and bleating instead
of grazing peacefully. Their eyes bulged from their sockets with fear and
their black hooves quivered, shaking in their fluffy white fleeces. Their
baby lambs, with teddy bear eyes and floppy cream ears, too, huddled
closely to their mother's tails. Will knew that a shepherd would never
have let sheep as young as those go out so far from the home field. The
crowd of grating baaa's unsettled William, and what didn't help is that
the livestock were two ram horns away from being the face of Satan
himself. He rolled the front wheels of his car forwards a little further into
the cloudy traffic, and that was when he saw that the animal outbreak
hadn't been constrained to just one species. Two giant Stallions stood a
stone's throw away, ahead along the road, saddle-less and without an
equestrian wearing jockey to straddle their dark brown manes. They were
a tad braver than the sheep, sniffing and snorting at the ground with their
smooth, black, *Pegasus* nostrils and stamping over daisy's with the force
of their muscular thighs. This was when Will opened his side door and
left his car to investigate the scene. He passed the terrified sheep, who
were all marked with red pigment as to avoid confusion with any
neighbouring countrymen, and headed into the forest that they had
seemingly appeared from.

There was a clear trail marked through the woods by way of squashed
plants and scratched bark, the undergrowth crushed as if the animals had
galloped over it in a hurry. Strands of sheep fur clung to low hanging
branches like checkpoints, guiding Will's path to the source of the
breakout. It didn't take long for him to identify the escape route, for atop
a ramp of shrubbery there stood a broken fence. Its splintered wood was

pried outwards and its iron nails were bent as if the animals had forced their way out in a panic. Less an Orwell uprising, more a beasts retreat, these guys must've really wanted to get away from whatever it was that had been in their field. A wolf perhaps? No. That wasn't it. Flies buzzed around the mangled carcasses of baby lambs that had been sacrificed in the stampede, their tiny, brittle bones crushed and their skin torn under the weight of their fellow sheep. Their eyes stayed wide open, gazing up at the skies as if to ask God why they'd been taken so young. The contrast between the red of their strewn guts and the white of their fresh, cotton towel fur was disturbingly stark. Will pushed forward through the gap of light in the torn fence, he needed answers. Through the break in the border, he found himself in a vast green clearing where the sheep and horses had fed, and at the centre of it, just beyond another small fence, was a solitary country farmhouse. *Geller Farm.*

William edged his way along the main road towards the house, it was muddy and marked with tractor wheels and poultry car skids. The air smelt strongly of manure and the hot summer sun seemed to marinate the stench, he could still hear the distressed cries of the sheep behind him. It was a dustbowl dry day, the kind where vultures circle, waiting for the dead. The building was decrepit and old, its walls peeling and its shuttered windows covered in dust. He'd felt small and weak looking up at the giant house, like it's corrugated bay doors would suck him in and swallow him whole. None of the lights were on and not a farm hand nor a hen was in sight. The only sound that came from the creaky shack was from the high pitched ringing of the wind chimes that had brushed to and fro in the summer air above the porch. Sandy lines of hay lay across the yard, a sack-headed scarecrow with a missing eye stared from a pasture of crops. Will stepped towards the closed main door to the farms living quarters, where the Gellers spent their days when they weren't grooming produce, and raised a fist to knock. He felt a duty to tell the farms owner, who at the time he didn't know was Marcus, that his livelihood had up'd and broken free from right under his nose. But before he could connect his fist to the door, he'd noticed a sticky substance leaking from under its crack and onto his workman boots. It was dark and thick and red and seemed to drip between the unvarnished floorboards of the porch. Will stopped dead in his tracks, and then turned and ran like he'd never run before, pummelling towards the nearest payphone whilst crows cawed around him.

William Blythe returned to the crime scene but this time he wasn't alone. Backup came in the form of three squadron police cars, the lead of which pulled up first outside the farm. Its front wheels cracked dried dirt and upended dust clouds into the air as it came to a standstill, before the right door swung open and the Grosmont Chief Inspector stepped out. Donning a tight, tucked in shirt, black trousers and brown leather boots, Detective Cole Simmons, Father of a certain Henry Simmons, who was clearly inspired and enthused by his Dads collection of mantelpiece accolades, walked towards the house.

'Over here' pointed a shaken Blythe, still in shock at what he'd discovered.

No wonder the animals had fled the scene. Judging by how scared they'd been, he was surprised to have seen that there'd been a farm house left at all and that it hadn't been blown to hell by a stray propane tank. A police officer slammed the door of his cop car shut, the impact sent a loose panel of rooftop tiling crashing down to the floor with a smash. Simmons Senior, followed by his subordinates, strutted his stuff up the rotting steps of the porch and removed his aviator sun glasses from the ridge of his nose, he looked like his son. Noting the pool of blood, that had increased in size considerably since Blythe had first identified it, he carefully side stepped around the dark red fluid, preserving it for when forensics arrived.

'Geller! Geller, it's Cole! Open up'' he yelled through the door, there was no reply. 'Geller! Geller!', still no answer. Cole knew everybody and anybody in Grosmont, a school kid couldn't so much as violate a '*Keep off the Grass*' sign without him knowing about it. Worried by now and with Marcus Geller still not replying, Cole made the call.

'Knock it in boys' he ordered. He made way for another officer who took the sole of his size 11 foot to the frame of the door, and after two strong kicks it gave way into the kitchen. Cole immediately covered his nose at the foul stench of decay that was released from the room, and then stepped inside with his men behind him.

What he saw, he attested to being the worst thing that he'd ever had to come across on all of his forty years on The Force. It would haunt him in is nightmares until the day that he died of dementia in 2006, absorbing him in a frenzy of screaming and cold sweats at 3am, tangled in his bed sheets. Holidays, Christmas, school assemblies, whatever the occasion, it would always be carved onto the underside of his eyelids, reminding him of the evil that he'd witnessed on that sunny July afternoon. Two of his men with weaker constitutions ran back out into the yard, they threw up into the pig trough next to the old leaky water spout and turned as white as the fur of the sheep fleeces just across the road. The rest of the officers who'd stayed just stared, fixated in disgust, eyes and jaws agape and stunned into silence.

Rose had Ted in the palm of her hands, she savoured the long pause before she made the treacherous reveal, and he hung on her every word. He begged to hear more with his patient silence, like a sinner praying for forgiveness at the hands of a pastor in a parish confession booth.

Immediately at their feet lay the decapitated corpse of Mary Jane Geller, Marcus's Wife. The circular shape of her neck where her severed head had once been, was the open wound from which the blood had dribbled under the door. Her rigor mortis body lay stiff and motionless on the kitchen tiles, as the pulpy stump that had been her face oozed out of the house and down the porch steps. Fly food. Her skull hadn't been severed by way of a blade laceration, instead it had been imploded, blown from her shoulders by what appeared to be the thick shell of a double barrel shotgun. What was left of her head was splashed around the kitchen floor, pieces of ripped flesh and mucus covering the yellowing walls whilst blood splatters soaked the curtains and hanging pans above the sink. Just across from her, her seven year old daughter had been spared the mutilation of *her* body, but was still dead never the less. Elsie lay face down on her backside, propped up against the oak kitchen cupboards. The blast, this time, had struck her chest, detonating straight through her infant torso and catapulting into her ribs and heart. Her tiny hands, too, lay still at the sides of her pink summer frock and shiny cream dolly shoes. Her beach blonde fringe protected the officers from the trauma of having to see her empty baby eyes, but Cole didn't have to put his fingers to the girls pulse to see that she was long gone.

But who could've done this? What kind of sick minded, cold blooded killer could've murdered an innocent, caring mother and her daughter in broad daylight in such horrific fashion? Cole didn't have to look far for the culprit. For at the kitchen table, wearing a forest green *Barbour* jacket and tweed cap, cradling the murder weapon and staring soullessly into space, sat none other than the father and husband of the victims, Marcus Geller. The guy gave a new meaning to the phrase; '*caught red handed*'. He hadn't so much as stirred or acknowledged the arrival of the officers, even when his country latched-door had been bolstered down. He had just sat at the mahogany table, gripping the iron funnel of his shotgun tightly and humming quietly to himself an old North Yorkshire Folk song, over and over. The melody was hummed through his gruff, constricted voice, round and around in a loop. Even when they'd driven him to the station in chains he'd sang it, a tune the officers would never again pry from their ears. His thick beard was stained with blood, and already traces of the liquid had begun to dry under his nails and cuticles. For Cole, the case was closed as quickly as it had been opened. Crushed, and his faith in humanity utterly decimated, he equipped his Taser gun and handcuffs, before reciting the legislation he'd come to know far too well...

'Marcus Geller, you are under arrest....'

The ends of Ted's neck hairs stood up on end and goose bumps rose on the pores of his skin. He wasn't one to scare easily but Rose's story had certainly stricken fear into the pit of his stomach. Ted thought about the

Geller man, surrounded by the massacred bodies of his family, sat alone in his kitchen for what might've been hours, just waiting in the middle of the countryside with nothing or no one for miles around. Who knows how long he might've sat there if William Blythe hadn't arrived.

The potential malevolent thoughts swimming between Geller's temples disturbed Ted, of upside down crosses, plucking the wings off insects, of stalking prostitutes who'd walk through dark Manchester alleyways alone at night. And now this man was at large, this man who'd taken a loaded gun to his daughters chest and pulled the trigger, this man who'd heard and ignored his wife's blood curdling screams as he'd killed the woman that he'd shared a bed with for years, this man was on the loose. And if Marcus was willing to commit such heinous crimes against people he'd supposedly loved, just what kind of atrocities was he capable of committing to a complete stranger…?

Ted mulled over the frightening permanence of death, the sickening finality of it all. It was the heart-breaking '*I can't take it anymore*' in a crumbling marriage, the burning of an old photo that was the last trace of a person's existence, the definitive full stop that signalled the final sentence of someone's favourite novel. It made Marcus's crime all the more terrible and suddenly caused Ted to experience a wave of frightful realisation for his own fragile mortality, the ease at which the slice of a knife could pierce his skin and end it all. He became very aware of the fact that he and Rose were alone in the corridor by the lockers and separated away from the rest of the group. He turned to suggest that they re-joined the pack, when suddenly he felt a hand on his shoulder grip him by the collar bone. He leapt out of his skin with a cry.

But, like a cheap 'jump scare' from a sub-par horror flick, the grab turned out to be a false alarm, not Marcus Geller at all, but Billy the Janitor.

'You scared the shit out of me!' yelled Ted, breathing with relief and putting his hands to the grass stained knees of his jeans to regain composure. Billy didn't seem to care though, in fact he took pleasure in almost making him defecate his denim.

'Good. I'm glad I scared you. Asshole. I'm looking for...' Billy's violent and hostile demeanour suddenly evaporated when he locked eyes on the beautiful Rose. He seemed to Ted to transform before his very eyes from the confrontational bully he'd run into earlier, to a reserved school boy with a serious case of the love bug, and was that a blush he'd spotted filling his slender cheeks?

'Oh hey Rose. I was just...coming to find you...' He stammered and stuttered his way through the sentence and Ted could've performed a beat poem to the kick drum of his heart, it'd sped up that much.

'Hey Billy, what's up?' she replied casually, now out of character as the maniacal story teller and once again off script.

'Oh...I went to see Perkins about the staff leaving for the night, and he told me to gather everyone up into his office for a chat'.

'Jesus. Wonder what the slave driver wants this time?' joked Rose, to which Billy laughed hysterically. She could've said anything and he'd have laughed. 'I'll be along in a minute, okay Bill?' she replied, pushing a lock of her hair behind her ear and not realising that she'd made his day.

'Sure thing Rose!' he smiled back, before realising he'd been smiling and staring a tad too long. He scurried away past the lockers and into the darkness to summon the rest of the staff, colleagues he'd have spoken to in a far less courteous manner. He nudged Ted again on his way out. He couldn't have had that kid thinking that he was some sort of soft-brained pushover now, could he?

'"Bill?" You're friends with that Jerk?' an unbelieving Ted asked Rose.

'He's never been a Jerk to me. It's just Billy. People give him a hard time because he's different, but all he needs is someone to be nice to him and poof, he's not so bad. People don't have time for weirdoes, but I do'. Her answer had been so sincere that Ted had restrained himself from telling the girl that Billy was clearly head over heels for her. He may have been a bully, but the brotherhood code was the brotherhood code.

'Well, you should count yourself lucky. He's given me nothing but trouble since I've got here', Ted said as he rubbed his bruised shoulder.

'Just stay out his way and he shouldn't give you any grief. He's harmless really. Now, do you wanna hear what happened next or don't you?' Rose tempted him, Ted took the bait.

'After Marcus was taken into custody he refused to talk, he wouldn't answer a single question for Cole or any of the other officers. Luckily though they'd had enough evidence to pin on him to fill a dump truck, so they didn't need a confession, if anything his non-talking just made him seem more guilty. As you can imagine, the overwhelming evidence and lack of any kind of remorse didn't play out too well in front of the Jury. Marcus got himself slammed up in *Full Sutton Prison* on a life sentence with no chance of parole and no one's heard from him since...

....until now that is. They had to move him into the *Vulnerable Inmates Division* after a few years though, prison isn't too kind on men who murder their families. One night, around nine months into his sentence, he got attacked by a group of crooks with home-made knives in the showers, he was lucky to have made it out alive.' Ted Gulped.

'Some of the kids in town say that if you cycle past the prison at dusk, you can see the light on in his cell up on the top floor. They say if you listen closely, you can hear the sound of him humming that folk song, carrying on the wind, the same tune he'd sung over and over again on that sunny day, when Officer Cole had found him covered in his wife and daughters insides'.

Ted processed the horrendous depictions that had been forced upon his brain for a moment, before his rationale took over and he began to poke holes in Rose's theory. 'Wait. How do you even know all this? How do you know he's the prisoner that escaped at all?'

'I've got a friend who works up in the prison', she bragged smugly, 'the police aren't revealing anything to the press to avoid panic, but it won't be long before everyone figures it out. A detail this huge wouldn't have been deployed unless someone really bad had broken free. Which they have.' Rose could see, despite his best efforts to look manly, that her story had frightened Ted. She put her hand onto his sore shoulder, he didn't mind when *she* touched him there. 'Don't worry, have you seen the amount of police they've got on this? They'll catch the guy in no time. He's got nowhere to hide, Inspector Simmons is right. You'll be out of here by morning to...wherever it is you're trying to get to'.

Ted could see why Billy had a crush on the girl. Her name was certainly appropriate, she was most definitely a prized English garden flower, the fairest in the land, with rosy cheeks, pale skin, supple pink lips and those shinning azure eyes. He'd bet she'd look even prettier with blonde hair, it saddened him that she'd thought she'd had to change herself at all.

'Pfft. I'm not scared of no crazy old kook. The guy's hip would probably shatter if he tried to take a swing at me. Thanks for the heads up about it all though, it's nice to know what we're up against' fronted Ted, as Rose pulled out a set of keys from her apron and moved to locker 291. They dangled from a silver, moon-shaped tag.

'It's no problem. I figured I still owed you one, since you didn't get to eat my world famous pesto/ham surprise. I didn't even spit in it or anything', she turned the key on her locker and left it inside without pulling open the blue metal door. 'It's awful though isn't it? Just how messed up does a man have to be to do something like that?'

'Does anybody know why, he did it?'

'Nope. How could they? Marcus hasn't spoken a word to anyone since the conviction. Not even his own son visited him...I can understand why.'

'There was a survivor?' asked Ted, hoping for a happy ending in some form or another amidst the misery.

'Not a survivor. Just lucky. Terrence was slightly older than Elsie, around twelve, he'd been out playing with a friend nearby when his Dad had...done what he'd did. If he'd been at home that day he probably would've had his own fair share of bullet holes too. It's terrible. But no. No one knows *why* exactly. Some say he found out his wife was having an affair and snapped. Others say that he went stir-crazy farming alone out there on the Moors, that the long days and early mornings of isolation wreaked havoc on the guy's head and drove him round the bend. I heard a rumour that one of his favourite cows had '*told him to do it*'. And then there's the third possibility...and quite frankly I don't even want to consider that...' Her face darkened then, as though the sun had been blocked and her English Rose complexion had wilted and withered in the winter.

'What?' pushed Ted.

'Well...maybe nothing happened. Maybe he was just born a monster, maybe there was nothing he could've done about it and since the day he was born he was always destined to kill his wife and kids. That scares me the most I think, the idea that any one of us could be a killer and can't do a single damn thing about it'. Ted didn't like this Rose, the sad, scared, defeated Rose. From what he'd seen of her, she was at her truest self when she was hopeful and happy, with faith in the world. She'd *need* it to have been pursuing an acting career, Jeez. It was his turn to comfort her now.

'Well, like you said, it's not something we have to worry about because he'll be caught any minute and shipped back to the big house where he belongs'. This worked, her smile returned. Hers was a face that smiles were made for.

'Thanks Ted. You're a good guy'.

'You too Rose. Hey, I'm sorry about your audition, that's a real shame', he commiserated. It reminded Rose of something that she'd wished she'd forgotten. She huffed and suddenly looked extremely tired, like the preceding nine hours of coffee pouring and bun glazing had caught up with her body in one go.

'Ugh. I totally forgot about that with all our murder talk. I'm gutted. There's no way I'll make it now, it's all the way on the other side of Manchester at 9am.'

'What's it for? A TV show? A cool new movie?' asked Ted, excited, spoken like a true fool without a bone of culture in his body. Rarely did such glamorous opportunities come Rose's way.

'It's for an all woman's rendition of "*Julius Caesar*" she replied, simultaneously sorry to disappoint him and slightly irritated by his presumption. Ted's face deflated.

'Oh'.

It was a face she recognised all too well. Friends and family who were oblivious to the true craft of performing always switched off whenever she'd mentioned the dreaded '*Shakespeare*'. He wasn't sexy, the Stratford bard didn't even write in modern English never mind have any hair. His plays wouldn't be on TV, his plays wouldn't have cool trailers and posters that proud aunts and mothers could share of *Facebook*. If she'd had to hear a relative ask her about why she hadn't landed a gig on a soap-opera, or how she shouldn't forget them when she was famous, one more time, she'd thought she was going to scald them with a piping hot cup of Joe. Clearly Ted was no different.

'Well that sounds...interesting' he lied.

'It's okay. You don't have to pretend. I know most people don't find Shakespeare interesting, but it's important to me and I really would love this part. I'm up for the role of "Brutus" and I've been going over his "conspirator speech" all week trying to get it perfect for tomorrow. Looks like I won't even get the chance now, it'd probably have been another "no" anyway...' She sighed, reminded of the hundreds of crushing rejections that she'd received thus far in her career.

'If you're tired of "No's" why don't you just...I dunno...apply for drama schools? That's a thing isn't it? Maybe that'd be a better way into it?' asked Ted, trying to help but continuing on his roll of ignorance, in a field that he knew nothing about.

'...and give my money to an elitist, pretentious institution that charges way too much to make you dance, choreograph dumb physical routines, memorise ridiculous vocal warm ups and channel your "inner truth" for three years and label it is as "art"? All under the supervision of washed up wannabee's who never succeeded in their own careers and so try and make a buck by squashing the hopes and dreams of up and coming artists by telling them that they aren't good enough? No thanks.'

Ted refrained from prying that particular can of worms open any further. Rose swung open the door of her locker, and out tumbled an assortment of goggle eyed, stuffed, teddy alien toys, ranging in colour from blue, orange, green and yellow.

'Erm....'

'Don't judge me. They're from the toy claw machine in the lobby. A girl's gotta do something to keep herself occupied on her lunch breaks.'

Ted held his hand to his mouth to stop himself from laughing. 'That's the saddest thing I've ever seen' he joked.

'Be that as it may, I've got every single colour of these bad boys, apart from the red one, never could clinch that bastard...haven't you got anything better to do then to make fun of poor, alien collecting girls at service stations? Oh yeah. I forgot. You don't. So you better get used to this here saddo'. She winked playfully, nudging his arm and closing her locker after getting the water bottle that she'd be searching for, replacing the abundance of fallen kids' toys inside.

'I better shoot off anyway "mysterious Ted who won't tell me where he's from", not that Manager Perkins will let any of us go home early anyways. I guess I'll see you around, it's a small station after all, try not to get too bored without me and my bedtime stories' Rose giggled, and then she was gone, leaving Ted alone by the lockers. After the safe haven of the pairs flirting had worn off, Ted began to replay the dastardly account of Marcus Geller in his head. The gruesome details chilled him to the core and at the risk of a shotgun wielding hand bursting from the lockers to get him, or of hearing the soft humming of the killers folk song through the overhead ventilation system, he decided to scram and to re-join the safety of the law abiding citizens in the promenade. He could already smell the refreshments that Perkins had guaranteed. The smell didn't seem promising, but anything was better than staying in that dark corridor alone. He sure did hope that they caught the killer soon so that he could be on his way to Middleborough. Once again, he chose to ignore another of his mother's voice mails, but if he *had* listened to it, it probably would've sounded a little like this…

'Ted. Teddy. I used that tracking app they have to trace your phone. I know where you are, and I know where you're going. Oh Teddy, why are you going there? Really? After all this time? Do you really think anything's waiting for you there? You promised me over and over that you wouldn't go. Please just come home will you? They're saying on the news that some dangerous prisoner has broken free around those parts, you're not caught up in any of that are you? Please Teddy, will you just call me? I Love You.'

…but of course, the messaged remained unopened.

Ted re-joined the masses, a lonesome hero looking for his place in the world, while a sick minded janitor, a wide eyed dreamer red head, a disillusioned police Inspector, an angry, raging gypsy, and a mysterious custard-coat wearing boy all readied themselves for a long night of waiting, unbeknownst to all of them, the horrors that it would have in store. What a curious selection of strangers the hands of fate had picked for the evening. But selected them they had, and there was no turning back now.

And so, with the passengers locked up inside the station, outside, the Yorkshire Moors had begun to claim back the world that they had left behind for themselves. The once clogged motorways, flooded by headlights that'd brighten the faces of hidden speed cameras and catch the light of amber studs on the outside of the carriage-ways, were now lit only by the glare of the street lamps. Weary eyes that would gaze hopefully at blue and white signs for the miles back home were long gone, only searching police who patrolled the borders stayed. The roads were empty even of the joyriding 3am stragglers, who'd coast smoothly along its lanes with open windows and open lungs. Just miles of winding, silent nothing. Leaves of the untended road-side trees floated onto the highway, awaiting raking by way of a lorry's whooshing that would never come. Overhead signs were stuck on loop, mindlessly flashing 'traffic ahead' in red and in green.

Families of rabbits who'd dare not ever cross the roads, for fear of fatal rubber wheels, suddenly hopped from the shrubbery, bright eyed and bushy tailed, and then trampled over the tarmac. Meanwhile, wild orange foxes, strangled the pit stops bins to the ground, scavenging through half-finished burgers and chicken wrappers that were sent cascading to the floor. When they'd had their fill, they'd skulk towards the twitching hares on the concrete, leaving the paper wrappers to drift across the wet lawn. The night wind howled like the lost voices of injured mountaineers carrying through ravines. Its force began to tug at a loose banner, advertising a kids '2 for 1' bargain in rainbow crayon colours. Manager Perkins had been on at Billy all week to tighten the ropes on that thing, but now it was too late. It ruffled and then came away from the brown wooden fence that it was attached to, struggling at first, and then surrendering to will of the dusk. It wasn't unlike a young, petite brunette, raped and then thrown into the icy depths of a city river. She'd fight the waves, before her lungs burst and her limbs would go stiff, her heavy bones sinking her to the depths of the lonely, black bottom, waiting to be fished out months later. Yes, just like that poor, hypothetical brunette victim, the promo banner resisted, and then tore from the ropes that had suppressed it, flying up into the white-dwarf sky, succumbing to the current of air. It was pulled away by invisible hands, across the road where the foxes slaughtered the rabbits, airborne like a voodoo magic carpet, and then up the ridge towards the Moors, before it vanished into the night. It belonged to the Heath now…

…they all did.

CHAPTER FOUR

They say there are other worlds. There are alternate realities that run parallel to our own, existing simultaneously on different plains of being, ones that are always concurrent alongside us. The paths we tread, the monuments we see; there are, at this very moment, exact replicas of everything that we have come to know, lying on the other side of some invisible, crystallised door of Technicolor, through a gap in space and time. This theory of course stretches to include ourselves, there are doppelgängers that are clones of us. They are the same in every way, from our freckles to the microscopic molecules that bind us together. They go on with their lives as we do; laughing, crying, working, mirroring, all within the confines of another dimension that remains always out of reach.

Perhaps it is this peculiar scientific phenomenon that best describes the transformation that occurred to the North Yorkshire National Moors between the sinking of the sun and the rising of the moon. It was almost a biological change, altering at a subatomic level like the fizzing cells of slugs under pinches of sodium chloride. For once the night time came, the tranquil peace and beauty of the pollinated fields, became a den of nightmares and fear. How could it be that somewhere so beautiful and inviting between the hours of 8am and 6:45pm, could become so frightening and hostile upon the watershed?

Mothers forbade their children from playing on the Moors once the solar wattage of the sun's battery had needed charging, for fear of loose footing, or careless slips down treacherous hillsides that would've otherwise provided the perfect slopes for mud sliding during the days. Dog walkers whistled their canines to reunite them with their leads, and then returned them safely to their kennels and warm bowls when the stars had begun reveal their faces. Even harmless animals reconvened to their burrows, when the fields, which had shone a hundred different shades of green during the day, like the varying prints of black & white newspaper clippings on the cork board of an obsessed detective, had changed to a formidable, singular sheet of black. Everybody knew to leave the Moors alone once the sun had begun to set. The heath was kind enough to let them wander its mighty pastures during the days, but at night, when this chemical change had occurred, it demanded its privacy. Woe betide the man who denied the Moors their solitude. Fifty-two year old Simon Berkley, was one such man.

Simon wasn't afraid of the Moors, not at night, not in the day, not in the morning, not ever. On that particular dusk he'd decided to hold a mini-coup of sorts against his wife. She did have a habit of worrying bless her, dearest Carol, so much so that she'd given old Simon, her hubby of forty years (*of which they were very proud*) a curfew for his walks. He was to be home and in his comfy chair in front of the TV and log fire for 21:00 promptly, or he'd face the iron wrath of her temper. Then it'd be him sleeping in the dog house, never mind his trusted border collie. But that night, Simon had found it to be a particularly beautiful evening, and he was sure that Carol would've felt the same if she'd been there. So, what the hell; *an extra 15 minutes wouldn't hurt.* He sure did love her. To Simon, his wife was as perfect and as radiant as she'd been all those years ago when they'd first met at the *Malton Weekly Village Dance.* If he'd have closed his eyes, he'd have still been able to picture the flower in hair, the white of her dress, the lavender soap smell of her skin. Well, he'd be with her again soon enough, back in the warm comfort of familiarity. But for now, he'd had a walk to enjoy.

All of a sudden, as Simon squished gloopy piles of mud beneath his feet, the glare of a bright white light filled a circle around him. It hovered over him for a moment, like a UFO prepping for an abduction, before moving onto the path ahead of him and fading over the ridge. It was another one of those police spotlights. Simon had counted five helicopters and over a dozen cars so far. Something was going on out of there, it was almost as if the Yorkshire Force were searching for something, or someone. He chuckled to himself then, remembering something that Carol had told him once. Whenever she'd heard the propeller blades of one of those choppers, she'd instantly felt guilty, like she'd had a sordid secret to hide, and that went for spotting officers out on the beat around the village watermill too. It right cracked Simon up, imagining his wife, his prim and proper wife, who'd always kept a jar full of all of her receipts and had baked for the village cake sale, slapped across a '*WANTED*' poster in the Malton post office. *Carol Berkley: Bank Robber Extraordinaire.*

The heart-warming glow of his fond memories made Simon yearn to sweep her off of her feet and to kiss her again. Who was he kidding? He'd have done anything for that crazy old coot, and that included making his nine o'clock curfew. He turned to go. And that's when he saw it.

'What's that old boy?' he asked his trusty dog, who began barking at a light in the distance, beyond the clustered branches. As Simon stomped closer, he saw that the light didn't belong to that of a scouting choppers spotlight, nor had it been the attic window bulb of a Duke's lonely country estate. Rather, it was from the headlights of a crashed Mustang. From the looks of things, it'd slammed bonnet-first into the bark of a lowly Birch, and was smoking from under the hood.

'Oh my God' gasped Simon, distraught. But as he scrambled with his dog through the forestry to check the welfare of the driver, and if necessary, to rescue them from the wreckage of the vehicle before it'd burst into flames, an unexpected guest decided to put an end to his well-intentioned plans. A hand grabbed Simon by the collar, and pulled him into the darkness. By the time the dog had turned to find his owner, he was long gone. The pup cried and whelped alone in the dark, before lying on his belly and waiting for his master to return. He didn't.

· · ·

Two hours after this incident, Ted was ten years old again, and sitting at his kitchen table looking out at the sea. The waves were rambunctious, nautically foaming and collapsing in and over each other like a flood of mermaid's tails. But up from the crow's nest of his kitchen window, ten year old Ted could see the beach as well as the ocean, and it was *this* that he had been watching that morning.

Barefooted children ran laughing along the sand bed, strings about their hands as they choreographed dancing kites, which soared on the summer wind like origami swans. Parents watched, smiling proudly from afar, on standby to wash clean their grainy feet, under the cold water taps beside the multi coloured beach huts. Photographers scanned the horizon through zoomed in lenses, their cameras propped on tripods, allowing them the steadiness to capture the focal point of the pier against the tides. Oh, the glorious tides, home to whales and seals and fishes and sailors trapped in Great White bellies. Wafer coned ice-creams of mint, strawberry and salted caramel could be easily traced back to the seaside café that overlooked The Bay. Business sure was booming. But the beach was merely on loan from the sea whilst the tide was out, sovereignty still, and always would, belonged to Atlantis. For tiny rock pools that were made up of salty seaweed and swirling shells and fossils, hosted pinching crustaceans, as if on day trips themselves, until the tide returned at dusk to fetch them back out with the sea fog. The delicious waft of battered sausage and chips in the sweltering summer sun wound its way up the cobble-stone streets, past the gift shops, cottages and pubs, right up to Ted's door. But instead, a bowl of piping hot porridge oats and raspberry jam was plonked in front of him, distracting him away from the sea view.

Breakfast had been served up by the same broad, anchor-tattooed, blue fisherman jumper-wearing man that had encroached upon Ted's last dream. His weathered, calloused hands placed it on the wooden kitchen table, along with a silver handed spoon and a glass of cold juice. This time though, Ted's imagination allowed him to see a little more of the man, an extra clue to piece together his likeness. A thick, prickly black beard around the lower half of the adults face stared down at Ted. His eyes were kept from view, in accordance with the nonsensical regime of *'dream rules'* that leave the sleeper at the mercy of their own brain. But this time around, the man spoke.

'I think we need to talk, Son'.

Then Ted woke up.

Oh yeah. He was stuck at a service station. He preferred the dream.

He awoke on his ass. He'd been napping on the floor against the back of a vending machine in the promenade area, which was hardly the comfiest of positions and had resulted in a very stiff neck joint. Going by his watch, he'd been out of action for twenty minutes. What had happened? The last he could recall he'd returned to the *O'Nowhere* lobby after his debriefing with Rose about Marcus Geller, and then had helped himself to the rather miserable buffet spread that had been put on by Manager Perkins. Tomato soup and crusty bread were the menu specials, with a choice of lemonade or apple juice to wash it down the hatch. With limited supplies available, a rationing had been put in place so that everybody had been given only a single chocolate bar each. Perkins was too much of a cheapskate to allow his guest's full access to the stations shops. On the whole, the food had been a disappointment, hardly worth the forty person queue to reach it.

If only he'd have boarded an earlier bus, that way he'd have made the crossing to Middlesbrough hours ago, before the police had even had the chance to seal off the roads. Now, even if they'd arrested or gunned down Marcus Geller there and then on the Moors, there'd have been no way that the bus service would've ran as normal until the following day. It looked like his plans had been dashed and that he wouldn't be reaching his secret destination until the cockerel cry of morning.

The little fear that had been instilled in him from Rose's tale of bloodshed had now been replaced by frustration and boredom. And truth to be told, it was difficult to generate any fear whilst being surrounded by the hum drum chit chat of Yorkshire folk and their children playing hand-held video games. The mood of the station had relaxed and it seemed that the guests had accepted the course of their night, in fact many of them had seemed to find it an exciting change of pace. No doubt it was soon to become an electric anecdote that they could exaggerate to their friends at their next BBQ gathering. Yorkshire folk sure did love to talk.

Ted hated being trapped. He could feel a burning itching on his scalp and on the inflamed skin of his wrists from being stuck in the same damn place for too long, and he couldn't do a thing about it. No one had left or entered the station since Simmons had officially announced the lockdown and at this point it didn't matter if Ted had been ten miles from Middlesbrough or ten thousand miles. The longer he stayed put, the longer he gave his mom the chance to work out where he was and to intercept him. No way was he going back to Birmingham, no way. He'd come too far and given up too much just to leave the North again. They'd have to drag him back by his hair until he was as bald as the day that he was born if they'd wanted Ted to move. But none of this changed the fact that Ted, sat on the floor with his back to the '*Out Of Order*' vending machine, was stone cold bored out of his young adult mind.

He began his crusade against his boredom by people watching, he could've answered his moms missed calls to pass the time, but decided against this tactic. He characterised a moustached Father as a Mexican drug cartel, assuming a false identity and living incognito. A middle-aged, vixen mother became a seductive temptress, stranded at *O'Nowhere* on her way home from a seedy motel where she'd met her lover. Ted even fictionalised one of the police officers as Marcus Geller himself, in disguise. The backstory saw the killer squeezing the life out of the young man that he was impersonating, until he'd turned blue out in the woods. He'd then stolen his uniform to blend in.

Once Ted had grown weary of real people, he'd switched his efforts to the imaginary. He'd spotted a large, red heating pipe running along the ceiling and had imagined a family of mini-soldiers crossing it, an unknown race of marble sized men and women who lived in the air vents and rafters. The tiny crew were climbing a rope of string onto the pipe, where they'd been forced to do battle with the evil, tarantula sized *House Spider of Doom*. It spit venom from its fangs and tried to trap the teensy heroes in its sticky web. But it hadn't been long before Ted had grown tired of this game too. He was bored. Bored. Bored. Bored. Bored.

That was, until he'd spotted the large flashing toy claw arcade machine on the other side of the lobby, and a lightbulb popped above his head. Ted defeated his aching joints and climbed to his feet. He honed in on the glass case of the machine, specifically, the tiny red goggle-eyed alien at the very bottom of it, buried beneath his colourful brethren. *Mission: Accepted.* The flashing lights and cheap coin sound effects of the claw machine did for Ted what the bright, neon signs of Las Vegas casinos did for gamblers, drawing him in. Ted always had to be doing something, moving forward, striving towards some kind of goal, and since reaching his secret '*X*' on the map had been out of the question, winning a stuffed red alien for Rose perfectly filled the vacancy in his empty schedule.

Already waiting there though, on the other side of the glass staring in, with eyes that had barely grazed the lower most quarter of the machine, was a certain 3 ft 2, Custard-coloured coat wearing boy. His short height had meant that he was at a perfect eye-line with the aliens at the bottom of the pile, namely, the red extra-terrestrial. But without a shilling to his name, being four years away from earning his very first pocket-money transaction courtesy of the '*Bank of Mummy and Daddy*', he'd had no chance of playing the game. The boy stepped to the right when Ted rocked up to the machine, but said nothing. The two locked eyes for a moment, before Ted turned to assess the mothership of a task that he was up against.

He could see why Rose hadn't managed to bag the red teddy. It was certifiably wedged at the very bottom of the tank, sandwiched between a blue and a green figurine, two colours that were plentiful and that could easily have been won be even the most amateur of players. But there was only one, red, Alien. If he were to stand any hope of clinching the fluffy trophy, then he'd have to move the other toys out of the way first, no easy task, but one that he was willing to undertake. Besides, there was hardly much else in the way of entertainment at the *O'Nowhere* that night. With each spin at the claw costing 50p a go, Ted had to be economical with the change in his wallet. He'd only had enough for seven turns. *But surely that'd be enough? Right?* He slid the first coin into its slot, equipped the joystick, and then prepared to do battle. The Custard-coloured coat wearing boy watched him silently. The silver, shinning pincers of the claw sprung into life with a robotic soundbite, and then began its descent.

But the game proved to be a little trickier than Ted had anticipated. He manoeuvred the claw down towards the body pile of toys. But despite wanting to at least move a handful of the creatures to clear a path to the top prize, the edges of its tweezer hands had just nudged the shoulder of a yellow doll, buzzed, and then died.

Game Overrrrrr, the retro font of the screen on top of the claw machine mocked. That was okay though, it was only a first try. Ted was just establishing his footing. He was sure that his second attempt would be far more in line with his ambitions, even the best of players stumbled on the first level whilst getting to grips with a new games controls. But boy, was he wrong. History repeated itself upon his second try and he failed to even move a single toy. *Game Overrrrrr*, flashed the screen.

Suddenly, all sense of wonderful nostalgia that Ted had experienced whilst playing the game was vaporised by a ray gun. Gone were the fond memories of hitting the Scarborough arcade coin machines with one and two pence pieces as a child. All that was left was a biting frustration. He only had five goes left....

The *O'Nowhere* speaker system powered back to sound, an attempt by Perkins to further relax his unexpected guests. 80's techno tunes began blasting through the PA as Ted inserted yet another heptagon silver and went for a '*three times a charm*' on the claw. Still, the boy watched. Yet again, rather pathetically, Ted failed a third and then a fourth time after that, gracelessly sliding the claw from left to right whilst synth chords played overhead. Both attempts, he didn't win a single toy.

Game over. Game over. Game over.

Disheartened and dejected, Ted gave in. Despite having slid a fifth 50p coin into the machine, he'd decided, unlike most Las Vegas gamblers, to cut his losses and to leave the machine behind before he'd emptied the entire contents of his wallet.

'Damn thing' he sulked, kicking its cartoon, solar-system decorated side and then marching off. Even *that'd* hurt his toe. *Perkins must've rigged the thing, yeah, that was it, he just didn't want anyone winning, or he'd have had to replace the aliens inside.* At least, that's what Ted told himself, despite being in possession of the knowledge that Rose had clearly beaten the game before. He'd just have to find some other means of entertaining himself for the night....

....that's when he'd heard it.

'*You Win!*'

To his disbelief, Ted turned around, only to see the young, silent, Custard-coloured coat wearing boy standing in front of the arcade machine. He reached his tiny hand into the black slot at the base of the front glass, something Ted would've had to bend down to do, and pulled out a bright blue, goggle-eyed alien toy. He'd done it, the plucky young kid had only gone and beaten the claw on what would've been Ted's fifth go! Immediately, Ted returned to present the space cadet with a deal, he had a bargain in mind. Not wanting to insult the lad by patronising him, Ted refrained from crouching down to his level, instead remaining stood and squaring him straight in the eyes.

'Hey kid. You won that thing?' he asked. The boy simply nodded, cuddling his victory alien close into the folds of his puffy coat.

'You used my 50p?'

Again, he merely nodded in response.

'What do you say you and me make a deal?' Ted proposed. He took the kids silence, and his not running away crying as an '*I'm listening*'.

'Look kid, we both have something the other person wants. I've got the cash, you've got the know-how. If I were to give you two 50p's worth of go's on the game, would you be able to win me that little red fella at the bottom?' Ted pointed at the object of his desires, the kid acknowledged the reward. He gave his young partner a moment to mull over his offer, and the boy took full advantage of this to consider the possibility as to whether or not what the weird guy was asking for could've been done. It could. The boy nodded his head, which in turn nodded his oversized hood along with it. He'd never liked wearing it up because it covered up his eyes, but his mummy always made him when it rained so that he wouldn't catch a cold. He innocently looked up at Ted, and then stretched out a hand to take the money. Game on.

'That a boy!'

The boy took to the joy stick. In two goes, the kid had managed to make more progress than Ted had in four. He'd put his skills to shame, despite being a whole sixteen years younger than he was. Months of playing his *Xbox* alone in his room after school and during the summer holidays with a glass of cold milk had honed his toddler thumbs. If he could vanquish the latest *Call of Duty* single player campaign on the hardest difficulty mode, mastering the primitive claw machine would be a cinch. What the lad lacked in height and age he more than made up for with his gaming abilities and on his second turn, he managed to quite easily win another Teddy bear. This time it was a green one, leaving a clear pathway in the pile towards the one and only red. Now the heat was on, Ted only had one coin left, which had meant that the silent warrior-child only had one shot at taking home the glory.

'This is it kid!' stressed Ted, sweat appearing on his brow and his chestnut eyes wincing. He could barely watch. The claw descended slowly and gently into the pile. The kid knew exactly the right amount of pressure to exert on the control pad to maintain a smooth handle on the thing, it sure was sensitive. He pulled down the lever of the mechanism and the silver-tipped pincers of the claw grabbed the outside of the red alien's faux, gelatinous skin. He had it! But one wrong move and the jig would be up. If the kid didn't extract the creature properly, it'd slip straight out of his grasp and tumble back into the mass, even further out of reach than it had been before. The 80's anthems were pulsating, Ted grinded his teeth, and then, within the fraction of a second that it took to blink, it was over.

The boy's high-five'd.

The night-time had done for the sleety Moors what black hoods did for the faces of cult members and home intruders, masking its landscape in obscurity. Transylvanian vampire bats swooped and circled over ground holes that would've made ample coffins for strolling strangers, burying them six feet under in subterranean hollows. The pure white moon, which resembled that of a rolled back eyeball in its socket, cast its Luna light over barbed wire posts that separated quadrants of grassland. Avenues of moonlight slipped between the gaps in poorly boarded barn doors like a cinema's solitary projector light, and one could see trails of white mist in their lanes. The green heads of carrots, onions, asparagus and butterscotch squash's shuddered, tucked firmly into their vegetable beds and wrapped in duvets of churned soil and seeds. The charred, burnt skies watched on, whilst inside the station, a storm was brewing.

The staff lounge was hardly fitting a place for the busy workers to unwind in, many chose to spend their breaks sat on the benches on the lawn outside the *O'Nowhere's* car park instead. Its grey ceiling panels were falling out of place, and the gaps revealed the mould ridden, rat bitten circuitry for the room's LED lights. Out of five, only two of the bulbs had worked. Years old magazines were stacked on a stained coffee table, and a rusty kettle and microwave were in the corner for lunch breaks. Without boiling though, the water that the leaky tap had produced hadn't been fit for consumption. The Union Jack flag mugs were chipped and each contained dubious looking brown marks at their bases which seemed un-washable, just like the sour odour of mature cheese in the room was un-cleanse-able and the dense aura of dreary misery was un-defeat-able.

'No. Absolutely not Billy, and that's final' said a viciously firm Perkins, who now, behind closed doors, was revealing his true colours to his employees. For beneath the veneer of his glossy, public persona, the one that he'd presented to the police and trapped guests in which he'd given them free food, he was a weak, dirty, conniving man. Billy involuntarily clenched his fists.

'Look. I've been working here all week and all I want to do is go home. I have a life outside this station you know. I'm tired of scrubbing floors' screamed Billy. He was making a complete scene in front of all of his fellow employees. It didn't matter though, they'd all already thought that he was a weird, creepy man. His reputation couldn't have been saved. He'd even forgotten about appearing kind and composed in front of his love, Rose, who was also stood in the staff room for the employee gathering.

'I've said no. I can't be any fairer than I'm being. The police have said you're staying and that means you're staying. Just because you work here doesn't mean you're magically exempt from the law Billy. Isn't being on double pay enough for you? It's bleeding me dry and *these* are the thanks I get?' Perkins roared back, his flabby, toad-like neck bulging from his shirt collar. It begged for him to undo his top button and to take off his burgundy tie, to release its greasy rolls like a woman undoing her brazier after a hard day's work. Rose watched the encounter unravel with forlorn eyes, there really was no chance of her making her '*Julius Caesar*' audition now. Although she'd admitted to Ted that she knew that this was the case, a small part of her had still clung onto the false hope that maybe the staff members would've been allowed to leave early for the night. She was wrong.

'Look, I know you're all tired, believe me so am I, but you are still employees of the *O'Nowhere* and you are contractually obliged to work. I'm sure this will all be resolved soon and the second it is you can go home...'

'...I'm due in tomorrow at 9am. What if I don't get out of this shithole until 3am in the morning? Am I supposed to just come back for another ten hour shift with three fucking hours of sleep in the tank?' raged Billy. He was pacing up and down the staff room, wearing holes in the fuzzy upholstery fabric. Perkins, away from the judging eyes of the public, lashed out.

'I'm getting pretty sick of your profanity and toxic behaviour Billy, it's just not very good for morale now is it? Am I going to have to put another strike on your record? You're already on three, one more and I'll have no choice but to take your case up to company HQ' threatened the manager. This silenced Billy. Though his feet stood still, his rage still seethed and burned at the timbers of his insides. He couldn't afford to lose his job, no matter how much he'd despised it. It was this fear of unemployment that muzzled Billy like a crazed rabid dog. Two young male staff members who'd worked at the station book store sniggered at him, the same two that had ransacked his locker only three months before and had written *'Billy the Freak'* on post stick notes all over its blue metal door. They'd never been caught of course, but Billy knew that it'd been them. *The pricks*. Rose shot the pair a disgruntled look, and then asked a question of her own.

'He's got a point though Perkins. What if we're in tomorrow?' she asked sweetly.

Perkins turned his greedy glare to Rose and licked his lips, the saliva in his mouth made a choppy sound. 'Well Rose my darling, because *you* asked so nicely, tomorrow the station will be closed, so all of you will have the day off anyway. Consider this...overtime, for the hours you'll miss out on tomorrow'. The other staff members were too busy planning their days off to notice the disgusting, sadistic manner in which Perkins had stared at Rose, not her though. She'd always catch him staring at her ass, her breasts, imagining sick fantasies of the two of them *'doing it'* after-hours in his office. He made her want to hurl.

'You hear that Billy?' provoked the tubby dictator. Billy looked up from his shoes, the promise of a day off hadn't calmed his anger in the slightest. He *had* to get back home that night or he'd be in major trouble.

'You'll be off tomorrow. So quit your moaning and grab that mop and get back to cleaning the toilets. While you're at it, maybe have a shower too? For someone so good at soaping up the walls you sure do struggle to keep your own pits clean. Don't you? You stink Billy', at this, Perkins released a thunderous laugh. The rest of the staff gathering joined in, all but Rose. They laughed and pointed at the janitor in a circle. Billy, blushing and furious, stormed out of the staff room, ramming open the squeaky doors with tears in his eyes.

At the same time that Ted had been inserting his first silver, fifty pence coin into the arcade machine, Billy had inserted £6.50 into the pay phone on the far west corner of the station. It was a seldom used device, especially given the digital, *iPhone* age that the pit stops guests had been living in. Billy's own phone, a *Nokia*, was out of juice. He dialled up the numbers in the privacy of the booth, he knew them by heart, and then he placed the mouthpiece to his chapped lips and the receiver to his ear as the connection was established. An electrical current surged through the devices lead and travelled out of *O'Nowhere*. It voyaged along the tops of telegram poles where black crows sat, and across the breadth of the lonely Moors, whilst lightning bolts clapped in the distance. It eventually settled in the cradle of an old, rotary-corded wall phone, in a house, on the other side of Egton. The voice of an elderly woman answered mid-way through the first ring, as if she'd been sat there, expecting his call.

'Where the hell have you been, dumbass?!'
she shrieked. Billy took a deep breath, and prepared for the scalding.

'Mum, look, I'm sorry, there's been a problem at work and I've had to stay behind. I...'

'A problem? A problem? What sort of problem? I'll tell you a problem. You were supposed to be home three hours ago with my dinner and now I'm starving to death. No more excuses. Get your ass home. Now!' she yelled down the phone. Her voice was grotesque and gravely, it was like her words had been struggling to climb up through her throat and could only come through in fragments, and not fully formed.

'But Mum, there's things in the freezer, can't you just put something in the oven and...'

'Me?! Put something in the oven and cook for myself? In my condition? How dare you speak to your Mother like that, after everything I've done for you? You know I can barely get out of bed with my back and legs. As much as I hate it I'm totally dependent on you, and after all the years I've spent raising you and feeding you and putting clothes on your miserable back, now that the time has come to repay me you want nothing to do with me.' The hideous voice began wailing then, sobbing and crying in a banshee-like moan down the phone receiver. It hurt Billy's ear.

'Mum please...' he begged, looking over his shoulders to make sure that nobody could hear him.

'No, not "Mum please". You're ashamed of me, your disgusting, wrinkly old mother. You don't love me. You just want me to die here all alone in this house and be rid of me. You're just like your useless Father, are you going to walk out like he did?'

Billy whimpered hysterically down the phone to persuade his mother of his devotion to her. It was a pathetic, high-pitched, childlike tone that someone like Ted would never have considered to be available to him. His frame crouched even lower than unusual so that his spine was hunched. He shortened in height and seemed to resemble a deformed, mutant child in a grown man's body. Even from across the phone she'd had the power to reduce him to nothing. This witch of an old woman, all the way on the other side of the Moors in her haunted house on the hill, sunken into her armchair in front of her static filled television screen.

'Mum! The police are here! They're not letting anybody leave, I swear! They've got the whole place locked down...'

Billy's mum raised a dusty, grey eyebrow behind her spectacles. 'Hmmmm. Smells like bullshit to me Billy Boy...'

'No Mum! It's not I swear! I tried asking Manager Perkins to let me go but he wouldn't. He won't let any of us go'. Billy could feel the tip of his manhood quiver and he was sure that if he'd had a full bladder that he'd have wet himself there and then all over the floor. It would've been like secondary school all over again.

'You wouldn't be telling Mummy porkies now? Would you Billy?' she pushed, leaning forward in her brown, vintage armchair. It smelt fusty, of World War Two bunkers and of ration boxes, everything in her house did, from the record player in her sitting room, to the false teeth on her dressing table.

'No Mummy...' whispered Billy

'Good' she replied, grinning evilly to herself. Though they say it requires fewer facial muscles to smile than to frown, doing this seemed to coax out all of her wrinkles and lines at once, she looked demonic.

'Because if I find out you are...you know I'll have to lock you in the attic again. And you don't want that now, do you?' she said, revelling in the vile deviancy of her threat. At this, Billy, despite not having a full bladder, did indeed feel a trickle of urine dribble down his left leg and stain the cover of his navy work overalls.

'I promise' he assured her quietly. 'I'll order you a pizza to the house, okay? How does that sound? Sardine. Your favourite. As soon as the police give me the all clear I'll be back home, for now, have your pizza and then try to get some sleep in your armchair. I'm off work tomorrow, so I can look after you. We can watch that film you like, "*Singin' in the rain*", I know it's your favourite'. There was a pause on the other side of the line before she spoke again, in the disciplinarian voice of someone who'd gotten what she'd wanted.

'Okay Billy dearest, that sounds perfect'. Her accent was extremely old-fashioned, the obscure, classic style of Yorkshire that would've sounded indecipherable to anybody outside of the county. And like her accent, the woman too was a traditionalist, stuck in her ways, of hating Jews, distrusting the *Labour Party*, and most frightening of all, punishing children. It was something that had clearly had a profound effect on young Billy, so much so, that one could've made the argument that the way that his Mother had treated him, had ruined his entire adult life.

Billy knew that his credit would soon run out, and quite frankly he was pleased about it.

'I should go anyway Mother, I have to get back to work. I'll order your pizza as soon as I go.' The cruel countess who'd birthed him suddenly took on a sweet and nurturing persona, like the dragon was now at bay and the mother in her had finally emerged.

'Of course Billy, you just be safe now for me, okay? I love you very much darling'. She blew a kiss over the phone, one that Billy had dodged before it could land and pucker on his bony cheek, and then hung up. He placed the phone back onto its cradle. He scrubbed at the wee stain on his overalls with a piece of cleaning rag that he'd carried in his pocket until it was gone. After this was done, he mundanely called the pizza restaurant and made his mother's order as if nothing had happened, and then hung up and left the booth to go back to work.

Boy, did Billy hate his Mum, but not as much as he'd hated the way that he'd allowed her to affect him. She seemed to hold some kind of demented monopoly over his mind, like his psyche was enslaved to her. Billy, despite what many people had thought, didn't have a dwindling IQ, he knew that his frail, decrepit mother wasn't actually capable of doing any harm to him. So why was it then that he'd pissed his little pants like a ten year old boy when she'd mentioned locking him in the attic? It was a paradox that he just couldn't comprehend.

More and more of late, Billy had begun to understand that all of the anger and hatred that had simmered away inside of him had been as a result of his mother and how she'd treated him. It was her that was the anchor that had kept him shackled to where he was, both literally, forced to work at the service station close by so that he could look after her, and figuratively, trapped within a prison of his own mind. Billy didn't want to be the monster that he'd become, he didn't want to harbour the hatred that he did towards everyone and everything. For years he'd searched for the source of the problem, trying to understand the fault in his wiring that had made him the way he was, the pivotal turning point in his life that had made him so dark and broken, like a smashed medicine bottle. Finally now he knew, it was her and had been all along, she'd ruined him.

The only solution was to leave. But how could he do that? She was his flesh and blood for God sake. One thing that she had said *had* been true. She *had* looked after him all of his life; washed him, clothed him, put hot food in his belly and a pillow beneath his weary head. Maybe all she was, was a lonely, kooky old lady. Billy couldn't remember what she'd been like before his Father had left, but perhaps there had been a time when she hadn't been so wicked. A happy time, a peaceful time, a time before the beatings and the burnings and the name callings and the manipulation. Perhaps she was a victim too, one that just needed looking after. No. There she went again, getting inside of his head, he hated it when she did that. Billy scratched away at the scars left from the wounds on his body, the ones that had been inflicted by her, and the ones that had been inflicted by himself, alone at night in the attic.

But what was he going to do about it? Would he finally confront his Mum? And tell her he was leaving her behind to start afresh, and to follow his dreams? No. Of course he wouldn't. Billy was weak and he knew it, he'd never be able to stand up to her, or to separate her from his being, like a malformed growth attached to his face. And so he would go on working at *O'Nowhere* and dancing to the beat of her croaky old drum until the day that she finally died. By then it would be too late too, her control over him would've become so engrained within his soul that it would've been past the point of no return for him to salvage the remainder of his existence, by leading a normal, happy life. The damage would've been done. He'd inherit her old, haunted house on the hill and live there alone amongst the peeling wallpaper, until the day that he passed on, and then she'd torture him all over again in the fiery pits of the underworld. It was better that he came to terms with his fate, and that he succumb to his own defective actuality. All the self-help *YouTube* videos that he'd seen *did* say that acceptance was the key to happiness after all.

Since all he'd known for all of his life was pain and rejection, every ounce of love and compassion had been gradually, forcefully squeezed out of Billy like juice from a stubborn lemon refusing to twist on its grinder, leaving behind nothing but a jet-black heart. And a man with a heart of darkness hates all, well, all except one.

Rose.

Rose wasn't like the others, no way. She didn't judge him, nor did she ridicule him or look away in the corridors when he'd walk past, Rose was kind. Billy's brief encounters with Rose, their small conversations in passing at the lockers in which she'd ask about his day, and where they'd make fun of Perkins together, had rather become the highlights of Billy's weeks. He'd remembered times that he'd arrived into work and checked the '*sign in*' sheet, only to see that Rose had called in sick that day. Instantly his shift would be cast into shadow. He'd often look forward to seeing her on the nights before he knew that they would both be working, and plan ways of making conversation in his bedroom, like asking her about her acting, her upcoming auditions. To Billy, Rose was the first and only person that he could remember ever showing any kind of tenderness towards him, and he had fallen in love with her.

But this wasn't just a childish crush, no. Billy saw Rose, with her immaculate red hair that had reminded him of the delicate petals of the plant that she was named after, as his redemption. She was his way out, his way of escaping the ageing clutches of his maniacal mother's long, reedy nails, his last shot at happiness. For Billy envisioned his life, as a closing, underground cavern with a dim, speck of light at the end of it. Stalactites and boulders were collapsing around him and the rocky exit at the mouth of the tunnel was closing. This was his window of opportunity to leave the lonely, miserable existence that had been imposed upon him by his mother, and if he didn't seize it soon by standing up to her and leaving with Rose, then it would seal forever, dooming him to skulk in the darkness, never cured of the ferocity that plagued his soul.

Through Rose he could be saved. In fact, for months now he'd been plucking up the courage to ask her out on a date, he'd had it all planned out. He'd ask her to go and see a movie at the local Malton picture-house with him. Billy knew conversation was hardly his strong point and so watching a film in silence for two hours would be the perfect way to ease himself into his first ever date with a girl. Conversation would only be required for roughly ten to twenty minutes in the lobby, as they'd decided between salted or sweet popcorn. Chit-chat after the credits rolled could be amateur-criticism regarding the movie itself.

Billy's infatuation wasn't creepy or perverted, the fact was, to him, she was the most beautiful person he'd ever met, and he liked who he was when he was with her. Gone was the anger and the rage, in its place, was a strange, glowing, pleasant feeling, one that made him hear the sweet chirping of the perching birds and smell fresh rosemary on the breeze. Not even the cobwebs and corners of the attic could touch him when he was with her, and if he'd had to have put money on it, he'd have labelled this mystical feeling, as happiness. It was settled, Billy would ask her out that night, what better time than when he couldn't leave out of cowardice or make up an excuse? He'd finally do the deed, and the thought thrilled him.

Billy had been walking through the station promenade to collect his mop and to return to work when he'd noticed Ted at the coffee shop. Ugh. There went that arrogant, *'know it all'*-prick again.

But wait, was that his beloved Rose talking to him at the counter? Billy didn't like that one bit. He watched from afar, hidden amongst the crowd of gossiping Yorkshire folk. He was probably just ordering a coffee, some pretentious, hipster, *Coconut Mocha Latte* with two cinnamon shots and whipped cream, that was all...but wait. Hang on. Why was Ted handing her that red alien doll? And why was she smiling? She didn't smile like that, with *'girl next door'* teeth, when Billy spoke to her, when he'd compliment her on her acting. Why was she touching his arm like that and blushing? And why did he look so damn smug and handsome? Why did they both seem so smitten, so happy? It was like some perfect scene lifted from a meet-cute ROM COM. Billy had seen enough, he could hardly bare to look any longer. He turned right around and stormed through the crowd, shoving people as he went, relapsing into his hateful self, until he'd reached the solitude of his private cleaning cupboard.

Once inside, he released a prehistoric scream and tore down the metal shelving units. He sent squirt-bottles of stain remover and mop handles crashing onto the floor with a wallop. Microfiber cloths floated gently behind them like handkerchiefs. He took the wooden sweeping brush from the corner of the room and repeatedly struck it against the wall until it snapped into splintered halves, before collapsing onto the floor himself with weepy eyes. And there, alone again, like he'd always been, Billy mourned for his life, and imagined doing terrible, unspeakable, illegal things to Ted with his bare hands. It was just like Bundy, Dahmer, The Ripper, and many more, had done before him, before claiming their very first victims.

CHAPTER FIVE

His garish, orange peel coloured skin looked absurdly counterfeit and streaky against the dull whiteboard. It would have looked false even in the natural light of daybreak, especially given the moist, overcast spring that Yorkshire had been experiencing that April, where temperatures had rarely risen above five degrees and the sun's ray's couldn't have put a dent in the sauna steam-room smears that had been the clouds. It was a time of year where coastal towns were empty, their gift shops shut for the season due to lack of business and where ice cream stands just weren't in *Vogue*. The only means then, by which the raging gypsy could've acquired a tan that loud, would've been by forcibly chargrilling his pore's on an ultraviolet sunbed twice a week. He had.

'Do we understand each other?' asked Henry J. Simmons rhetorically, standing over the giant. The traveller in question had wrists so chunky that they'd barely fit into the cold restraints of his handcuffs. His protein shake frame bulged from the chair that he was sitting on, but that didn't intimidate Simmons. He repeated himself when the gypsy didn't reply.

'I said, do we-'

'-I heard what you said Simmons' the bulge spoke. His hair was waxed into a perfect quiff, he'd dyed that black, like he'd dyed his skin brown. 'I get it. I'll play nice. Can you just take these fucking cuffs off of me now? They're hurting my hands'.

'Well you certainly didn't think about anyone getting hurt when you smashed that window in the lobby.'

'What can I say, I get stressed in closed spaces. I act out.'

Simmons put his hands to his hips. He'd taken off his policeman's hat by now, a sure sign that he'd settled into the station. Perkins had allowed him and his men to temporarily borrow his office whilst the search for Geller had been ongoing, he'd converted it into a makeshift basecamp. The gypsy squirmed and huffed in his seat. 'I wanna talk to a lawyer. I want my phone call. I've seen the shows. I know what I'm entitled to'.

'Smithy you don't need a lawyer. I'm letting you go. I just need an assurance that you won't "act out" again. There's a lot of scared people out there, tensions are running high, and the last thing they need is a crazy thug smashing up the place and causing havoc, you get me?'.

'You can't force me to stay here, let me out! I ain't afraid of no prisoner, I'll probably recognise the guy from one of my stretches. Who knows, maybe I'll be able to help you catch him. You didn't think of that one, did ya?'

'Somehow I doubt that Smithy...'

This wasn't the first time that the pair had crossed paths. Henry and Smithy had had their fair share of run in's before, too many to count. The latter had become rather the household name amongst the boys in blue down at Malton station. The two men were rivals, nemesis. Oh, Henry had definitely come close to jailing the delinquent, almost pinning him on a suspected arson, and an insurance fraud. The word on the grape vine was that the local Grosmont village pub and chippy that his wealthy family had owned, had in fact been masquerades for a criminal drug enterprise, both used to launder profits from shifting the white stuff across East Yorkshire. But nothing ever stuck, nothing was ever concrete, and the petty charges for pub fights and public indecency were never enough to get Smithy incarcerated for anything longer than a few months at a time. The streets would've been a much safer place without him on them, and that's why Henry couldn't quite believe that he was about to let the guy go.

His Reasoning. The people that he had locked down in the station were subdued and calm, for now, but pretty soon, he was certain that an uninvited bout of cabin fever would be settling in for the night along with them. He needed the panicky Yorkshire folk on his side, to trust him, and if he started arresting men, husbands, son's, when they inevitably began growing rowdy, then that would be a sure fire way to blow a hole straight through any mutual respect that the people had for him, respect that wouldn't be so easy to win back. The last thing he'd needed was a riot, Simmons had enough to contend with. Releasing the gypsy, though it killed him inside, set the precedent, that the Inspector was a friend of the people, there to help, not a military dictator sent to control them. Smithy was of course, naturally suspicious that the man who'd been on his ass since he was sixteen for hijacking ponies from Mr. Gunther's farm was letting him go. But ultimately, not being one to look a gift-horse in the mouth, nor one to say no to a box full of designer perfumes that had '*fallen from the back of a lorry*', he agreed to the terms.

'Alright, alright. I promise. No more smashing up shit. Jeez. If you're not gonna let me outta' this place, I may as well be stuck here with my hands free.'

'I thought you'd see things my way.'

The Inspector gestured to his officer who unshackled Smithy and then led him back out to re-join the crowd.

'I hope you've got some hotties locked in here with us', winked Smithy over a lateral pull-down juiced shoulder. Then he was gone. Simmons was sure that his first port of call would've been to push his way to the front of the food stand and to have wolfed down an entire bowl of tomato soup, no spoon required. But Smithy had darker designs. Letting him go would soon prove to be a huge mistake on Simmons's part, a mistake that would have dire, even fatal consequences.

Alone, Henry took to his leased desk chair and stared into the mess of maps, coordinates, notes and felt-tip pen scribbles that were charting their, as of yet unsuccessful, efforts to bring Marcus Geller to justice. Simmons was tired, operating on five hours shut-eye, all he wanted to do was to return home to his wife and to spoon her to sleep, and to kiss his daughter goodnight. But he knew full well that he couldn't. He had a killer to catch, and he had to stay strong. For he was the wood of the dam that was holding back the flood, the backbone of the operation, the man that his officers turned to, relied on, for leadership and for strength. If he fell, they all did, like dominoes, and that was a tough cross to bear. It wasn't just his duty to his men that had kept him powering on like a bottomless black coffee though, no, it was his duty to his late Father, Cole Simmons, who some-thirty years ago, had first caught and arrested the infamous *'farmhouse killer'* himself, Marcus Geller.

Henry had witnessed first-hand the unravelling of his father after that awful summer's day. The late nights drinking, the nightmares, the unrelenting rising of his blood pressure. Marcus Geller had unwittingly initiated a countdown on his Father's life that day, and he wasn't going to let him get away with it. He deserved to be punished to the full extent of the law, and since England's justice system didn't extend to the use of the electric chair, rotting in a prison cell for the rest of his life would do just fine. At sixty-six, he was sure that Geller hadn't had long left before the grim reaper had come knocking anyway, but until then, he was going to make sure that he served every damn second of his sentence. Ever since the red alert alarm had first been issued on Geller, Simmons had sensed the watchful gaze of his Dad from above, somewhere on the other side, and in truth had felt closer to him than he had in years. He wasn't about to let him down. As of yet though, things weren't looking too hopeful. Prior to his interrogation with Smithy, Henry had contacted his officers at the borders, and there was still no sign of Marcus '*the family killer*' Geller; where the hell was he?

He supposed that murder was like the dropping of a pebble into a still body of water. When one took a life, the aftermath of the death would ripple out, and shake the lives of everybody around it; the victim's family, the brave men and woman tasked with tracking down the defendant, and dare he say it, the relatives of the executor too, confronted with the brutal reality that the child that they'd raised was a monster. Even from behind bars, the sick-minded perpetrators of these crimes continued to do irreparable harm and damage to the innocent parties involved, and Geller was no exception. Many a time Henry had racked his brains to try and understand just what had compelled Marcus to so brutally deprive his wife and daughter of their lives on that sunny day, how he'd selected his *modus operandi*. But every time, his cerebral autopsy on the matter had fallen flat. For despite the snappy one-liners and sexy, chiselled, '*troubled*' detectives that could be seen on the True Crime Drama's plastered all over *Netflix*, Henry didn't deem it possible to truly '*Get inside the Mind of a Killer*'. Even with a clean-cut motive, he just could not fathom, nor comprehend, how somebody could resort to such heartless barbarism, and take away another person's life. Marcus had had it all, why had he thrown it away?

Through the disintegration of his Father, Henry had learned a hard truth about the world, that it was an evil, dark, unforgiving place, and that it was the people who populated it, who were chiefly responsible for making it that way. Since then, Henry's faith in humanity had never quite been the same, and upstanding citizens like Smithy, and the assortment of other wrong-doers that he'd encountered throughout his years on the

Force, had done little in the way of discouraging him of this grim philosophy. And though he craved the blissful ignorance that he'd had as a child before witnessing his Father's fall from grace, he knew that he'd always see the world in this sombre, bleak way.

'I'm coming for you Marcus, wherever you are' he muttered under his breath.

As Simmons cracked on with his terrible search, a fashion-disaster of a single silver studded earring was making its way, not to the rest of the crowd, who were gathered in the lobby like a band of extra's on a movie set, but to the storage lockers. Smithy knew that the police would be searching them soon, and so needed to act fast. Once there, he slid a hand over his steroid enlarged calf muscle and slipped off his left sneaker. Inside, hidden under the sole, was a locker key, labelled '*64*'. Taking care to survey his surroundings first, he opened the container carefully and then pulled out a brown parcel, one that contained approximately 3.5 Kilograms of pure, sugary white cocaine. Smithy had been sent to *O'Nowhere* by the powers that be, a drug baron operating within the Scarborough area, the coastal line by which the supply had been smuggled in. But now, he found himself in the awkward position of being stuck with the Class-A stockpile in a service station full of policemen. Not the sharpest knife in the drawer, he'd tried to escape by smashing the window as not to be associated with the bundle. But now he was trapped, and had no idea of what to do with the stash. With the parcel under his shirt, tucked into the buckle of his stolen, brown leather belt, he sauntered back towards the lobby to formulate his next step. Perhaps there was a loose ceramic tile in the toilets that he could store the contraband in, until the whole thing had blown over.

Unbeknownst to Smithy though, he hadn't been alone. Like a fly on the wall waiting for a corpse, Billy had seen the whole incident unfold from the corner, mop in hand.

'Perfect', he smiled to himself in the darkness. This was exactly the blackmail that he'd needed to recruit Smithy into his ranks, he'd require his man-power for what was coming. A deadly love triangle had formed between himself, Ted and Rose. Its three pointy edges were sharp and deadly. So razor-like were they that they could have cut quite nicely through a succulent artery on a man's neck. Billy had wretched plans, which had meant that Ted, was in grave danger.

'Hello Smithy', Billy whispered from the shadows. The hardened crook froze on the spot.

. . .

'Are we almost there Rose?'

'Yes, yes, almost there, just quit your moaning.'

'Ow! I think I just stubbed my toe.'

'Okay. Right. Stand still. That's it. Now, you ready? Look!'

She removed her coffee perfumed fingers from his eyes. And what he saw, floored him.

'Ta-Da!'

After giving her the alien doll, Rose had been so flattered and taken
aback that she'd insisted on taking Ted on a secret whistle stop tour.
She'd led him by the hand, something he'd enjoyed very much, down a
service corridor, where delivery trucks had dropped off supplies once a
week, and into an old, storage locker. It had been the very locker that had
been used to house the benches that Perkins had prematurely ordered out
onto the *O'Nowhere* lawn, despite the April showers. Billy had
assembled them. From there she'd guided him, still by the hand, through
a hole in the plastering behind a broken, vertically propped up bench, and
then down a narrow ventilation passage, up a ladder, and through a door
into a small side chamber. That's where she'd covered his eyes, she'd
wanted him to be shocked when she'd led him through the boarded up
hole in the wall and outside onto the grassy hill, he was.

Ted was lost for words. One minute his feet had been on concrete, but
now he found himself suddenly stood on top of a mound of grassland,
brushing shoulders with the back of the station. It overlooked the
highway on the east side. Still confused, he turned back to see the cavity
in the bricks that they'd emerged from. It was true, he was outdoors
again.

'H-how...'

'This place has been my little secret for years. A while back there was a

128

storm so bad that a tree fell down and smashed a hole straight through the wall. Perkins had it boarded up and planned to get it fixed, but since it wasn't a north facing wall and his customers would never see it, he'd figured why bother? The cheapskate. You like it?' she asked, already knowing the answer.

Ted was dumbfounded. 'But wh-what about-'

'the police? They don't know about it. Unless Perkins told them. But I doubt it. This place is my little secret hideaway. I come here to go over lines sometimes, and sometimes just to think. Here, pull up a seat good sir!'

She took his hand and lowered him onto the grass. It was wet on his bum, but it felt good.

'Rose. I love it, it's....'

'Amazing? I know. You can thank me later. Beats a pesto/ham toasty, right?'

'I'll say' he laughed.

'You're the first person I've ever brought up here. You'll be leaving soon when the lockdown ends anyway, so you can't steal it. You're no threat to me, then again, no boy whose name is an abbreviation for a Teddy bear ever could be' she playfully nudged him. 'I figured, what the heck, it might be nice to have some company for once'.

Once the initial shock of his new surroundings had begun to placate, and he saw that Rose was at ease, Ted relaxed too. This was the first time since his arrival that he had breathed in Yorkshire's air, the small space in which he'd been exposed to it when he'd gotten off the bus hadn't been anywhere near enough. He inhaled and let the crispness of it massage his lungs, he felt free again, he was home. It somehow tasted even fresher than it had before, like the rainfall had cleansed it of any impurities, leaving a refined, earthy scent imbedded in the oxygen. It was the kind that humans had breathed before a time of car exhausts and pollution, the kind that would make trees grow tall and green, the kind that made the wandering heart of an intrepid adventurer grow wild.

From up on the secret hill, Ted could see far and wide across the Moors. It was the landscape that had been hidden from him by the ridge when he'd stood in the car park, at ground level. But now he felt on top of the world. He scoured the richness of the image for the mysterious figure that he'd seen out there hours before, but saw no one. A trick of the light. That's all it had been. Yes.

The view was as terrifying as it was beautiful, like the ocean, spectacular to view from the shore, but mercilessly deep and inhospitable past the shallows. These were the off-road Moors, free from the vanilla public footpaths and hiking routes that gift shops had sold pamphlets and guided tours for, rules didn't apply here. The Moon, though full, and undoubtedly converting the DNA of bitten men all across the county into feral wear-wolves for the night, offered no illumination on the land at all, it was completely pitch-black. Gone were the silhouettes of sparrow wings that usually graced the horizon, instead they were snuggled safely in their twiggy nests atop Sessile Oaks, those that hadn't fallen that is, with their trunks blocking trails and brooks. The scene was made all the more gothic and horrifying knowing that he, Geller, was out there somewhere, perhaps even watching Ted and Rose right at that very moment, fantasising about cannibalising their entrails. But something about being there with Rose, it made the fear electric, the risk exhilarating, the danger irresistible, like they were flirting with death and laughing in its face. They were taunting it with their presence and screaming '*we're young and we're dumb and we just don't care*' into the black, like a serial killer writing letters to the press.

'I bet you weren't expecting this were you, eh?' Rose said, very pleased with herself.

'Pretty amazing, isn't it?' She sighed, even though she'd seen it a million times before it still never got old.

'It sure is' Ted said back, but he wasn't looking at the Moors.

Though Ted had found Rose attractive before, her rebellious breakout and the thrill of the two of them going somewhere that they knew that they shouldn't, seemed to heighten how he felt, like damsels in distress falling for the heroes who'd rescue them in movies. In fact, he was starting to think that Rose was actually pretty damn cool. Whether he'd still feel that way when they'd returned to the station he couldn't say, but that didn't matter, in that moment he felt it, and that's all that counted. The artificial glow of the highways lamppost's seemed to reflect in her iris's as they stared out at the Moors, as though she were sat by fireside, like the eye of Jupiter. With her ruby red hair, Ted thought that she resembled a timeless English monarch, a princess, immortalised only in medieval paintings or in church stained glass. But he'd have wagered that with her natural, peroxide roots that she'd have looked even more ravishing. Blonde haired and blue eyed, the kind of beautiful '*ideal victim*' that the media always flock to. She didn't need layers of make-up to look pretty, she was the '*girl next* door', simple but definitely not plain. Her lashes short and her nails unpainted, hers was a natural beauty. Why meddle with what didn't need changing?

It had crossed Teds mind to run on first instance, to leap from the ledge and to escape the police at *O'Nowhere* and to continue his journey to Middlesbrough on foot. But not only did he soon realise how extremely stupid that was, but after seeing Rose and how perfect she'd looked, he'd decided that there was no place on the earth's axis that he'd rather have been, than sat by her on the grass beneath the starlight. He could definitely see how Cathy and Heathcliff could've had fallen for each other in a place like that. The Moors, that shits romantic.

'So, I gotta admit Ted, you going out and winning me that alien...' Rose spoke quietly, in case any nearby police officers heard them.

'I know. You're impressed, right? I'm surprised you'd not won it before. I'm mean yeah, I'm not saying it was easy but...'

'Actually, I was going to say it was pretty unexpected. I mean, we'd only just met and then you went and did that for me...what, you think this is some kind of romantic comedy or something?' she teased, not being too far off the mark. Ted shrugged it off, badly, faking disinterest.

'Pfft. You wish. Don't flatter yourself Rose. The truth is, I was bored and wanted something to do. I don't like sitting still for too long, staying static, I always have to be moving towards something' he confessed.

'Is that why you're here? Because you're moving towards something?' Rose asked, daring to readdress the nerve that she'd struck earlier by the lockers. This time she'd used a more sensitive approach. But still, at the mention of his destination, Ted battered down his hatches. *Why did she have to go and ruin a perfectly perfect moment by bringing that up?* They could've spoken about anything, the meaning of life, debated the chicken and the egg, and maybe even kissed under the constellations, anything but *that*. He pivoted his shoes to the left away from Rose and stared off along the highway. Car-less, it rolled on towards a cluster of twinkling city lights in the distance.

Rose persisted, 'C'mon. I mean, I don't know anything about you. Where you're from. Where you're going. For all I know *you're* the one who could be a killer....'

Ted still, looked off into the trees, their buds beginning to bloom with the coming of the spring. The jealous wind rustled their branches, sending pink and white blossom petals, not yet strong enough to fight the gale, floating down to the ground like wedding confetti. Rose edged closer along the high ground towards Ted and placed a chilly hand on his shoulder, a purple bruise had sprouted under his shirt from where he'd been shoved by Billy. 'Please. I've shown you my secret place. How's about you give me a little something too?'

He hated to admit it, but she did have a point. Aside from tree surgeons, workmen and Perkins, Rose was the only person alive who'd ever sat upon that hump, and it was one hell of a spot. It was the treehouse, the hidden sanctuary in the woods you'd play in as a kid with friends. It was the one that only you and your gang were ever allowed to know about, blocking the entrance to the clearing with a password like '*spaghetti face*'. You didn't give up gems like that for nothing. It must've taken a lot for her to show it to him, and for that, she'd deserved a morsel of information. He could tell what she was doing, guilt tripping him to the max, and though her tactics had been dirty, he'd just become her catch of the day, because he'd fallen for it hook-line and sinker.

'Birmingham' he admitted, turning from the dreary motorway lanes and back to her innocent, marine blue eyes. They were much nicer to look at.

'What?'

'I came from Birmingham.'

'You don't sound like you're from Birmingham...you should count yourself lucky.'

Ted chuckled. 'Thank you, I take that as a major compliment'. He spoke in a deliberately eccentric black-country twang, pronouncing his '*you*' as '*yow*' and descending on his '*ment*'. The two laughed. Their sounds echoed out towards the vastness of the land, the barren Moors ominously repeating their laughter back to them. It was as though theirs were golden Major notes, but the Moors spat out Minors. Rose wasn't satisfied with just that though, she wanted the whole story, not just the prologue.

'And where are you going?' Ted resisted the vulnerability of telling her anymore. 'Let's face it, we're probably going to die tonight, do you really want to spend your last night on earth with things left unsaid?'

It was true that Ted's chest had ached from the weight of all of the heavy truths that he'd wanted to offload from it. He was just so used to trapping things inside, that setting the words and thoughts free would've been like going against his habitual factory settings. But there was something about Rose's smile that had told him that he could trust her with his revelation. It was a true smile. Not the kind that you shape voluntarily out of politeness, but the type that the mind dictates to the body, kind thoughts that trigger the mouth muscles to curve whether they want to or not, like when someone calls you 'beautiful', and you can't help but grin like a fool. Not a crack of inauthenticity lay on her lips that night, and like a family member confirming the corpse of a loved one, he'd identified nothing but sincerity in her eyes. And that's why he'd told her his trilogy of truths.

What he'd run from. Where he was running to. And what was waiting for him there.

'I'm going to Middlesbrough to find my Dad'.

'Your Dad?' Rose asked, fascinated but huddling her arms around herself. It was a cold night and the high altitude of the hill meant that not bringing a jacket had definitely been a mistake.

'Yep. My Dad. I'm going to find him. I mean, not that I'd lost him. You can lose a lot of things, your keys, your phone, but not your Dad. I got separated from him when I was young by my mom, and I haven't seen him since.' Once he'd broken the safeguard over his story, Ted was surprised at how easy he'd found it to tell, it felt good to share. He'd never see Rose again after-all, so what harm could it have done?

'I see...and when you say "young..."'

'I was ten when I last saw him. So I haven't seen my Father in eleven years. But tomorrow, I'm finally breaking that chain baby' he said raising a fist, as if toasting to *Orion's Belt*.

'And your dad, he lives in Middlesbrough?'

Ted chuckled, 'Oh. Not quite. That's just where my bus was dropping me, it didn't go any further than that. I guess those narrow Moor roads just aren't the right terrain, not mega bus-friendly. No. From Middlesbrough I was planning on getting a train in the morning, across to a seaside town, a place called Whitby. From there, and yes I know it's a hell of a journey but I'm crazy enough to trek it, from there I'd get another bus to a point on the coast named Robin Hoods Bay. And that, Rose my dear, is where I'll find my long lost Dad. Have you heard of it?'

Rose was amused by this, as if Ted's amateur map trotting had been meant to impress her. 'Have I heard of Whitby? Please. Who do you think I am? You're talking to a born and bred Northern Lass here Ted. Of course I've heard of Whitby! I love it there! Can't say I've ever been to The Bay though....'

Merely mentioning its name conjured up warm feelings of home inside of Ted, and like all heat rises, those feelings too, ascended to his face, which erupted in a wide, charming smile. Boy, he couldn't wait to get there. His happiness was infectious.

'Yeah?'

'Yeah! My parents used to take me all the time as a kid! I'd go on the beach and visit the ruined abbey and walk across the pier! I used to love getting ice cream there and looking at all the cool *Dracula* stuff. That's where Stoker wrote it, right?' she asked with a cartoonish nostalgia, reliving times that she'd waded into the sea without shoes, joyfully squealing at the cold.

'He sure did' spoke Ted with an air of pride. Though he loved hearing about people's enjoyment of his childhood home, he was always quick to remind them that *he* had a superior connection to the place, a deeper one then they had, a birth right. He was very protective of his Whitby. 'If you think you loved it just going for a day, imagine living right by there all of your life'.

'Didn't you get bored of the sea though? Part of the fun of going was that I never got to see it. I imagine the magic of it would wear off if you saw it every day' Rose asked. To Ted, her red hair had perfectly complimented the green of the hill, like the best of the autumn and the summer combined.

'No way in hell. You never get tired of waking up to the ocean every day. It beats traffic jams and homeless dudes spitting on the floor that's for sure'. He spoke with disdain for Birmingham, like it left a foul taste in his mouth, whereas Whitby tasted of candy and cream. 'And if you think Whitby's nice, you ain't seen nothing, Robin Hood's Bay is even more awesome. It's the town where Dad lives, a little further up the coast. Way fewer people know about it, so it's quiet, peaceful, it was our little slice of heaven'.

Who was Ted kidding, any reckless thoughts he'd had about staying on that hill with Rose were mere fantasy. The crosshairs fixed on his objective had wavered for a moment, but now they were once again on target. Perhaps though, he could bring her with him, a sidekick. What a heroes return that would be, to arrive at his Father's cottage door and to shake his weathered hands, the prodigal son with an English Rose on his arm. The urge to skid down the embankment and to sprint through the valley of empty motorways to Middlesbrough, hand in hand with her, gripped him by the heart again. To hell with Geller.

'So, if it was so perfect, why did you leave your Dad behind in the first place? Why did you move to Birmingham'? Rose asked carefully. She dissected Ted as she might've approached a character in a script, unearthing his backstory. The lost son stood and crossed his arms, the drop to the bottom of the hill was a lot steeper with the extra six foot.

'It's my mom. She made me leave. They split up and she dragged me all the way across to the other side of the country. She fed me some bullshit story about how my dad was "bad news". As I got older it evolved into more R-rated lies, apparently he'd had a "drinking problem" and he was a "deadbeat". What horse manure. Well, now I'm putting it right Rose, I'm going back to where I belong, with him, by the sea!' Ted shouted to the Moors, as though he were the king of the hill, the master of his own fate, and the world his Whitby oyster.

Rose couldn't explain it, but when Ted said this, she had known that everything that his mom had told him had been completely, categorically the truth, he was just too blind to see it. He was setting himself up for one hell of a fall for when he was finally reunited with the guy. There was a reason she didn't hang out at the backstage doors after theatre shows, '*never meet your heroes*', or so the expression went. She felt incredibly sorry for him.

'And your mum doesn't know you left?'

'No way in hell. I just booked my bus, packed my bags and went. She's left me a bunch of voicemails but I haven't answered them. She'd just try and persuade me to go back home, I know her'. Ted was becoming increasing excitable now, he was one slip away from tumbling headfirst from the rise to a broken spine. Rose stood up, she felt as though she were talking down a suicide attempt.

'But why now? You've had years to go back to him. What made you suddenly decide to go back to The Bay?' The dark made the top of the hill hazardous. It was deep and thick, like liquorice or Jet, hiding the edge of the drop. Rose tread carefully.

'Because I couldn't breathe Rose! I was suffocating in that city, I was trapped and enough was enough. Uni. That was the thing that finally pushed me over the edge.'

'Uni?'

'Yes. Uni. That's where I'd been when I'd ran away. I'd been studying in Birmingham and living in halls of residence. I'd thought that moving out from home might've made living in that city a little more bearable. But I was wrong. The lecturers must've reported me missing to my mom when I didn't turn up to my seminars, she was listed under my emergency contact number'.

Rose cocked her head, confused. 'What was so bad about Uni?'

'What was right about it? Explain this to me Rose. How am I expected to make a choice, to choose one subject, one course to study for three years that will totally alter the rest of my life? I was studying English, but what if I'd suddenly decided two years in, that I'd wanted to be a painter? Or a dentist? Or a carpenter? I'd be locked into a course that I didn't even want to do anymore, completely pigeon-holed. You're an actress, it's kinda like being type-casted I suppose, and that just doesn't sit well with me. I hate being...'

'...stuck in one place, I know. But if you're always moving towards something, what if you miss out on something good that's right in front of you?' she asked, conscious that Ted was raising his voice and that they might've been discovered by a policeman on a cigarette break at any moment.

'Look, when things get serious I panic. Commitment scares me, not because I'm afraid, but because life's too short to spend it just doing one thing. And that was what finally made up my mind. I'm going back to The Bay where I can be free with my Dad, the way it used to be, and we'll answer to no one, living by our own rules. No one can stop me, not my mom and certainly not yo-

'TED!'

Suddenly, Ted lost his footing and plunged towards the bottom of the hill. Rose quickly ran to his side, yanked him by the jacket, and then the two fell with a clonk onto the grass, sunny side up and facing the stars, panting. A moment of silence passed.

'I got a bit carried away, didn't I....?' said an embarrassed Ted, staring up at *Gemini*, *Capricorn* and the gang.

'Yep.'

'I just made a complete ass of myself, didn't I....?'

'Oh most definitely.'

Ted hauled himself to his feet, wiped grass stains from his denim, and then turned to re-enter *O'Nowhere* through the boarded up hole, his tail between his legs and his ego bruised along with his left arse cheek.

'I think I'd better go inside. I'll leave you to it. I'm sorry Rose, I didn't mean to make such a scene. Thank you for showing me your secret spot, it's really cool. I-'

'I think you should call your mum back and let her know you're safe' Rose interrupted, climbing to her feet as well. She'd been wearing a skirt and so had scraped all her knee's when they'd hit the grass.

Frustrated and annoyed, Ted raised his voice. 'What? Are you crazy? Did you even hear anything I've just told you? That woman is trying to stop me from going back! She's the one who encouraged me to go to Uni in the first place and took me away from my Dad! Why would I-'

'-I'm not sure I want to be an actor anymore Ted.' It was Rose's turn to disclose a painful admission.

'What?'

'Wow. That feels weird to say out loud. But yeah, I don't think it's what I want anymore.' Ted gestured her to go on, the two stood facing one another.

'I mean look at me Ted. I give everything to this thing. I dye my hair, I spend all my time travelling across the country to go to auditions I never get, I work every hour under the sun behind that God damned coffee counter, just for all my wages to go on train tickets and subscriptions to casting websites. When I do get roles, they're for free, unpaid student films or for profit-share *am dram*. When's something gonna to give? All of my friends are buying houses, or getting married and settling down, all of my friends are happy. And then there's me, poor, lonely, desperate me, learning monologues to perform in front of middle aged white men, just for them to tell me to come back when I've lost some weight, or that I'm not "pretty enough".'

Shocked, and guilt-ridden with the realisation that he'd done nothing but talk about himself for the entirety of their time together, Ted spoke.

'Then why do you do it?'

'I've been doing it for so long that I don't even know what else I could do. People who see me struggling say "you could do anything you like" to cheer me up, as if it's this good thing, as if there's all these limitless possibilities out there. But the truth is, it just terrifies me. I have no idea what else I can do with my life Ted' she replied. There was something about the night time that had made the two of them reflective and confessional. They were sure that these were conversations and emotions that they'd regret revealing when the morning broke, but for now, these were things that needed to be released.

Ted didn't know what to say, fortunately Rose did the talking for him. 'But there's one more reason why I haven't given up Ted, why I haven't thrown in the towel and gotten a "normal" job like everyone in my family keeps telling me to do. Regret. If there's one thing scarier than wasting my life in pursuit of something I'll never attain, it's looking back at seventy, from my rocking chair on my porch, and asking "what if?"'. What if there's a big break around the corner? What if just beyond the next script, just beyond the next rejection, there's something good worth fighting for?' She came close to him and looked him in the eyes. 'What if Geller appeared over that hill right now and cut both of our throats? Could you honestly say, as you lay there dying on the grass, that you'd be glad that you'd never called your mum? How many victims do you think are looking down from heaven right now, wishing that they'd have had one last chance, one last chance to say a proper goodbye to their loved ones before their lives were taken? You have that chance. Don't waste it.'

Ted looked to his feet, ashamed.

'We have choices in life Ted, there are plenty of paths we can take, and once we've decided on one, we close off the others. Like Geller, he made a choice to kill his family that sunny afternoon, a choice that meant he'd spend the rest of his natural life as a criminal. I choose to act, which means I can't have the things that other people have. They may be things I want, but as long as this is my path, I have to sacrifice them. I guess we're sorta like Priests...'

'Priests?'

'Yeah priests. You're telling me a man of the cloth has never locked eyes with a pretty woman across the bar and wanted to dance with her? That he's never felt electricity in his stomach that's made him want to revoke every vow he's ever taken and marry that girls ass right on the spot? But he can't. Because he's made a choice to seal that path. Yeah, I guess we're a little like Catholic's in love aren't we? Forever wishing we'd chosen something different to what we have. You can do whatever you want Ted, but you can't have everything, all you need to do, is decide which path it is you want to take.' Ted thought about the concept, but the theory was wasted on him, flying over his head and out onto the Moors. He hoped that he'd understand it one day though, it seemed important, whatever it meant. Rose continued her soliloquy.

'You were right about one thing. Life is too short, way too short to hold onto grudges. I get you're scared of commitment and I get you feel lost. So do I. Go to The bay if you think you'll find what you're looking for there, but just let your mum know you're alright. Just pick up the phone...'

He smiled at what an ass he'd been. The girl sure did know how to make him feel small, but all she'd done was a hold up a mirror. He didn't need to confirm to her that he'd call, she knew that he'd do it. 'Are you coming in with me?' he asked as he turned to re-enter the station, he'd memorised the route back.

'Nah. I think I'll stay out here for a while until my breaks over. I've got fifteen minutes left until I have to take Millie off, that's prime line learning time. Who knows, maybe they'll let me send over a self-tape instead. I'll catch you later Ted'. As he pulled back the sheet of ply-wood to return to the station and make his call, he watched as Rose began reciting her 'Brutus' lines, and from the sounds of it, though he was by no means a Shakespearean scholar, she was pretty damn good.

'It must be by his death,
and for my part I know no personal cause to spurn at him but for the
general.'

He re-covered the tree-smashed gap behind him, and then proceeded to search for a hotspot where he'd get signal, not noticing the muddy, brown boot prints that had been left at the base of the hole beside the outside of the door. It was as if someone had come in from the Moors.

Neither him, nor Rose, had been wearing boots.

Ted made his way through the empty service corridor, past the conveyor belts where goods would've been loaded from the delivery trucks; cardboard boxes of magazines, fizzy drinks, and coffee beans. He pulled out his phone before he could change his mind, took a deep breath, and then moved his thumb to dial his mother, as the trapped guests had called their loved ones hours ago. But before he could, a sharp blow was dealt to back of his skull and he fell straight to the ground. His phone flew, spinning out of his hand and across the floor.

Ted smashed his chin upon impact, but before he could identify the man behind his assault, the perpetrator continued his GBH by taking a clenched set of knuckles to his face. Ted was jabbed in full force across his right cheek, punched so hard that his head was propelled to the side, dislodging his jaw bone which cut into the lining of his cheek and gums, causing an outpouring of blood and saliva to spurt from his mouth. His back teeth loosened and their crowns tussled. From the floor, this time he was able to trace the hairy fist to its owner, for leaning over him, through blurred vision, he could make out the bench-press plated figure of the gypsy who'd taken a chair to the *O'Nowhere* doors earlier that night. Why the hell had he been released from custody? And what had Ted done to him to deserve this? Before these questions could be answered though, the gypsy took his right foot, and with a strength equal to that of his punch, kicked Ted twice in his stomach, narrowly missing his rib cage by a hair both times. Ted let out a cry of agony for his sore gut as the traveller grabbed him by the lapels of his jacket and dealt a final blow to his nose, the tacky gold ring on his finger catching the skin under his eye and tearing it open, the strike itself bursting his nostrils but thankfully avoiding any septum breakage. Already, swelling had begun around his lips and his sinuses were draining with gory blood all over the ground, but it seemed like the beating was over. Ted, dazed and confused and in excruciating pain, began sliding himself along the concrete to escape, but a boot on his back halted him in his tracks. The satisfied face of Billy slithered in front of him and grinned diabolically.

'Stay away from Rose, prick. Or next time, you don't get off so lightly'. His breath stank of filth, like the giant wheelie bins full of food wastage that had been dotted throughout the passage.

Billy then spat in his face and slapped him, his preferred method of combat given his puny figure. As Ted's vision began to fade and he started to pass out, his eyes allowed him to witness Billy kick his smartphone, still logged onto his moms contact number, down a drainage grate on the far side of the corridor. It slipped straight through the grid and fell down into the station sewage system, the screen cracking on collision.

'Nice slap. You sure showed him whose boss. We good now, yeah?' asked Smithy, waving his sore fist as though he'd just sat an exam and was suffering from writer's cramp.

'Good work Gypo. And yeah we're good, I'll stash your dirty drugs in my cleaning cupboard until this shit storm is over'. The palm of Billy's hand had turned bright red. Weak and feeble, he'd hurt it clouting Ted but wouldn't let it show.

'No more dirty work. We had a deal, remember? Now keep your fucking mouth shut about that stash or it'll be you I'll be dealing with next'

'You've got a big mouth Smithy. I'd like to see you go for me with cuffs around your wrists. If I want you again, you'll help me, or Officer Simmons will bag a murderer *and* a drug dealer on the same night' Billy replied, finding confidence and gusto as by-products of the adrenaline pummelling through his veins.

'Freak'. The gypsy pretended to attack Billy, stomping his foot and lifting a fist, to which the caretaker winced and cowered. Smithy sniggered a dirty snigger and then turned to leave, walking past the blood-splattered breeze blocks. He knew full well that the lanky janitor had him by the balls and that he'd do whatever he asked in exchange for him keeping his powder cache concealed.

Billy took one last look at his degraded victim, broken and squirming on the floor, and experienced a sensation he'd rarely felt in his life. It was gorgeous, seductive power. Oh, if only the school bullies and Perkins and his Mother could've see him now, they'd soon shut their mouths. Billy was in charge. Billy was the man.

'I mean it prick. Rose is mine. Back off', and with that, being the honour-less worm that he was, he too kicked Ted in his torso. Though far less powerful than Smithy's roundhouse, it had been enough to finish Ted off. With this, he was knocked unconscious, and left to bleed on the cold, hard floor.

As Ted fell into a deep, fist induced slumber, his mind drifted into another, oceanic dream from his youth.

Ten years old, young Ted unlocked his duck-egg cottage door in Robin Hood's Bay to take out the rubbish. He placed the black liner in the bin on the patio. From inside his house he could hear the rowing voices of his parents, his sober mother and his ferociously drunk Father. He hated it when they argued. Before going inside, he decided to stay out for a while until the name-calling and the plate-throwing and the mom-beating had died down.

He watched the last of the magic hour sun slowly set over the briny horizon of the sea, which was still and calm, as it usually was in the evenings. The triangular red rooftop tiling's of the Robin Hood's Bay cottages, like bricked tent canvas's, shielded his eyes from the suns dwindling glare, which tinted the sky with an orange and mango coat as it descended. The cobbled streets were empty and hushed, all the townsfolk inside, though with a population of 800, it wasn't often that the Bays boulevards were full. It had meant that Ted never had very many friends to play with, that he was often very lonely, and bored. The breeze was gentle, caressing the sea's waves like a soothing breath, puffing lightly upon them as if cooling hot soup. They plopped and splashed quietly, the beach submerged beneath the tide for the night. Dangling flower baskets and stationary bicycles too, trembled and wobbled in the evening wind. With kettles boiling under every rafter, the Bay was a ghost town.

Whilst his future self, had lay battered and bruised in the *O'Nowhere*, dying to return home but his memory of his childhood and how unhappy it had been distorted and clouded with age, young Ted had stood alone, gazing out to sea, dreaming of the day that he could leave that Bay forever, and never, ever come back.

CHAPTER SIX

'I'm singing in the rain, just singing in the rain. What a glorious feeling, I'm happy again.'

Billy Ocean? Nope. Billy Joel? Not quite. Ladies and gentlemen, performing for one night only, it's Billy the Janitor!

Billy sang Gene Kelly's famous number as he rubbed moisturiser into the pores of his face. Almost all of the notes were out of tune, bouncing between key changes like a pinball. He'd laid claim to the *O'Nowhere* male showers, locking the door and transforming the tiled wet-room into his own personal en suite. He'd taken Perkins's advice and had a nice hot shower, complete with a charcoal body wash, anti-frizz shampoo and conditioner. As a result, he smelt like a sudsy masculine dream. The water had turned black when he'd rinsed himself, there had been a little red mixed in too, from where he'd gotten pesky Ted's dirty nosebleed on his hands. He couldn't have that. His skin was bright and reinvigorated on account of the free moisturiser samples that he'd taken from the station pharmacy and he'd even sprayed some musky aftershave on the glands of his neck and wrists for good measure.

'OI! You've been ages in there! Let me in!' cried an angry northern bloke from the other side of the shower room door. Billy had indeed held the chamber under siege for the better part of 45 minutes, but just as Rome hadn't been built in a day, rugged good looks and proper male grooming didn't just happen overnight.

'Shut the fuck up prick or I'll come out there and eat your face off' screamed Billy, hunched over the sink where black hairs and shaving foam were clogging up the plug. He had a towel around his waist. The man didn't reply. With his peace restored, Billy turned back to the mirror, smiled pleasantly to himself, and then ploughed forward with his make-over, singing as he went.

'I'm singing in the rain, just singing in the rain.'

Next, now free of flakes and crusty dandruff, Billy took a dingy comb to his scalp and neatly scraped the strands of his greasy hair into a 1920's style side-parting. He'd seen the '*look*' in old movies and in magazines before and had thought that it was very distinguished. Though the rest of his body appeared to be wasting away, with the lines of his ribs and bone tissue protruding from under his skin like gristle on a steak, his hair had remained thick and full well into his early thirties. He'd supposed that he'd had his mum to thank for something at least, or maybe it had been his Father. If only he'd have been able to remember what he'd looked like. Good genes. He brushed, flossed and then mouth-washed his yellowing teeth, applied deodorant, and then turned to the outfit that he'd hung neatly on the door of an unused shower. The hot steam had ironed out the creases. These were his Sunday best, his smart clothes, ones that he'd been saving on a hook in his locker for a day just like today. Bought from a charity shop in Egton, the outfit was comprised of a pair of neat, denim slacks, and a cream, sand coloured, smart-casual, long sleeved shirt. He slipped his malnourished legs past the hem of the jeans, and put on the top, making sure to roll down the sleeves and to button the cuffs to hide his scars. *The ladies didn't like a self-harmer!* A condom machine attached to the far left wall flogged contraception and endurance gel.

Though Billy never would've called himself a looker, staring into the cracked bathroom mirror he had been moderately surprised at the scrubbed up bachelor that had been looking back at him. He posed, practising smiling into the reflection, and then twirled in his outfit.

'Just wait until they see you' he muttered to himself, imagining the smiles wiped off the faces of his bullying colleagues, once they'd seen his transformation. It would be just like those reality shows, the ones where the presenters would take a nerd or a fat person and totally turn their lives around with a team of glamorous stylists. Billy would often watch shows like that alone in his room on his television, sometimes treating himself to a jar of strong pickles as he did. The lady-killer took a deep breath, he was ready. Like a cop on a stakeout, he'd waited and waited, but now his time had come. He collected his toiletries into his brown leather man-bag, and then left to place them back in his locker, making sure to take the back corridors so that his new '*look*' didn't receive an early debut. Now, it was time to find Rose.

'I'm laughing at clouds,
So dark up above.
The sun's in my heart,

and I'm ready for love', he sang.

Billy strutted into the promenade, pushing on a set of double doors like the life and soul of a downtown bar, and then made his way to the coffee shop counter where he'd find his belle. For the first time for as long as he could remember, he'd felt really good about himself. With the hour being late, and with it seeming more and more unlikely that the police would be catching Marcus Geller out on the Moors, many of the guests had gone to sleep, napping on benches, using folded up coats for pillows. Billy, with his head held high, walked past a group of irritating Leeds hipsters who were blogging their experience at the *O'Nowhere* via a video livestream, to their equally gross social media followers. Though he didn't notice the looks of his fellow employees, they sure noticed him. The two book store clerks who had made fun of Billy during Perkins's staff meeting, witnessed him walking towards the coffee shop in his spanking new get up. They burst out laughing and took photos of him behind his back, others did the same.

Billy clamped sight on his conquest, pumping cinnamon shots into a latte cup to-go. Cheesy as it was, time appeared to slow down around Rose; the flicking of her infrared locks, the blinking of her blueberry eyes, the pouting of her tender lips. It seemed unfeasible to him that a girl so inwardly beautiful and kind could exist within the skin of someone just as faultless, but lo and behold, she was the trial-changing evidence that blew the case wide open, and proved that it could be true. She was beyond perfection, his one-way ticket to the life he'd always wanted, and with that troublesome prick Ted firmly dealt with, she was finally about to be his. He re-slicked his hair and straightened his shirt, before going in for the kill.

'Hey Rose' said Billy confidently. At the time she'd been bent over a crate of condiments, arranging the brown and white sugar behind the counter. She stood and turned to reply, answering without seeing him as she tied her hair back into a tail.

'Oh hi Billy,I-'

Rose had to double-take, not registering at first that the man that was stood in front of her was not the poorly dressed, scruffy caretaker that she'd grown accustom to. No, this was someone else. It was the look that Billy had pre-empted and longed for, for her to finally look at him as something more than just a friend, to actually *see* him.

'Wow. I didn't realise we had a new starter here. Billy you look...well, you look amazing! Check you out, I'm very impressed' she beamed, happy that her friend had revamped his image, not knowing that it had all been for her.

'Thank you, I thought it was time for a little change, you really like it?' Billy asked.

'Honestly, I think you look brilliant, look at that hair! Very handsome' she continued, unaware that she was fuelling his delusions.

Did you hear that? She thinks you're handsome.

She clearly wanted him as much as he did her. Billy smiled, but it was shambolic. It seemed wrong on his face, somewhat artificial and unsettling. The bend of the curve didn't appear to fit, like a circle in a square shaped hole on a child's toy.

'Really well done Billy, I'm gob-smacked I really am. You look like a totally new guy, a million bucks. You shouldn't let Perkins see you out of uniform though, you know what he's like. He'd go ballistic.' Rose knew he'd had it in him, finally he'd stuck it to the bastards who'd made fun of him for all those years. This would be a real turning point for Billy. She hoped that the bullies would finally leave him alone now that he'd refashioned himself. She hated the way that they'd treated him. Was being different really such a crime? In fact, she foresaw Billy standing a much better chance of meeting a nice girl now that he'd completed his metamorphosis into a gentleman. Yes, that's exactly what he needed, he deserved someone special to look after him and to love him for who he was. Everyone did.

'So, what inspired the makeover? Were you really that bored? Maybe we should be locked in *O'Nowhere* more often, hopefully it'll rub off on me and I'll decide to use the time to spruce up myself too. You can be my personal stylist. Got any tips?' she joked.

Billy had certainly administered a well needed feel-good factor into her miserable shift. After Ted had left her on the hilltop Rose had struggled to muster the motivation to rehearse her lines knowing that she'd never make her Manchester audition. Who was she kidding? They'd never have let her self-tape, by the time the day was done they'd have found their 'Brutus'. Around the tenth iambic couplet, roughly where her character had finally decided to assassinate *Caesar*, she'd given up, sat down and forlornly watched the stars. But seeing Billy, the underdog, defy the odds, had certainly put a spring in her step. At least *someone* was doing well.

Billy's confidence was at an all-time high by this point and his weedy fingers couldn't have been more enveloped around the sticks wrong end. It was time to face the music.

'Actually Rose, I had something I wanted to ask you.'

'Oh sure Billy, what is it?'

'Well Rose, we've known each other for a long time, and we really get on. So, I was wondering if you'd let me take you out on a date to the cinema after all this is over? I think you're really lovely, and I think we'd have a great time together' he said.

There was a spacey, long silence after he'd extended the invitation. Rose's face dropped. *Oh no.*

'I'm sorry Billy, as in, you're asking me out on a date? Just us? You and me? Alone?'

'That's right Rose. Would you like to?' He continued to smile, he should've taken the hesitation as a caveat, a red flag to match her hair that things weren't going to go his way.

'I...Billy...I'

'Yes? I've already checked the screening times for next week at Malton picture-house. I thought we could go on Saturday night if you'd like? I checked the time sheet, we're both off that day. There's loads of films to choose from.'

It all made sense to Rose now, why else would Billy have gotten so dolled up whilst still on shift? She had always found it infuriatingly unfair when men had asked her for her number whilst she was working, after all, she couldn't escape, she was trapped behind that counter and had nowhere to go. But for Billy she felt nothing but guilt. Had she lead him along? Shown any signs of interest? No, she knew that she hadn't. She was guilty of nothing but being nice to the guy, and though it was hard, to set him free she knew that she'd have to destroy that friendship forever. It sucked.

'I'm really, really sorry Billy. I think you're a wonderful, smart, lovely guy, I really do, and you're a great friend. But maybe we should just keep things that way. Just friends.'

Billy stood motionless, his arms by his sides and his smile unmoving. Perhaps he'd misheard her? Or he'd failed to explain himself properly? He wasn't the most of articulate men. 'Sorry Rose, no. I don't think you understand. I'm saying, I don't want to go to the cinema as friends. I want to go as more than that, I really like you' he professed.

Rose, as much as it had killed her inside, was left with no choice but to be brutal. 'Billy, no. Look, I did understand. I guess...argh this is really hard. I guess what I'm trying to say is that, I don't see you in that way

Billy. I'm so sorry, to me you couldn't ever be anything more than a friend'.

This time there could be no grey area, he'd been rejected. She didn't want him. He fought the falling of his tears, but as anyone who has tried this knows, when the body wants to cry, it cries, resisting is as futile as holding back vomit when sick, or sweat when stressed. His eyes began to water and his bottom lip wobbled. He suddenly became very aware of the giggles of his work colleagues, who'd watched the scene unfold from behind their till points in the opposite shops. He turned as red as the hair he longed to touch.

'Are you okay? I'm sorry. I don't know what to say' Rose asked kindly, genuinely so sorry that she'd had to hurt him, but understanding that there was a kindness in her rejection. Billy however, was heartbroken. All that was left to be done, was damage control.

'Thank you for being honest. I should go. Sorry to disturb you Rose. I'm sorry for being so silly. I have to get back to work now' he sputtered. His voice cracked on 'work'. Billy quickly turned to leave, ignoring her pleas to 'wait' so that she wouldn't see the extent to which she'd gutted him.

'Oi! Watch it mate!' Not looking where he was going, the hapless caretaker reversed and walked straight into a customer's table. It capsized, tipping over onto the floor and taking Billy and a large chocolate mocha along with it. The coffee spilt all over his nice cream shirt, scalding him as the brown stain spread across the lining.

'I'm so sorry', he pleaded with the man whose coffee he'd knocked.

Unable to bear the shame of meeting Rose's eyes, Billy instead looked to his left, only to see the station book clerks in fits as they recorded the incident on their phones. The pit stop had fallen silent. Guests were awoken from their dreams of home by the ruckus, and those who'd already been awake merely stared at Billy, who was spread out across the floor and covered in caffeine. Like Victorian's gawping at a vaudevillian circus they watched, marvelling at a conjoined mutant in a cage and thinking '*I'm glad that isn't me*'.

Rose, unabashed by the amusement of her colleagues, raced to Billy's side to help him up, but the look in her eyes as she moved around the counter proved to be one stab too far for Billy, it had been pity. He chose flight. His best shirt and special trousers ruined, he struggled to his feet and then hobbled as fast as he could past the spectating crowds, to the solitude of his cleaner's closet as the tears began to stream. No one could hurt him there. Rose watched him vanish around the corner in bits.

'What are you looking at? Shows over!' she shouted at the crowd as she tore off her apron and left for the kitchen, disgusted at their cruelty.

'Who was that freak?' asked one hipster to the other, quietly, as not to incur the wrath of the feisty red head, who'd clearly held an affinity for the weirdo in question.

'I've seen his name badge. "Billy", I think it is'.

But Billy was no more. For through the steely hot anvil and hammer that had been his suffering, that night, a monster had been born.

Just as Billy had been putting the finishing touches on his new '*look*' in

160

the men's showers, and had struggled to recognise himself, Ted too, if he'd have had access to a mirror, would've struggled to make out *his* own likeness. Gone were his boyish good looks. A stormy purple hurricane of a bruise had formed on his right cheek, taking over his face and rising like a soufflé from the swelling. His boxed, popped nose had ceased to bleed, but the downpour had dried into the thickets of his moustache and surrounding stubble, turning it red and crusty. His head throbbed like no migraine he'd ever had before, and as he came to on the cold service-corridor floor, there were screaming, piercing pains in his stomach and lower back. His first attempt to stand was a failure, his arms giving way and sending him crashing back down to the ground. His second was a small victory, him barely managing to climb up to his feet. Beneath the midnight bags under his left eye, he felt a stinging pain from the open wound that had been left behind by Smithy's tacky signet ring.

The harrowing memory of Billy's boot kicking his phone down the service drain returned to him and the stress of it inflated his headache like a hot air balloon. He could've done with a medieval apothecary drilling into his head, to expel the ache. Clutching his poorly, beaten stomach, 'Ted the undead' limped his way towards the drain and then peeped inside. Thanks to a well-timed ninth missed call from his worried mother, his phone screen had lit up. Through the grating he could see it, cracked but still functional, somewhere in the bowels of *O'Nowhere's* sewers. He *had* to get that phone back. For one, he'd need *Google Maps* to navigate his way to Robin Hood's Bay once he'd finally reached Middlesbrough. His memory of the area hadn't been as fresh as it used to be. He should never have tried to call his Mother, Billy would never have seen his phone otherwise. Even without knowing it she'd managed to thwart his quest to reach his Father all over again.

Ted left the grating and followed the nearby metal wall piping, in the hopes that he'd find an entrance to the sewers. The winding pipes took him through a labyrinth of tunnels, past fire doors and wooden pallets, until eventually he arrived at a copper man-hole cover in the ground. Using a considerable amount of strength and his one good arm, he used a rod to the left of the trap door to prop open the passage, revealing a set of rusty ladders that lead down into the cistern. A stomach churning stink was unleashed from the hole, forcing Ted to cover his mouth, it was as though he'd robbed the grave of an ancient mummy in its sarcophagus. The toxic odour had come from the collective smell of the stations urine and excrement, of which there had been plenty given the nerves of the guests that had been trapped there for the past few hours. But into the cloud of green Ted went, gently lowering himself down the rungs of the ladder, step by step, until he'd reached the bottom. It was a task not made easy by his pounding head and agonising stomach. Billy had definitely gotten his money's worth out of Smithy.

Once inside the sewage system, Ted followed the sound of muddy running water through the darkness. He felt his way along the sticky walls, grabbing onto slimy metal valves to guide his way but always being petrified of an unseen hand meeting his before it landed on a surface. What little light there had been had come second-hand, via the gratings in the passages ceiling, originating from the dim bulbs of the rooms above. Legions of grey, matted, beady-eyed rats scurried past him as he moved, the slinky vermin tails tickling his ankles and climbing over his shoes, occasionally nibbling on his laces. The roof was low and tight, making Ted feel claustrophobic and very much aware of his limited oxygen supply, he was after all, treading beneath ten feet of solid concrete. At times, Ted would be forced to wade through deep puddles of brown water, they would soak his trainers, seeping into his socks and freezing his feet. After limping through what must've been a hundred yards of filth, Ted finally arrived at a point that he'd recognised. Above him, he could see through some grating into the service corridor where he'd been served a heaping can of *whoop-ass*, courtesy of the gremlin and his pet troll. He crouched down and searched through the darkness with his bare hands, cringing as he did, until, after sliding over God knows what, he latched onto a familiar shaped object. Success! He had his phone back!

Eager to get the hell outta' that creepy place as quickly as possible, Ted made to trudge his way back along the drainage pipe, but stopped when he'd heard a pair of voices. He recognised one, but where from? Instead of turning back, he followed the passage a little further down. The voices grew louder and the diction more precise, until he was able to piece choice words together, like 'murder' and 'disaster'. When the sounds didn't seem like they could get much louder, Ted gazed up, only to find himself staring straight up into the hairy nostrils and trouser zippers of Inspector Henry Simmons and one of his officers, through another grating. He was directly under Manager Perkins's office. Like a Russian spy, he eavesdropped.

'Two?! You've got to be kidding me'. The cool and collected Simmons that had delivered a rousing speech and had calmed the crowd when Ted had first arrived, was gone, replaced by a clone, who was vexed and on edge.

'Yes sir. Two men. Vanished on the Moors' replied the officer, who'd drawn the short straw of telling his boss the bad news. Simmons's tie was loosened and his top button was undone, the edges of his white shirt were hanging from his trouser waist and his under eyes were dark.

'What do we know?' he asked, dreading the answer.

'The first of the two is forty-eight year old Mr. Steven M. Brooks, an Ex-champion swimmer. He had been driving home from his job, at Dalby Commercial Law Offices, leaving the building at around 6:36pm. His wife reported him missing two hours later when he didn't come back home on time. Officers investigated and found his crashed Mustang, around two miles from here, in a ditch, smashed into the bark of a tree.'

'Any sign of a body?'

'None.'

Ted gasped, and then quickly put his hand to his mouth and hid around the corner of the cistern passage, remembering that he shouldn't have been listening in. Once he was sure that he hadn't been caught, he returned to his spot under the office to hear more, monitoring the sound of his breathing, by only doing it through his bloody nose.

Simmons leant on the front of his desk. 'And the second?'

'The second is an older gentleman. Sixty-two year old Simon Berkeley, a

Malton resident. He had been walking his dog earlier tonight across the Moors and was due home for twenty-one hundred hours. Again, his wife reported him missing when he was a no-show, claiming it was extremely out of character for her husband ever to be late back. We sent two officers to investigate and found no one, only his border collie with the tag still tied around its neck. It had been crying on the ground sir'.

Simmons put his hand to his weary face. It was happening again. He didn't need to see the bodies to know that they were there. Sooner or later they'd turn up; a mangled corpse hidden beneath a tree, a disfigured body placed in a degrading position under another. Geller knew the Moors like he knew the shape of his own testicles, he'd been raised on that land all of his life, if anyone could hide a body from the police it would be him. Two men. Two innocent men had lost their lives because of that bastard, two deaths that Simmons could've easily have prevented if he'd actually done his job and caught the monster. He could already feel the crushing responsibility of having to ring the two men's wives at 3am to inform them that their husbands had been slaughtered. He could already hear their animalistic cries down the receiver as he made widows out of them, paraphrasing procedural bullshit talk like '*I regret to inform you*'. He rose from his desk.

'So let me get this straight. We've got two hundred young, fit, able-bodied officers out there searching for this guy, and in three hours we've not been able to find a single hair, not a single shred of evidence as to where he might be? Yet, he's managed to kill two completely innocent men and hide their bodies, all whilst we've got choppers circling the summit, sniffer dogs under ever trench and road blocks on every rural and highway exit for fifteen square miles?!' he asked rhetorically.

'We don't actually know that the men are dead yet sir. We've had no confirmation th-'Simmons silenced him with a single, stern look.

'This Guy is making a fool out of us, he's making a fool out of *me*, running rings. We need to double our efforts officer. I want this man caught by sunrise. If we haven't got him by then, I don't know if we'll ever catch him.'

Henry dismissed the officer then and returned to his desk, defeated, slumping into his chair and taking a swig from his fifth coffee of the night. Ted could no longer see him and so turned away from the vent grid, he'd heard enough anyway.

Simmons lent back into his chair and then contemplated the black and white photograph of his Father with his war buds, the one that he'd propped up on Perkins's borrowed desk as a reminder of the stakes. His legacy was on the line. If he'd have been half the Inspector that his Dad had been then he'd have caught Geller by now and would've been shipping him back to *Full Sutton Jail*. Maybe he just wasn't cut out for the job like *he* had been, he thought, staring into his eyes, sat in the boot of a camo-army truck in Nazi occupied France, with his arms around his battalion.

When would it end? The answer was never. Even if he were to catch Geller, which was seeming less and less likely by the second, there'd always be another, another rapist, another thief, another killer. Because people were evil. Killing had been going on all throughout history, ever since Cain had taken a rock to Abel's head. No wonder the UK legal system still adopted Latin expressions. As long as man existed, so would murder, and Simmons wasn't sure just how much more of it that he could take. Yes, once all this was over, once Geller was back behind bars where he belonged, Henry thought that he might be due a serious change of career, something simple and quiet, anything to get away from the glaring reminder that humanity, at its core, would always be rooted in a deep, dark, evil. It was something that he'd thought he could change, once upon a time, but not anymore. He saw now that it was a pointless, endless war to wage, that the dark would always extinguish the light. He was tired of trying to make it otherwise. He returned to his feet and left the office to continue the manhunt. This was the longest night of his life.

. . .

'It was awful mummy' cried Billy, snivelling and choking on snot in the pay phone booth. He'd ran straight there after his promenade meltdown. The cackling voice of his ragged mother replied.

'I know my baby, I know. Tell mummy what happened next.'

Billy recounted the scarring events. 'Then they all laughed at me. That nice girl tried to help me up, but I...I just couldn't bare it, I had to run, I had to get out of there'. Billy, at rock bottom, paused and held his head in his hands, the coffee had dried into his shirt now. He'd never get that stain out. 'It was so awful Mum, they all just laughed, they all just laughed at me. How can I ever face them again?'

His Mother, who looked as though she were five years past her due date for death, grimaced to herself. Her clipped, silver hair had been pulled back poorly, with crazy strays flying loose like a sinking ship shedding cargo to keep it afloat. Her overgrown nails clicked against the handle of the phone when she moved it. The skin on her hands was thin and shiny, and covered in brown moles.

'That girl wasn't trying to help you, you fool, don't you see? She was in on it. She was laughing at you too, behind your back. The dirty bitch. You should've known better than to try and fraternise with a whore like that Billy boy, I've raised you better than that'

Billy, his nose dribbling with mucus and his eyes sore from rubbing, clutched tightly onto the handset of the phone. His lips were so close to the microphone that whoever had used it afterwards would've had to wipe his saliva away from the plastic. 'No. Not Rose. You're wrong mummy. She's not like that. She's different to the others. She's-'

'can't you see she's against you like everyone else Billy? You really are fucking stupid, aren't you? They all hate you and she's the ring leader, her and that Ted boy. They planned this, they've planned this all along. They're probably laughing about you and committing all kinds of sin in that coffee shop kitchen right at this very moment'. The manipulator, covered in pizza crumbs, leant forward in her stagnant armchair. She lived in the English equivalent of a trailer park or a Louisiana bayou, spending her days on the marshlands with the gators that she'd so closely resembled.

With this, Billy began to overload with a conflicted passion. 'No. No that's not true I-'

'you know its true Billy. You know it is. Your mummy is right about everything. I'm the only person who cares about you in this world. The only person who's ever cared about you. That girl and boy are against you, they've made you look like a complete fool in front of everyone. And what are you going to do about it?'

'Well, I-'

'-NOTHING!' she screeched down the phone, deafening her son. 'You won't do anything. Why? Because you're weak. You're gutless. You have no balls, just like your Father didn't when he walked out...'

'Mum, please, I-'Billy started, becoming increasingly agitated and upset. He'd reverted back to the child inside of him after his rejection. All he'd wanted was for his mother to comfort him. If she turned on him too, he'd truly had nobody left.

'No Billy. You're not going to do anything. You're just going to let them walk all over you like you always do. Because you're a coward. You're pathetic! You're-'

'Mummy please. I love you!'

'I think somebody needs to go back to the attic when he gets home...'

'STOP!!!!'

Billy screamed at the top of his lungs and began bashing the phone violently against the frame of the booth. 'SHUT UP! SHUT UP! SHUT UP!'

He bawled over and over again as he whacked the phone, its case splitting and wiring short-circuiting, sending spiky golden sparks into the air like fire crackers. He was imagining that it had been Teds and Roses and his mothers and the bullies' heads that he'd been pummelling against a pavement, their brains spilling out onto the floor through their broken skulls and their eyeballs popping.

After the carnage began to subside, and the repetitive beatings of the phone became slower and slower until they'd stopped, Billy had stood alone in the booth, panting heavily. It was safe to say that the line was dead. Untethered from his mother, and now truly alone, Billy was flying off the grid, a law completely unto himself, like a raver at a silent disco. He'd done it, though not in person, he'd finally stood up to his Mama, and boy, had it felt good to shoot the bitch down. The only thing left on his mind, was revenge. He'd crossed a giant X through his mother's name on his naughty list, but there were still many more on there that had needed to be taken care of, starting with Rose and Ted. If they'd thought that they could get away with humiliating him and toying with his feelings like he was some sort of marionette, then they were sorely mistaken. Oh Rose, he'd given her a shot, they could've been so happy together, he would have treated her right, spoiled her, and made sure that she'd never wanted for anything ever again. But she'd thrown it all away, and for that, her and her prick of a boyfriend would have to pay with their lives. He'd been so dumb to think that she'd actually cared about him, all along it had been nothing more than a game, a twisted prank at his expense.

Billy, who hadn't realised that he'd wet himself again whilst obliterating the *O'Nowhere* payphone, walked hunched back towards his creaking cupboard. Once there, he clipped open the white bucket of cleaning products that he'd been storing Smithy's cocaine stash in. He pulled out the brown parcel, and reached between the paper folds. He wasn't looking to snort the drugs himself, no, that wasn't Billy's style. For you see, Smithy hadn't just been afraid of being lumbered with a sentence for '*Possession with intention to market illegal substances*', no, he'd have been put away for much longer if the police had found the other materials that he'd been smuggling through the *O'Nowhere*. Billy smiled as his bamboo fingers wrapped themselves around the handle of what he'd been searching for. He pulled out the black handgun and loaded its bullets.

. . .

Try as he might, Ted couldn't pick an answer from his brain. How could it be? How could it be that criminals and delinquents like Billy and Smithy and Geller could come to materialisation whilst growing up against the mise-en-scene of the glorious Yorkshire countryside? What terrible event had occurred between their births and adult lives that had transformed them into such diabolical beings? Surely, being raised amongst the rolling hills and great Dale lakes, and spending a childhood foraging for riches amongst the Pennine valleys, would've inoculated chivalrous virtues into their character? But clearly this had not been the case, the wonders of Yorkshire had been wasted on them.

Geller was the worst of the bunch, senselessly murdering his family in

171

grisly madness when he'd had everything to live for. The notion that one is a product of one's upbringing, seemed to Ted therefore to be debunked, like a false supernatural sighting. These three hadn't known how lucky they were. The high violent crime rates in Birmingham, with its collapsing community centres and deprived council housing estates, Ted had understood, but in wide open Yorkshire? The idea seemed preposterous. Perhaps then, true evil, transcended man-made constructs like class and wealth and environment. Perhaps then, it could take root anywhere, able to plant its corrupted seed inside of anyone, regardless of the quality of the soil. The thought chilled him.

Now there were two more corpses to add to that ever growing pile, and having seen behind the curtain of Simmons's police operation to stop the killer, Ted had discovered that it was nothing more than a complete shit-storm. Freaked out, Ted decided that he'd spent long enough in the *O'Nowhere* subterranean, it was time to scram. But since he hadn't left a trail of bread crumbs to the sewers entrance, pretty soon, he'd found himself lost.

Was that a left he'd taken back there? Or a right?

Panic set in. Dead end after dead end steered him as he limped through the caverns, like a lab rat in a maze. He desperately felt through the corridors for a beacon that he could recognise, a sign post to let him know that he'd been that way before, but found no such signal. Eventually he found himself instead, standing ankle-deep in a free flowing passage of boggy water, with no clue as to where he was. Trinkets and pieces of trash floated past his legs; coins, plastic bottles filled with questionable yellow liquid, and the shaved head of small girl's doll. The rounded shape of the tunnel that he was in had meant that the air flow had been funnelled into a 'hooting' sound, like a late night barn owl.

Ted had an episode, palpitations and dizziness kicking in. The conical vessels of his lungs expanded and deflated at a rate that made his stomach bruises ache. He knew that shouting for 'HELP' until his throat had been red raw would've been wasted energy, the bustling guests directly above him in the lobby would never have heard his cries. Alone and enclosed, he began to wonder whether or not he'd ever escape the sewers and see the light of day again at all, and that's when he stopped. He suddenly became astutely aware of the sound of feet shifting through the water behind him and a faint breathing over his shoulder. Turning around towards the darkness, Ted's heart continued to beat well past its usual *BPM.*

Boom. Boom. Boom.

As Ted faced the black of the *O'Nowhere* underworld, the heavy footsteps stopped, and like *Pennywise the dancing clown*, a pair of piercing pupils appeared amidst the shadows. The eyes were striking and blue, not the soft, beautiful, South Pacific of Rose's eyes, but frosty, vacant and unblinking. And unlike the time that he'd thought he'd spotted a figure lurking atop the ridge of the Moors, this was no mistake, it was all too real. The grey-bearded mouth below the eyes spoke, in the gritty, hardened voice of a man who'd seen far better days.

'Hello there.'

Ted knew exactly who it was that he was trapped with. Truth be told, he'd known ever since he'd heard the watery footfalls that had been tailing him.

It was him.

It was Marcus Geller.

CHAPTER SEVEN

Falling into, and then abruptly awakening from a deep sleep was becoming quite the habit for Ted that night. This was the fourth time that evening that it'd happened. While Smithy's brute-force induced slumber had been as a result of three back to back roundhouse kicks, Marcus Geller had taken out Ted with one simple smack to the face. It was as though he'd known exactly the right area to strike him in in order to knock him out cold. This made sense though, he was after all, far more proficient in the deadly art of the taking of a man's life than the petty gypsy.

To Ted, it seemed to him that the passage of time had spanned hours. He expected upon opening his eyes to see that the golden crest of the sun had risen and had dispersed its light all across the Moors. But this was not the case, unfortunately only 15 minutes had elapsed since he'd been passed out, and the night was still young. It was 12:45am.

On any normal weekday, four hours from then, at 5am, graveyard staff members would've been arriving at the *O'Nowhere* like zombies, to begin preparing for the onslaught of early morning lorry drivers that would soon dock at the station once it had opened. They'd spend the morning readying ingredients for the cafes breakfast menus; frying eggs, sizzling bacon, and unloading the fresh, black coffee beans. But thanks to the generosity of Manager Perkins's public persona, this time, the station would remain shut-up shop until the day after next, empty, quiet and alone, its walls patiently waiting to resume their normal functions.

Ted wondered though, if normal life would *ever* go on, or if what had happened at the *O'Nowhere* that night would linger like a ghost. After all, could one ever really, truly, fully cleanse a crime scene once a murder had been committed there? Sure, high salaried clean-up crews, dressed head to toe in white protective gear, would scrub every inch of surface, ridding them of blood traces and hair follicles and fingerprints until they appeared the same as they had before aesthetically. But perhaps there were some stains that couldn't be cleaned, ones that would be forever entrenched into the soul of a place, the echoes of the horrors that had happened there. There *had* to be some kind of reason as to why state-side solicitors were required by law to divulge to American buyers if a death had taken place on a property? It was high time that that particular piece of legislature was introduced into the British legal system, thought Ted. Something told him that the service station would never be the same again, and it was all because of Geller.

The dank, putrid stench, mucky brick walls and impenetrable darkness told Ted that he was still somewhere underground. His hands and legs were tied with rope. The more he struggled to undo the tightly wound knots though, the tighter they got, rubbing and burning his wrists and ankles in the process, so he stopped. He'd awoken to the sound of a single dripping, coming from an unseen pipe somewhere in the darkness. It seemed to him to be like the ticking of a clocks hands, counting down the minutes, maybe the seconds, until his execution. Once his eyes had adjusted to the lack of light, he gazed around, and saw that he wasn't alone in the cavernous hole. Sat upon a rock, staring at him intently with his dagger-sharp eyes, was the bulky, colossal figure, of Marcus Geller. It was as though he'd been sat there the entire time, waiting for Ted to come around. It confirmed the fears that Ted had had when he'd first bumped into him, but why the hell was he inside the *O'Nowhere*? How had he slipped past the police? His body temperature plummeted upon seeing the murderer, like the room were an abattoir. The two men stared at each other in silence for a long time; two gun slinging cowboys from the west, waiting for the other to make the first draw. Eventually, the killer spoke.

'Morning kiddo' he grinned, through his unkempt beard. No response from Ted.

'What? Cat got your tongue? I mean yeah, it doesn't feel like morning, but last I checked we were just coming up to 1am. So yep, dark as it may be out there, it's definitely not "good evening" anymore' he chuckled, perched on his rock, which was way too small for him. Clearly the prison life, and years of eating cafeteria slops, hadn't taken any toll on the felons physique, the man was a brick-house of muscle. He'd certainly made productive use out of the *Full Sutton* gymnasium facilities during the last thirty years, he'd needed *something* to pass the time Ted had supposed. Still, the captor didn't reply, terrified for his life, and for

177

which one of his veins Geller might cut into first. Perhaps his pulmonary system would be the one to go, no longer connecting oxygenated blood from his lungs to his heart just as Hammersmith had connected passengers to Oxford Circus.

'Not much of a talker, are ya?' Geller stood up and Ted felt extremely small beneath him. He'd thought that legends were always supposed to be far shorter in real life; TV stars, celebrities. Not this guy.

'I er....apologise for the living arrangements. Believe me this wasn't my first choice, but as you probably know by now, I have quite...limited options. It ain't so bad though, once you get used to the stink'. Geller laughed to himself at his own joke and began walking slowly around the space, inspecting the mossy walls and running one hand along them, the other stayed in his pocket. He was wearing Steven Brooks' clothes, stripped and taken from off his back out on the Moors, like a true Dick Turpin.

'Argh well, eh. Beggars can't be choosers. Better a free man in here, than locked back in there...if you know what I mean' he winked. Ted knew what he meant.

'Are you going to kill me?' he finally asked, petrified. He could feel his knee's quaking together and his teeth nattering. Ted had never been so scared in his life. He wished he'd never left Birmingham. Marcus spun around towards his hostage, at first surprised that Ted had spoken at all, and then, greatly amused.

'He speaks! Kill you? Oh kid. You're the one killing me here, you really are'. He threw his head back, and with nowhere for the sound to go, his gruff, psychopathic laughed filled the room. To Ted it wasn't funny. 'That's a good one. It really is. Kudos to you kid. I ain't laughed like that in a long time'. The giant stopped and then walked towards Ted, each step of his shoe's clapping against the stone floor as he got closer, and closer. Ted rived with fear and tried to back away from the killer by lifting his body with his elbows, but there was nowhere to go, not now. He was about to become Gellers third victim of the night.

Geller crouched down in front of Ted, stretching his ginormous thighs, and then leant in close so that the boy could see right into the lenses of his icy blues. Ted was instantly reminded of a quote, about how if one's stares into the abyss for long enough, the abyss stares back into you, though he couldn't quite remember who'd said it. The man didn't blink once. Ted, squirming and afraid, could smell soil and rain on Gellers skin, no doubt from hiding in the wilderness as he'd evaded the police and dragged bodies through the mud. Marcus lifted a huge, veiny hand, the same that had pulled the trigger on his wife and daughter, and what little life that Ted had had left, flashed before his eyes.

Was this truly the end? The man could've crushed his throat there and then if he'd wanted to, and marvelled as the asphyxiation turned Ted lips to violet. He'd perish, never having known his Father, in the depths of a service station, alone in the dark. But instead, Geller tore open the collar of his own shirt and revealed an inky black tattoo of Christ's crucifix on his muscular shoulder.

'"Thou shalt not kill". God's sixth commandment kid. I ain't gonna murder ya, I ain't allowed' the ogre grinned, and then he returned to sitting on his rock on the other side the cave. 'Although, it looks like somebody has already tried...' he joked, in reference to Teds bruises, as the boy breathed a sigh of relief that he hadn't been throttled.

'They failed' Ted replied bluntly.

'I can see that.' Marcus went on. 'I'm not surprised you'd thought I'd kill you though. I mean, I can hardly blame you, with the reputation I have. I'd rather thought everybody would've forgotten about poor old me by now, rotting away on the top floor of that reeking old prison. But I guess not....' Ted listened carefully, all the while discretely assessing the dirty room for an escape route, or something that he could've used as a weapon, anything.

'In fact, it seems my years in prison have only made my notoriety grow. I'm quite the celebrity these days, aren't I? All my fellow "murderers" are. Nobody remembers the names of the victims, do they? God knows what's happened to the world, but being a serial killer, if I'm not mistaken, appears to me to be the "in-thing" at the moment, it's sexy. Christ knows how many times a prison guard has told me that "he's just watched a fascinating documentary" or a *YouTube* video about what I'd supposedly done to my family, on that hot, summers day. I must say I'm quite flattered, I've never been a *star* before. The whole worlds obsessed with killing. And you think *I'm* the sick one-'

'I said, are you going to kill me?' Ted courageously interrupted, Gellers rant going over his head. At this, his captors face darkened and a spark went out behind his eyes.

'Listen here kid. You've asked me that already and I've told you the answer. At first, it was funny, now it's just rude, so I suggest you drop that particular line of enquiry and we move on.'

Ted complied. In that moment he'd peered beneath the facade and was offered a glimpse at Gellers true, slayer form. Sure, he'd been charismatic at first, magnetic even, but that's how they got you. They'd disguise themselves as the most wonderful of people to draw you in, and then they'd eliminate you, bury your body beneath their floorboards, and then go about calmly cooking themselves a delicious, hot lasagne for dinner as if nothing had ever happened. *Murderers*.

'Now, I'm going to untie your ropes. Just so you know, you do anything that I don't like the look of, make a run for it or try your chances at taking me down, and I'll just knock you back out and tie you back up all over again. You're looking pretty bruised already though so I wouldn't recommend it, you're not far off a concussion kid, and I'm a lot of things, but a doctor ain't one of them. Understand?' Ted nodded silently, and then held out his wrists. Geller untied the knots with ease and then let the ropes fall to the floor, before returning to his stool on the rock. He watched as Ted rubbed the sore, red marks on his wrists and revolved them in circles to return feeling and blood flow to his veins. It was healthy blood, blood that Ted hoped wouldn't be spilled all over the stone floor of the sewers anytime soon. His hands and legs free, he'd felt like *Pip* from *Great Expectations*, sitting with the convict, *Abel Magwitch*, amongst the Marshes. It was a book he'd had to study at university back in Birmingham, before he'd run away that is.

'That's much better isn't it? See, if you behave yourself and play by my rules we can get on just fine.' Ted had thought that Gellers elderly age, with his grey hair and wrinkling skin, would've made him more pathetic than scary, nothing more than a bitter old man with a grudge to bear against the world. But it had had quite the opposite effect. He instead seemed experienced, seasoned in the methods of killing, only concerned with himself and his own sordid routines as so often older people are, which made him even more of a threat.

'What's your name kid?' asked the violent pensioner. Tired of being referred to as 'kid', the detainee answered.

'Ted'

'Cute. Like a stuffed bear, or Bundy. Well, listen closely Ted, I'm going to tell you a story now. It's one I've waited to tell for a very long time, thirty five years in fact, and so as you can imagine, I'm very eager to tell it. I would ask that when I'm talking, that you please don't interrupt until I've finished, or I may just have to knock you on the head again. Am I making sense?' Ted agreed. Geller's overt, English politeness unnerved him.

'Good. You comfy? It's a real corker of a tale. Excellent. Well then, let us begin....

...I didn't kill my wife and daughter.'

Ted, shocked, his short-term memory failing him, instantly forgot their pact and interjected.

'What! But I thought-'

'-come now Ted. I thought we'd agreed to no interruptions. I'll give you that one, but that's it. Two strikes and you're out.' Remembering himself, but bursting with questions, Ted reluctantly held back, realising that the best way to get answers would be to remain patient, until Geller had elaborated on his bomb-shell announcement. He knew that he was lying, of course he'd killed his wife and daughter, the evidence was overwhelmingly beyond '*any reasonable doubt*', he'd been caught red handed in the act for God's sake. But at the very least, perhaps Gellers delusional take on the events might've offered Ted a way out of the mess that he'd found himself in. So he'd indulge him, what other choice did he have? With Ted acting as the midwife for his festering revelation, the confession of a convict began.

'I suppose you think you know how the story goes, but you don't. Crazy old farmer, going raving mad alone out there in the hills, finally snaps and murders his entire family? Textbook. But also, completely wrong. I'll tell you what really happened....' The inflamed red marks on his wrists, like those left behind from a hangman's noose, and the anaesthetic-like fuzziness that had come as a side effect from Ted's blow to the head, hadn't been enough to stop him from giving Geller his full, undivided attention.

'The year was 1978, not on a "cold and stormy night" like how one would expect a scary story to start, but on a hot summer's day in July.

That part of the story, you've got right, that's true. But I'm afraid everything from that point onwards that the news stations reported, was completely wrong.'

Weighing the two deadly eco-systems, Ted concluded that he'd much rather have taken his chances out on the Moors than inside of the claustrophobic passages of the sewers with Geller. The pitch-black Moors, black like a funeral veil or the lipstick of goths who'd so often frequent the famous '*99 Steps*' of Whitby, in commemoration of Bram Stoker. As a student of the sea, Ted knew all too well that the ocean often took on the colour of the sky. And so, that dark night, he'd expected that the view from his beloved Robin Hood's Bay would've taken on the form of a screaming, shadowy vortex, mimicking the brooding of the Moors, its waves building momentum before committing mass suicide by crashing into the sharp shore rocks. It was the home that he might never see again. But Ted abated his fear by listening to Gellers story. If he truly was to die, and these, were the last words that he'd ever hear, at least he could take some final comfort in scratching the itch of his curiosity. Who *had* killed the Gellers? Marcus carried on in melodramatic fashion.

'I woke up that day in the same way that I'd woken up every day before it, with the strong smell of manure in my nostrils and the sound of summer birds tweeting outside of my bedroom window. I'm a farmer, dealing in the currency of the land, I always have been, like my father before me and his before him. We trade in livestock mostly, Daddy Geller had been in the potato ploughing business when I'd been just a little boy, but we'd made the move into animals somewhere around the early 50's. Don't get me wrong, we still grow a little grain here and there for some side-income, but we mostly leave that to the Malton bread mill in town. It was a day just like any other, I'd had no idea that it was about to become the worst of my life'.

'I vaulted out of bed. The cuckoo clock on the wall had read 12:30pm and I'd woken up alone. Now, before you go about accusing me of being a lazy lay-around, hold your horses. My wife hadn't been gallivanting off with another man either, I know that's a rumour that a lot of the true crime *YouTubers* love to toss around. This wasn't at all an uncommon occurrence for me and the misses. You see, I'd get up at 5:30am every morning to feed the pigs and to let the sheep go out for a wander. I'd always used to joke to Mary Jane that they'd looked like Japanese flags with their red painted fleeces. I'd return to bed after tending to the animals at around 7am, and then Mary would get up at 9am and leave me to sleep until midday. That's generally how our weekends would go, so that day didn't seem out of the ordinary at all when I'd woken up and Mary wasn't by my side. Oh how wrong I was.'

'I made my way downstairs to the kitchen and Mary was nowhere to be found, neither was my daughter, Elsie. Again though, I'd figured that Mary must have gone and taken her down to the farmers market for a spot of strawberry jam shopping, in fact, I remember feeling pretty damn happy that I'd had the farmhouse to myself for a little while. I kicked back, put my feet up onto the kitchen table, something I'd never usually have been allowed to do, and then read the Malton times with a cup of hot coffee in my hand and a *Neil Young* track playing on the radio. It had been a glorious morning, and I remember feeling utterly content, drinking tea with my family's photos up on the walls and the summer sun shining in through the window above the sink. I was happy Ted.'

Geller breathed a foreboding sigh then, as if he'd known that the warm, nostalgic portion of his tale had been over, and that he was about to wade into far more sinister territory. He was past the point of no return now. 'It was when I'd reached the crossword puzzles and horoscopes at the back the paper that I'd realised just how much time had gone by. It was 2:30pm by then and there was still no sign of Mary nor Elsie. So I'd decided to go searching for answers instead of waiting for them to fall into my lap.'

'Now, it's here we that arrive at a lie. It was a subtle, barely noticeably lie, so small in fact that it had managed to sneak through into the press's publications, but it was a lie none the less. You may or may not remember, I'll assume that you don't, that the newspapers printed that I'd had a son, a twelve old lad named Terrance Geller. Apparently, he'd managed to avoid my "murder-spree" because he'd been out playing with a friend nearby, at the time that I'd supposedly done it. This, Teddy boy, is complete fiction. Terrance wasn't playing with his friend at all that day, no, he'd been at the farm with us...'

'...I realise that this is a lot to take in and that I'm throwing a shit-tonne of information at you within a very short window of time. Please do try to keep up, you're doing great' said Geller to his prisoner. These were the words that he'd been longing to say for three decades, agonising over every tiny detail long into the night, as he'd tried to sleep through the deranged sounds of crazed madmen and repenting criminals in the jail-cells next door to his. '*I didn't do it!*' they'd scream through their bars, until they'd had no voice left to do it with. Ted gestured Marcus to continue with a nod of his head, it hurt to move even slightly.

'I put on my boots and my Barbour jacket and then stepped out into the yard to see if I could find out where everybody was. Bear in mind that this was a Saturday, so the hands were off work for the weekend. The courtyard was completely empty. You should've seen it Ted, what a perfect afternoon it was, not a cloud in the sky, the flowers in bloom, and the birds singing. I imagine that if my family hadn't been killed that day, we'd all have fired up the BBQ and whiled away the hours spraying Elsie with the garden hose, laughing until it'd hurt. My girl used to love the sunshine. And that's when I'd heard it....'

Just then, Ted had noticed that Marcus's eyes were full to the brim with a deep, agonising pain. It wasn't like the physical hurt that Ted himself had sustained from his blows to the head and stomach, no, this cut far deeper. It was a kind of crippling suffering that Ted hadn't yet had the awful misfortune of experiencing, and he'd hoped that he never would. It was the affliction of knowing that someone you'd loved more than anything in the world had had their life deprived of them by another. That they'd been murdered.

'I followed the two bullet sounds to the farms backfield, running as fast as I could, but by the time I'd got there it was too late...'

The mammoth man's eyes started to water, and he began to totally break down at the memory of what he'd seen out in the field that day. It was a memory, that up until now, he'd thought that he'd managed to tame throughout his years of incarceration, only for it to have snuck back up on him and to have stabbed him straight through the heart all over again. The pain of the wound was as fresh as it had been thirty five years ago.

'I'd tried to tell him. I'd told him so many times, never to use my gun' Marcus cried, as he placed his sizeable head into his hands. Even Ted had begun to well up, he'd hardly expected to sympathise with Geller when he'd awoken to his wrists and legs in bonds, but since when had anything that night at the *O'Nowhere* made any sort of sense? It's a particularly biting breed of sorrow to see a grown man cry, especially one as masculine as Geller. It's rare, like an eclipse, but when it happens, man is it a kicker. Marcus shuddered and whelped and his agonising sobs echoed through the ant colony burrows of the sewers. The acoustics of the yucky ducts propelled his wails out and across the Moors where they'd catch the ears of scouting police officers. They'd put the haunting sounds down to nothing more than the howls of the late night wind.

'Terrance. I saw Terrance standing there with my shotgun in his hand. The bodies of Mary and Elsie at his feet'. Ted looked away from Geller for the first time since his abduction. Somehow he'd known what Marcus was going to say, even before he'd said it, but it hadn't made it any easier to hear.

'It had been an accident. A total freak accident. Mary, just like I'd thought, had been shopping at the market that afternoon and had left Terrance to look after Elsie. The two of them had been playing out in the fields all morning when Terrance had had the idea to steal my gun and to use it to practice shooting tin cans off of the scarecrow poles. Goddamn it. I'd told him time and time and time again not to mess with it, but he'd always been fascinated with the thing, he just wouldn't listen. He hadn't realised that the barrel was loaded and...Well...please don't make me say it....'

'As soon as he'd shot Elsie in the chest, he'd heard the voice of his mother behind him. Mary had arrived back from shopping at the market and seen the two of them playing in the field. She'd decided to sneak up on them, to surprise them with a can of fizzy-lemonade each. He'd turned around, shocked, with the weapon still in his hands and...Well....then she was gone too'. Marcus had used a precise and factual delivery of his story to steer him back towards a state of comprehension. He had a tale to tell, and by God was he going to tell it. It was his truth, and if Ted was the only person ever to hear it, then so be it, but he'd make damn well sure that it was told in the right way, his way, even if it *was* through snot and tears.

He looked up then, and spoke with a pride and conviction. 'I did the right thing Ted. I did what any Father would've done. I took the blame. My boy was twelve for Christ's sake. Do you have any idea how long they'd have sent him away for? For a double manslaughter? And, on top of that, for the possession of an unauthorised firearm? His life would've been ruined. I'd already lost two thirds of my family, I wasn't about to lose what was left of it. So I told him to run, to run as fast as he could back out into the fields as if he'd been playing, like nothing had ever happened, and to leave everything to me. I'd take care of it. And that's exactly what I did Ted, that's exactly what I did. Carrying those bodies back into my kitchen and placing them along the floor was the worst thing I've ever had to do in my life. But I did it. For love, I did it for Love. Because that's all I had left, it's all we ever have.'

'Officer Cole Simmons turned up not long after and the rest is history. The police had enough evidence on me that they hadn't needed to conduct a wide spread investigation out into the surrounding area, if they had they'd have found the blood traces and spilt lemonade out in the barley fields. I think they'd just wanted the case as open and shut as quickly as I did. The court hearing was swift, especially since I'd refused to say a single word during the entire proceedings. And then there I was, locked up in *Full Sutton Prison* and my son scot-free. All that mattered was that my plan had worked. I won't tell you how I've managed to escape, a magician never reveals his tricks. But this wasn't no *Shawshank* Job, no hidden tunnels behind posters here Ted. Now, flash forward three decades later, and I'm sat in the sewers of a service station that couldn't be more slap bang in the sticks, face to face with a boy I've never met before, and firmly placed at pole position on the *North Yorkshire's Most Wanted List.*'

Ted was lost for words. He'd begun the night believing that Geller was a villain, a murderous scumbag of unparalleled evil, but now, though he'd have hesitated to admit it, he'd come to respect him as a hero. The tale had completed reversed his opinion, as though the needle of his subconscious, like on an old wireless 1930's radio, had been oscillating between two distant stations, before finally coming to settle upon a channel of truth. He believed him. But he still had questions for Marcus. He read the room and permitted himself the chance to speak, it was his turn now.

'What about Steven Brooks and Simon Berkeley?'

'Who?'

'The two men you killed tonight out on the Moors. I overheard some of the officers talking about it' highlighted Ted, believing he'd caught Marcus out.

'Oh, were *those* they're names? Funny, I'd pictured them more as a "Ronnie and Clive". How many times do I have to tell you Ted? I ain't no killer. You may have noticed I'm a dab hand at knocking people out though, you've got my scrappy, country boyhood to thank for that skillset. They're both fine, unconscious, but safe and sound, hidden in a cave somewhere out on the Moors. They'll be able to find their own way back home once they've come around at daybreak. It's a pity I'll never get a chance to thank Steven for his clothes though, he has good taste. I traded his for mine, a bright blue jumpsuit is hardly the best of attire for a prisoner out on the run'.

Ted was relieved by this, though he'd had no idea why it had been the first question he'd posed. Perhaps it had come from an instinctual sense of moral obligation to his fellow man, he'd wanted to make sure that the pair were okay.

'If this is all true....then why, Marcus Geller, have you broken out of prison? It doesn't make any sense. From the sounds of things, you'd have done anything to have gotten yourself banged up instead of Terrance. Why are you out?'

'Cancer' the man replied, in a very 'matter of fact' way. The letters were as prominent and as glaring as the *Hollywood* sign.

'I...I'm sorry I-'

'Oh pack that in you fool. I've come to terms with it already, I'm not after any sympathy. Terminal lung cancer, that's what the prison doctor told me. I was diagnosed around two months ago, so I don't have much time left. And it's this Ted, this mortal coil, which forced my hand, and finally made me get up off of my wrinkly old ass and break out of that joint. I want to see my family again, my Terrance, all grown up, to meet *his* son, one last time before I go. The truth is, I could've broken outta' *Full Sutton* years ago. That place is a cinch, '"maximum security" my arse', Marcus laughed.

Ted admired his ability to muster humour even in the face of such hopelessness. No wonder the man's hair had gone grey and white, Ted expected that ageing hadn't been the only contributing factor to his 'silver fox' look, not after all the stress that he'd had to contend with.

'Why don't you just ask them to visit you?' Ted asked. He'd only now just realised that he'd inadvertently slid across the floor and was sat much closer to Geller, who was still upon his rock.

'And say my farewells through a glass case? Like I'm some sort of animal? Ted I want to hold Terrance in my arms, I want to shake the hand of my grandson without having to worry about armed guards thinking that I'm smuggling contraband into my cell. I want to feel the cold wind blow, just one last time. These last 8 hours have been the most exciting that I've had in thirty five years, and now it's been cut short. I'm so close, yet so far'.

Ted was astounded by Marcus's spirit. So often he had viewed adults as stuffy and dull, jaded by life, all of their youthful vigour extinguished, his Mother being as a good an example as any, but not Geller. Despite the horrors that he'd endured, horrors that no man should ever have had to go through, he'd retained hope. That hope seemed to dwindle though. Geller lowered his head and stared at his throbbing size twelve feet, the blistered feet that had carried him for miles and miles across muddy Moor-land and that so badly needed rest, but that were prepared to carry him further still, as far as it had took them, to reunite him with his son.

'It seems more and more likely now that it's never going to happen. A few miles back I ran into a police squadron across one of the eastern passes, to avoid them I was forced to flee into the *O'Nowhere*. Don't get me wrong, I know those heaths like the back of my hand, but even *I* couldn't dodge the sheer number of Bobbies that they'd had out searching. They must really want me bad. I couldn't go back Ted, I just couldn't, not before completing my mission. I panicked, and that was when I noticed the station. I was able to get in here through a boarded up hole atop a hill-face. And now I'm trapped, with no hope of getting out at all. They've got me Ted, they've got me. It's over.' Ted could hardly blame Marcus for becoming so forlorn, after all, by trapping himself in the sewers, all he'd really done was exchange one prison cell for another, only one, was wrought with paranoia and danger, and the other, had been equipped with a pillow, hot food and a working loo. 'You're too young to know the pain of being separated from the person you love the most Ted, you have no idea how much it kills a man inside'.

'Actually I do' Ted said back abruptly. It seemed that the two of them had more in common than he'd first thought. 'I'm actually here at the station tonight because I was on the way to find my father, over in Robin Hood's Bay. I haven't seen in him eleven years'. Though it had taken hours for Ted to entrust Rose with his secret, Geller's earnestness had made him feel as though they were in fact old friends instead of strangers, like he'd known him all of his life.

'The Bay?' The spritely sense of fun that suited Marcus so well returned to him.

'You know it?'

'Do I?! Why, Mary and I used to take Elsie and Terrence down to Whitby all the time, there's no place quite like it. Ah, I remember it fondly, strolling along the pier at sunset, drinking a cold pint in "The *Duke of York*" overlooking the harbour, struggling to pick which ice cream flavour we wanted from…Erm…what was it called now? Cl…Cl…'

'Clara's!' the two men shouted gleefully, in sync. The pair burst into a jovial laughter that seemed to momentarily light up the grimy, clammy basement. But when the dust had settled and the harrowing reality of their situations had returned to them, an elephant had been left behind in the room. Its humongous greyish hooves, trunk and ivory tusks rivalled that of even Gellers size, with his tight boxer's muscles and bodybuilder frame. It was one that Ted had realised he had no choice but to confront.

'What happens to me now?' he asked.

Marcus knew this part had been approaching. He had grown so accustomed to having paedophiles and sociopaths for company within the concrete walls of *Full Sutton* that it had been somewhat of an unexpected delight to have been able to talk to Ted, a nice, respectable young man, who'd listened and cared. He had reminded him of Terrance in many ways, but now, he knew that he had to let him go.

'Of course. You're free to leave whenever you like' he said reluctantly, gesturing towards the doorway of the hole.

'Just like that?' replied an astonished Ted. He'd almost anticipated a surprise *Game of Thrones*-style twist.

'Just like that. I'm sorry I dragged you here kid, I really am. I just couldn't take the chance, I saw you out there in the tunnels and panicked. I hope you can understand'. Geller arose from his stone seat then. Ted imagined that it must have been rather painful on his rear end. 'I'm pretty good with directions. If you head through that door and make two lefts and then a right, you should arrive at a set of ladders, that'll take you back up to the surface'.

Ted slowly limped towards the exit. But there was something other than his bruised leg that had stalled his leaving the room, guilt.

'If you go to the police I won't try to run, they'll find me down here. I have nowhere else to go' said Geller after him. Being the incredibly versatile piece of machinery that the human body is, Ted's eyes had adjusted to the darkness of the underground by now, and had been able to easily make out a likeness of disappointment on his captors face. 'I've had a good run, eh? I was lucky to have gotten as far as I did. I was heading for the farm, my old farm where it all happened. Terrence lives there now with his wife and my grandson. I was so close, so damn close'.

195

Ted stopped at the threshold of the doorway with his back to Marcus, as if some invisible force shield were preventing him from going any further.

'Hey Ted. Thanks for listening man. I really hope you find your Dad' said the ex-prisoner, soon to be shipped back to perhaps an even higher security penitentiary, one even further from his lost son and family.

At this, Ted turned around. How could he leave? How could he wilfully turn in a man who he knew to be innocent, separating a father from his son whilst he was reunited with his? It wasn't fair. Marcus's story had touched Ted, so much so that he was willing to break the law and to help him escape the *O'Nowhere* if it had meant allowing him and Terrance, one last goodbye. Ted had an entire lifetime of adventures ahead of him with *his* Father to look forward to, once he'd tracked him down, but this was Gellers final hope to see his son before the cancer invaded his respiratory organs, and his curtain came down. What kind of man would that've made Ted, if he'd knowingly gone through with aiding the police in his arrest? He knew, a man that his dad wouldn't have been proud to meet. To hell with it, he didn't even care if there had been an £100,000 reward waiting for him in the commissioners vault. He was Marcus's lifeline. He was the one thing standing between him and his dying wish, and he wasn't going to let him down, in the way that his own mom had let *him* down by dragging him away from Whitby, all those years ago.

'I'm going to help you. We're getting you to that farm Marcus.'

Geller frowned his sooty brows.

'What? What are you talking about? I-'

'There's no way you're gonna be able to get back out of this station alone, but with my help, you can. If I can get you back out onto the Moors, would you be able to find your way to your farm?' quizzed Ted, standing tall and proud in the knowledge that he was doing the just thing. Geller hesitated, the scene appearing too good to be true. He looked as though he were about to keel over with disbelief.

'I....yes....yes I could find my way back. But Ted, I can't pull you into this kid, this is *my* mess, I-'

'I'll be fine. In the worst case scenario that we get caught by the police, I can always say that you coerced me into it. I'll get you as far as the Moors and then you're on your own. You can say your goodbyes before you're recaptured and then I'll be able to leave this fucking place and finally reach my own Dad'. Ted, chewed up and spat out by the *O'Nowhere*, raised a trembling hand to shake Geller's, whose eyes once again, were beginning to glitter with tears. This time though, they were tears of hope, hope, that he might have finally been able to see his Terrance again. The two shook on it, a pact of abandoned Fathers and sons.

'You're full of surprises, aren't you kid? I don't know how I'll ever be able to thank you.'

'You can thank me by getting back to your son Marcus.'

Geller grinned away in the dark. After all, he'd had every right to. Ted had believed every single word of his story, even though every single word, had been a complete, and utter, bare-faced lie.

CHAPTER EIGHT

They had the makings of their very own 'buddy-cop show', Yorkshire's answer to '*Starsky & Hutch*' or '*True Detective*'. '*The courageously daring Ted and his beloved sidekick; The Custard Coloured Coat-Wearing Boy*'. Except this pair, instead of fighting crime, were perpetrating it.

Inside the book store, which also doubled up as a sandwich vendor, the two clerks who'd bullied Billy at the staff meeting and when he'd failed to ask Rose out on a date, were doing anything but working. The majority of the staff at the *O'Nowhere*, as the night had worn on, had slowly become more and more relaxed in the carrying out of their employee functions. The first of the two assistants was stood behind the book store counter. A spotty-skinned lad, sporting a conventional 'short, back and sides', he was leafing through a porno magazine that he'd helped himself to, from off of the stores top shelf. As he stared at a pair of silicon implanted breasts, his colleague, a ginger lad with pasty skin and acne scars, sat on an upturned apple crate, playing video games on his phone. The pair were bored out of their minds, but their elongated shifts were about to get a hell of a lot more interesting.

Ted, still horrendously bruised around his facial area, positioned himself at the back of the store in the food aisle, and pretended to peruse the goods on offer. He'd gone relatively unnoticed, customer service was hardly high on the mandate of the two clerks on duty that night. Meanwhile, as according to plan, the Custard coloured coat-wearing boy, whom Ted had recruited earlier in his arcade machine shenanigans, was stood at the front of the store, next to a tower of packet sweets. *Yummy*. Ted had run through the plan with the boy numerous times. He'd picked it up relatively quickly though, he was a surprisingly bright lad for his age.

Ted raised a closed fist to his mouth, and then fake-coughed once. The young boys ears pricked up, it had begun. Then Ted coughed a second time. The clerks paid it no mind, but the boy knew that this was his signal to inhale. He took a deep breath. There was a long pause, filled only by the sound of cheap pop music playing at an inoffensive volume over the shops speakers, and then Ted coughed for a third and final time. *GO! GO! GO!*

The Custard coloured coat-wearing boy, a lad of many talents, began crying and wailing at the top of his voice, spluttering and sobbing at the front of the store. He'd had many years of practise, perfecting the art of crocodile tears. It rarely worked on his father anymore, but the two books clerks fell for it like dominoes. Looking up from a pair of plastic surgery-butt cheeks, the first of the two noticed the young boy crying and raced around the counter to his side, his colleague joining him shortly after from the apple crate, putting down his round of '*Snake*'.

Unsure of what to do, the boys looked at each other apprehensively. 'Hey there little guy...' said the first, embarrassingly.

'What's the matter? Are you lost? Are you hurt?' said the other, bending down, as the child continued to cry. It was as though they were talking to an alien species, instead of one of their own. The spotty faced lad reached a hand towards the child.

'Do you...erm...need a hug?'

'WAIT!' The other clerk grabbed his friends hand to stop him.

'What man?'

'Don't touch him dude! Seriously!' the other stressed, bloodshot eyes, wide with fear.

'Are you crazy? Why not? I don't see you doing anything to calm him down!'

'Look man, if you touch that kid who knows what you'll be accused of. Trust me, parents are crazy paranoid these days. You may *think* you're helping to cheer him up...but then BAM! Before you know it you're slapped with a molestation charge. Touching that boy even slightly is as good as putting your hand onto a poisonous mushroom and then licking your finger dude, he's toxic' the stoner teen explained, speaking holy truths that he'd read on conspiracy websites at 2am in the morning, whilst sprinkled with nacho cheese-dust and high on energy drinks.

'I guess you're right man, good call! I ain't ending up on no "Sex Offenders Register". But what in the hell do we do with the thing then?' replied the other, equally clueless, his spots flaring up from the stress.

'I don't know dude! Do I look like I know anything about kids?'

As the boy continued to howl with an impressive stamina, and the two idiot shop assistants remained completely distracted from everything but the child, Ted set about completing his half of the mission. He yanked on the metal keychain on the zip of his backpack, pulled it wide open, and then began emptying the shops shelves of food into it. Supplies were middling but by no means depleted. Many of the *O'Nowhere* guests had grown weary of the complimentary soup and bread that Perkins had had on offer and so instead had decided to shop elsewhere for sustenance. Fortunately the book store had been quiet at the time of the great '*Flapjack Robbery*'. Sandwiches, wraps, crisps, biscuits, fizzy drinks, water, fruit, packets of meat, cookies, sweets. Anything and everything went into Ted's bag. Geller was a huge unit, and just as monster trucks required more fuel than *Mini Coopers*, the fugitive would need a particularly massive quantity of food to restore his strength for the *O'Nowhere* breakout that himself and Ted had been planning.

When his bag was full to the brim, Ted, who was sure that the child would be ruining his throat by now, ran back over to the two panicking book clerks. They had begun singing the infant a lullaby in an effort to subdue him.

'...and all the kings' horses, and all the kings men, couldn't put humpty together again!' they finished together, singing horribly out of tune and key, as Ted arrived on the scene.

'Toby! What are you crying about now? C'mon, let's get you back to Dad' he said, giving Rose a run for her money in the acting department, as he took the lad by the hand.

'You know this pip-squeak?' asked the ginger dork, hopefully.

'Know him? He's my little brother. Little shit more like. Sorry about the trouble fellas, I'll take him off your hands', Ted led the boy out of the store.

'You ought to keep that midget on a leash' shouted the pervy shop assistant after the pair. He spoke with a Doncaster twang, an area that in a recent poll had been voted the *'least attractive accent'* in the county by *'Yorkshire Readers Digest'*. But the dynamic duo, with another heist under their belt, were already gone.

Their success was short lived though. As Ted and the Custard coloured coat-wearing boy waltzed victoriously across the surface of the promenade, they suddenly heard a stern 'Hey! You there!' from behind them. Turning, Ted's heart sank like a stone once he saw the source of the summoning. One of the police officers stationed at the *O'Nowhere*, with his hands on the hips of his trousers, slowly approached the two vagabonds.

This was it. Ted was going to get caught. He'd be asked why he'd been stealing so much food, and he was sure that he'd crack under the pressure of a harsh interrogation from Inspector Simmons. He'd fess up all about Marcus in the sewers and then it'd be game over. Geller would be arrested and returned to prison, and then he'd die alone of lung cancer as he stared up at the grey, concrete ceiling of his cell, never having been reunited with Terrance. Not only that though, but Ted would be charged and taken to court for *'aiding and abetting'* a known serial killer. With a case this huge, he'd be plastered all over the television, and his Fathers first update on his son in over a decade would be that he was a criminal, about to face a stretch in jail for assisting a child killer's escape. He'd be so ashamed, he'd never want to meet him then.

As Ted gulped and sweat began to drip from his forehead, the luminous jacket wearing officer stalled in front of him.

'What happened to your face son? Are you hurt?' he asked, concerned.

Relieved, but with no time to enjoy it, Ted thought fast.

'Oh this?' He pointed to the extensive lesions of blackening on his cheek from Smithy's thwacking. 'Rotten luck. This happened to me just before I came here. I was mugged by a couple of low-life scumbags back in Brum, the day before last. The bastards stole my watch and scarpered, I was devastated. My Dad had gotten me that for my 21st. It's killing me'.

The officer studied the bruising on Ted's face, with his mouth shaped into an 'oooo that's sore' shape, and then nodded in commiseration. 'Oh man. That looks nasty. That is rotten luck. You've got a hell of a shiner. I've heard about the muggings in Birmingham. It's a real problem down there, isn't it? Hey, at least your prisoners *stay* in jail once they're caught though' the jolly cop chuckled. Ted joined in.

'They do officer. To be honest, knowing what Birmingham's like, I think they're probably better off locked up inside'. At this the two laughed in the promenade. The young child, still holding onto Ted's hand, stared up at them and shook his tiny head. *Adults.* It hurt Teds jaw to laugh, but he did it anyway, fully committing to the role.

'Well, you get some ice on that and take it easy. I hope they catch the two thugs who did that to you and you get your watch back'. At this the officer returned to his duties around the station. Ted's smile instantly left his face and he rubbed his sore cheek. That had been a close one, too close. He and the boy looked at each other then, and with the Bobbie off their back, finally enjoyed their hard-earned success. The pair performed their signature high five, and then Ted handed the lad, as per their agreement, a tasty chocolate-fudge nougat bar from his bag.

'Pleasure doing business with you again kid' said Ted. The boy nodded back and then vanished to chow down on his sugary reward, another raid in the bag.

Returning to Gellers lair in the sewers to deliver him his stolen banquet, Ted had felt a rush of adrenaline flooding through his veins. So this is what it felt like to commit a crime? To get away with hoodwinking the authorities. He hurtled at full speed through the unsanitary gangways of the sewers back to Marcus, not because he was afraid of being caught, but because the pump of the thrill of stealing had given him a whole heap of energy that he'd desperately needed to burn off. It felt naughty, it felt wrong, but boy did it feel good, and for that brief time, Ted had almost understood the appeal of why criminals stole in the first place. It was kind of addictive. He was sure that he'd feel an even more potent explosion of endorphins once he'd sprung Marcus out of the station, and he couldn't wait. The whole experience, had made Ted feel completely alive.

He'd rushed so quickly back to his prison-hopping compadre that Ted hadn't noticed the altering climate of the guests in the lobby of the pit stop above. They were becoming agitated. The irritability and the tensions of the guests were not unlike another occurrence that was taking place in Yorkshire. For across the kelp-green Moors, past the kissing gates and brimstone, where the cold wind had whistled like a jolly milkman, a natural change was transpiring on the eastern coast. Centuries of the ocean crashing into the cliff faces had slowly begun to eat away at the sedimentary of the walls, so much so that holiday-goers who would regularly return to the likes of Scarborough and Whitby on an annual basis, would always comment on how much closer the edges of the cliffs footpaths had become. The asking price for houses that had sat atop the cliffs had plummeted drastically, each one of them slanting, and on the verge of collapsing into the ocean to join the bedrock beneath them. One could say, it was almost as if the vicious sea was slowly but surely, chip by chip, gradually reclaiming man's world for its own. And like those chilly splashes that had been incrementally gnawing away at the shoreline for years, the night's events too, were taking their toll on the passenger's patience. Cabin fever had arrived, and soon, a pitchfork riot would ensue if Henry Simmons wasn't careful.

'Special delivery!' shouted an excited Ted as he re-entered the revolting, nauseating hidey-hole that Geller had come to call home. The giant hauled himself to his feet in anticipation for the delectable meal he was about to be served.

'About time. I was *this* close to biting the head off one of these rats', he said. Ted had thought that he was joking, he wasn't. He emptied the contents of his backpack onto the floor and an assortment of delicious, multi-coloured, packeted snacks fell onto the ground. Ted watched with the satisfaction of a gourmet chef or a soirée host as Marcus tucked into the mouth-watering goodies. He chewed and munched and bit upon the food as though he were starving, the stench of the cistern not being nearly enough to put him off his meal. Ted considered a conundrum. If he himself were a death row inmate, what would *his* final meal on earth be? He settled on a starter of garlic bread, a main of 'meat-feast' pizza and a chocolate cheesecake for dessert, served with creamy vanilla ice cream and a beer to wash it all down with. *Bon appetite.*

He'd been correct in his assumption that Geller would eat a lot, the beast of a man swallowed half the rucksack whole. When he was finally stuffed, his muscles and his belly full of some much needed carbohydrates, he sat back against the sewage chamber wall and released a mighty belch. It stank, but he was fed. Crumbs had clung to his bushy beard, it was grey and white and black, like the feathers of a silver winged bird. Ted wasted no time in getting down to business.

'So, I've been coming up with an idea to bust you out of here, and I think our best bet is almost definitely how you came in, through the boarded up hole, on the eastern side.'

'In agreement' voted Geller. He was still seated against the dungeon wall, in a food coma. He'd undone the buckle of his borrowed belt and had let his bloated belly hang loose over his waist, like Henry the 8th slobbing out in his royal four poster bed. Geller had an unusually shaped body, in that while his frame was rock-solid and muscular, his stomach was flabby and flubber-some. Somehow though, this misshapen, imperfect appearance, had made him seem even more threatening, in opposition to the waxed and chiselled six-pack anatomy of a meathead like Smithy. Ted knew who he'd back in a cage fight that was for sure.

'The only problem is, last I checked, it looks like the police Inspector running the show here at the *O'Nowhere* has decided to deploy a patrol of officers along the service corridor that we'd usually use to get to it, blocking our way completely. That means, going by my reconnaissance, that the only other way to reach the furniture locker, and the ladder inside that'll take us up to the hill top, is via a back entrance, on the other side of the promenade'.

Geller pointed out a slight flaw in Ted's logic.

'Unless you've forgotten kid, there's over fifty stranded guests sitting right above our heads in that promenade. How the hell are you proposing you sneak me past them all? Not to mention all the armed officers.'

Ted had been looking forward to this. He'd hoped that Marcus would pose that very problem, only so that he could solve it and dazzle him with his genius. The lightbulb of his idea brightened the moist dugout that they were sat in as he pitched his partner the scheme that he'd devised, how he'd stow him past the crowded lobby and out onto the

Moors. The resulting smile on Gellers lips from hearing Ted's plan curved like the lower half of a ships anchor. He raised his paw-like, mud-caked hands and applauded them together three loud times.

'Bravo kid. Bravo. That's quite some plan you've cooked up there. I might actually get back to my farm after all'. A reminiscent glint of nostalgia flickered in Marcus's eyes then. 'I have a feeling you and Terrance would've gotten on like a house on fire, he would've liked you a lot. It's a shame you won't join me in returning to him.'

'I'm sorry Marcus, but it's just too risky for me. I stand by what I said, I'll get you out of the *O'Nowhere*, but then you're on your own I'm afraid. I have my own Father to get to'. Ted couldn't believe that he'd been petrified stiff of Geller only a matter of hours ago. He'd thought of him as a Category-A prisoner, but now saw him as a Category Z. It didn't make what he was about to say any easier though, and Geller could sense Ted's angst.

'Alright, what's wrong kid? What aren't you telling me?'

Ted stood up and walked tentatively to the other side of the unlit room, crackling litter under his feet from the feast that he'd provided as he went. He turned.

'I think we need to bring someone else on board'.

'WHAT?!' Despite his abnormally swollen belly, the statement immediately upheaved Marcus onto his feet and away from the brick wall that he'd been sat against. His legs sprung to life suddenly, like the spasm of a corpse that continues to jolt even after death, before settling.

'I know, I know what you're thinking. But please, hear me out. Her name's Rose and she works at the coffee shop here. I know her, we can trust her, and she'll understand everything' reasoned Ted. But Geller was having none of it.

'Look, I like you kid. But this isn't some sort of game, this is my life we're talking about! You get to walk away from all of this, but if I get caught it's over for me. We have a good thing going on here, we trust each other, why risk ruining it by bringing someone else into the fold?' Geller was visibly upset. Ted could see that his dreams of reuniting with his son were slipping between his fingers, but he needn't have been worried, they could trust Rose.

'We can't do this alone Geller! You talk about risk, but this entire breakout is based on nothing *but* risk. You risked being caught out on the Moors, you risked me ratting you out to the police when you offered to let me go earlier. The only way we're going to get you out of here is through taking risks.'

'No. We're not doing it. And that's final. We stick to the two of us.' Marcus dealt his ultimatum. But Ted pushed forward. After all, a man that had been capable of keeping his composure and staging a crime scene only moments after discovering that his wife and daughter had been blown to pieces, must've had a great breadth of patience. Geller could handle it.

'She can be trusted, she's really cool. I haven't known her long, but I know-'

'-Ted, look. Your intentions are noble and I respect you wanting to help me as much as you can, but I'm telling you, I'm begging you to understand that this is a huge mistake!'

'Think about it. You need me. Without me you're not going anywhere, I could walk away right now and leave you down here alone and then you'd never be able to escape. I wouldn't hand you in, but how long do you think it'll be before the police come searching down here? I'm the only person you've got. I'm the one holding the cards here, so if I decide Rose is on board, she's on board. Or this whole operation falls apart and I leave'.

Geller never would have suspected that Ted had been hiding such bowling alley worthy sized balls between his legs. The kid was right, he needed him, and so he'd have no choice but to go along with his silly ploy and pray that this Rose girl would agree to join their squad, and not turn him in. He exhaled and re-tasted the creamy mushroom pasty that he'd just wolfed down.

'Alright. I guess you win, Ted. I don't have much of a choice, do I? Bring her in. But I hope to God you're right about this, you know how much is riding on it for me'.

'She won't let us down Marcus, I won't let you down. We'll get you to that farm by sunrise' Ted confidently spoke. 'Rest up for now and wash down your supper with a drink.' He pointed to the fizzy, grape flavoured beverage that he'd stolen from the book store. 'I'll be back to collect you in an hour, and I'll be with Rose. That's when we execute our escape plan. 3am on the dot. So, do what you need to do to prepare yourself. Once it begins, there'll be no going back' he instructed ominously.

'Your Dad must be a brave man Ted, you must have gotten that courage from somewhere. He'll be very proud when he finally meets you' said an admiring Geller.

'I like to think so' replied Ted, and then he vanished into the sewers to go and find Rose. He had some convincing to do.

Marcus stood in silence for a long time until he was certain that Ted had gone, he gaged his absence by the fact that he could no longer hear the clipping of his shoes against the icky sewage pathways. And then he was alone, a shadow amongst shadows. He moved to the wall, crouched down, and then dislodged a loose piece of black bricking. He reached inside. When his hand emerged again, it was clasped onto a small, homemade blade, the same one that he'd *almost* deployed on a certain Steve M. Brooks, from the passenger seat in his 1970's Mustang. Marcus had become quite the 'handy man' during his time in *Full Sutton*.

When the kid returned to collect him for their escape, Marcus would be taking his sharp souvenir along for the ride too. It was no lie that he liked Ted, but he'd waited for far, far too long to let a ballsy young punk like him get in the way of finishing what he'd started, all those years ago. If Ted, or this Rose girl, assuming that she'd join them, were to get in his way, even in the slightest, he'd plunge that knife straight into their stomachs and gut them like it were sport. Just like he'd murdered his family before them. In fact, maybe he'd do it anyway. After all, once he was safely out onto the Moors again and on his way to the farm, his use for the pair would've duly expired. He placed the weapon under his shirt, and waited in silence for his nicked wristwatch to strike 3am. Ah, the witching hour, the dichotomy of Christ's crucifixion, the dead of night in which folk law dictates that the spirits and demons are at their most powerful. Appropriate, he'd be right at home then, Marcus thought.

At the same time that Marcus had been sheathing his dagger, Billy the caretaker, had been taking anything but care, and handling a weapon of his very own. But this bad boy was not handmade, *no sir-eee*. It was a fully loaded black pistol, with two metal bullets inside of its firing cylinder labelled 'Ted' & 'Rose'. He was going to make them pay for the way that they'd treated him. But to say that this vendetta was purely about killing the star-crossed lovers, would've simply been inadequate. By putting a bullet into the brains of Ted and Rose, he was putting a bullet into the brains of everyone and anyone that had ever mistreated him, exacting his long overdue revenge against the world that he'd come to hate so fiercely. But why leave it at metaphorical vengeance? Maybe once he'd killed the lovers, he'd catch the bloodlust, and continue his murderous rampage on the rest of the *O'Nowhere* workers who'd forced him through a living hell for most of his adult life. And then perhaps, he'd trek across the misty Moors back to Egton, and send his mother from the cradle to the grave too. There were enough bullets to go around, one for everybody's brain. But he was getting ahead of himself. First things first, came the girl who'd broken his heart, and the man she'd broken it with.

He marched towards the lockers, firearm equipped, to where he knew that Rose often hung out on her breaks. He'd gotten changed back into his navy blue jumpsuit. He'd torn open the upper front Velcro, so that the yellowish vest that he'd worn underneath it was on show, it had been white when he'd first gotten it. He'd wait around the corner in the darkness until she arrived, and then BANG. *Bye Bye*. But when he got there, he was startled to hear not only Rose's voice, but Ted's too, coming from around the corner.

This was perfect, *two pricks for the price of one*. Seeing them together only fuelled the fires of his rage. They were probably talking about him, laughing at how he'd asked Rose out on a date and how she'd brutally rejected him in front of everybody. As he hid behind the lockers, Billy mused on which of the two of them he'd kill first, before finally settling on blowing Ted's head clean off and making Rose watch as he did it. But before he could execute his dastardly plan, Billy stopped in his tracks. The pair seemed to be talking about something rather intriguing. He decided to delay his justice, and to eavesdrop on whatever it is that they'd had to say first. What he heard, was better than anything he ever could've imagined…

Before Ted had dragged Rose away from the coffee shop kitchen to talk, she had been sat alone on the metal counter at its centre, having completely given up on rehearsing her 'Brutus' audition script. She had, in fact, gone one step further, and emailed her agent notifying him of the situation, that she'd be unable to attend the casting at all. She had been surprised at how little she'd cared when it had come down to it, that she'd been robbed of the chance to perform her soliloquy and to prove herself. Years ago she'd have bawled and cried and lamented all night long that she'd been unable to go, but not this time. Maybe she'd just realised, after months of relentless rejection, that even if she *had* have been able to read her lines for the powers that be, she wouldn't have been offered the job regardless. But maybe there had been a far more definitive reasoning behind her apathy towards the entire affair, perhaps, she just didn't care about being a thespian at all anymore. The thought truly terrified her, because if this was true, and she really did no longer want to perform classical texts to sold out venues up and down the country, then what *did* she want? What *was* she meant to do now? Fortunately, her new friend Ted had arrived to provide a much needed distraction, luring her away, with the insistence that 'it was a matter of life and death'. And she'd thought *she* was the dramatic one...

'Okay, Rose. What I'm about to tell you might come as a slight shock, but I need you to promise me that you'll hear me out, and that you won't run off screaming before you've given me a chance to explain myself' Ted begged her in front of the lockers. He'd traipsed dirty chute shit all over the floors, stinking out the hall, as if the foul essence of Marcus himself were lingering about them.

'Ted. What are you talking about? And will you please tell me what the hell happened to your face now? She gestured towards his injured features.

'There's no time to explain, but everything will become clear soon. I need you to promise me Rose.'

'Ted, I-'

'Rose, I need you to promise me'. She reluctantly nodded, surrendering to the fact that she hadn't the strength to argue with him, and that like a dog with bone, Ted wouldn't back down on this one.

'Alright, but this better be quick because I'm exhausted. I'm really not in the mood for messing around'.

And so, with her assurance in place, just as she had relayed *her* cautionary tale about Geller stood in that very spot a mere few hours ago, Ted relayed his, warts and all, not sparing any details in recounting how he had discovered him in the *O'Nowhere* underground and how was planning to bust him out. As he spoke, Rose's jaw was lowered like a drawbridge by what she heard. Billy too, who was spying on the pair from the shadows, was utterly gob-smacked by the revelation, something that didn't happen too easily. He loosened his finger on the trigger of Smithy's pistol.

'So, you see, that's why we need to get him back to the farm, to reach his family! We need you to help us Rose. What do you say?' Ted finished his pitch and then took a step back. He awaited her enthusiastic response, the 'oh Ted, of course I'll help you! We have to get him out!', but it never came. Instead Rose just stood in silence, speechless and appalled.

'Is this your idea of a joke, Ted?' she whispered through gritted teeth. She hoped that it was, no matter how offensive the gag would have been, it couldn't have been as horrifying as it being the truth, please, anything but that. She had deep, heavy bags below her eyes and her skin was even more porcelain than usual, lifeless. Perhaps what Ted had said to her had been a part of some kind of strange mid-nap dream that she hadn't known that she was having? Or, that in her exhausted delirium she had totally imagined his confession? Unlike her though, this theory was quickly put to bed.

'A joke? No, Rose, I'm being deadly serious. Geller is here, hiding in the *O'Nowhere*. He's innocent and he needs our help to escape.'

This time she believed him. That did it.

'Ted, what the fuck? What the fuck? What the fuck? Are you crazy? Are you fucking crazy?' She had, in all fairness, honoured her vow of keeping her cool during Ted's chronicle. But now that it was over, she was free to go nuts, bonkers, completely bloody mental at the guy.

'Rose, look, I know this is a shock but-'

'A shock? Ted, you're helping a fucking murderer escape from the police! I cannot believe how stupid you've been, I mean, I knew you weren't the sharpest tool in the box, but I had no idea you were this much of a moron. What? Just, what? He could've killed you, he could've torn you apart with his bare hands! Why the hell didn't you run when you had the chance and tell the police straight away? They could've arrested him by now and this whole shit-storm would've been over!' She put her left hand to her temple and began pacing between the lockers that stood on either side of them, as if this would somehow help her to assimilate the deplorable tale that she'd just been told. Their circular black padlocks resembled empty eyes.

'Didn't you listen to a word I just told you, Rose? Marcus is innocent, he didn't kill his family, and he's not any danger to me at all!'

'Oh, I listened to every word, that's the problem. That's what he told you, is it? And you're actually dumb enough to believe the word of a fugitive that has half of the Yorkshire police looking for him?'

'I know it sounds bad, but if you'd just come with me, if you'd just meet him, you'd realise he's not lying!' Ted grabbed Rose by the arm then as if to pull her in the direction of the sewers, but she jerked it free and then pushed him away, slamming him into the lockers and disturbing their contents (*books, family photos, makeup*) with a metallic rumble.

'Get off me!' she cried. Still, Billy watched on, under the cover of darkness. It pleased him to see Ted hurt.

A new bruise had been added to Ted's ever-growing collection. Now that the initial blow of the news had settled into her brain, Rose was now able to approach the mess through a more rational lens, it allowed her to uncover all sorts of new reasons as to why Ted's plan was pure idiocy. 'All these people, all these people trapped here, when you could've ended this hours ago, all these people kept from their loved ones...'

'And what about Geller, Rose? Hmm? He's been kept from his loved ones for over thirty years for a crime he didn't even commit! What about him? Can't you see we have to do this? We can't just stand by and do nothing and let the man die alone.' Ted spoke passionately, as if he were a lawyer, advocating his client's freedom to a judge.

Rose, the prosecution, gladly volleyed retorts back to him. 'That's not our call to make Ted, its Inspector Simmons's. It doesn't matter whether he's innocent or not, this isn't our job'.

'Well, maybe it should be. The legal system failed him, he made the ultimate sacrifice and now all he wants to do is to see his children one last time. I don't see anybody else rushing to his side. You know as well as I do that if I took this to Henry Simmons he'd just slam him back in

Full Sutton and throw away the key.' The two could tell by now that there was no hope of convincing the other, they'd already made up their minds.

'You know, I really thought you might understand, I really thought you were different...' started Ted vindictively, resorting to dirty blackmail tactics now that his main attack had failed to convince her. This enraged Rose though, she stormed right to him, confronting him head on. Her dyed red hair covered her face as she shouted, it was greasy and matted like a foxes hide.

'Ted, you can drop the act. This isn't even about Geller. This isn't about breaking him out of the station at all, why pretend? This is about you. It's always been about you. This is just another beacon, just another checkpoint for you to aim for. Just like winning my toy from the arcade machine, just like getting to Whitby, just like finding your dad. You really will come up with anything to distract you, won't you?'

'Yeah? Distract me from what, Rose? What exactly is it that I need distracting from *so* badly?' Ted invited back, pettily.

'...You'll do anything at all to distract you from the fact that you're lost, that you don't know what you're doing with your life. You said it yourself, you always have to be doing something, aiming towards some goal, but what you don't realise is, is that it's all just temporary. You're terrified of commitment, of actually facing anything permanent that might last and lead somewhere, isn't that why you ran away from Uni? From your mum? Chasing a father who you know deep down is no good for you. Well, if you want to make Marcus Geller one of your little projects, be my guest, but if you ask me, it's about time you grew up and started making choices in life instead of hiding behind horizons. You convince yourself that life will be better if you can just reach "this", or if you can just do "that", only to find that there's always something else to do, waiting on the other side of it. I think it's just plain selfish, and it's a disservice to the people around you that care about you and give you everything they can, like your mum, back home, worried sick. I bet you haven't even called her, have you? Wake up Ted. Stop chasing better things, and enjoy the life you do have. Because this time, I think you're going to get yourself killed'.

It was as though she'd been granted a search warrant into Ted's inner most self. Could it be true? Were the things she was saying correct? If they weren't, then why did he suddenly feel like crying? It felt as though she'd struck a nerve that had never been struck before, one that Ted hadn't even known had existed, it had been buried *that* deep beneath his tissue. No matter how much it had hurt though, whatever this bizarre, visceral emotional reaction had been to what she'd said, it could wait. These were issues that he could resolve later on his own. Nothing would stop him from helping Marcus escape, and then from finding his Father, however rousing Rose's recital had been.

'And I'm not the answer to your problems either Ted. I'm not some quirky, "manic-pixie dream girl" that you can introduce to your Dad and make everything okay. I can't save you. Only you can do that. You need to find your own way.' With this, Rose had nothing more to say.

The blueish hue of the corridors light seemed to cast an air of destiny or mysticism upon the scene, as though both characters were standing on the verge of a precipice, at turning points in their stories. The choices that they made that night would echo throughout their lives, forever.

'Are you going to tell the police?' Ted replied quietly.

'I don't know. I just don't know anymore. I have to think. But I do know that I can't help you Ted, if you do this, you do this alone'. As she went to leave, Ted tried one last time to convert her to his cause.

'3am. We're escaping through the hideout, the boarded up hole in the wall that you showed me. If you want to turn us in you can, if not, we're doing this, with or without you. I hope it's with you…

'..Oh and Rose…' he added, as a final, lowly footnote.

'Maybe I am lost. Maybe I don't know what I'm doing with my life anymore. But I have a feeling, even if you try really hard to hide it, that you're just as lost as I am.'

And then the two parted ways.

Billy was the only soul who remained by the lockers once the war of words had ceased. This couldn't have worked out any better, Ted's plight, was his glee. What could've been a more fitting punishment than putting a bullet between his eyes and sending him straight up to Saint-Peter? Why, catching him in the act of helping Geller escape and brandishing him with a life-long sentence of course. He'd stop the pair in their tracks and deliver them straight to Inspector Simmons. Billy would shed his skin and return as a hero, heralded as the man that had captured Marcus Geller on his own.

It sounded like there had been trouble in paradise between the two love birds too, clearly Rose wasn't as smitten with Ted as he'd first thought. She'd need a shoulder to cry on once the dust had settled, and Billy couldn't think of more appropriate candidate for that role than himself, emerging like a cockroach from the fallout. She'd see the error of her ways for rejecting him and fall straight into his arms once he'd collected the bounty on Geller's head. And he wasn't scared of no convict, he had a gun. He didn't care whether what Ted had said about him being innocent was true or not, he'd turn in him, and in turn, deliver himself from his own miserable existence, just like he'd always wanted. He couldn't do it alone though, and he knew just the gypsy for the job.

And so, like chess pieces on a board of black and white, the three players all went their separate ways. Ted went towards the sewers to collect Geller for their escape, Billy went towards Smithy to recruit him and to intercept them, and Rose, torn between logic and loyalty, went roaming the *O'Nowhere's* corridors, searching for answers. As she moved through the station, she felt a vibration in her right hand pocket from the buzz of her phone. Clearly she'd been positioned under one of the rare hotspots of cellular activity in the *O'Nowhere* that had allowed her mobile to connect to the nearest mast. She'd been sent an email, a reply from her agency that began with the words...

'*We regret to inform you, that as an agency we can no longer represent you...*'

The final showdown, had begun.

CHAPTER NINE

The rocky coastline of Maine had the howl of wild loons. The dreamers' skyline of the Los Angeles Mountains had the prowling roar of coyotes. The rolling welsh hills had the grating baa of fluffy sheep, and the grand Alaskan Alpine Lakes had the ferocious cry of black bears. But the monstrous sound of the West Yorkshire Moors, was made not by an animal, no, it was in its deadly silence that the heath was able to hail *its* terror. So quiet was the green expanse that night that even the patrolling officers who had searched the foothills for Geller's prints had felt the need to lower their voices, lest they disturb some sleeping wrath, waiting to be incurred upon them.

What hadn't been quiet though, were the profanities and complaints of the angry mob inside the *O'Nowhere*. They had become like butterflies in a bell jar, head-butting their antenna and fluttering their wings against the glass in a bid to escape their reasonably priced prison. Gone were the soft Yorkshire folk, the kind that would invite one round for a cuppa' tea and a plate of *Custard Creams*. Instead, the interior of the station had become somewhat of a demonstration, a social experiment into what would happen if you got on the wrong side of a Northerner. It wasn't pretty, that was for sure. Enough was enough, the guests were through with being polite. They were tired and grumpy and wanted to go home. And as anybody who knows a Northerner knows full well, just as their bouts of kindness are exaggerated and know no bounds, their sulking and crabby-ness too, happen to the extreme.

Inspector Henry Simmons's worst fears had come true, cabin fever had come to stay, and he'd completely lost control. The waiting angry guests had all gathered in the promenade of the *O'Nowhere* in a bulk, as the time had just struck 3am. Simmons was once again standing upon the wooden framing of an artificial plant at the centre of the lobby, attempting, and failing, to ease the impatient jeers of the masses.

'Right, I need everybody to calm down. We know this has been a difficult and tiring night, but believe me when I say, you're far better off in here than you are out there' spoke Henry to the rowdy group. His upstanding silver badge no longer had any effect on the people though. Once, it had inspired respect and confidence, but now the guests were over answering to the law.

'You've been saying that all night! When are you going to let us go? I've got a wife at home whose worried sick!' cried one angry man, up at the officer.

'My kids are exhausted here. We're on our way back from a holiday in Scotland and all we want to do is go home! It's a five hour drive as it is!' screamed a displeased mother of three.

Simmons, in the face of wild feverishness, maintained his professionalism. 'I understand that tensions are high, but our prisoner escapee is still on loose. He's out there somewhere, and if we let you go-'

'What have your officers been doing all night? Sitting with your elbows up your arses? It's one man, there's hundreds of you, why haven't you caught him yet?!' yelled another passenger. More joined in. The guests seemed to conform to the social cliché that the English are a nation of queue-makers, each one of them stirring up their own volatility to replicate that of the others.

'Yeah! How do you know he's even out there anymore? If you haven't got the guy by now, he's probably miles away! He's clearly got more sense than you!'

'Exactly! What harm can it do to let us all go? Keeping us here isn't doing any good!'

'Oh this is a fucking joke!'

The scene was a mess, so much so that Henry couldn't even trace the shouts to the mouths that made them anymore. Young children bawled and cried on the floor and in their parent's arms. Seething passengers veins burst from their flustered red necks as they shouted curses, and hot headed men began sashaying up and the down lobby, squaring up to the anxious officers who lined the perimeter with their hands on their batons. It was North Yorkshire's answer to *The Lord of the Flies*, and Simmons watched on in despair as the societal microcosm of the *O'Nowhere* began to break down and the hooligans descended in a protesting chaos.

'Everyone! Please! Just calm down! Losing your temper isn't going to help anyone!'

He was wasting his breath, no one was listening anymore. Even the father of the Custard-coloured coat wearing boy heckled at the desperate lawman. The son stayed silent, standing at a slight distance as not to be associated with him, embarrassed.

'We know our rights! You can't force us to stay here! We demand to be let go!'

Manager Perkins meanwhile had deserted Henry and his own employees. He was hiding in his office behind his desk, watching the scene unfold from the comfort of his plush leather chair on the CCTV monitors, nervously chomping on the nails of his chubby fingers as he did. He'd locked the door to the workroom and barricaded himself in by pushing a bookcase in front of it too.

'I can't breathe in here! I've got a bad ticker, it's no good for me being cooped up inside for too long!'

'Is this what we're paying our taxes for? So much for having faith in law enforcement. We're the ones being treated as criminals here, locked up like animals!'

'Let us fucking leave!'

The grievances of the people piled higher and higher. Negative, violent energy from the vibrating fists of the guests at the front of the mob, seemed to ripple to the ones at the back, until the entire promenade was ignited into a blazing uproar. When the frequency of the craze had reached its peak, a line in the sand was crossed, tipping the yobs from mere anti-social behaviour, into a full blown mutiny. A particularly unsatisfied gentleman on the left-hand side of the gathering, influenced by the heat of the moment, decided to take it upon himself to spark a more physical revolt. The words he'd been about to utter, he couldn't take back. Once he'd shrieked them, the idea would no longer be his, but it would belong to the hive-mind of the horde. Despite knowing this, he said them anyway. Damned to the consequences, he wanted out.

'Hey! There's far more of us than there are of them! I say we all make a move and just walk out! They can't stop all of us!' he suggested.

'That's not a bad shout. There's over fifty of us, and only thirty or so of them. I say we smash in those glass doors and break out of here! That Gypsy earlier, he'd had the right idea!' lobbied another.

'Yeah! What are they gonna do? Arrest all of us? Let's do it! We haven't done anything wrong!'

Simmons watched in horror from his podium as the stir-crazy guests charged towards the exit doors, acting as human battering-rams. Officers and station employees alike stared at the ferocity-engorged group, unsure of how to conduct themselves. The angry man's proposal had indeed been, the stray *Jenga* brick that had toppled Henry's tower of order to rubble. Two officers who had been stationed in front of the *O'Nowhere* entrance, guarding the fractured glass that Smithy had taken a chair to earlier in the night, made way for the stampede of disgruntled detainee's out of fear of being squashed. Once there, the group began pounding on the doors, those stood at the back of the crowd cheering on those at the front like mascots.

How had it come to this? Simmons wondered, as his men looked to him to tell them what the hell they should be doing. When the investigation had first gotten underway, it had been a well-oiled machine. The night had gotten off to a barn-storming start, with a rousing speech that had earned him the patience and full cooperation of the *O'Nowhere* passengers. He'd had hundreds of Yorkshire's finest policemen at his disposal, both inside and out of the station, ready to ensure that justice was served and that Geller was returned to the prison where he'd belonged. And he'd acted fast, taking action well-within the twelve hour window of Marcus's escape, sealing the roads and immediately initiating a thorough search of the Moors which had meant that he'd had the upper hand. So, why now, had things gone so disastrously awry? Here he was, six hours later, with nothing to show for his efforts. There was still absolutely no sign of Geller, who at that very moment was escaping with Ted beneath his feet, and the guests who'd once respected him had turned, smashing on the glass of the doors with their bare hands, about to break free.

What kind of an Inspector was he? He didn't deserve to wear that badge, he wasn't fit to wear his uniform. Because of him, a brutal, double-time killer was about to get away and get back out into the world. Any blood he'd spill, would be on his hands and his alone. Oh, if his Father could've seen him now, he'd be ashamed to call him his son. He'd let him down, he'd let all of Yorkshire down. Yes, once all this was over, whether he'd caught Geller or not, Simmons thought that it was high-time that he hung up his hat and bid farewell to the Police Force. He was past it, all he was doing now was getting in the way of a more able-bodied Officer from taking his job, and doing it a damn-sight better than he ever could. Who was he kidding? He wasn't cut out for this, he wasn't no Cole Simmons, he wasn't his Dad. And if this really was all he'd got, maybe Geller had deserved to get away. He was beaten, bested. Game, set and match.

The hinges of the double doors began to give way as the guests beat on them harder and harder, the once courteous and well-mannered citizens, converted into lunatics. It was then that Simmons felt the gentle patter of a cold water drop land on his cheek. That was odd, he definitely wasn't usually a crier. Could it be that his emotions had seen it fit that this were to be the day that broke the mould? He hoped not, failing his men was one thing, but losing his dignity by crying in the process, that would've been far worse. No, it wasn't a tear, that's not right. He felt another droplet land on his forehead, and then on his right ear and then on the back of his neck. Simmons wasn't the only one experiencing this peculiar spell of precipitation either, the other officers in the promenade too, began to notice tiny drips of water falling onto their skin, leaving dark spots on their nice, clean white shirts.

The rusted metal tubes of the *O'Nowhere* sprinkler system hadn't been used in some time, thankfully. The only ever recorded fire in the station had been reported in the summer of 87, when a kitchen grill had been left unattended and had sprung into flames. It was this underuse that had meant that the sprinklers had been slow to crank up into action, only releasing a few drops at first. But once the cogs had been dusted off, the heavens opened and the caps of the seven nozzles dotted across the ceiling of the lobby emptied unlimited litres of cool water from the hydrant tank, and onto the people below.

The guests were drenched to the bone instantaneously, after-all the sprinklers had been designed to extinguish a fire as quickly and efficiently as possible. They yelped from the cold as they attempted to seek refuge from the artificial downpour, hiding under canopies and sheltering their heads with purses and bags. But no matter where they went, the water followed. Lightweight clothing became thick and heavy from absorbing the gallons, black eyeliner ran down the faces of screaming women and hair became soaked like that of drowned rats. What the hell was going on? This certainly snapped Simmons from his state of self-deprivation. He leapt to ground level, which was already starting to fill up like a pool.

'What should we do sir?' yelled his nearest policeman, he'd had to shout over the drum of the waterfall to be heard.

'That's a good question officer. You there, in the uniform, what is this?' Simmons asked the redheaded book clerk standing just inside of his shops doorway. He chose to ignore the irony in asking a ginger for help regarding the putting out of a fire.

'Erm...it's the sprinklers sir', the hapless assistant replied.

'I can see that son. But why have they been set off? And more importantly how the heck do we turn them off?'

The dorky stoner, whose pale white eyebrows were only made visible by their dripping, gathered himself. 'I'll be honest sir...these sprinklers have never gone off whilst I've been working here. Th-there's never once been a fire at the *O'Nowhere* as far as I know'. He stuttered and stammered his answer, he wasn't anywhere near as tough in front of Simmons as he had been bullying Billy. 'Maybe…erm…there's been a…malfunction on the switchboard? I dunno. But the only way to turn it off now is manually, in Manager Perkins's office. It's just that W-'

'-yes, I know where his office is' interrupted Henry. The kid quickly lowered his hand, which had been pointing to show him the way.

'Simmons! We need to get these people out of here, it's just not safe' a female officer pleaded to the Inspector from over his shoulder.

One look at the lobby and it wasn't hard to see what had prompted her reaction. Simmons witnessed guests slipping and skidding on the wet tiling's as they rushed for shelter. Young children continuously fell and bumped their limbs and the elderly passengers shuddered and shook from the freeze, a flu at that age wasn't so easy to fight. Empty, unused coffee cups were overflowing and the thick, full beards of overweight truckers were sodden. And yet, there was not the lick of a flame, nor the eye-burning scent of any grey smoke at all, and the alarms were silent too. One thing was for certain though, the sprinklers weren't stopping, and if there had been even the remotest of chances of a combustion somewhere in the *O'Nowhere* then Simmons had no choice but to evacuate. Health and safety trumped a serial killer whose whereabouts were currently unknown, and so he made the call. It looked the like guests would be getting what they wanted after all.

'Officers. I want you to rally everyone together and let them out of the front door. Gather everyone into the car park, if they have towels in their car boots and a spare change of clothes then they can sort themselves out. But no one, and I mean no one, goes any further than that, the roadblocks are still in place. This isn't over, not by a long shot.' Henry threw a rounded set of keys to the nearest policeman, the gold pointy one of which would unlock the partially shattered doors that would allow the passengers their freedom.

'What about you?' asked the ambitious young constable who'd caught them. He was a newbie to the force and eager to earn his stripes, already unbelieving in his luck that he'd landed work on a case as big as Geller's.

'Myself, I'll to head to Perkins's office and turn these bastard sprinklers off. You three! I want you to search the premises for any sign of a fire, it seems odd to me that the alarms haven't sounded. I'm willing to put money on the fact that the fire service haven't been automatically summoned either. No, it looks to me like these sprinklers were set off independently'.

The three officers who had been assigned the task of surveying the pit stop for fire, or rather a lack of it, moved off in separate directions. The others barged past the panicking guests and made space for the constable with the keys. He rushed up to the door, inserted them into the lock, and then for the first time that night, the *O'Nowhere* had been open for business once again.

 'Now, if everyone wouldn't mind leaving in an orderly fashion I-'

The guests ignored the well-intentioned rookie, they fled from the tempest into the outdoors like a flock of doves being released from captivity. Finally, they were outside, if only in the parking lot. Simmons meanwhile, made his way through the raining corridors towards Perkins's barricaded office, to manually override the seemingly malfunctioning sprinkler system.

'Somethings not right here', he muttered to himself, sensing foul play as he fought against the fake drizzle, leaving the promenade completely deserted. It was exactly as Ted had wanted it.

Like a dodgy stalker in a black and white film noir, peering through cut-out holes in a newspaper, Ted looked around the corner. His plan of triggering the sprinklers had been a resounding success, the lobby of the *O'Nowhere* had been cleared of all the guests and officers.

'Okay. 3. 2. 1. Move!' he ordered, as him and Geller left their hiding place behind the locker corridor corner and began swiftly crossing the promenade. They had been victims of their own plan, caught in the cross-fire of liquid and dunked in water, but it would be worth it to break Geller loose. Speaking of which, Marcus's size had meant that he was much slower than Ted in reaching the other side of the room, luckily the guests were pre-occupied in the car park, as were the officers sent to supervise them. The waterlogged passengers were frantically drying themselves with beach towels whilst the policemen, rather comically, ran around like headless chickens, attempting to coordinate a kind of system of control amidst the bedlam. Both parties were too stupefied and befuddled to enjoy the fine, brisk northern air that they had been deprived of for the past six hours. Mothers rub-dried their children's hair and other numb guests fired up the warm AC of their cars, drinking what little hot caffeine they'd had left out of flasks. The omnipotent, all-seeing, deity-like Moors gazed with a curious indifference at the panicking humans below them.

'Hurry up will you! We don't have time to slow down' shouted Ted to Geller as they sprinted through the falling water.

'Hey, you may or may not have noticed this, but I'm sixty six years of age kid. Go a little easy on me' the convict bantered back. 'I'm one slip-up from a hip replacement. I'll go as fast as I can' he wheezed.

Despite their bickering, the pair were able to evade detection and slip through a back door at the rear of the commercial area, it led them to the service corridor that they'd needed to reach. The sprinkler system hadn't been working in that quadrant of the station, which had meant that the resulting image was like that of some kind of freak weather anomaly. There was pouring water, cascading down, in one half of the corridor, but just a few yards further, it had been as dry as a bone. Ted thought that this was pretty cool. The two didn't stop to take in the sights though, wasting no time in jogging into the furniture storage unit, folding their way into the exposed ventilation passage in the plastering, and then scaling the rusty ladder inside. The convoluted route, which Ted had committed to memory ever since Rose had first shown it to him, led the fellows back to the boarded-up hole in the wall of the *O'Nowhere's* east side.

They'd done it, they'd made it to the hilltop.

'Oh boy, is it good to be outside again. You taste that Ted? That's the finest damn air in the country' said Geller proudly, arms outstretched as if receiving a '*welcome home*' from the starry heath.

'It is pretty amazing, isn't it?' said Ted, finding great fulfilment in Geller's joy.

'Amazing? Talk about an understatement. I'd never thought I'd see these Moors again, this is perhaps the single greatest spot I've ever set my feet upon'.

Ted was stunned by the view all over again, the Moors certainly were as enchanting as they were terrifying. Though the dark, restricted view he had from the hilltop had meant that he could only see the outskirts of the land, he knew that the further one trod towards its black frontier, the wilder the terrain would've surely become. The shrubbery denser, the rivers deeper, the tree's more gnarled. The space above the ridge therefore was just a teaser, a misleading taste of just how precarious and lethal the Moors would become a little further afield. Ted knew that there was a menacing darkness lying behind its beauty, and quite frankly he couldn't wait to see the back of the Moors for good.

But there was no time to marvel at the landscape, for from around the corner of the *O'Nowhere*, Ted could hear the hum drum of a crowd, no doubt the evacuated passengers from the lobby. This of course had meant that they'd been escorted out by the armed police officers, which placed the pair in a rather vulnerable position. They'd have to move hastily.

'Okay Geller. You're out. This is where I leave you I'm afraid, I've done my part. It's been a pleasure Marcus, it really has, but there's no time for

234

a long farewell, the police could turn that corner any second! Now, you get of here and go find that family of yours, it's the end of the road for us. I've got a father of my own to meet'. As he spoke, Ted trembled. His wet clothes had begun to cling to his body, and the moist, damp April air had meant that they'd had no chance of drying. 'I'll head back into the station and pretend that I got separated from the evacuation. By the time they realise you're out, you'll be long gone. I figure you've probably got a half hour head start on those police'.

He extended a hand to shake Gellers. 'You're a good man Marcus. Even if the whole world is against you, I hope it brings you some comfort to know that you'll always have a friend in me. Your family are lucky to have you, even if it is only for a little while'. Ted could practically hear the fond laughs and picture the teary smiles of Marcus's reunion with Terrance, he hoped that his own father would be just as overwhelmed to see *him* when he'd reached the Bay.

'I gotta say, we've been through the quite the ride, you and me' smiled the man, unbeknownst to Ted that he was evil incarnate.

'Thank you for everything you've done. You're a damn good kid, your father would burst with pride to know what a fine young man you've grown up to be. It's a real shame you can't come with me, I'd have loved for you to meet my family, and to show you the best hiding spots on the Moors. But I understand, you've got your own way to go' commiserated Geller as he shook Ted's hand with his right arm.

His left hand though, was otherwise pre-occupied, fiddling with the sharp, homemade shiv that was in his shallow jacket pocket. Ted had served his purpose, he'd saved him from the *O'Nowhere*, and so Marcus no longer saw any necessary rhyme nor reason to keep the boy alive. Besides, it had been a while since he'd taken a life, thirty five years to be precise, and a murderer needs to kill, like a vampire needs to feed. He played with the stone hilt of his dagger as he toyed with potential methods of butchery, approaching the predicament with a pleasurable determination, like an architect might've approached his blueprints before breaking ground.

If he were to be kind, he'd have equipped the weapon and sliced Ted straight down the wrist as he shook his hand, like he were gutting the cold blue stomach of a haddock out at sea. At least his death would've been quick. But no, Marcus's notorious comeback to the news headlines couldn't be with a stifled whimper, he'd needed to return with a sucker punch, to make a powerful statement, that he was ready to hunt and to stalk and to rule the night once again. Instead, he opted to cut through Ted's ripe young throat with the blades back end, from ear to ear, like a bloody clown's smile carved across his neck. He'd then proceed to kick Ted in the stomach and watch him helplessly roll down the hilly face, like he were a tumbling barrel of cask ale. His fatal wound would spurt crimson vein-juice in a spiral until he'd landed at a heap at the bottom, dead. Marcus licked his top teeth in delight at the prospect of a satisfying stripe of red trailing behind Ted's corpse, like the painted lines that marked out the borders of some kind of hellish football field. Yes, plunging into his jugular it would be.

'...it's just such a real pity you'll never reach *your* father' the wicked Geller spoke, as he prepared the virgin blade, eager to break her in for her first kill of the evening. Ted looked back confused.

'Huh? I don't get it? I-'

'FREEZE!'

Just as Geller was about to quench his insatiable thirst for murder, he was stopped by the prescription of a feeble, northern voice behind him. Both he and Ted instantly turned, fearing that they'd been busted by a cop, only to see that it hadn't been a policeman who'd shouted at all. It was a two-headed band of vigilantes, taking the law into their own hands. There, standing at the edge of the hole in the *O'Nowhere's* wall, stood none other, than Billy and Smithy, the former of which, was holding a gun in his hand.

'Billy!' said Ted, being sure to keep a suppressive lid on his surprise, as not to arouse the suspicion of the police escorts just around the corner.

'Who the fuck are these jokers?' laughed Geller. Billy and Smithy too, were soaked and dripping, having been caught in the sprinkler monsoon.

'I'm the joker who's going to hand you into the police, so you better watch who you're talking to' threatened Billy. He'd talked a big game back inside the *O'Nowhere*, but now that he'd been confronted by the huge, almost inhuman, Goliath-build of Marcus in the flesh, he was rather terrified. He'd half expected to fire his gun and for the bullet to have simply bounced off of his plated chest.

'Oh are you now?' replied an amused Geller. Ted was far more worried about the unforeseen development in their circumstances than he was.

'You got that right you old motherfucker. So you better show us some respect or we'll knock those false teeth straight outta your mouth. Gummy'. Smithy was far more effective in the delivery of his threats than Billy was, despite being the unarmed one out of the two. But one sharp, stony look from Geller instantly shut him up. It was those eyes, thought Smithy, those ice-blue, empty, dead eyes, they were crippling. It was like they'd belonged on a slab at the morgue.

'You're coming with us. So I wouldn't do anything stupid if I were you...or I'll shoot you where you stand, Grandpa. I think the term is, "self-defence"'.

Marcus was not petered by Billy's demands. 'Oh really? Do you even know how to use that thing? I bet you don't. But I do...'

Ted shot his partner in crime a questioning side-eye, but then remembered that he'd been a farmer prior to his incarceration, of course he'd fired a gun before. Of course he had. Marcus continued his dismantling of Billy's status.

'...why don't you hand that pistol over? Before you hurt yourself, you scrawny prick'.

Billy's drawn, sunken face became infuriated. 'Prick' was *his* word. 'I'm afraid it's not gonna work like that. You don't scare me. I may not have fired a gun before, but I know how to point and shoot, and that's all I'll need to know bullet you down. So keep that mouth shut'.

He hated to admit it, but Geller knew that the skinny freak standing in front of him had him by his wrinkly Yorkshire ball sack. Oh, he was in no doubt that he'd have been able to rush the pair, and taken down that Billy fella with his bare hands. But what he couldn't have guaranteed, was that his pistol wouldn't have gone off. This was a variable that he simply couldn't risk. Not because he was worried that the stray bullet might strike Ted's face, no, he didn't give a flying fuck about that kid, it was more a case of the unwanted attention that a gunshot would attract from the policemen waiting around the corner. Without the blare of late night motorway traffic to drown it out, that shot would've been as blatant as a bum-note in a symphony. They had the upper hand, and it killed him. He fantasised about severing their heads with a buzz saw, and then mounting them on his wall for trophies, like stuffed stag heads in a woodland lodge.

'Look, Billy, you don't understand what you're about to do here. We haven't spoken properly before, and I know for some reason you seem to despise me, but I'm telling you, you're about to make a huge mistake! Marcus is-'

'Innocent. Yeah, I heard your conversation with Rose. But I don't buy it Ted, I've been around enough scum in my life to know it when I see it, and this guy is the real deal. I'm handing him in, and you along with him' interjected Billy. The slippery heels of Ted's and Geller's shoes were tittering on the edge of the hilltop. Over fifteen feet tall, it would've been a mighty fall for the two of them, they'd have been lucky to get away with just one broken leg. A fat lot of good that would've done Marcus in fleeing from the police.

Ted persisted, questioning the intentions of the gun-slinging caretaker. 'This is bullshit. You don't give a damn about justice, about doing the right thing. Let's face it Billy, this about getting back at me, about Rose'

'Maybe it is. Maybe I didn't get Smithy to beat you hard enough last time, because you clearly didn't learn your lesson. Either way, you're going to be going away for a very, very long time Ted. Say bye bye to your Daddy. He'll be dead and buried by the time you're let out, and even if he's not, do you really think he'd ever want to meet a son who helped a child-killer escape?' Billy smiled a deliciously evil grin then, revelling in seeing all of the elements of his plan finally coming together, this was the revenge that he'd been waiting for. Oh, if only his Mother could see him now, he was really starting to get the hang of this 'power' thing.

'Now, are you going to come quietly? Or am I going to have to start busting organs?'

Geller and Ted looked to one another. With nothing more than a sheer grassy drop behind them, that would've greeted them with an upward view of the moon and a smashed up limb, they had nowhere to go. It was hard to believe that only a few hours ago, Ted had been perched on that very hilltop, gazing up at Gemini and Sagittarius stars with Rose and sharing enthusiastic plans for the future, for seeing his Dad again, in Whitby. But now, the jig was up.

Or was it?

Just then, when all hope seemed to be lost, a third party entered the fray.
It was one that had had a far more feminine touch, but by no means any
less testosterone than the quarrelling lads.

'Ted! Move! NOW!'

Rose swung the plank of plywood like it were a baseball bat and she
were scoring a home run. It collided with the backs of Billy's and
Smithy's heads, sending them flying. Whilst Geller had managed to side
step out of their way, Ted's reactions had been dramatically slowed
because of his fatigue. It had meant that Smithy had been able to grab
him by the collar as he'd fell forward. Ted, Billy and Smithy, all went
souring over the brow of the hill, sliding along its face until they hit the
bottom with a thump. *Ouch.*

'Rose? I take it?' asked an impressed Geller.

'You got that right', she replied feistily. Her wrung wet hair had brought
out all of its shades of red, varying from crimson to cherry.

'Let's get one thing straight, I don't know if you're innocent or not, but
Ted's my friend, and he seems to believe in you. I'm not about to let him
fuck up his life and get hurt, I'm here for him, not you, I...Oh my God,
Ted-!' Rose peered over the edge of the hill and saw the three men lying
on their fronts at the bottom. Marcus resisted the urge to grab her by the
neck and to throw her down headfirst, surely snapping her spine. She'd
earned a morsel of respect from him.

'I suppose we better go check on the kids, c'mon' said Geller with a fatherly sarcasm. The two of them sat on their asses, and then slid down the muddy Ted-shaped trail that he and the others had left behind.

Meanwhile, back at the ranch, on the other side of the *O'Nowhere*, the ambitious young officer whom Simmons had tossed his keys to, had distanced himself from the rest of the crowded officers and passengers. A jumpy, and nervy young man, his bladder had betrayed him, and so he'd wandered to find a piece of shrubbery to relieve himself on in privacy. He'd fined many a gross-dude for pissing in the Pickering streets, but he'd figured that the given circumstances of the night had allowed him a little legal leeway. Once he was done peeing, he slipped his manhood back into his soggy trousers, and then zipped them up. His warm wee had steamed in the cold. And that's when he'd heard it.

Rumble. Rumble. Rumble.

It was an odd sound, one that had seemed altogether a trifle unnatural, one that was coming from the very rear of the station.

He switched on his trusty flashlight, which had been hanging from his belt. Being the boy-scout that he was, he knew the protocol, and thus, he moved to shout for backup, but then stopped. No, this was *his* scoop. If he really wanted to prove to Simmons that he meant business, he'd have investigate this one solo. Besides, it was probably nothing and he didn't want to embarrass himself by bringing Henry to a false alarm. He crept warily around the perimeter of the station, it sure was an ugly building once you'd gotten past its front doors. He shone the beam of his torch, scanning the bushes slowly.

Miraculously, the three had managed to hit the deck without breaking a single bone. But that didn't mean that it hadn't hurt like a bitch. Ted lay to the far right. His body might as well have been 99% bruise from all of the contusions that he'd suffered that night. His Dad would hardly recognise him at all at this rate. Billy lay stiff and in pain on the far left, with Smithy in-between the two of them. The gun had been launched across the ground. Both Ted and Smithy, once they had patted down their bodies to check for shattered limbs, locked eyes on the firearm, and then on each other. They darted for the gun on their bellies like crocs, but only one was victorious.

Smithy struggled to his feet whilst holding the weapon to Ted's cranium, who remained on the floor, defenceless. 'Looks like your little girlfriend couldn't save you after all. It's nice to see the beating that I gave you earlier has held up nicely though. You look like shit.'

'So do you, and you haven't had a beating, so what's your excuse?' wise-cracked Ted, whose legs were throbbing with pain. Smithy's low IQ didn't take too kindly to this.

'Either you come with me, or I shoot you in the leg and drag you with me to the police, along with your prisoner friend. He's next. Billy told me that there's a pretty hefty bounty on his head...'

'I don't suppose there's any point in me saying "you don't have to do this", is there?'

'Not a chance in hell. Now get up, before you're not even able to stand. I really am not in the mood to carry you to Simmons, but if I have to I-'

Smithy suddenly stopped mid-sentence.

He was experiencing a rather alien sensation in his gut. Looking down, over his stubbly chin, he saw something that surprised him. *That's weird*, he thought to himself. That definitely hadn't been there before. Why was it sticking out like that? And why did it hurt so much? And why was it bleeding?

Geller pulled out the knife and then re-inserted it a second time, twisting it and cutting through Smithy's stomach glands like warm butter. He tore out the blade once he was satisfied that it had done its job, sending a splatter of blood across his own face, like a *Jackson Pollock* piece. It had been particularly visible on the white patches of his beard. Smithy fell backwards onto the grass, and Geller placed the spoiled knife back into his jacket pocket and picked up the gun, a far more sophisticated tool than his crude blade.

If Geller had been *Pollock*, then Ted, Billy, and Rose, who'd also arrived at ground level, had been *Edvard Munch*, their jaws dropping in disbelief at what Geller had done and the colour evaporating from their cheeks.

'What? He was going to kill you Ted. I had to do something... I-'

'HEY!!'

Before Geller was able to fully justify his violence, a certain plucky young officer struck gold. He'd hardly expected to stumble upon the fugitive himself whilst he'd been emptying his night's coffees onto the road side. He ran towards them, baton in hand.

'MOVE!' yelled Geller, disregarding any sense of volume.

Panicking, and not in his right mind, Ted followed him and grabbed Rose by the arm, who was still frozen with shock. The whole time he pulled her, she never once looked away from Smithy's bleeding torso. He was mouthing 'help me' to her with watery eyes, as Ted Yanked her away. Billy, upon seeing the officer, immediately raced towards the nearby treeline and hid. Once there, he threw up. The final thing Smithy would ever see, as his vision began to fade and his soul departed from his body, was the sight of Ted, Rose and Marcus, disappearing over the ridge that overlooked him, and out onto the Moors.

And then it all went black.

CHAPTER TEN

He pressed the creased edges of the map against the car bonnet. An underused art in this modern age, a time that prefers *Satnavs* and *Smartphones*, Simmons was old fashioned, and always favoured the use of his trusty map. The faint lines and squiggles on the pages signified the roads and villages that were dotted around North Yorkshire. Haworth, Pickering, Kirkby Fleetham, Malton, many more. But there was a vast, green, blank space of uncharted territory where the Moors lay waiting, and that, was where he'd needed to send his men in order to find Geller and the missing kids. His black tie, which was unbuttoned at the top, dangled over the plot like it were a pendulum, counting down to zero hour. The neon-soaked flash of the police cars' rotating lights doused Henry's face as he studied the map, like he were some kind of ice sculpture. But cool and collected he was not, because now, not only did he have a carpark full of panicking passengers, two missing persons and a killer at large, but he also had a fatality on his hands, Smithy.

Though most of the guests were dry by now, in fresh, creased clothes that were meant to have been unpacked on holiday beds hours ago, the officers were still drenched. More a squadron of deep-sea divers than police officers. The biblical-like shower had soaked the team, as though one of the guests had been a secret shaman and had performed an unauthorised African rain dance in the *O'Nowhere* broom closet. But they persevered despite their shivering uniforms, ready at Simmons's hand to finally bring Geller to justice for the wrongs that he'd done. They were gathered around their commanding officer who was staring down at his map of the Moors against the car hood, they were waiting to be told what to do next. After hours of idle-standing and friendly-talking to the citizens, Smithy's brutal stabbing had bolstered the officers into focus-mode like an old hotel bell summoning a concierge. No more games.

'Right, I want men here, here and here, spread out, covering every section of the Moors within a fifteen mile radius. I don't want a stone un-turned in the finding of this guy. Geller's clever, he knows these lands, and you don't. Don't take it personally, very few men know these Moors like Marcus does. But that means he could be hiding anywhere. If something looks strange, call it in, it could be important. Likewise, don't go anywhere alone. Geller's proven he's not afraid to add more bodies to his life sentence tonight, now's not the time to be a hero' commanded Simmons, his men huddled around him.

Barricades had been erected in the form of lesser officers, preventing the waiting guests with hands outstretched from entering Henry's new, outdoor office. None of them had yet caught wind of the fact that Smithy had been murdered, with the officers taking extreme care as to transport the body bag in which his corpse had been lying, out via the *O'Nowhere's* rear exit way. The guests were already in a volatile state and knowing that someone had been killed, even someone as morally dubious as Smithy, it would've sent them into a hurricane of panic and madness. Simmons was rather ashamed to have admitted that a slight irritation had crept its way into his head at the realisation that Geller had killed Smithy before he'd had the chance to see him taken into custody, he'd have liked to have done those honours himself. But a life was a life, no matter the way that it had been led, murder was murder.

'Now, I reckon he's got about a twenty minute head start on us, so he can't have gotten far. Plus, he's got baggage with him, two kids, that'll slow him down.' Henry had quickly determined that the whereabouts of Ted and Rose were unknown once a headcount had been performed on the guests, they'd been made to sign a register upon entering the station that night. It had led him to deduce, that the two youngsters that the officer had seen with Smithy, had indeed been, the unaccounted names.

'Speaking of the kids...there are lives at stake now, immediate ones. We can't forget that he has two people with him. Whether they were taken by force or not we're yet to determine, but proceed with caution, he may plan on taking them as hostages or using them as leverage in the instance that he's backed into a corner. We don't need any more dead bodies this evening'.

Two kids. Two missing kids. The thought terrified him. Simmons had a child of his own and the thought of her in danger, well....best not to think about that. It was a common maxim in law enforcement that the odds of finding a missing person, once they'd been off-the grid for twenty-four hours, were slashed by half. Forty-eight hours, and another 50% would be taken off those chances. By seventy-two hours any hope of finding that person alive would be nothing short of a miracle, or misguided, painful parental optimism. What wasn't clear though, as not something mandatorily included as a precedence within the police officers handbook, were the chances of rescuing a missing persons once they'd been abducted by an escaped-serial killer. And Simmons didn't like the unknown.

He couldn't quite believe just how much things had escalated. Henry hadn't the time to allow guilt to cripple his senses though. He knew that Smithy's death was on his hands, on his failure to catch Geller, but he also knew not to allow himself to be distracted by his remorse, not now. He had a criminal to catch, and any excess feeling other than cold-blooded determination would do nothing but deter him from doing so. He could wrestle with his conscience later over a bottle of whiskey. In fact, the murder and subsequent sighting of Geller fleeing had somewhat reinvigorated his fading tenacity for the case, his thirst to bring Marcus to justice. This was the breakthrough that he'd been searching for, he'd only wished that it hadn't taken the death of a man to cause it.

'I need you all to act fast, and swiftly. This is it guys, we have to catch Marcus Geller, once and for all. Now, move out'. His men watched, quite to the contrary of what Simmons had believed, with an ambitious sense of admiration for their leader. 'I wish *I* could be like him' they all thought, surely to be heartbroken if they were to have learned that he was contemplating retirement post-case. One thing was for sure though, they'd do their damned best to catch Geller out on those cold, lonely, ominous Moors. They'd do Simmons proud.

When the men dispersed, split into search parties to track down the knife-wielding killer who haunted the misty heath, Henry turned to two officers that remained behind.

'Anything on the CCTV in that rear section?' he asked, in reference to the site of the murder.

'No sir. We've managed to pull footage from every other camera in and around the *O'Nowhere*, but for some reason the exterior cameras on that side of the wall weren't operational' the young officer replied. He wore glasses. They were slightly smudged from where he'd wiped sprinkled water from their lenses, using the cuff of his shirt.

'Not operational?'

'No sir.'

'But...'

It was then that Simmons turned to the porky, sorry-state of a man that was Manager Perkins, who was shivering and sniffling beside the car bonnet. He'd been desperately clinging onto the arm of the officer who'd escorted him out of his office, once Henry had barged in and disabled the sprinkler system. It had been hard to tell whether the water droplets on his face were from the shower, or his eyes, the dark stains on his trousers from the sprinkler, or from his own bladder. The few strands of white hair that he'd had left on his egg-shaped head were soaked and slicked back and his unseemly grey suit had shrunk from the downpour, making him look larger than ever. Boy, was he large, as though he'd gorged on the profits of the stations bank account until his buttons had popped and his breeches had split.

'Care to explain Perkins, why the CCTV isn't working in that quarter of your building?' asked Henry, hands on his hips.

'Well....I...erm...you see...'

'Spit it out Perkins. There's a dead man and two missing kids out there. I'm not in the mood for your bullshit anymore. Tell me why, now, or so help me God I'll....'

'Okay, okay!' squealed Perkins. The Police rulebook had been torn up, blended, and thrown out of the preverbal seven-story window, murder had a habit of doing that. Henry reckoned that he'd have had no problem with bending Perkins over and spanking him like a misbehaving child with his baton, if he hadn't told him what he'd wanted to know.

'A few years back there was a storm, a real bad one. It knocked down a tree and it smashed through a wall on the stations east side. It made one hell of a hole in it. It took out the power box and some wiring in that quadrant, totally shutting down the electricity too, including the CCTV.'

It all made sense now.

'And you didn't think to get it repaired...?.'

At this point Perkins burst into tears and began wailing, he turned to the officer standing next to him and attempted to bury his head in his shirt.

'I want to go home, this is a nightmare' he sobbed in a babyish tone. His employees, who'd been segregated into the crowd of waiting, anxious passengers, watched and laughed at the whimpering man with pleasure. Simmons meanwhile, pieced together the puzzle.

'That entrance then, that hole in the wall, that must've been how Geller broke into the station, how he escaped. He's been hiding here all along...all this time we've been searching, and he's been here, right under our noses'.

The concept infuriated him, of sending brave men and women out onto the freezing cold of the Moors to search for a man who'd been quietly laughing at their expense, beneath them the entire time. Aftermath patrols would soon locate the food wrappers of Geller's stolen feast, hidden in the sewers. What tore up Simmons the most though, what really upset him, was the notion that he'd endangered the lives of the *O'Nowhere* guests, by sealing them inside the station with a killer.

'There were children....for Christ sake...children in there!' he hissed to himself.

'What was that sir?' asked a nearby officer. He'd just pushed off an advance from the hysterical Perkins, who was trying to hug him.

'Nothing, I'm just tired of being made a fool of that's all. No more playing around. It's time we bring Geller home to the cell where he belongs' replied Henry, speaking loudly over the sounds of Perkins blowing his snotty nose into his hanky.

'I want my mummy' he was saying, over and over. The antithesis of adorable.

'I suspect Geller might be trying to go back to his family farm, where he committed his first murders. His son Terrance still lives there with his wife and son. God knows why after what happened in that place, the profits from the land too much to turn down I expect. Send a police detail over there too to guard them, in case he turns up.'

The officer complied and turned to pass on his instructions via a radio call.

'We've got you now...' said Simmons quietly to himself, as he surveyed the dark ridges of the Moors that loomed over him. 'I'm gonna do you proud dad, we haven't lost this yet'.

Whilst on the topic of fathers and sons, as Simmons departed the scene to search for Geller, leaving a subordinate in charge of supervising the stressed out passengers, a pair of tiny eyes watched him go. At knee-height of his *own* Dad's leg, his custard-coloured coat hood almost blocking his view, Ted's little helper had been studying Henry's speech as it had been unfolding. Though of course he hadn't known what he was saying, none of the guests had, he'd watched as Henry had rallied his men into action, mouthing words of valour and pulling expressions of unwavering bravery and strength. He'd then, in turn, witnessed the faces of his officer's morph from that of a petrified fear into determination, and had seen how they had been willing to march into the dark unknown and to face horrifying evils, no matter the cost, in order to bring them to justice. Whatever it was that Simmons had been saying was immaterial, it was the manner in which he'd said it that had inspired the Custard-coloured coat wearing boy. Plus, his hat had been pretty cool too...

And it was there, stood in that car park, wearing his dripping mackintosh at his father's feet, that the tiny lad had turned his back on his short-lived career as a shop-lifter, and his destiny had been sealed.

'Daddy' the boy said, looking up into the nostrils of his pa.

'...when I grow up, I want to be a policeman, just like him'.

· · ·

The Moors weren't pleased. Their blank, wet, grassy faces were used to the polite, occasional footprints of wandering walkers in their midst. But the multitude of police officers that had been dispatched to stalk their hills for Geller were not welcome guests. They abruptly tore through branches and rudely pried open purple thistle bushes in their search, trampling over shrubbery and disturbing sleeping swallows in their nests in the pursuit of justice. The sheer disrespect that the officers showed to the environment angered the watchful ridges, who they themselves had bear witness to many a crime in their centuries of existence. They'd seen bodies buried out on those lonely fields that had never been found, and most likely, never would be. But as far as the Yorkshire hills were concerned, they'd never hush a word about them to anyone. After all, that was mankind business, they were as indifferent to the laughs of exploring humans as they were to their cries of pain. The Moors simply watched, and they simply were. These people would come and go, but the Moors would remain forever, fixed, constant, always.

And too, in the search for Geller, they did not participate, continuing to watch with anger and curiosity as the men lumbered over filled-in badger holes, like blocked pores on the skin of a teen, in their quest for a killer.

The time was 4:47am and by now, like blonde roots beginning to show in the hair of a fake brunette, glimpses of yellow sunrise had begun to pierce the clouds above. If the policemen had thought that with the break of the day an increased visibility of their path would come, then they had been mistaken. A dense, grey, foggy mist had descended over the Moors, and the torches of the weary officers floated through them like sunny orbs, as they tried and failed to locate Geller in the wilderness. Their beams would pass over badlands, revealing untamed nature, as though the Moors had once been a prim and proper topiary; hedge animal dogs and cats and lions that had been left to their own devices. Uncut, and abandoned, they had grown outwardly into all manner of bizarre and terrifying shapes, until eventually the vines of their borders and the claws of their greenery had become something unrecognisable and wrong, something that no longer resembled the animals that they had once been at all. This wasn't a place meant for humans. And yet, there was still no sign of Marcus, Ted or Rose.

The tired men who longed for their warm beds, wives and hot chocolates couldn't find him. The riled, stiff eared sniffer dogs who burrowed their wet, black noses into every puddle and every corner of every winding path couldn't find him. The spinning blades of the birds-eye view helicopters, with their spotlights couldn't find him either. Where the hell was he?!

Panting. Sweating. Grunting. Panting.

These were not sounds that the local wildlife were used to hearing. They were the sounds made by the three runaways, Ted, Rose, and the evil Marcus Geller, as they tore through the forests. Using paths and shortcuts and hidden trails that only *he* knew about, Geller led the trio as they were propelled by adrenaline over the undergrowth, past twisted tree's and misty frog-spawn ponds as they evaded the searching police.

It hurt to breathe in, for the air was cold and spiked. The gallons of oxygen that Ted inhaled froze his teeth, the soft palette of his mouth, and the back of his throat, before reaching his lungs and then freezing them too. They had been running non-stop for what felt like hours, evacuating the scene of Smithy's stabbing and scaling the ridge of the Moors to escape Simmons and his men. They'd collectively covered four kilometres worth of land beneath their feet, yet still, no matter how long their marathon had lasted, they'd constantly felt under threat of detection. They ran and they ran until they felt as though their legs might give way, but they didn't. It truly is impressive the lengths that the body will go to in the name of self-preservation. It was Rose in fact, who had decided that enough was enough, putting the brakes on their getaway.

'Stop!' Stop! Wait!' she shouted, using the last of her breathe to do so. When one is running as fast as they were, one does not simply stop. Their feet, which had been locked into a cycling motion, gradually decreased in momentum until they came to a rest. She bent over and placed her hands on her knees, desperately trying to regain her breath. The other two stopped a little further ahead of her, and then turned back.

'What? What is it? Is someone there?' asked a gravely concerned Geller, his eyes wide with a crazed look, like the bulging stare of *Jack Torrance*,

Patrick Bateman and *Hannibal Lector*. Ted put his hand on Rose's back as he regained his own regular pattern of breathing.

'No....there's no one...I just need a minute to....'

'Then why the hell did you stop us? We need to keep moving. They could be on us at any minute sweetheart! If you can't handle it, you can stay here alone, but I've got no intention of getting caught' snapped Marcus. The threesome had stopped in a forested clearing, on a pathway of mud and woodchip. It was silent, but it wouldn't be for long, the sounds of chattering policemen and barking dogs would soon fade into ear-range if they didn't move quickly. Ted reassured Rose.

'Yeah Rose, we need to keep moving, they're right on our track!'

Rose pushed Ted's hand from her shoulder and returned to standing straight, her red-hair once again dangling around her face.

'Ted, what the hell are we doing here? Are you crazy? Did you see what I see? Or am I the only sane person here? That guy, that monster, he stabbed Smithy, he stabbed him Ted...he...'

'Look, I'm getting tired of talking about this. You're really starting to tick me off little girl. I've already told you, he was going for him, a lunatic like that doesn't know his own strength. I just saved Ted's life, you'd think you could at least show me a little appreciation...'

'Saved his life? You murdered someone Geller, I watched you stab a man through the stomach, you're crazy!' Rose cried, hoping for the slim chance that a police patrol might've heard and inadvertently stumbled upon them again.

'I used to gut animals all the time on my farm sweetheart. I know a thing or two about anatomy. Where I shanked him I'll have missed any arteries and organs, the guy will have a nasty scar on his stomach but that's it, he'll make a full recovery, not that he deserves it....now can we please just get moving?' Marcus anxiously looked around the tree line for any unwanted policemen. He was sure that they'd never find them where they were, no one knew the canopy coverage like he did. But with so much at stake, he wasn't taking any chances.

'Bullshit. Ted, you don't really believe this guy do you? He's a killer Ted, and if we don't run now he's going to kill us too...'

'...oh come on Ted, I thought you said this girl was cool? Seems to me she's nothing but a headache. If I'm so guilty darling, then why are you here? Why did you run with us? Why didn't you go along with that officer back at the foot of the hill? Hmm? If you're so noble and righteous.'

'I....I don't know...I was scared...I....well now I'm putting things right, I'm going back to those police and I'm telling them exactly where you are. Are you coming Ted?'

The heat coming off the arguing pair seemed enough to splint a campfire in the clearing. Ted all the while stood between them, his loyalties torn in two. Geller could sense that he was losing his hold over the boy. Back in the sewers he'd been like white wine in Marcus's glass, gently swirling

him around at his will to do as he'd commanded, but now his grip was
loosening.

'Look Ted, we're not far now...my farm is only three more kilometres
ahead. We can do this. I'm sorry I did what I did back there, but I had no
choice, can't you see that? That giant gypsy was going to bash your
brains in, and I couldn't let that happen to you, not after all we've been
through.'

Ted's ideals faltered. Geller's huge, bulking body made him look like an
otherworldly apparition amongst the trees. It was like he was the last of
his kind, a lost species, a violent Sasquatch that terrorised nearby
villages, dragging goats on his back to devour in his lair.

'...all I want to do is reach my son Ted, you know what that's like, don't
you? To be this close to the one you love, this close. Let me have this...I
beg of you. If you tell me now that you want to go back to the police, I
won't stop you, by God I won't, I swear it. But if they find you, they find
me, and then everything we've worked so hard to achieve, everything
I've been dreaming of for thirty five years will have been for nothing I...'

Marcus, a true bloody showman, began coughing violently into a closed
fist then, reminding Ted of his phoney diagnosis.

'Please I need you, please son...' Geller spluttered.

It was a colloquial northern phrase, 'son'. It was one not limited to
fathers and their boys, commonly used, say, by milkmen dropping off
pints to the young lads who'd collect them at their doorsteps. 'Thanks
son', they'd say as they tipped their hats. But Geller had known exactly

what he was doing when he'd dropped the 'S' bomb. It had instantly reminded Ted of the relationship he'd longed to have, with the man waiting for him in a Robin Hood's Bay cottage.

'Rose, I can't leave him.'

Rose's heart sank, she'd lost him, and Geller had won. The mist and the low-light of the daybreak, combined with Ted's turned back, had offered Rose enough vision and Marcus enough time for the two to exchange a look. He was smiling, she wasn't.

'Ted, listen, I-'

'No Rose. You don't get it, you don't get the pain he's feeling, you can't, but I do. You heard him, we're so close to the farm now. He needs me and I'm not leaving him. You've done more than enough, saving us from Smithy and Billy back there on the hill, but if you want to leave us here I'll understand. *I* just can't.' He turned and walked back to Geller's side, who placed a gigantic hand on his shoulder.

'Just a little further I promise. Then once I've seen my family, I'll hand myself in, you have my word', he lied.

'Promise me though Marcus, promise me no one else will get hurt? I know you were just trying protect me back there, but please, no more hurting' pleaded a very naive Ted.

'You have my word kid...' the man replied, as the devil lied to Eve in the Garden of Eden, ruffling his hair.

Rose desperately wanted to run, but how could she? She knew that by the time she'd reached the police that Ted would be mince-meat. There was no doubt in her mind now that Marcus was truly a killer, not after what she'd seen him do to poor Smithy. He'd poisoned Ted's mind, manipulated and used his love for his Father against him. If she were to leave him now, she'd be signing his death warrant. No, she had no choice but to join them. At least if she were there, together they might've stood a chance at defeating Marcus once he'd finally revealed his true colours, like she knew he inevitably would.

'Fine. I'm coming. We'll help you reach that farm Geller. But then that's it, you hand yourself into the police, and we say you forced us to come with you, we walk' she announced reluctantly, as the tree's whispered in the wind. Instead of the feel-good endorphins often released via exercise, the running had left Rose with a soreness in her side, toxic lactic-acid that had given her a painful stitch.

The three of them then, their bodies barely refreshed at all from the break in their running, resumed their sprint east-bound towards Geller's old farm, into the shroud of the mist ahead. They were frightened rabbits, fleeing the prowling foxes, only, one had been amongst them, disguised with painted fur and stuck-on ears, licking its lips, all along.

On and on they went, three black silhouettes against the rising orange sun on the horizon, dodging the pine trees, as a brand new day was ushered in. A fine day it was, a truly fine day to die if it were to be the case. Marcus had been true to his word about at least one thing, the farm had been close. The three characters docked into a cluster of woodland and then stopped at Marcus's lead. It was the very spot that a certain

William Blythe had left his jeep to investigate, on the edge of the 80's, queerly picking at sheep fur on branches, unknowingly moments from discovering the worst crime scene that the North side of Yorkshire had seen in just under a century.

They'd arrived, they were at Geller Farm.

'...and there she blows...' said Geller. He said it not to the others, but more to himself, after all, this was *his* plan, one that had been over thirty years in the making. Crouching down, the three of them had a perfect view of the building through the backfield of the farm. *She hasn't aged a day*, thought its former owner, nostalgically. It was the very same as it had been all those years ago, back when he'd blown his wife and daughter to smithereens. His senses took in the entirety of the scene, the broken tiles of the roof, the robust smell of manure in the air, the dusty track of mud that led up to the front porch, the rotating rooster weather vane above the door. Then finally, he smiled at the warm glow of the kitchen lights through the thin, netted lace curtains in the windows. It was just how he'd imagined it, night after night as he'd closed his eyes to shut out the cries of the sex offenders in the cells next door to his. He couldn't help but let a grin escape his lips, imagining the sick and twisted goings on that he'd be bringing about once he'd finally gotten inside the farmhouse. But then he quickly remembered himself, and erased the grin. He'd had a part to play in front the boy. However, his look of glee had actually acted in his favour, with Ted catching sight of it and mistaking it for an unconditional love for his family, not knowing that his mind had instead been full of violence and bloodshed.

'They're in there...' Marcus whispered to himself, too pre-occupied with his dark fantasy's to consider why the farmhouse lights had been on and why his family had been up at 5:30am in the first place. Rose hadn't been.

'So what's the plan now, dumbass? Bet you didn't account for this did you? Huh?' she said with a snarky satisfaction, arms folded to try and warm her shivering body.

Marcus, confused, looked up to realise that she had been referring to the police cars and officers that were parked up a little way in front of the house. Simmons's gut-feeling had paid off it seemed, he'd worked out that he was coming for his son and his family, to finish what he'd started, that sunny July afternoon. Luckily, Geller had had a plan B.

'You do make me laugh sweetheart. You really think I didn't know that this would happen? Darling, if there's one thing a man has time for in prison, its thinking. I've thought about every conceivable scenario and possibility and figured out a way around each one. This, is no exception'.

Boy, would he have loved to have cracked open her skull and to have wiped that smug bitch-smirk off of her face. To have taken a log to her cranium with full force, and then to have watched the juice dribble from out of her brains and onto the leaves, prematurely changing their colour from a spring green to an autumn red. But no, he couldn't go spoiling the grand surprise now could he? Killing her then would've just been plain indulgent. As orgasmic as it would've felt, nothing could've compared to what he'd had in store for the pair at the farm. It would be his crowning achievement, his magnum opus, the vile, unspeakable act for which he would be remembered for and studied about in criminology lectures from Scotland to Cornwall. That first summer had only been a warm-up, now, Geller was in the business of history-defining, legacy-building killing, anything less simply wouldn't do.

'What's our move then man? They're crawling all over the place, we'll never be able to sneak past them. No way' asked Ted anxiously.

Rather than verbally replying, Marcus chose to show, not tell. He walked a few yards to the left, through ivy leaves and nettles. He mentally counted fifteen steps, whilst Ted and Rose watched him, perplexed, until the crunching sound underneath his stolen boots ceased, and a metallic-like texture of a noise replaced it.

'Ah. There we go.'

He stepped back, and then swept away a layer of dirt and plantation, that, come to think of it, had seemed a little oddly grown in its pattern when held in comparison to the nature surrounding it. Geller scraped back the soil, revealing what appeared to be a secret, horribly rusted, steel bunker door beneath it. There was a dusty porthole-shaped window, like on the starboard side of a ship, on its face. With what must've taken unparalleled levels of strength, Geller finally unleashed the maximum power of his biceps and traps by pulling open the hatch with his bare hands. It's hinges squeaked and screamed and Marcus's face turned bright red until the trapdoor finally gave way, revealing a long drop and a set of ladders that led downwards into the darkness below.

'This, is how we get in boys' and girls'. Marcus stood proudly over the hole, he, like many of his serial killer predecessors, had a liking for the dramatic. The combined strength of Rose, Ted and Billy couldn't have lifted open that portal, the man was truly super-human. Super-villain more like.

'What...what is that?' asked Ted.

'An old service passage. Back when the farm was first built, it allowed for the transportation of goods, to and from the road and into the house, whenever it were to get blocked by snow in the winter or by flooding. Kept things ticking over nicely and business blooming you see. This little gem of a secret, will take us straight under those prick-police men and right into the basement of the farm'. Geller then turned around and began descending the rungs of the ladder. 'You coming? Or are you too scared?' He laughed as his grey head slowly disappeared through the gap in the ground and into the earth, knowing full-well that Ted would follow him like a lap-dog.

Before Rose had a chance to talk Ted out of the suicide mission, as predicted, he'd already bounded after him, and too, was following Marcus's lead into the pit. It left her with no choice but to follow them into the darkness too. As she watched the yellow morning daylight at the mouth of the bunker disappear, getting lower and lower and closer to the bottom of the ladder, she wondered whether or not she'd ever see the outside world ever again.

Ted was having flashbacks to the many trips he'd had to make through the dank, foul smelling passages of the *O'Nowhere* sewers. He'd hoped that he'd never have to revisit such an unpleasant journey again, but the tunnels under the farm were unnervingly similar. They seemed to go on endlessly, for miles and miles through the pitch-black. He wondered about the northerners who must've unwittingly stumbled upon the deadly network and then gotten lost, never to be found again. And then he decided not to think about that, they did after all, have Marcus, who guided Rose and him through the corridors with an incredible ease. The more he relaxed, the more he began to experience a kind of thrill at walking beneath the unsuspecting bobbies, the same he'd had when he'd stolen from the *O'Nowhere* shop for Marcus. He felt like Guy Fawkes with his band of merry men, sneaking beneath the houses of parliament, gunpowder barrel at hand. Crime was kinda fun. He held onto the back of Marcus's fleece and Rose held onto him, until eventually the uneven *Ghidorah* of adventurers, with only one evil head, arrived at a wooden door. Golden light was peeking through the crack at the bottom.

'Beyond this point, I need you all to remain extremely quiet, okay? I mean it, not a peep. This takes us into the farm basement. I don't want my family to hear me...it'll ruin the surprise. I can't wait to see the look on their faces' whispered Geller, picturing the unspeakable atrocities that he was about to commit and becoming giddy with excitement. 'Just stay close to me, follow my lead, and remember, whatever you do....don't make a sound. Okay?'

'They're going to be so happy to see you. You've done it Marcus, after all this time, you're finally going to see them again. Make it count my friend, you won't have long, so you show them all the love you've got big guy. Give them something to remember you by' replied Ted, rallying him on and nodding. It was a pointless movement, seeing as Marcus couldn't see him at all, it was *that* dark.

'Thank you Ted. I can't quite believe this is happening. This isn't a
dream is it? I'm not going to suddenly wake up back in my cell am I?
No. This is really happening. We did this Ted, you and me, and you'll be
next lad, don't worry, your Dad's waiting for you.'

Marcus gently pushed open the basement door then and stealthily crept
into the chamber. All the while Rose's heart was pounding like a drum
and sweat was pouring from her temples, she knew that something truly
awful was about to happen and she hadn't a clue about how she could
stop it. She desperately searched for preventative measures that she could
take to stop Geller from doing whatever it was that he'd had planned, but
all of the trial simulations that she ran in her head ended with both her
and Ted as corpses. She was powerless, all she could do was bide her
time, wait, and pray that when the opportunity to stop him finally
presented itself, she would recognise it and then take it. The basement
was a cramped, sooty, dingy room, with a set of stone stairs against the
far side that matched the granite walls. Shelves of opened paint tubs,
garden sheers, and other tools were propped up against the south and
west side. A lawnmower, with its parts dismantled, stood in the corner,
beside it, a work bench, with a glue gun and pieces of palette wood. The
room smelt of varnish.

Marcus slowly but surely made his way up the stairs towards another
wooden door, one that would take him straight into the house where he'd
murdered his wife and daughter. He could hear northern voices
emanating from the other side and could smell sizzling bacon, eggs,
sausages and coffee beans. They'd have been warned by now by the
police officers about his escape, and will also have been informed that a
dispatch would be guarding them outside and that 'everything would be

okay'. Bullshit, they were about to die, all of them, including his son Terrence. He found it mildly amusing that even at 5:46am, in the face of life threatening crisis and danger, that his family had decided that the best course of action would be to cook a full-English breakfast. Classic Northerners. At least they'd die with full stomachs, the eggs yolks would scarcely have had time to digest before he'd cut up their limbs and gauged out their eyeballs. Closer and closer he got to the top of the stairs, with a mortally terrified Rose and an excited Ted following closely behind him, the latter of which feeling as though he were about to be part of something truly magical, the reuniting of a Father and a son, something he himself would soon be doing, at the Bay.

But then, a rather disturbing thought edged its way back into Ted's mind, as he did his best to remain silent, ascending the stairs. He'd forgotten about it up until now, what with all the commotion of Billy and Smithy's ambush, falling down the hill, and then the tearing away from the police. But like a bobbing buoy out at sea after a storm, it resurfaced, the catalyst being the contemplating of his *own* return to his Father. Hadn't Marcus said something rather weird back on the top of that hill....just before Smithy and Billy had attacked...?

Yes...he believed he had.

'...it's just such a real pity you'll never reach *your* father' it had been.

Yes, that's what he'd said just before he'd been interrupted. But what had he meant by that? It had been a somewhat strange thing to say seeing as Ted hadn't been planning on joining Marcus in running across the Moors, very strange indeed. But before Ted had had time to think about

Geller's peculiar off-handed comment in any more detail, the man in question had reached the door at the top. He'd been psyching himself up for the evil that he was about to unleash. Even madmen got nervous, but now, he was ready.

'Here we fucking go!' he screamed. He swung open the door, flooding the basement with light, and then pulled out the gun that had belonged to Smithy from his left pocket, the one that he'd been sure to pick up from off of the grass before they'd fled from the police. He dragged Ted and Rose along with him into the country-home, where Geller's family, including his son, Terrence, had just been sitting down to a cooked fry-up in the kitchen. Now a man deep into his forties in his own right, Terrence and his son, Jacob, who had kept the family name despite the heavy stigma that had come with it, both looked up from their breakfasts and cutlery with a disbelieving look of shock and horror. Margery Geller, Marcus's daughter-in law, was carrying her own plate to the table (*she always served herself last*) when the killer burst into the pantry, causing her to scream and to drop it, shattering it on the ground.

'Honey, I'm home!' jeered the eldest of the Geller clan, as he waved his loaded pistol in the air. And then the horrible, awful truth suddenly dawned upon Ted, the truth that Rose had been begging him to see all night. This wasn't going to be the cosy, touching, long awaited homecoming that he'd hoped it would be...

All hell broke loose.

CHAPTER ELEVEN

Her face was stern and harsh, yet soft at the same time. An acquired taste, she had an uncanny ability not so dissimilar to that of *Dr. Jekyll and Mr. Hyde*, to be able to shape-shift from kind hearted and warm, to terrifying and paralysing within the space of a blink. Margery Geller was not a woman to be trifled with, nor was she one who suffered fools gladly. She'd always be on hand to serve up fresh, green granny smiths to the children of the village, but would never fail to add a footnote after doing so; warning them not to eat the pips, for danger of an apple tree growing inside of them. The Malton locals would loathe her one moment, for scolding them with her wrath; '*don't you know how to keep that dog quiet*?!' And then they'd adore her the next, relishing in the glory of her compliments, which were all the more moving and worth so much more than that of anybody else's, given just how hard they were to come by; '*I must say Mabel your hair looks delightful today*'.

A sturdy and house-proud woman, in a greasy, dough stained apron with pushed back hair, she knew that her men, her son and her husband, were in dire need of a full-Yorkshire breakfast in their hour of helplessness. And so that's just what she cooked that morning.

'He's got some balls I'll give him that, after all these years. But if he thinks he's got a snowflakes chance in hell of slipping past our police out there then he's in for a rude awakening. Ent he?' Margery shouted over her shoulder, competing with the sizzling hiss of full-fat bacon. She stirred her men's scrambled eggs in the pan, soft and milky and fluffy, she knew just how they liked them. Sweat dripped slightly from her brow but she paid it no mind as she moved from drawer to drawer with ease, she could've cooked that meal blind-folded.

'Food'll be ready in a minute fellas. Don't you worry. If I'm being frank, I'm more pissed off than anything. Breaking out of *Full Sutton* and making us get up at this ungodly hour. I've been tending to those cows all week, this were supposed to be my day off, my *only* day off!.'

She seemed to be stirring the tea, serving the dishes, squirting the sauces (*Terrance had ketchup, Jacob had brown*) and buttering the toast all at the same time, like she were some six armed Indian Goddess. Maybe she was, a deity of domesticity. One didn't win the prized title of '*Malton Vegetable Patch of the Year*' three years running by just idly sitting around, no way. No sir.

'Well, if he does somehow manage to reach here, I'll clatter him with me handbag a good few times round the head before the police get him. No one disturbs my day-off, no one'. She demonstrated the seriousness of this statement by slamming a cupboard at the exact same time, it made the hanging knives and decorative ivy plant leaves shudder around the window. Although her courage was admirable, and she was certainly making herself feel a lot better, the same effect couldn't have been said for Terrance and their son Jacob. The pair were sat next to each other at the kitchen table, the one that Marcus had been sitting at when Chief-Inspector Cole Simmons had arrested him, on that awful, sunny day.

The clock read 6am, and two guarding police cars were waiting outside in the farmyard, protecting the family from any sign of Marcus. They'd arrived only half an hour before, awakening the remnants of the Geller clan to apprise them of the situation, that a certain bloody relative of theirs had escaped, and could've well been on his way to slaughter them all in their beds. Of course, the officers hadn't used those exact words as such. They'd tip-toed around the sleepy family, down-playing the severity of it all. But Terrence knew full-well that things were bad, really bad, and if his Father truly had broken out of *Full Sutton*, then that could only mean one thing. He was coming, coming for them all. Margery had of course, in true Margery form, gone ape-shit at the nervous officers for not informing them that Marcus had escaped hours ago, when it'd first transpired. But once she'd vented her fury and realised that this hadn't been a decision that the officers had been privy to, she'd let it go, and returned inside to await further news. Terrence though, was shaken to his core.

'Well, I for one hope they gun the bastard down. I'm certainly not afraid of him, if anything he's done us a favour by breaking out. It'll mean he gets shot making a break for it instead of dying a natural death in prison. You know what these jails are like now anyways...penthouse suites most of them, these murderers live in luxury they do. It's far better than he deserves...'

'-Marge. Please' interrupted Terrence. He knew what she was trying to do, defusing the tension with her humour and the 'no-nonsense' attitude that he'd fallen for back in 96. Usually it would have worked. But not this time.

'I'm sorry Terrence, but I'm not afraid of your father, Christ, even saying that seems wrong. He's no father of yours, he's no man at all...that thing...whatever he is...I'm not going to let him scare me. Let him have his little moment in the spotlight, let him perform his little show, I ent giving him the satisfaction of letting him get to me' Margery announced, spatula in hand.

'...Dad, should we be worried? They wouldn't have sent out those police to guard us if they hadn't thought that there was anything worth guarding us against' asked an anxious looking Jacob, sat opposite his Father at the kitchen table. Wearing oversized white and blue PJ's, with scruffy hair and baggy eyes, Jacob was a dog-eared lad of eighteen, and was particularly tired given that he'd spent the vast majority of the night playing video games and drinking energy drinks, when he should've been sleeping. A few days prior he'd actually been gaming on the exact same server as the two nerdy book store clerks that'd worked at the O'Nowhere. Their usernames; *'Ladykiller19'* and *'CheesePuff X'*.

The pantry was warm and stuffy from the combined heat of the gas stove and the boiling kettle, it steamed.

'-Of course we don't need to be worried' snapped the boy's mother, frustrated that nothing that she'd said had settled into his adolescent brain. 'He's a hack, a coffin-dodger. You think a man like that stands a chance with half of the Yorkshire Police Force out there looking for him? You worry too much Jacob. Tell him Terrence, tell him there's nothing to be afraid of' she urged her husband.

Jacob, quite to the contrary of what his overbearing mother had believed, had heard and soaked up every word that she'd said about Geller's escape, and would've found comfort in her rant, if not for the look on his Father's face. It was a look that he'd never seen grace his old man's features before. Make no mistake, he'd witnessed his father stress many a time, the autumn of 2010 for instance, when a nasty case of influenza had wormed its way into the farms water supply and had exterminated half of their cattle only weeks before an auction. But this particular expression, this wasn't no case of stress, Terrance's face read; *I'm scared shitless.*

The man of the house remained silent. He looked not unlike the haggard, painted portrait of a fisherman that one might've found hanging outside of a pub, dangling and peeling from a wooden sign, welcoming punters with a classical Yorkshire name like '*The Salty Sea-Dog*'. Terrence had had very little to say at all since he'd first been informed by the visiting officers that his father had escaped from prison, leaving Margery and Jacob to do all of the talking for him. The truth was though, was that Terrence had been dumbfounded, struck completely speechless. Like most Yorkshire men, years of toxic masculinity had trained him into somewhat of an expert in the bottling of emotions. But this was the bottling of all bottlings, and it was becoming increasingly impossible to stop his crippling fear from escaping from under its cap and out of its glassy neck. He was back, the man who'd murdered his mother and sister in cold blood was back, to finish the job.

'Well?' demanded Terrence's wife, 'tell the boy there's nothing to be afraid of and that he's just being silly. Terrence...honey?'

'-I can't' Terrence whispered through his bushy, brown sea captains beard. Margery stared back aghast. This hadn't been the 'yes dear' response that she'd grown accustomed to, and so based on this, she hesitated.

'What? Stop goofing around honey, tell the boy everything is going to be okay. Just tell him'. Whether Margery was begging her husband to assure Jacob, or herself, was unclear.

'I'm not going to sit here and bare-face lie to the lad Marge. He's eighteen now, he's a man. He's old enough to know the truth' said Terrence, becoming upset.

'What truth Dad?'

'That we are all going to die!'

The kitchen table that the threesome had been gathered around was usually a conference centre of fun and merriment; family meals, catch-up's and board games. But tonight, it was an epicentre of conflict and despair.

'What? Are you scared now Marge? You should be. We all should be. Don't you get it? This isn't some petty crook we're dealing with here, some graffiti artist or some shoplifter. This is the man who murdered my mother and sister, and he would've killed me too if I'd have been there!'

'Honey...please don't say things like that, you're upsetting Jacob' pleaded Marge, tears gathering in her stony eyes, something that was no easy feat given just how tough the old bat was.

'Good, he should be upset, because I know *I* am. I know that man, he's not like you and me, or anyone else for that matter. He's a monster, and he won't rest until he's put me, and you, all of us in the ground and finished what he started.' Terrence had stood up by now, his thick bushy beard and high-neck Guernsey jumper disguising the lump in his throat. His arms flailed as he spoke, unable to keep trapped the heart-stopping fear that he'd been stowing inside of him, ever since the officers had first told him the terrible news.

'...You say he doesn't stand a chance against the police, the ones out there. If you ask me Marge, they're the ones who don't stand a chance against him. You don't know him like I do, you haven't seen what I've seen...you...'

The solid northern soul burst into tears at the PDST memory of his family's violent massacre, and then collapsed back into his chair, unable to speak any longer. At once, all animosity was forgotten, and both Margery and Jacob rushed to his side to hold him as he wept.

'I can't lose you too, I just can't. I can't let him take you too' Terrence sobbed as he held them both close, as though it were the last time he'd ever touch them. The watchful policemen in their high-visibility jackets stared on from the farmyard, as the family huddled together in the light of the breaking dawn. Already, even from afar, Marcus was tearing the Gellers apart, as though his rusty shotgun were firing bullets from the sepia-soaked crime scene photos of yesteryear and straight into the hearts of his relatives-to be. They, all of them had bounties on their heads, and Marcus was on his way to collect them.

'I'm scared Dad' wept Jacob, a boy usually far too *cool-for-school* to cry.

'Me too Son.'

'We all are. But at least we're scared together, and we're going to weather this storm the way we always do. As a family' said Margery proudly, her momentary lapse of confidence over and her bravery returning. Her strength, gave them strength too. And as their tears began to dry, a sudden foul smell pricked the nostrils of the farmyards mother.

'Oh shit! My sausages are burning' she shrieked, rushing back to the blackened pork on the hob. At this the father and son shared a look, and then roared with laughter. It was a welcome island of comic comfort for the two of them, before the coming danger of the dark.

One could hardly blame Terrence for his emotional reaction, after all, for lack of a better term, the man had been through a hell of a lot of shit.

So often used as a starting point in the re-telling of the story; that bright sun-shiny day in July, when the incident had occurred, had indeed been baking warm. It hadn't begun on a 'dark and stormy' night as so often scary stories do, but in broad daylight, somehow making it all the more terrifying. It had been the kind of hot weekend that had cooked cracked egg yolks on patios, a truly sweltering day, and thus, a truly perfect Sunday for the local children to play out. Young Terrence had been no exception, and at the very moment that his Father had been carrying out his long-gestating killing spree on his mother and sister, he had been lost in a world of twig swords and shields. Being twelve years old had meant that Terrence was just on the cusp of losing the last of his 'make-belief', in exchange for girls and the *SEGA*, and so him and his school friend Charlie Macintyre had been duelling down by the Malton Brook that afternoon, making the most of their six week summer holiday. After finishing with a jousting competition in a neighbouring field that had led to Charlie being crowned the *'Lord Crusader Of The Land'*, the two had parted ways with a fond farewell and Terrence had started back home towards the farm.

His journey was longer than usual, the boy understandably favouring the shade and a slower pace under the scorching sun. He was rather looking forward to an ice-cold glass of his mother's world famous iced-tea when he returned, to help him cool off. Maybe his Dad would spray him with the garden hose too. Terrence had always pretended that he'd hated it but secretly found it to be extremely fun. On his way back he passed riders on horses, click-clocking along the road, and could hear the sweet bird song of lapwings, foraging for worms. He yawned and stretched as he passed berries that had fallen from their bushes, worn out from his playing and eager to recount the day's adventures to his parents and sister.

When he did finally make his way back to Geller Farm though, to his great surprise, his arrival was marked not by the welcoming smiles of his family, but by a slew of police cars and ambulances, gathered around the porch. What were all these officers doing outside of his home? And what was inside that funny-shaped bag that the men in white had been wheeling out of his kitchen, on that squeaky trolley? He wondered, as the police turned to notice him, walking curiously down the road. Their hearts breaking.

When Geller had murdered his wife and daughter on that uncharacteristically tropical day, he'd also ended the life of his son, whom, unbeknownst to Terrence, Marcus had been watching from the back of Cole's police car in cuffs, as the officers had struggled to tell him that his mummy and sister had been killed. Terrence was never quite the same after that.

Though the standard procedural custom in these cases, when a truly unspeakable act of violence were to have occurred on a premises, is to demolish the building, in the case of Geller farm, things had gone quite differently. In an appeal to the council tribunal, Terrence's uncle, Jack Geller, had persuaded local authorities of the public benefit of keeping the farm intact. He'd used the argument that to destroy the building would've been directly against the public interest, that the destruction would've been depriving Malton of its primary source of livestock. Seeing things his way, the authorities ruled to save the business. Jack Geller, a farmer himself in Pickering, was to oversee the running and maintenance of the farm, until young Terrence came of age and inherited it, at which point it was his to do with as he saw fit, be it selling or otherwise.

But as it happened, the farm was to remain in Terrence's possession, long after he came of age. Once he had been adequately trained by his uncle, he took over the mantle of the head of the farm himself at age twenty-six, and business resumed as per usual, the bellies of Malton fed. Make no mistake, this hadn't been a decision made on Terrence's part through some deep love of agriculture, no, rather, he had decided to stay on at the farm, because he had been too afraid to leave it.

Despite Jack Geller going above and beyond the call of duty of his 'Uncle' title, and stepping into the shoes of Marcus with all the love that he could muster, Terrence was a very, very broken boy. Jack had kept him away from the publicity and court proceedings as best he could. But Terrence refused to speak a single word until a full year had elapsed after the event, preferring instead to keep to himself and to bury his head in his work around the farm. When he finally did decide to put his voice box back to use once again, it would only ever come in the form of single words, mumbled phrases, quiet replies, and only ever when he was spoken to first. He lost weight too. Weekly therapy and child counselling sessions became a part of his routine, in a bid to help him overcome the nightmares that awoke him every night in fits of tears and screams. Jack would often overhear the lad praying in his room alone, begging the heavens above to return his family to him;

'He loved us. He loved us so much. I don't understand why he did It.' he'd repeat, over and over again.

Prone to walking alone amidst the wheat fields in his free time, no longer talking even to his closest childhood friends, Terrence isolated himself more and more. So reclusive and alone had he become, that Jack had seen it fit that the lad became home schooled. As the years rolled by, Terrence spent every one of them tethered to the farmhouse, like a dog lurking at his masters grave, until eventually his friend Charlie stopped coming round to ask him out to play at all. He was a ghost.

Marcus Geller had set his son on the course of a life-long battle with depression. As he grew into his teenage years, Terrence's pain matured with him, manifesting itself into darker thoughts and darker behaviours; drinking, driving, fighting, smoking, fucking, the way grown-ups deal with things. This wasn't your sexy, 80's, leather-jacket, bad boy-style breakdown either, there was nothing cool about it. Many a time Terrence had found himself feeling envious and resentful of his deceased mother and sister, often believing that they had in fact gotten off lightly by being shot down that day. He had been forced to die a thousand deaths, them, only one. It had made him wish that he had been killed along with them, leading to a handful of failed suicide attempts around a hangman's noose in the old barn out back. For years the same question tormented him; why? Why had his Father done what he'd done to his mother and sister? But with both parties refusing to see each other, and his Father not so much as writing a letter to the boy explaining his bloody crimes, Terrence had no hope of ever finding any answers. This only made him more lost.

If not for one thing, one precious, life-altering thing, Terence's hatred and sadness would've only continued to feed on his past, growing to potentially self-destructive levels of misery. But it was the love of a young village belle, a local barmaid by the name of Margery that had done just the trick. It had been her patience, her kindness, and her rock-solid belief in Terrence's strength to defeat the demons that had ruled his life that had saved him. Before long, the all-night drive-by's spent watching the *Full Sutton* top-floor prison cell had stopped, as did the bar fights and the drugs and the endless loathing. She had bathed him in so much love and care that Margery had been able to do the impossible, to reform and to deliver him from the sins of his father. And for that, he had put a ring on her finger.

Margery and their unborn son suddenly gave Terrence a renewed sense of purpose in life, a reason to overcome the darkness and to get sober. He vowed to put right his father's mistakes, to provide his son with the childhood that he'd wished he'd been given. Boy, would that have been a life that would've made his mother proud. He now was content with never having known why his Father had done what he did, he didn't need those answers anymore, and so he'd let them go, like caught fish back into a pond.

Terrence knew that they'd always be there though, the demons, that they'd never truly, fully go away, and that he'd probably spend the rest of life doing battle with them until he was old and grey. But that was fine. He'd come a long way from fighting Charlie Macintyre with wooden swords, he was strong enough to take them on now, his family made him strong.

Now, business on the farm was blooming, Jacob was growing up, his marriage had never been better and the terrible echoes of his past had become but a mere whisper, no longer defining him. Many a cool, summer evening would he spend drinking iced tea on his porch, looking out over the golden glades as the sky turned purple and the air perfumed with lavender. He'd find great comfort in hearing the final chime of the nearby station, announcing the last train of the day as it departed for Whitby. And it was in these peaceful moments of tranquillity, as Margery called him to bed from the pantry, that he'd think to himself; 'yeah, life is good'. His Father was gone...

...until now.

When those three knocks had awoken Terrence in his bed that morning, and he was informed that after over thirty years of incarceration that his Father had sprung himself from prison, he had just *known*. To '*just know*', the intuitive feeling in the boot of the human brain that tells us that something truly earth-shattering is about to occur. The way parents '*just know*' that something is amiss, when their children don't arrive home after school at their usual time. The way patients '*just know*' that their days are numbered after their doctors assure them that there's 'probably nothing to worry about' at their preliminary examinations.

Despite there being no immediate evidence pointing to the worst case scenario, and despite there being a myriad of far more likely, harmless explanations that should be ruled out first, for some unknown psychological reason, humans are always able to sense when tragedy has come to haunt their doors. And so, as every reasonable possibility is slowly struck off and debunked, one by one, eventually all that can remain, is the gutting, gutting truth. It was the kind of truth that only ever happened to other people, never to you. It was that death had come. And as much as you had tried to deny it, you had felt his skeletal fingers and the brush of his long black cloak, tickling the back of your neck, and had heard the sharpening of his ice cold scythe in your ears, all along.

Terrence had '*just known*' the second that he was told about Marcus Geller, that this was the end. His Father was coming, to slaughter them all. *Rub, rub*, went the hands of the ferryman, eagerly awaiting his and his families arrival onto his barge, ready to lead them across the river of the damned.

No.

No longer would his Father continue to rule his life, no longer would he let the wrathful legacy of Marcus Geller poison the ones that he loved. That creature of a man had already claimed enough of Terrence's years. He'd worked too hard for too long to give in now, and he refused to be frightened by his escape. As Margery and Jacob had gathered around him, holding him close whilst he'd cried at the kitchen table, it had summoned the strength within Terrence that he'd needed to keep the demons at bay once again. His wife had been right. The time for running was over, it was time to make a stand. The police would stop Geller senior. All would be well. Death would not come today.

Oh, how wrong he was.

'Hey kiddo, how's about you grab us a board game from off of the shelf to pass the time?' suggested Terrence.

'A board game? Dad are you kidding me?'

'Not on my watch. I haven't slaved over this breakfast just for you two to let it go cold throwing dice' said a strict Margery, picking out the burnt sausages and throwing them into the bin, sifting through and then rescuing the edible ones. She'd been sure to remove the batteries from the smoke alarm before it had gone off, that infernal noise went right through her.

'C'mon, if we're gonna be stuck here we may as well have some family time. I don't think I can bare listening to your mother drone on. Go ahead, pick a game lad, we can eat as we go along' Terrence insisted. 'Don't worry, we don't have chess, I know it's a little above your IQ'.

'Can't we stick on a movie or something?' moaned Jacob.

'A movie? Where's the competition in that? Ah, I see, afraid your old man will whip your ass, huh? You may be the king of those damn video games, but this is old-school stuff, your quick thumbs won't help you here kid' his father laughed. Jacob rose to the challenge.

'Alright, you're on. But don't come crying to me when a lad half your age beats you at your own game.' He looked over at the shelf to pick. Terrence reclined back into his chair.

'Keep talking, keep talking. It'll just make my victory all the sweeter.'

'You do realise that one day I'm going to be picking your retirement home, right? You might wanna show me a little more respect...'

'How's about we make things interesting then...?' Terrence cocked an eyebrow, '...the loser has to muck out the cow shed, for all of next week...'

'Oh you're so on, old man' teased Jacob.

'That's enough you two. There'll be no board games until after we've eaten and that's final. So here. Eat up.' The trousers of the house had spoken, placing the men's early breakfasts down in front of them.

'My cholesterol doctor won't be too happy about me eating this Marge...' flirted Terrence, as his wife dished up her own portion. She'd gone without sausages, giving the only brown ones left to her men.

'I can always replace that with a nice bowl of granola and half a grapefruit if you like...'

'And let this go to waste? That would just be plain rude' replied Terrence cheekily, already shovelling beans and scrambled egg onto the same fork.

'I wonder if those police men out there would like anything to eat?' considered Marge, 'they must be starving, working all night like this. I'll rustle them up some tea and biscuits on a tray when we're-'

'Honey! I'm home!' said a deep, thundering voice, coming from the back door. All three family members jerked around just in time to see the hulking Marcus Geller barge into the pantry, with two young kids trailing behind him, and a loaded pistol in his hand. Margery screamed at the top of her lungs, holding her hands to her cheeks, which sent her plate crashing to floor. Terrence and Jacob immediately rose to their feet.

And then the gun went off.

CHAPTER TWELVE

It was a real damn shame. Six months it had been waiting, hibernating beneath the snowfall and the frozen lakes for its time to shine. But now that April had finally rolled around, the orchid bulbs and the blossoming tulip petals and the greening ash-tree leaves, all of them had been robbed of their time in the spotlight. Spring had had its thunder stolen. The culprit? Well, there had been many. The neglectful searching policemen, a dangerous serial killer at large, two missing youngsters. And of course, the most distracting of the bunch, the ultimate offender, the rip-roaring of the revved police car engines that had rocketed down the country lanes between the *O'Nowhere* and Geller Farm. There was always next year, spring supposed.

There had been six cars in total, all driving in a straight lane, one after the other down the forested road, fronted of course, by Inspector Henry Simmons. Like good manners and polite professionalism, the speed limit had also been a nicety that had been ditched in light of the most recent development in the case. Back at the *O'Nowhere* car park, Henry, who at the time had been trying to calm the crowd of rioting guests, had received the radio call that he'd been waiting for all night.

'We've got him', the static filled voice on the other side of the line had said.

His fevered, determined eyes never left the road, as Simmons steered to the left and right towards his destination, leading the convoy behind him. A Polaroid photograph of his wife and daughter, pinned to his dashboard, violently shook as he drove. As the vehicles passed break-off lanes, more police cars joined them in their mission. The cars were filled with officers who had been stationed all across the Eastern North that night, places like Middlesbrough, Haworth, Goathland, and Pickering. All of them were banding together now to defeat their common enemy, their services no longer required in their allocated villages. By the time that Henry had finally reached Geller Farm, he'd had an army of twelve police cars behind him, racing at 75 miles per hour.

Like his father, three decades before him, Simmons rolled his car down the old, dusty road towards Marcus Geller's farmhouse. And like his Father before him, he didn't plan on leaving without the murderer in chains. As he drove, the soaring of the car engines and the combined screeching of the police sirens awoke sleeping animals; sheep, cows, horses, in the fields on either side of them. Not built for such terrain, Simmons put the pedal to the metal on his clutch to help his ride across the potholes.

'C'mon old girl' he whispered to the wheel. She only had to make it through one more mission, before he'd retire her to the depot, as he hung up his own hat up for good. He pulled into the farmyard, upending a storm of brown and grey chicken feathers into the air, and then swung open his door. The other cars did the same, and then a fleet of armed police officers exited their vehicles and formed a line around the perimeter of the building.

'Talk to me' Simmons said bluntly, to the officer who'd called in the sighting. Police-talk for; 'tell me everything'.

The officer, one of the two that had informed Terrence and his family that Marcus had escaped, filled him in.

'20 minutes ago sir. We heard a scream and then a gunshot coming from the house. We approached the building, and looked into the window. We saw....' the officers face turned white, '...we saw him sir. Geller was in there. Holding a gun'.

The air tasted of morning dew. Local news outlets had already caught wind of the commotion, and much to Simmons's irritation, were flooding the scene in white satellite vans and helicopters, each hoping for the latest scoop. 'I'm here at Geller Farm...' he overheard a reporter saying into a camera and microphone. *Vultures*.

'Was anyone hurt?' he asked.

'Not that I could see sir. From what I could tell the bullet was a warning shot. Nothing more. All five victims were fine' replied the officer.

'Five?'

'Yes sir. It's the reason we didn't breach the building and apprehend Geller straight away. We have a hostage situation sir. He's got five of them inside, at gunpoint. It's the Geller family, and the two young kids from the *O'Nowhere*, Ted and Rose'.

'How the hell did he get in there? You've been guarding the place!'

Mistaking his tone as accusatory, the officer defended himself. 'I swear sir, there's no way he could've snuck past us! We'd have seen him. He must've known another way into the farm'.

Simmons at first felt relief that the hostages hadn't been hurt, and then a bitter frustration. Of course, it had all seemed too easy, he should've known better. Geller wasn't about to surrender without a fight. Henry only prayed that he didn't plan on taking anyone down with him. The inspector grabbed the blue and white police-issue megaphone out of the hands of a nearby rookie and then spoke into it. Simmons hated the sound of his own voice, and was always the first to leave the room upon realising that a family video was being recorded. He could just about tolerate his graduation photo on the station wall. His northern nuances filled the valley, and the journalists and officers fell silent as though at a Mass, hanging on his every word.

'Marcus Geller, we have you surrounded. Come out with your hands up, and let the hostages go.'

No response.

'I said, come out with your hands up. There's nowhere for you to go now.'

He spared Marcus the 'good cop' routine.

A: Because he knew that it wouldn't have worked.

And B: Because the bastard didn't deserve it, not after what he'd done.

Still, with no reply, he gave Geller one last chance, not that he'd expected it to work.

'Come out with your hands up Marcus. We know you're in there. There's no need for this to get messy'.

He took a five minute pause, in order to give Geller enough time to surrender and to release the hostages. The entire field stood with baited breath like cricket fans at *The Ashes*. But when there was still no activity from the farmhouse, Simmons hung up the megaphone, and then handed it back to a nearby officer. He'd tried the diplomatic method, the easy way, and so now he'd have no choice but to go about things the hard way. In truth, it had always been his preferred option.

'What's the plan of action now sir? We can't just storm the place' asked an officer.

Simmons suddenly felt the weight of a hundred eyes upon him, not only from his own men, but from the local village Bobbies and constables that had volunteered to help him with the arrest in any way they could. Used to dealing with stray goats and runaway teens, these countryside officers were completely out of their depth. Their presence hadn't been necessary, no one had called upon them, and yet they'd wanted to help anyway, for their families, for the Force, for Yorkshire. Now that they were turning to him for guidance, he couldn't let them down. What would his father have done?

It was true, though they undoubtedly bested Geller in terms of numbers, using brute force to raid the farmhouse would only result in fatalities. Simmons knew that at the first sign of threat, Geller would have no qualms with putting bullets into the brains of all five of his hostages, including his own son, and then finishing himself off too. The only way to defeat Geller would be to beat him at his own game, it was time to get dirty, it was time to cheat. Thinking like an officer of the law wouldn't get them anywhere, not against a villain like him. And with this new line of inquiry in mind, Henry Simmons hatched himself a plan.

'It's clear we're not going to get through to the guy with negotiation. Talking is off the cards. But if a small task force were to sneak up to the house without him knowing...I'd bet we'd be able to take him down before he'd have chance to harm the hostages'.

The officer that Simmons had been treating as his second-in command nodded. 'How small a task force are we talking sir?' he replied, to which Simmons said;

'One man'.

The officer looked to the faces of the others, hoping to discern whether or not he had been the only one to think that the plan was lunacy.

'Sir...you can't...it's too dangerous...it's not protocol to go into these situations alone...I...'

'Don't tell me what I can and can't do. I'm in charge here. And to hell with protocol. Sometimes, the smart route isn't always the best route. I want you and the others to stay here and to keep the perimeter secure. I'm going in. I'm ending this. You're in charge while I'm away...'

'But Sir-'the officer started, but Simmons was already gone. He slipped away from the reporters and into the right-hand cow field. It was just out of eye-shot of the kitchen window, where Geller had been hauled up with his prisoners, but wide enough that it would take him right up to the house without detection, *if* he was careful enough. Crouching down, and then turning off his radio, Henry started moving slowly through the grass and soiled puddles, hugging the stone wall that separated the livestock from the road and treading stealthily as not to be seen. Disguised amongst the shrubbery, when the wall became too short, he crawled towards the farmhouse on his belly commando-style instead, dragging himself in the direction of the light in the kitchen window. The safety latch on his pistol was off. His crisp white shirt and ironed knee's soon became muddied and covered in filth, he desperately hoped it hadn't been manure. His wife was going to love him when he finally reappeared back home, head to toe in muck, treading faeces all over the rug. Henry was completely camouflaged within the bushes, and one might say, it was almost as if he had become at one with the Moors themselves. History was repeating itself, and it seemed very fitting that he be the one to march into the gates of hell alone. Simmons knew that he could never have asked any of his men to risk their lives in the same way that he was doing, it had to be him, it was always meant to be him. Whether he'd be coming back or not though, was a very different story...He got closer and closer to the farm, clawing handfuls of worms and earth with his fingernails, hoisting himself along the ground and squashing hoof prints, his shoes filling with water. He spat out mud, but accidentally swallowed some of it too.

• • •

Geller's iceberg eyes peaked out from behind the kitchen curtains. As he did, he gently fondled the lace, as if it were the dress of a lover. All those police officers just for him? He was so flattered, he didn't think they'd cared. They'd updated the uniform since they'd last arrested him, the world had moved on it seemed. He preferred the old one. Not only that though, but what a pleasant surprise to see that a very old acquaintance of sorts had been stood amongst them. He was honoured.

'Isn't that poetic? Little Henry Simmons, all grown up and in a uniform of his very own? Daddy's little star. How touching' he mused to himself.

The giant of a man turned away from the window then, towards the kitchen, and then redirected his attention with a maddening smile, back onto his artistic vision come true. Like Michelangelo admiring the ceiling of the *Sistine Chapel*, Geller revelled in the beauty of his twisted creation. Ted, Rose, Jacob, Margery and Terrence were all tied up with rope to the kitchen chairs and lined up against the wall, like lifers on death row, queuing for the gas chamber. Each of them frantically rived and struggled in an attempt to break free, but this only made their knots tighten even more. Geller hadn't bothered with gagging them, they could scream all that they liked, it wouldn't do them any good. He actually quite enjoyed it. No need for a see-through rain coat or rubber gloves here, he'd wanted their blood to rain all over him. He wanted everyone to see what he'd done. Marcus had known all along that the police would eventually catch up with him at the farm and so made no effort to mute their cries for 'HELP'. This wasn't about evading arrest anymore, this was about completing his plan, thirty five years in the making. No one was leaving that farmhouse alive.

As the little piggy's helplessly twisted and turned and the tears rolled down their cheeks, Marcus watched with great pleasure, fantasising about all the endless ways that he'd be able to inflict pain on them. The limitless methods of misery spiralled through his brain, like rollers in the hair of Liverpool girls. It was everything he'd been dreaming of, they were fodder for his demented urges. In an ideal world, he'd have wanted to *really* drag things out, to have tortured them for days and days until finally their bodies could've taken no more, their bones on show and yellow puss oozing from their infected wounds. But he knew that time was not a commodity that he had the luxury of, the police would stop him soon. Whatever he was planning on doing, he'd have to do it quick.

With a giant, size eleven foot, he took a step towards the group. They were immediately silenced, all five of them petrified of what his next dastardly move might be. He smirked an evil smirk, getting off on their panic, before opening the kitchen-side drawer and perusing the cutlery inside. The group's fears that a steak knife would be drawn proved to be false though, instead, Geller reached in and grabbed a metal fork. He then plunged it into one of the uneaten sausages that Margery Geller had so lovingly prepared, and began chewing on it slowly.

'Win a man's stomach. Win his heart. I can certainly see what Terrence here saw in you...Margery is it?' He knew her name.

'You'll have to give me your recipe, this is delicious'. Marcus savagely munched on the fry-panned meat as the group watched on in terror.

'Well, I must say you've grown up into fine man. You've definitely inherited my looks son, if I do say so myself. Not sure if I agree with what you've done with my house though...those drapes are horrendous'. Geller pointed to the curtains, they were floral, like the front of a summertime blouse.

Terrence refused to speak. He'd been a fool. If only he'd listened to his gut, it had been trying to warn him. Though Marge would've undoubtedly protested, he knew that he'd have been able to force her and his son out of the house before Geller had burst in. Now it was too late, and they were all going to pay with their lives for his complacency.

'Still a farmer eh? Well, I do suppose it's in your blood. I must say part of me is disappointed though....' continued Geller, who'd by now finished his pre-killing snack. Slashing limbs was hungry work. ....'after all, there's something so, predictable, about following in the footsteps of your Fathers profession. I mean, Henry Simmons I can understand, the kid was always a pushover. But I don't know, I guess I'd always hoped for more from you....I hoped you'd get outta' this town and do something exciting with your life. I guess you're not so different from your old man after all'.

At this Terrence growled. It was all he could do to vent his rage without verbally attacking his Dad, he knew that that would've only put his family in even more danger. But to compare the two of them, to even suggest that they were alike in anyway, it was treason of the highest order, and it warranted all the burning anger that he was feeling. Of course, Geller was toying with him, a lion with its prey.

'What's the matter? Do you not speak? I heard you talking plenty before I came in...Why the shyness now your Daddy is here?' asked Geller, faking offence. Terrence had burnt every photographic trace of his father once his uncle Jack had taken him under his wing, and as for the pictures in his head, well, he'd let the erasing hands of time take care of those for him. But seeing him now, standing in his kitchen, it was as though no gap had passed at all, and all of the memories that he'd fought so hard to eradicate had come back flooding into his brain. Of course, all of the recollections that he'd had of his Father had been happy; summer trips to the Whitby coast, piggy-backs in the fields at dusk, bad jokes that had made Mum laugh way too hard at the dinner table. But these were poisoned now, all of them ruined, like ink spilling over fresh bed sheets. Terrence knew that it had all been a lie, every second of it, and that the entire time, his father had secretly been fantasying about ripping out their insides. Margery had been right, this man was no father of his, he never had been, this man was a stranger.

'You don't see your Dad for thirty five years and you have nothing...not a single word to say to him? Not one?' pushed Geller, with no joy. He sighed to himself, he certainly hadn't *raised* a stubborn child.

'Well, in that case. If you don't want to talk...maybe I'll have better luck with your wife.' Geller lunged towards Margery with his pistol and held it to her temple, she screamed.

'Terrence make him stop! Terrence!'

'LEAVE HER ALONE' ordered Terrence, that had done the trick. He could take a lot, but to threaten his woman was too much to take. The thought of his wife in pain stabbed his heart. 'Kill me instead. Do what you want to me you fucking sick bastard. But don't you touch a hair on her head.' He spoke a big game for a man in ropes, it was the Northerner in him, fighters until the end the Yorkshire folk.

Geller found great amusement in his son's little show of bravado, as if he were a toddler that was refusing to go to bed.

'Oh, I'm sorry, am I not allowed to touch her? You should've said.' He lowered the gun, he'd held it so tightly to her skull that the funnel of the bullet chute had left an imprint on her skin. 'I guess I'll just go for the grandson instead...'

'NO!' screamed Terrence. Tears poured from his eyes as he sat powerless, watching Marcus replace one target for another, standing over Jacob with the pistol pointing at his face.

'DAD! Dad! Help me Dad!'

Jacob screamed a guttural scream. The policemen outside even heard him, each of them desperately wishing that they'd had the authority to storm down the doors.

'We have to DO something!'

'We have our orders! Simmons said stay put!' said one officer to another.

The scream was so bloodcurdling, that they'd never forget it for the rest of their lives.

Terrence shouted so hard that it hurt. 'Don't you fucking hurt him! Don't you hurt my family you fucking bastard! Don't you-'

'I'll DO WHAT I LIKE' roared Marcus, moving back to his estranged son, his eyes mad with rage. He grabbed Terrence by the collar and pulled all sixteen stone of him up into the air with a remarkable strength, even the wooden kitchen chair that he'd been tied to followed him. 'I'm in charge here. I'm your father. I made you, and I can end you if I want to. So how's about you show me some respect and stop IGNORING ME?' The murderer yelled so closely to Terrence's face that he'd been able see right down into his throat.

'Leave him alone you bully!' A fourth voice joined the scene. Marcus, surprised, turned and cocked his head. He let Terrence fall to the floor. He landed on his side still tied to the chair, marooned on the kitchen tiles. From there, he could see under all of the cupboards, where the rats liked to hide.

Geller walked slowly over to the source of the defiance. It of course, had been Rose, who despite putting on a brave face in front of the killer, was now deeply regretting what she'd said.

'Looks like you got me darlin'. You should've listened to her Ted, when she warned you about me.' Marcus lightly slapped Ted's face three times on his way to the girl, he was tied up next to Rose, and to the right of Jacob. He didn't move an inch. The entire time, Ted had been sat in silent shock, staring blankly into space.

'...but luckily for me, you ignored her. Is it any wonder though? You really are an annoying little bitch, aren't you? I've wanted to kill you ever since I first laid eyes on you. I told myself I'd save you for last, but now that you're here, with that stupid fucking face and that grating voice, I think I'll just kill you now'.

Rose was brave no more. Geller fiercely grabbed her by her long red locks and yanked back her head like she were getting the shampoo and rinse from hell, exposing the sumptuous white flesh of her neck. Bullseye. Her breathing and heartbeat reaching levels that they never had before, a single salty tear rolled down the side of her cheek as she faced upwards at the splintered rafter ceiling, her hair tugging at the roots. It was excruciating.

'Kill me then. If you're gonna kill me just do it and stop talking about it. I think we could all do with a rest from your psycho ramblings. You'd be putting me out of my misery'.

Geller hadn't liked this one bit.

'You cocky little bitch. I'm gonna rip your fucking head off and-'

'You lied.' The final of the five spoke. Ted.

'I was wondering when you were gonna pipe up' laughed Marcus, releasing Rose's crimson hair. Her head fell back forward. Terrence meanwhile, was just glad that the man hadn't been terrorising *his* family anymore, like when the school bully finally tires of you and moves onto their next nerdy victim. As cold as it had sounded, he'd barely known these kids at all. The more time that Geller spent hurting them, meant the more time that it would buy him and his family before the police came and rescued them.

'C'mon then Ted, what did you say? Speak up for the group. My hearing isn't what it used to be'. Geller perched himself on the kitchen table facing Ted, a front row seat to his latest plaything. It was a wonder that the table had been able support his weight at all, and that its wooden legs hadn't snapped beneath his muscle mass. Ted still, stared blankly into space.

'You lied to me....' he whispered. Rose looked at him, not feeling irritation that he hadn't listened to her, just, sorry, so, so sorry.

'About...' encouraged Marcus, gesturing for 'more' with his hand, the one not holding a gun.

'Everything. About being innocent...'

'Correct.'

'About having cancer.'

'Also correct.'

'About wanting to see your family one last time.'

'You're on a roll here' Geller smiled. Ted looked up then, straight into Marcus's deep, blue eyes.

'I trusted you', he said, so full of hurt and betrayal. 'You were supposed to be like me...all you wanted was to see your son again, like all I wanted was my Dad. I thought...'

'...you thought what? That I "understood" you?' mocked Marcus. 'Please. I used you Ted. And you were so obsessed with finding that precious Daddy of yours that it was like taking candy from a baby'.

It was Ted's turn to cry now. Tears raced each other down his face. What had he done?

Geller hopped off the table, the whole room seemed to shake when he did. He was still wearing Steven Brooks's boots. A perfect fit. Ted had forgotten to ask about him and Simon Berkeley, perhaps that had been for the best. If everything else that Marcus had said had been a lie, then there was an uncomfortably large possibility that what he'd said about them would've been too. Maybe they weren't safe and sound like he'd promised...

'...say Ted.'

'Yeah?'

'...how long did you say it had been since you'd last seen your father?'

'I don't see what that has to do with-'

'Just answer the question.' Geller could switch between 'cult leader'-charming and then terrifying seamlessly, at the drop of a hat. He'd often used such a skill whilst in prison to win over the guards, the resulting perks had made his life there slightly less unbearable. Extra food. Longer breaks.

There was a pause, before Ted replied.

'11 years.'

Geller nodded. 'Wow that is a long time. I guess you probably don't remember what he looks like too well, do ya?'

'Where are you going with this?' Ted replied, growing tired of his games. He could scarcely believe that there had been a time not long ago in the sewers beneath the *O'Nowhere* when he'd admired the man, even looked up to him. Now he found him to be positively repulsive. Maybe the stench fumes had polluted his brain, but now his sinuses were all too clear.

'...well...I'm just saying if you don't remember exactly what your Father looks like, I suppose in theory you might not even recognise him if you were to pass him on the street. Maybe, just maybe, he's a little bit closer than you first thought...Teddy boy'.

Geller leaned in close, smiling a satanic smile, an evil glint fixed in his eye.

Ted's heart plummeted like a snapped elevator wire. No. Surely not? He couldn't be. It didn't make any sense. The timelines were all wrong. And yet, it seemed like the sort of strange and shocking and heart-breaking twist that could been true. Now that he'd mentioned it, he did see a slight resemblance... No. That was crazy! This whole thing was crazy! Ted began involuntarily shaking his head, as if trying to rid his scalp of a blood thirsty mosquito that had latched its fangs into his bloodstream. But it wouldn't let him go. It couldn't be true, it just couldn't. It-

'Ted. It's me. I'm your Dad.'

A true *Darth Vader* moment. Silence.

Suddenly, Geller burst into hysterics, leaning on the kitchen table to stop himself from falling to the ground. Rose and Ted exchanged an incredibly puzzled look.

'You should've seen your face...' laughed Geller maniacally. 'You actually believed me. You're even more gullible than I thought you were, kid'. Marcus then proceeded to smack Ted around the jaw with the barrel of his pistol. Blood ejaculated from his mouth, flying all over Margery's clean upholstery, along with a back tooth that landed inside of an empty dog bowl.

'TED!' screamed Rose, her arms straining to hold him, but her ropes having other ideas.

'I'm afraid Terrence is my only son Ted. Looks like you'll never be seeing that Daddy of yours after all....' Ted had been in too much pain to hear him. The rope had been the only thing to keep his limp body from collapsing to the ground. His neck slumped to side as if his vertebrates had been removed and all that remained was skin. Blood and saliva trickled from out of his mouth and seeped between the cracks in the floorboards, into the basement that they'd used to sneak in. Another bruise for Ted's collection, the night had not been kind to him.

The first blow had been dealt. But Marcus was just warming up.

It was at this point that Henry had emerged from the swampy fields outside the farm, like the *Creature from the Black Lagoon*. Although, you'd have been hard pressed to have recognised the man. He was caked from head to toe in mud, smothered in brown muck and filth from wriggling through the undergrowth. That aside, his plan had worked, he was directly outside the kitchen window. He lifted himself to his feet, and like a cheesy American FBI agent, threw his back against the wall of the farm beside the window. He drew his gun. Unlike an FBI agent though, he was well aware that his firearm should've only ever been used in extreme last resorts. The UK police department weren't nearly as lenient as the cops across the pond. But with retirement looming, and the threat of him losing his badge no longer carrying any weight, Henry told himself that if it were a choice between saving the hostages and shooting Marcus, then the former would come up trumps.

He peered in through the window, and his worst fears were confirmed. Inside he saw the stupendously huge figure of Marcus Geller; his long greying black hair, his silvery bushy beard, and of course, his signature albino eyes. He was pacing back and forth in front of the hostages, who were tied tightly to the kitchen chairs like damsels to train tracks. From what Henry could gather, Terrence had been knocked to the floor, and the boy, Ted, he'd been the first to experience Geller's fetish for violence. He was bleeding heavily from the mouth.

Though Henry had made a pact with himself, many moons ago, never to let his personal feelings interfere with a case, this deal had become immediately very difficult to honour when confronted by Marcus Geller in the flesh. It was him. It was actually him. It was the man that had ended his father's career. He'd only ever heard about him in stories, and now here was, completely unaware that Simmons was right behind him. Henry had the perfect opportunity to avenge all of the lives that he'd ruined, all it would take was...

...No. As much as he'd wanted to put a bullet through the kitchen window there and then, he knew that he couldn't. That wasn't him. That was how *they* thought, the ones that Henry went after, not he. Geller was going to rot in prison like he deserved. To kill him would've been sinking to his level, no better than the backwards thinking Americans who still lobbied for the death penalty. And so Henry waited patiently, for the perfect moment, the perfect opportunity to smash through the glass and to arrest Geller without anybody getting hurt in the process.

The air was quiet and cold outside. The dried mud made his chin itch.

Back inside, Marcus ran the front of his gun along the hanging pots and pans, they made ugly metal sounds in different pitches, like a twisted xylophone. Then, after eyeing up the butchers knife on the kitchen side that Margery would often use to prepare lamb, he took it by the hilt and then stared into his reflection on the blade.

'Why?' asked Ted suddenly. The cavity in his mouth where his tooth had been was agony, his cheek had already begun to swell from the thwack. At this point, even his bruises had bruises. He pictured his mother identifying his terribly mutilated body at the morgue, she'd hardly recognise him anymore. He wished he'd called her. He wished he'd never tried to find his Dad.

'Why, what?' replied Geller.

'Why? Why did you kill your family?'

Geller sighed and rolled his eyes. 'Oh please, Ted. Let me guess, you're trying to "relate" to me? Understand me? If you're thinking of trying the whole; "you're a good person, you don't have to do this" routine it won't work.'

'No games. I just...I want to know why'. Talking was hard and painful, Teds mouth could barely open. Though Marcus pretended to be irritated by Ted's interrogation, deep down, the showman in him could hardly resist the temptation to reveal the truth, his story.

'Fine. If it'll make you shut up...I'll tell you why. Besides, you're all going to die soon anyway.' He paced the room, the pistol in one hand, the butcher's knife in the other. 'I know Terrence over here is probably curious to know too. Well, let's just say, your mother and my daughter weren't exactly my first rodeo son...

...I'd killed before'

The ears of the group stood to attention. Outside Simmons watched on, the sound from the room was muted by the glass. The revelation was to be their little secret. What happens between a murderer and their victims, of course, is always meant stay between them. It's a special sort of bond, those final few moments of life, only ever to be recounted in law reports, books and movies, but never truly known.

'...1978. What a year. You're probably all too young to remember this. I'm showing my age here, aren't I? There were a string of disappearances around the Scarborough area between May and June. Three women, all prostitutes. All of them were found dead and naked, floating in the sea beneath the cliffs. In fact, that's not quite true, one had washed up onto the shore and was spotted in the early hours of the morning, by a photographer who'd been hoping to capture the sunrise across the beach. Well, I've never told anyone this before...but I take great pride in telling you that that had been my work. I killed those women. Now, don't you go thinking that there was some kind of sexual motive. I'm not some dirty pervert. I never laid a finger on those women...well...I mean I did, but you know what I mean. I didn't rape them. It's just, prostitutes are so easy, aren't they? Easy to lure away into the darkness, where nobody knows where they're going. Yes Terrence, 1978, your maths is correct, that was the year that I was arrested. Which means I'd killed those lovely young women, and then returned home to you, your mother and your sister, acting like nothing had happened at all. I used to tell Mary Jane that I'd been out late, meeting prospective cattle buyers.'

Marcus circled the room like a Shakespearean actor delivering a soliloquy. *Hamlet*, or perhaps *Richard III*. Two plays Rose had seen live, performed at *The Globe Theatre* on the Thames. He continued, the five prisoners listening with contempt.

'Now, I must confess I did tell Teddy boy over here a slight porky not long ago. I told him that Mary Jane had been out on that hot, sunny, July morning, at the farmers market, shopping for strawberry scone jam. My favourite. I also told him that Elsie, my daughter, had been playing in the fields just outside of the farm. Not true. Both of them had been at home. Mary Jane had had the unfortunate luck of cleaning out my office that day, when she'd noticed a loose floorboard beneath my desk. My office was where I'd taken care of the farms paperwork, ordering goods and such. The nosy little bitch just couldn't resist looking...'

Geller clenched his fists around both weapons then, they turned his knuckles white.

'...I was going to burn the clothes...get rid of them when I'd had the chance. I didn't think she'd find them, all bloody and smelling of whore perfume like they do. She came straight to me and demanded answers. The poor little bitch looked terrified. Even right up until the end, she'd never have suspected that I'd have had anything to do with it, she'd thought that it had been one of the farmhands, up to no good. I sat her and Elsie down at the kitchen table and said that I'd be right back once I'd called the police. But instead, as we know, I came back with a shotgun.'

Terrence winced and shut his eyes.

Margery mouthed 'it's okay, honey', over and over to him.

'Aw. What's the matter Terrence? Story a little too scary for you? It was her fault. She's the one who got herself and Elsie killed. If she'd have just kept her nose out of my business, I'd have been able to carry on

309

killing and everything would've carried on as normal. Let's be clear. I didn't kill her to keep her quiet. That wouldn't have made any sense. I shot her and my daughter because they'd ruined everything, ruined my killing spree before it had really gotten going. I was just getting started. Oh, and Terrence? When the police had broken into the farm that morning, and found me sat at the kitchen table covered in blood...I'd been waiting for you son...to get back from playing with Charlie Macintyre. So I could end you too.'

His speech done, Geller felt a twinge of regret that his story would never leave the farms walls. He was denying himself the notoriety by not allowing at least one of the hostages to go free, and to spread the evil word of his legacy, like a door to door Satanic Bible salesman. Alas though, the overpowering pull inside of him to kill was too powerful to tame, like a fat kid eating crisps. Once he began slaughtering his prisoners, he'd never have been able to stop at four.

Margery spat at the madman, her saliva missed by quite a mile. 'You deserve to burn in hell'.

'You're no Father of mine', Terrence joined his wife's side.

'You're a monster!' shouted Rose, ever the brave one.

At this though, Marcus appeared flattered. 'Yes! Bravo Rose! You're exactly right. I am a monster. A real big bad monster. Rotten to the core. I suppose you're all wondering why it is I kill? Well, I hate to break it to you folks....but I'm not mentally disturbed. I didn't hurt animals when I was young. My uncle didn't touch me in the closet. The brutal, honest truth is that I just like killing. People like you, the media, they like to label things, to come up with all these explanations as to why people like me are the way they are. But the harsh reality is, is that some people are just born to be evil. They could've had the best upbringing in the world, been raised by the kindest of the kind, and yet they'd still end up like me. Since the moment I left the womb, it's been my destiny, my purpose is to kill.'

Geller moved in front of the round bullet hole in the back wall that had appeared from his warning shot, a single beam of morning light had been shining through it. 'We're a dying breed, us serial killers. We can't survive in today's modern climate, what with technology having come as far as it has. We all get caught before we've had a chance to fulfil our true potential. But make no mistake, people like me, they're out there, lying dormant, waiting to attack. I'm under no illusion, I know this is my last night on earth. But I take great pleasure in leaving it, knowing that even after I'm gone, another will take my place, that mankind will never defeat the evil. We are everywhere. We-'

'Oh shut up you nut-job'

That did it.

'You're deranged. Not part of some movement. You're just a sick and twisted old man with a grudge against the world. There's nothing special about you. Freak'. If Rose was for the chop, she'd figured that she'd at least wanted to die being true to herself. Aka: *a loud mouthed bullshit detector.*

Furious, Geller left his gun on the counter-top and then wrapped a massive hand around the young woman's throat. It was tiny to him, and he could almost meet his thumb and his finger at the base of her skull. He was about to spread the red of her hair to her entire body.

'You're right. No more talking. You go first. Bitch.'

As Margery and Jacob and Terrence and Ted all screamed 'NO!' Marcus raised his butcher's knife. He was seconds away from slicing a deep line right through Rose's pretty face, when he suddenly stopped. It was as though someone had paused the shower scene from *Psycho*, the blade in mid-air and the infamous string arrangement halted. 'No, this is too good for you. I'm going to find something else...'

At this, Geller threw the meat cleaver to the floor, kicked it aside, and then left the room in search of a superior death bringer. The five were alone.

Immediately, the group all began working their way out of their restraints. Terrence tried in vain to slide himself along the floor, moving towards the dropped meat cleaver that had landed beneath the sink. Jacob gnawed at his ropes like a rabbit whilst Rose wriggled erratically in the hopes that her knots might come undone. Margery meanwhile attempted to hop her chair across the room to reach the pistol on the work surface, although one could've argued that without the use of her arms or hands that reaching the gun would've been useless anyway. We should cut the old girl some slack though, one often doesn't think coherently when kidnapped by a serial killer.

Marcus had inadvertently knocked shut the kitchen curtain when he'd been ranting, and so Henry, who had been waiting outside the entire time, could no longer see into the room at all. If he *had* have been able to, he'd have noticed that Geller had left the kitchen and that this had been the perfect opportunity for him to smash open the window, to untie the hostages, and to end the entire bloody affair. But going in blind was just too much of a risk, and so he remained stationed outside, desperately hoping that he wasn't too late the save them. Henry had decided though, that if he'd heard the sounds of screaming one more time, then he'd have jumped through the glass, regardless of what was waiting for him on the other side. The time for playing it safe was over. A leap of faith.

Back inside, the only one of the bunch who hadn't been trying to seize the golden opportunity, was Ted, who all the while sat still, silent and motionless.

'Ted. Don't just sit there...' snapped Rose, '...do something. Try and break free! He'll be back any minute!'

'...there's no point Rose. It's over.' Ted replied hopelessly, as the sounds of Marcus's ransacking began in the room next door.

'Ted. This isn't the time for giving up. It only takes one of us to break free and we stand a chance against him! I think my knots are loosening a little.'

'This is all my fault' Ted said introspectively, his eyes welling with tears, not from fear of death, but from crushing guilt.

'Ted, stop feeling sorry for yourself and-'

'Rose I'm so sorry', he looked at her then, and she at him. The boy had something to make peace with before he faced the end.

'You're right. You were right about everything. I am coward. I am lost. At the first sign of any commitment I just run away like a baby. I just jump from one thing to another, without ever settling on anything meaningful. That's why I ran away from my mom, from university, why I've been romanticising Whitby and why I've been so obsessed with finding my Dad. When I couldn't reach him, I just replaced *that* diversion with freeing Marcus instead. That's all this mission to get to Robin Hoods Bay has ever been, just one big diversion. Anything, I'll do anything I can do to keep myself distracted, anything to stop myself from standing still with my thoughts, because I know if I do that, I'll just start thinking about what a colossal fuck-up I am and I won't be able to stop. I'll have no choice but to confront the truth, that I have absolutely no idea what I'm supposed to be doing with my life. And that scares the hell out of me...'

Rose stopped struggling with her bonds and gave Ted her full attention.

'...and now, because of me, because of how headstrong and arrogant I was, because I wouldn't listen to you, everyone is going to die. If it hadn't been for me, Geller would never have gotten out, Smithy would still be alive, and none of us would be in this mess in the first place. I'm so sorry Rose. I'm not struggling, because unlike you, all of you here, I actually deserve to die for the way I've acted. Let him kill me, it's no more then I deserve'.

The trashing din that had been coming from a room upstairs on the farms second level suddenly ceased to be, Marcus had found what he had been looking for. And as none of the hostages had managed to escape, they all readied themselves for the coming slaughter, as the heavy, slow sounds of Marcus's boots coming down the wooden stairs began to grow closer and closer.

'Well, Ted', began Rose, 'if you deserve to die. Then I do too.'

 'Look, I appreciate what you're doing but-'

'Shut up. This is my turn to speak' she said quickly, realising that she hadn't much time left to say something that Ted desperately needed to hear.

Thud. Thud. Thud. He was coming.

'The fact is, I could've walked away from all of this, back when you'd first told me about Marcus and your plan to break him free, by the lockers. But I chose to come back, I chose to come back Ted, because...because I don't want to be an actor anymore, I haven't for a long time. Which means I'm just as adrift as you are. We all are. But you know what? That's okay. Everyone finds their path in the end, it's the being lost that helps you find it. It's okay to be lost.'

Rose then, performed quite possibly the single greatest act of rebellion that she could've mustered in the face of such darkness, she smiled. Thinking she were about to die, she'd chosen to spend her final ounce of strength not trying to escape, but easing Ted's conscience. Ted smiled back.

'Catholic's in love, right Rose?' he whispered, as the door creaked open.

'That's right Ted. Catholic's in love.'

Character revelations aside though, it didn't change the fact that Marcus had returned to the kitchen, and was finally ready to complete his plan. He stepped back into the room, with a weapon that had made his meat cleaver look like child safety scissors. He was wielding a giant fire axe in both of his hands.

'That's more like it!' announced Geller, marching towards the prisoners. Terence had often used the axe to cut wood during the biting cold of winter, he could never have foreseen that one day it would've been the tool with which his family would be murdered. The group all spiritually held hands in solidarity, realising that there was nothing more that they could do. They were like village locals, protesting against the demolition of a landmark building, standing synergistically against the spade of the oncoming bulldozer.

'Now, where were we Rose?' asked an extremely excited Geller, raising his weapon of choice.

'Rose!' yelled Ted.

But the fiery-haired coffee shop girl just turned to him and said, 'Ted. It's okay. It'll be okay.'

The axe came higher and higher over and behind Geller's head, ready and primed to swing right into Rose's face. He wound his throwing arms back as far as they could go in order to ensure maximum disfigurement of her mouth, nose, eyes and skin. He planned to carve up her face and then to hold a mirror up to her eyes so that she could she just how grotesque she looked, before finishing her off completely.

'God, I've missed this' said Geller, in an almost sexually aroused manner.

Rose closed her eyes and....

Everything went black. Oh. Well, that hadn't hurt nearly as much as she'd thought it would. In fact, it was almost as if she hadn't be caved in the face at all. At least it had been quick. So, this was what death felt like? She supposed that she'd arrived into the afterlife, and that if she were to have opened her eyes, she'd have been greeted at the ivory gates of heaven by Saint. Peter. Forests of candy floss and rivers of chocolate and fluffy white gowns galore. She wondered if old Mr. Nicolson, her nice neighbour who'd died only a few months ago, might be around. But when she did unclench her lids, she was rather disappointed to find that Geller was still standing over her. Not only that, but that Ted was still sat to her left, tied up, along with Margery, Jacob, and finally, Terrence on the floor. The only difference was, was that now an unexpected sixth member of the party had joined the fray. It was a man, standing by the door, a man that went by the name of Billy. And Billy had a gun.

The silence hung in the air like a severed telephone cord. The thin, wiry Billy looked daft holding the gun, having clearly never handled a firearm before. But those perhaps are the most dangerous kinds of people, the inexperienced. Ever resourceful, something often overlooked on account of his creepiness, Billy had trailed Geller, Rose and Ted through the secret passages of the Moor forests, ever since he'd darted from the scene of Smithy's demise at the foot of the *O'Nowhere* hill. His low body weight of course had made him light on his feet, meaning that he'd been able to follow the threesome through the woods, the basement tunnel, and into the house without detection, where he'd sat by the kitchen door, and eavesdropped on every word of Geller's dreadful tale. And now, though it had seemed like the weight of it were about to have snapped his twiggy arm, he had snagged Geller's pistol from off of the kitchen side, and was pointing it right at him.

'D-D-Don't move' he said nervously, sweat dripping from his forehead, making his face shine. His usually slicked-back hair had fallen forward. Geller though, much to Ted and Rose's surprise, didn't look panicked at all. Instead he seemed pleased, joyous even, about the janitor's impromptu arrival.

'Brother?!' he asked hopefully.

'W-W-What?' stammered Billy.

'You're...you're one us, aren't you? Yes...You're just like me.'

Billy, who's sweaty finger slid on the trigger, was extremely confused, an emotion that when added to terror, made for one hell of a deadly combination.

'What the hell are you talking about? I said...I-I said don't move. Or I'll shoot you!'

'You're not going to shoot me...' Marcus replied smugly.

'Yeah? What-what-w-what makes you so sure about that?'

Geller's signature *Grinch*-like smile filled his cheeks, his hypnotic blue eyes never left Billy's.

'...because you're a killer just like me. You may not have done it yet, murdered someone, but it's inside of you, waiting, yearning for blood. I can see it in your eyes...Billy is it? You're fucked off with the world. You've been spat on and trodden into the ground for all of your life. Society doesn't give a damn about us, we're the outcasts, left to fend for ourselves on the outskirts. It's enough to make a man go insane, isn't it?'

Billy nodded slowly, the straightness of his gun-holding arm weakening.

'I know what it's like Billy, to have a rage burn inside of you, a rage so strong that it almost kills you. Well, a rage like that needs to be released, it needs to be set free. C'mon, haven't you ever wanted to make all those people pay? All those people who've laughed at you and made fun of you and put you down? The same people who seem to have everything while you have nothing? It doesn't seem fair, does it? They deserve to die'. Marcus dug his claws into Billy's psyche, manipulating him in the same way that he had done to Ted back in the sewers.

'...don't kill me Billy. I'm the only person who understands you. I'm a friend. Help me, help me to finish what I've come here to do, see how good it feels to get your own back.'

'Billy don't listen to him!' reasoned Ted.

'Shut the fuck up, prick' Billy ordered, silencing the prisoner by pointing the gun to his head, taking its sights off Marcus.

'Billy please! You're not a killer, you're a good person' Rose said next, desperately appealing to his sense of humanity, *if* he had any left.

'You can shut up n'all!' Billy aimed the gun at her then too.

'Ah, I see there's some bad blood amongst the three of you...' Geller laughed. 'Let me guess. She's not interested in you, right?'

Hearing it again only resurrected the resentment that Billy had felt towards Rose and Ted. The gun wobbled in his hands with anger, as if struggling to contain the limitless fury inside of him, a fury that could've quite easily been released like an orgasm by pulling on the trigger. It had been building and building for so, so long now, the hatred, boy would it have felt good just have to let it all go. All he'd have to do was click.

'What's Ted got that you haven't? What's so great about that kid? I say you finish them both off, make them pay for what they did' taunted the killer, shooting the pair a sideward glance and winking. Geller was never usually one to deprive himself of the pleasure of taking a life, but he'd won big with Billy, convincing and manipulating someone else into doing it for him would be even more gratifying. Besides, as soon as he'd shot the pair, he'd plunge his axe straight into the caretakers stomach anyway, and so he was only really missing out on killing one of his prisoners that night. He was a parasite, feeding off hatred, and Billy was a banquet.

'You broke my heart Rose!' Billy cried, tears streaming down his cheeks and mingling with his sweat.

'Here, let me show you how it's done' Geller propped up the butt of his axe's handle then, and began smacking Rose and Ted around the face with it, interchanging between the two of them. 'See, look how easy it is! I'm warming them up for you Billy boy! All you need to do is squeeze'.

'STOP!' begged Jacob and Margery. But it did no good, Geller beat the two of them to a pulp, all the while relentlessly seducing Billy into emptying his rounds.

'Don't let me have all the fun kid, they'll be dead soon if you don't hurry up! Make them pay for what they did to you!'

'Billy!! Please!! Stop him!! He's killing us!!' Rose wailed in-between blows, as blood exploded from her nostrils and her feet tensed in agony. Ted had been beaten so badly by now that he hadn't even had the strength to say anything at all, he just took the strikes, one after another, the bright white light of death getting closer and closer.

Though Rose had rejected him, and had torn out his heart and had stamped all over it in front of everybody at the *O'Nowhere*, it hadn't changed the fact that she had always been nice to Billy up until that point. When Billy had been alone, she'd always been the one to talk to him, to tell her about her day and to ask him about his, sometimes bringing him a free coffee on the days that she could tell that he'd been particularly down. When the others had made fun of him at work, she'd always been the one to ward them off, and to tell him to ignore them and that he wasn't a 'freak' or a 'weirdo' or any of those other names that they'd called him every single day. And though she'd categorically stated that she had no interest in taking their friendship further, something that he'd so desperately longed for, it hadn't changed how he felt about her. She was the love of his life, something he couldn't just switch off. And so, seeing someone that he cared for so deeply, deeper than he ever thought possible, being hurt so badly and begging for his help, it tore him up inside.

Why didn't it feel good? He should've hated Rose for what she'd done to him, despised her guts and wanted her to burn in hell. But he didn't. He loved her, and though he was as experienced with girls as he had been with handling Geller's gun, Billy knew that you didn't let the people you loved get hurt, even when they'd hurt you.

'Billy please. This isn't you!!' she screamed as the axe handle collided with her jaw.

'My arms getting tired here Billy. Don't be the weakling everybody thinks you are! Prove them wrong! Shoot them' said Marcus.

Ted too, Billy thought. Make no mistake, he hated the guy, loathed his guts. The pretty-boy prick had robbed him of his one chance at happiness, the only woman that he'd ever truly cared about, and thus, had become a symbolic amalgamation of everything that had ever gone wrong in his life. But despite this, seeing him beaten and bloodied at the hands of Marcus, it didn't feel satisfying in the slightest, not in the way that he'd thought it would. It actually made him feel rather sorry for Ted, feelings he'd never thought he'd feel.

'I don't know what to do...'

'*Shoot him.*'

'Wait, Mum? Is that you?'

'*Yes Billy. It's your Mother. I'm here*', the husky northern voice said in his ear.

'What? How is this possible? You're supposed to be at home...this doesn't make any sense.'

'I'm here Billy. I'm always here. No matter where you go or who you're with, I'll always be here, ruling your life. Even when I'm dead and gone and buried and the maggots are eating the flesh from my bones, I'll be in your head, until the day you die, and join me in hell.'

The entire room seemed to slowdown, Marcus's swipes and Rose's cries and Ted's jolts halving in speed. All that remained was Billy, Billy and the voice.

'No. You're wrong. I don't need you anymore Mum. I don't want you.'

'Pull the trigger Billy.'

'I don't want to. It's wrong.'

'Pull it. Don't be a pussy. You've been one all your life. When are you finally going to man up and do something for once? You're just like your Father, gutless, you'll always be gutless. You'll always be a nobody and continue to let everybody walk all over you unless you pull that trigger!!'

Her voice had been the same one that had come through the phone. Though it was upsetting and spine tingling to hear face to face, something about the static filled airwaves of the telephone connection had made it sound even more terrifying.

'Do it.'

'I don't want to Mum, I don't want to be that man. Rose is right. This isn't me. This is wrong, this is...'

'*Do it!*' The voice no longer even sounded like that of his Mother's, it was deep and pitched well below that of any humans. It sounded demonic, evil.

'No!'

'*Give in, become the killer you've always been meant to be. Or am I going to have to send you back up to the attic again?*'

'No. Please Mum. Anything but there!'

'*Do it.*'

'I WON'T'!'

'*DO IT!!!!!!!!!*'

Simmons smashed through the kitchen window, unable to wait any longer. He crashed into the room just in time to witness the gun going off.

Bang.

CHAPTER THIRTEEN

The orange dawn peeked over the hillside from across the bay. It was its windows that did it, their arches. The shape of them worked in tandem with the sunlight to create the illusion of two glowing blood-red eyes in the windows of the old, ruined abbey. Once a former monastery, undergoing extensive rebuilds as it passed through the hands of various Christian sects, the windows now stood empty of their stain glass designs, leaving the invading sunrays free to occupy their stony sockets. From the wooden bench outside the *Royal Hotel*, just opposite the *Khyber Pass*, one had had a perfect view of this eerily uncanny phenomenon. And it was here that Bram Stoker had sat, and it was this view that had given way to the creation of his 19th century gothic masterpiece, *Dracula*, all those years ago, as he'd desperately clambered for writing inspiration in the early hours of the chilly seaside mornings. Of course, he'd gotten quite a wet bottom in the process, on account of the morning dew. But he didn't mind.

The sunrise gently stroked the grave stones in the cemetery just outside the abbey, by St. Mary's Church. It pulled back the cool shadows like sheets over furniture to reveal the epitaphs of bygone sailors, buried close to the sea in the hopes that their souls might've been carried back outwards to the blue, where they'd spent most of their lives. Sea-legs weren't meant for soil. Now overcrowded, fresh grave plots weren't ever dug out in the yard anymore. Incense burned inside the pews. The church bell above peeled to signify the beginning of a brand new day in Whitby.

Returning to the bench though, just a mere fifty yards away, stood the infamous Whitby whale bones. Two giant ivory replicas of the mammals jaw, they formed a doorway overlooking the harbour. They guided tourists, once they'd taken their holiday photos, down a twisting ramp that led to the arcades and gift shops and ice cream parlours. A Captain Cook memorial too, presided over the West Cliff. In the early morning hours, as we so find ourselves, eager eyed seagulls circled his bronze lapels, ready to deposit their droppings all over his self-assured pose, only for the pavilion caretaker to have scrubbed him clean once the day was done again. A collection of scrolled sea charters beneath his arm, the statute immortalised Cook looking out to sea. He appeared confident and bold in his ventures to conquer the new world, free from the deadly foresight that Hawaiian tribesmen would eventually end his quest in blood. The morning sunrise too, revealed his determined glare, knee-high boots n all', for all the world to see.

Whitby was waking up.

In his long black coat, cane and top hat, the town's resident tour guide wrote in chalk on a blackboard beside the bones. It read;

'Assemble here for the Ghost Walk. 7:30pm. £5 per head'

A retired doctor, the elderly man had carved out quite the niche for himself and his grandkids, regularly hosting the tours two to three times a week. It was free from cheap thrills and pop-out goons in costumes, the doctor relied solely on his passion and knowledge for Whitby's spooky history to draw in custom. He'd guide tourists down the cobbled streets of West Cliff as he recounted disturbing stories from their past. The translucent apparition of a lighthouse attendant who'd suffered a heart attack on the steps of the pier, a small bakers daughter who'd ran screaming through the streets as her golden blonde hair had gone up in flames, the creaking footsteps of a wandering Dutchman who'd hung himself after going bankrupt, when his attempts to introduce Denmark architecture to the town had fallen flat. Each of these were favourites within his repertoire, they were met with both nervous laughs and private gulps from the crowds when his deep, monotone voice described them. One would think that years of telling the same stories over and over again would've worn thin on the pensioner, but in fact quite the opposite had been true. So passionate was he about the history of Whitby that he never grew tired of sharing the macabre fables. At sixty-five, he still felt as excited about his tours as he had been when he'd first begun them, continually searching for new ways to make them better, more terrifying. The man wanted everyone to share in his love for his home. But was he a believer? Or just a cheap peddler of follies? It was a question that would often arise in the final moments of the tour, when he'd invite the guests to take part in a supernatural Q&A. The answer was always the same;

'You bet your sweet ass I believe. After all, how could I not? I've seen the ghosts myself'.

He took in the cold morning air like a smoker takes in a cigarette.

'It's going to be a good day' he mumbled to himself, adopting a pose of pride as he looked out to the choppy seas, a pose not too dissimilar to that of the Captain Cook memorial standing behind him.

The ghost man wasn't the only of Whitby's businesses stirring into life that morning. On the cliffs that overlooked the Western beach, the staff of *Clara's Cafe* were removing the covers from their freezers, showing off an array of colourful crystallised ice creams; mint, strawberry, and caramel. A little further down, the projectionist at the *Whitby Pavilion* carefully handled film reel inside of the back room of the cinema, testing out the week's releases ahead of their premieres; a family film, a blockbuster and an obscure indie.

Up the road, amidst the never ending maze of terracotta-roofed B&B's, each one proudly displaying their *TripAdvisor* star reviews in the front windows of their dining rooms, *Botham's Bakery* too, was prepping itself for the day that lay ahead. It's all-female team, with their hair done up, their tucked-in white shirts and black aprons wound tightly around their waists, each played their part in readying the shop. They squirted cream into flaky pastries, they lightly sprinkled flour over warm doughy treats, and they removed jam scones (*a snack for which they were renowned*) from the oven and placed them one at a time into the front window displays, beside the children's cookies and cakes and iced fingers. They had been lifted straight from the set of a period drama. Yum!

Around the corner, on the aptly named Flower-Gate Street, the *Whitby Deli* had also prepared its breakfast menu. The staff buttered fresh sandwiches and plumped up packets of larger flavoured crisps. On the back shelves stood bottles of ale from the *Brewery*; 'Abbey Blonde',

'Whitby Whaler', 'Jet Black', each one containing no less than 4% alcohol. They were a noticeable product amongst all of the independent vendors. The multi pack of three was a particular best-seller for the *Deli*. One might think that the sandwich store and the bakery would've been rivals. But this was not true at all, each shop knew their place, and every shop supported each other.

The charity stores arranged their musky leather jackets into size order, the Jet jewellers dusted down their high-priced necklaces and bracelets, and the bookshop, with its spiralling staircase and postcards, watched on, as its keepers arranged the promotional stand for the week's brand new release. It was a book of poetry about bumble bees; the store had capitalised on this by offering honey-scented candles and stuffed toys, free with every purchase. The candles had been supplied courtesy of the *handmade soap shop* next door.

The entire town smelt of hot fish and chips, as if its buildings had been fried and battered along with the potatoes. The salty sea air seasoned its places and people.

Whitby was waking up.

The rusted drawbridge that had connected the shops and restaurants on the Western side of the bay, with the shops and restaurants on the Eastern side of the bay, parted with a heaving grind of its cogs, allowing the cargo vessels safe passage to sail through and to leave the estuary. On and on they'd chug towards the unreachable distance with their goods, until they had become nothing more than dim, grey specks, balancing on the line of the horizon like tightrope walkers. Locals paused for them to go. They were in no rush. The waters were kind that morning, calm and forgiving, perfect sailing weather. But as the signs around the pier forewarned; '*Do NOT swim in the sea*', and as the Yorkshire-dwellers had known full well, the Whitby waves had been more than capable of brewing up a ruckus when they'd wanted to.

Fun fact. Did you know that Whitby's port is the only coastal point in the whole of England that allows for a direct, unobstructed sailing route to Antarctica? It's true. One could, in theory, though heaven knows why any fool would do so, embark from Whitby harbour, and, travelling in a dead-straight line, reach the Polar icecaps without ever having encountered any other land at all.

It was perhaps this glacial link, to which Whitby owed the presence of its ferocious, sporadic storms. Freak tempests would often plague the town, beginning as foreboding, dark, and rumbling skies before erupting into typhoons that would shake it as though it were inside of a snow globe. The wind would scream and howl, tearing out great stone chunks from off of the cliff faces and upturning fudge-shop signs, whilst children and parents alike would cower inside of their locked houses. The ocean would contort itself into wild, liquefied shapes; fists, spears, and stallions, kicking legs, all of them slamming and smashing and charging into the Whitby coastline, demanding to be let into the kingdom. They were the kind of storm-tossed waters that the *Demeter's* crew would've struggled to cross, as they'd transported the sleeping Vampire Lord in their hull. It was the gargling spit in the back of a giant's throat, being projectile spat over the red-tile rooftops of the town, threatening to topple those that had lived closest to the beach, otherwise referred to as the *Crescent Apartments*. Frightened seals with kind-dog eyes would flea in terror from the safety of their colonies, in search of calmer seas. The skies would boom in an orchestra of thunder.

When the sea had finally settled, the morning after, locals would emerge from their houses to find their gardens raped and pillaged by the angry waters. Gnomes smashed, plant pot soil scattered, fences knocked down. The washing lines would be speckled with water droplets that would fling into the air like mass bungee jumpers when boinged. But with the sea returning to its sedated state, the Whitby folks would of course, always forgive it, how could they not? It had every right to blow off steam, to the odd-hissy fit, given that humanity had commercialised its shores. They accepted its moods and strops like understanding parents, it was a way of life.

This wasn't the cool, sunny, palm tree-style sea of LA. With its roller skaters, weed smoking hipsters, purpled tinged skies, boom-boxes and blonde surfer dudes. No. This was the sea where rough, smoke-smelling sailors taught their young sons to fish. It was where plastic bags could be spotted floating amongst the slurping of the waves, where chavvy teens would cycle and spit wearing tracksuits, where late night strolls would take place to reflect and to clear one's mind, where old married couples would spend their twilight years, a life by the sea being a life that they'd earned. This was an English sea. This was a Yorkshire Sea. And the Whitbians loved it because of this. It was home.

Whitby, had woken up.

At the Whitby station, a little after 9:05am, a three-carriage train from Middlesbrough pulled onto platform 1. It only had two platforms. From the train, two people, a girl and a boy alighted, and then made their way out. They stepped through a stone arch at the station entrance. It took them out onto the harbour front with a perfect view of the abbey, and they were greeted by a congregation of hungry seagulls. The town was quiet that morning. The pair, who were very tired from their travelling, strolled past a local *Weatherspoon's*, a hotel, and the barricades of the public toilets, the ones that had rather outrageously required 10p per pee for entry. It wasn't long before they'd reached the Whitby bus stops, and not long after that, until they'd boarded the X3 Arriva, scheduled to depart at 9:23am, on the dot. They were the only ones on board.

The bus swayed from left to right as it passed the local school, a touchstone that had told them that they were leaving Whitby behind. Instead, the pair found themselves travelling through tiny, remote villages, so obscure that even the most seasoned of Yorkshire pub quiz players would've struggled to have named them. Easy-going pensioners sat in deck chairs with cups of tea in their front gardens, some watered plants, and others cleaned their cars. The ocean occasionally revealed itself in brilliant flashes of bright blue and white like a strobe, between the intermittent coverage of the trees. But the teasing soon ended as the pair descended a hill and the forests cut short, laying bare the shore that their leaves had been concealing.

'We're here' said Ted, as the bus parked up to the left. The pair departed with a 'thank you' to their driver.

He was back.

In a far less tranquil setting, 48 hours prior, Billy had fired his pistol. He had triumphed over the voice of his mother and had aimed his bullet straight at Marcus, in an attempt to try and stop him from killing Rose and Ted. He of course, had missed, instead smashing one of Margery Geller's favourite pieces of fine China into tiny chips, the kind that she only ever took down at Christmas. The bullet had been deafeningly loud in the closeness of the farms kitchen, leaving a debilitating ringing in the ears of both Geller and his prisoners. But once the murderer had recovered, and unlike Margery's China, had managed piece together a picture of what had just happened, he had raised his axe to Billy instead. It was clear that his dark attempts to recruit a violent apprentice into his ranks had failed, and so Geller, like a dejected scientist disposing of a tray of test samples, had decided to do away with his disappointing experiment, by chopping the janitor into bite-sized pieces. For someone with such blue eyes, Geller sure was seeing a hell of a lot of red. At the sight of him approaching, axe-in hand, with an intention that surely wasn't to cut raw firewood, Billy had dropped his handgun to the floor and screamed. The sharp metal axe would've had no trouble slicing straight through the trembling wimp. Geller fantasised about stringing his body to a spit-roast like a pig, about stuffing an oversized cooking apple into his tiny jaw and waiting for him to become fit for consumption.

Before Geller's second murder of the night could've been carried out though, Henry Simmons had burst into the room through the kitchen window. He was a far better shot than Billy. He fired three bullets straight into Marcus. The first only slowed him down, penetrating his upper right shoulder and momentarily dazing him. Geller quickly shook it off, a wound that would've surely incapacitated a lesser-built man, and then carried straight on towards Billy and the officer, hoping to swipe both of their heads clean off in one foul swing. Henry fired a second and then a third time, once to the stomach, and then another to the leg. And then Geller toppled to the ground with an agonising roar, only narrowly missing Terrence. The room went quiet.

It had almost felt too easy to Henry, not quite right that it been a man-made weapon that had brought down the legendary Marcus Geller. A silver bullet, or perhaps a crucifix and a stick of garlic would've been more fitting, the man after all, had become so infamously evil that ending his reign of terror with three shots to the torso had seemed almost anti-climactic. But this was real life, Marcus wasn't a monster or a werewolf, he was just a man. A sick and twisted and fucked-up man, yes, but a man never the less. And in real life, away from the TV shows and the movies and the stories, no matter how frightening Marcus's reputation had painted him out to be, that's all the bad guys ever ended up being, men. And bullets beat men like rock beats scissors.

'NOW!' commanded Simmons into his pocket radio. In what felt like a matter of seconds the kitchen was flooded with policemen and paramedics. Officers untied the prisoner's ropes and immediately began shuttling them outside into the cool night air of the farmyard, where open ambulances had been waiting to provide emergency medical assistance. By God, did Ted and Rose need it.

Henry though, moved straight to Geller. He'd kicked away the fire-axe from his lifeless body and then slowly held up his fingers to the side of his neck, exercising extreme caution. Though the others in the room had all breathed easy knowing that Marcus had finally been bested, Simmons had known all too well that the unexpected should've always been expected in the case of Geller. If the night were to have taken another deadly twist, it would've been courtesy of him. Detecting a faint pulse, he ordered three armed officers to lift the giant onto a stretcher, however the sheer weight of the killer had ended up requiring five. The ambulance carrying Marcus had departed sooner even than those carrying the injured survivors. Though nothing would've pleased Henry more than to have watched the man bleed out on the farmyard kitchen, he was adamant that if there had even been a chance, however remote, that Marcus might've pulled through, then he had to take it. He wasn't allowed the sweet release of death, not for what he'd done, that would've been the easy way out. A ruthless new jury pool was what he deserved.

'Don't you die you bastard' Henry had said through gritted teeth, as he'd sat beside the silent ogre in the back of the ambulance, speeding towards Middlesbrough hospital with blue lights blaring. But Henry's prayers were to no avail. The coroner's report delivered the day after clearly stated:

'Marcus Geller, died of blood loss and organ failure in hospital transit', *'as of 6:57am'.*

The beast was slain. There were no menacing famous last words, no shocking revelations as one might've expected from a villains final moments, only one concluding puff of breath, before Geller had gently slipped away into the morning light, his cold blue eyes gazing up from his blood covered gurney. A shake of the paramedic's head was all that Henry had needed to see to know that it was over. He slumped back against the doors of the speeding ambulance and sighed. Perhaps though, this had been for the best. Geller was gone, and the world was a better place for it, he couldn't hurt anybody ever again.

Those who might say that they were disappointed with the straight-forwardness of Geller's demise, may find this chilling morsel of information slightly more satisfying. Henry had passed his right hand over Geller's ice blue eyes when he'd died, shutting them for good, before his corpse had arrived at the hospital morgue. However, or so the tale goes, the mortician from the hospital, when summoned to inspect the remains, later reported finding Geller's eyes wide open again. The eyes were empty, cold and unblinking, just as they had been when Marcus had been alive. Needless to say, the terrified mortician had quickly sealed the body away on its metal slab and locked the tomb for good. Not only that though, but ever since that night many of the East Yorkshire locals have often told stories of seeing a huge, ghostly figure walking slowly across the Moors, wandering in the distance, somewhere between Pickering and Haworth.

'It had blue eyes', the young children would say, 'such cold, blue eyes...'

'It is with great relief, that we are able to tell you tonight, that Marcus Geller, has been killed' said the well-dressed reporters of the news outlets, each reporting *Live!* from the farmyards muddy front, and all of them secretly worrying about their expensive shoes and designer trousers being ruined. But one detail that had slowly trickled into their newscasts, keeping the watching public on the edges of their seats and thickening an already unforgettable plot with a much-needed heroic angle, was this; '*Local Janitor helped defeat serial killer!*'

Word had spread of Billy's stand against Marcus, his following him through the woods and then the firing of the gun that had helped the police to finally bring the killer to justice. If there's one thing that the British public love more than a scandal, it's an underdog, and Billy fit that bill. When Billy finally emerged from the back of one of the stationary ambulances outside the farm, a blanket draped around his shoulders, the waiting crowd of police officers, reporters and Yorkshire locals had all erupted with a thunderous applause. Not used to such positive attention, Billy had at first been confused. Was this a joke? A hoax? But no, the standing ovation had lasted for longer than that of the audience of an art-house film at the *Cannes film festival*, and things were only going to get better for Billy.

Upon his return to work at the *O'Nowhere*, after a paid leave of absence that had allowed him the time that he'd needed to recover, as well as to take part in numerous tabloid interviews that had labelled him a 'hero', things were very different. He was greeted with handshakes, hugs, smiles, and cheers from the co-workers that used to ignore him. No longer did they laugh and mock and bully, now the *O'Nowhere* staff held nothing but respect and admiration for the wiry caretaker, something that, in the months to come, would slowly but surely work it's wonders on Billy's confidence. All that, as well a promotion from the *O'Nowhere's* new manager (*Perkins had subsequently been fired by the board*) to 'Head Groundskeeper', and it was safe to say that things were definitely changing for Billy. In fact, his first official act as the new head of his department was to organise and then to oversee the fixing of the hole in the wall on the *O'Nowhere's* eastern side. Oh, and as for that mother of his...

...Billy's dramatic rise in salary had meant that he had finally been able to move out and rent a place of his own. Whenever he *did* visit his Mum back home though, his newfound sense of self-worth had meant that he'd certainly had no trouble putting her in her place anymore....

Billy was considered a hero, a title he was worthy of, not only to the Yorkshire folk, but also to Inspector Henry Simmons, albeit, for perhaps more private reasons. When Simmons had returned home to his wife and daughter after the longest shift of his life, and after he'd held them so tightly and closely that he'd thought that he'd might never let go, the man hadn't gone about doing what one might've expected from him. He didn't begin writing his retirement letter, like he'd told himself he would, after returning to work from his paid leave of absence. Nor did he begin writing it once he'd completed all of the required, painfully dull paperwork from the Geller case. Instead, when the new week had rolled around, and the dust from the *O'Nowhere* incident had begun to settle, he'd returned to work at the Pickering police station as though it had been any other average Monday. Retirement wouldn't come for Henry, not for a very, very long time.

When Henry had witnessed Billy resist Geller's seduction, and then fire at him to try and rescue his friends, a light had been switched on inside of him. It was a bright light, a burning light, one that up until that moment, had been extinguished. It had been the entire reason behind why Henry had become a police officer in the first place, the lesson that his Father had taught to him since boyhood. It was the lesson that there was *good* in the world, and that though sometimes it might have been hard to find, and though sometimes it would often hide and appear as though it didn't exist at all, it was there, and it was a *good* that was worth fighting for. When the world seemed to be the darkest and most hopeless of places, and every sense of humanity had been stripped bare, there it would be, the *good*, revealing itself within the most unlikely of places. It was this endless, desperate quest, like priests searching for God and astronauts looking to the stars, this longing search for the goodness in the world, which had gotten Simmons out of bed every morning. It was the force that had inspired him to keep on going when he could see nothing but shadows and the worst in people. Because when he'd found it, that rare speck of hope, well, then that would've made everything worth it again. He'd forgotten it for a long time now, lost touch with the *good*, but in Billy that night he'd seen it again, and that had kept his fingers at bay from typewriting his letter of resignation.

Whenever he'd visit his Father's grave, something that he'd always try to get around to doing at least once a month, now he'd smile. He'd smile because he finally understood, the old bastard had passed it down to him. He'd inherited the condition, the clawing need to find kindness in the world no matter how hard it tried to hide. Maybe the two of them weren't so different after all...he *was* a Simmons, through and through.

In other good news, shortly after Geller's demise, police officers had stumbled across none other than the missing Mr. Steven M. Brooks and sixty-two year old Simon Berkley, both safe and sound and very much alive. The pair had been tied up inside of a hidden cave, a rock formation that had been tucked away behind a thrush of forestry, around mid-way up a cliff face, on the Moors. Geller had knocked them both unconscious and then dragged them in there prior to breaking into the *O'Nowhere*. Why Marcus hadn't chosen to slaughter the gentlemen though, had remained a mystery, but with the two of them very grateful and lucky to be alive, especially having heard the news about Smithy, they'd decided not to look their gift-horse in the mouth. Instead, they'd returned home to their wives, and kissed them and held them in ways that they hadn't for a great many years. Steven never drank again, and from then on out, Simon would aways make sure that he was home in time for tea whenever he'd walked the dog, as per his wife's strict orders. His furry companion licked and cried and snuggled his master like he never had before when the pair were reunited.

At last, the guests of the *O'Nowhere* were permitted to leave. Granted, the congestion of the car park had been a nightmare to navigate, but before long, an army of new cars, as well as the Megabus, had joined the flow of the motorway lanes and were driving off in their own separate directions, back home across England. Exhausted children fell asleep on backseats, their chubby faces pressed up against frosty, condensation covered windows and their snoring breath steaming up the glass. Fathers drove for miles and miles alongside truckers and early-bird commuters beneath the rising morning sun. Their eyes were heavy, but they fought the urge to pull into the passing service stations for coffee. They'd made that mistake before. Part of them never wanted to step foot inside of a pit stop ever again.

What was true though, was that the temporary memories that they'd all made at the *O'Nowhere* had already begun to fade. The finite friendships, fleeting moments and isolated panics, all of them would continue to dim throughout the years until they had become nothing more than a '*hey, remember when...*' They had happened in the station, and that's where they would stay. The travellers had come together like white blood cells repairing a wound, only to break apart again, and to carry on with their lives. And in that sense, that cold night of terror at the *O'Nowhere* service station, hadn't been so different to that of any other. It was, after all, only an in-between place.

It was on the fourth day, post-Geller, that Ted and Rose had made their way to Robin Hoods Bay. The pair had been admitted straight to Pickering Hospital upon their rescue to receive immediate emergency treatment. Rose had sustained contusions and heavy bruising to her face, but luckily had managed to escape Marcus's beatings without a broken jaw. Ted hadn't gotten off quite so lightly. The lacerations to his cheeks and mouth had required stitches and his broken ribs had meant that he'd have to wear a chest brace for at least two months after the attack. But the doctors assured both him, and Rose, that they would make a full recovery, prefacing it with a; 'you're extremely lucky Billy fired that gun when he did...' Their bodies healing processes would be sore and slow and ugly, but they'd get there eventually, and day by day they grew in strength and health.

Once the laborious police interviews had been taken care of, something that Henry Simmons had insisted on conducting himself, Ted and Rose had made their way back to her parents' house in Malton for shelter. They'd kindly offered to put Ted up for as long as he'd needed until he'd gotten better. From there, he'd called his own mother back in Birmingham, who all the time had been going out of her mind with worry. He assured her that everything was fine and that he'd be back home soon, but that he'd just had some unfinished business in Yorkshire to tie up first. It had probably been for the best that his Mother hadn't seen him, given the gruesome state that his torn up face was in.

Ted liked living with Rose and her family a lot. They were very kind to him, doting on him hand and foot with whatever he'd needed. Ted began to feel guilty for all the attention that they were giving to him. There were warm baths, hot meals in bed, clean linen and fresh pyjamas every day. They had kind smiles, Rose's parents, northern smiles. The pair had spent the days sat drinking hot chocolate with whipped cream and marshmallows, and watching horror movies under blankets from the comfort of the sitting room. Where Rose lived there was an abundance of greenery, so when the injured twosome weren't gorging on treats and watching flicks, they would go for long walks with Rose's dog through the cow fields and forests. Rose's mum had insisted that the fresh air would do their wounds 'the world of good'.

On the fourth morning though, when Rose had awoken to find Ted standing in the garden looking out over the Moors, with a hot cup of coffee in his hand, she had known that it had been time for him to go. It was time for him to find his father.

'It's this way' said Ted, pointing towards the town.

'You know, for someone who hasn't been here for over a decade, you sure do know your way around' replied Rose, following.

'I know right...it's weird. I thought I would've forgotten. But it's almost like I'd come here yesterday.'

Ted led Rose past the infamous *Victoria Hotel*, with its garden and veranda that overlooked the coast. It had been the location where thespian extraordinaire Daniel Day-Lewis had shot scenes for his final ever movie, *Phantom Thread*. With the hour still being early, inside the hotel rooms, lovers had snuggled each other naked beneath the covers of their king sized beds, their alarms set for 9 as not to miss the 10:30am cut off for breakfasts. The honeymoon suite too, on the top floor, had been occupied. It was by a newly engaged couple, who'd spent the morning making love and then drinking earl grey on the *Victoria's* only balcony.

Rose and Ted descended a steep hill into the town, nice enough on the way down but a bitch to climb back up again. They passed *Bertie's* gift shop to their right, a rustic emporium that stocked fishermen jumpers, raincoats, beard oils and more. Aside from that though, the Bay was lacking in the abundance of gift shops that attracted guests to Whitby. It hadn't needed them. Robin Hood's town was different, peaceful, tranquil, quiet, and these traits alone drew in tourists and persuaded them to fork out the extortionate price of an Arriva bus ticket from the train station. The streets were silent that morning, though Whitby had woken up, her wiser, older sister was still fast asleep. Ted and Rose were the only souls around.

'Oh man, it's so beautiful, isn't it Ted? You weren't wrong. I can't believe I've never seen this place before. I can't imagine what it must've been like to live here, you were so lucky. It must feel amazing to be back' said Rose, drinking in the sights that the bay had to offer. Hers was a reaction common to all first-timers visiting the town. Ted though, seemed distracted.

'Huh?'

'Aren't you listening? I said it must feel amazing to be back home...Ted? Are you okay? What's up?' she asked, taking notice of Ted's very un-Ted-like state.

'What? Yeah...yeah no I'm fine...it's this way I think' he replied, before carrying on. Confused at his lack of excitement, Rose followed, until eventually Ted stopped outside a small cottage with a duck egg-blue door, a little away from the shoreline.

'This is it, the house, this is where your Dad lives, isn't it? Where you grew up, Ted', said Rose. The two stood still, side by side, staring at the thatch-roofed building. Rose expected that Ted was merely overwhelmed with memories and nostalgia, and it was this that had been the rationale behind his anxious, elsewhere nature. But when he'd remained standing, instead of rushing up to the cottage door and banging on its golden knocker, she had begun to suspect that something else was afoot.

Truth be told, she had been dreading their trip to Whitby, secretly hoping that Ted would've abandoned the idea of searching for his Father completely. But that had been a long shot. She couldn't shake the feeling that her friend, after all this time, would've only been disappointed with what he found there waiting for him. His Mother after all, *had* to have had a good enough reason to have migrated to the south and to have taken him away from his Father at such a young age. '*Apparently he'd had a "drinking problem" and he was a "deadbeat". What horse manure.*' And of course, nothing had stopped his Father from reaching out to *him* for the entire past decade that he had been gone, so why hadn't he?

Luckily though, she was spared the sadness of having to see her friend, her close friend, heartbroken.

'You know, after…everything…Inspector Simmons gave me a little insight into Geller's upbringing', Ted finally spoke.

'Yeah?' replied Rose.

'Yeah. Henry told me that he was a victim of years of abuse, beatings at the hands of his Dad when he was just a kid, really bad apparently. I guess what he said, back in the farms kitchen, about just being "born evil", wasn't quite true after all.'

'I guess not', replied Rose over the sounds of seagull song, 'in a weird way, that brings me a little comfort'.

Ted continued, now saying what it was that he'd really wanted to get off his chest.

'I've been thinking a lot about what *you* said too…back at the farm'.

'Erm…"help us? We're going to die?" replied Rose. The salt in the air was like balm to her bruises, as was it, to Ted's scars.

'No silly, I meant when you said, "it's okay to be lost".

'Ah yeah, that.'

Ted seemed unmoved by the charm and the beauty of the townhouses and scenery around him, like an art critic writing a poor review of a collection. Instead he remained still, hands in his pockets as he spoke.

'You were right. I think...I've spent so long dreaming of coming back here, that now that I am, I kinda just feel sort of...'

'What?'

'Nothing.' He looked at Rose then, despite his long-lost father's home being a mere five-something steps away.

'I think all along, this whole time, it was more about the getting here, more about the journey than the actual destination. The truth is, I don't think I ever really cared that much about coming here at all, I just wanted to run away, to be moving *somewhere*.'

Rose nodded. The cold spring air made her eyes water if she went without blinking for too long. 'Look Ted, if you want to go in, I want you to know that whatever you find in there, I'll be here for you.'

Ted smiled and looked out to sea, it was a different kind of smile to ones that he'd smiled before. It wasn't the childish grin that he'd had back when he'd booked his Megabus tickets to Middlesbrough, nor had it been the one when he'd delivered Geller his successfully stolen feast. It was the kind of fond smile that one often has when reflecting on one's former self, picturing ourselves as teens and hardly believing it to be the same person, when the worries and fears that we'd had seemed as important as the end of the world. It was a smile of finally understanding, a smile contentment, a smile of growing up.

'Hey, how's about we get out of here?' he asked with ease, like they were leaving a boring dinner party.

'But, you've come all this way Ted? Don't you want to...?'

'Nah.' he replied, still smiling. 'Robin Hoods Bay will always be here, so will my Dad, there's no rush. I think it's time to stop running. Don't you?' He turned to go.

'But, what will you do now?' Rose asked, stopping him with a hand to his shoulder. Her dyed-red hair had begun to fade back to her natural blonde colour. She'd washed it out when the two of them had been recovering at her parents' house in Malton. It suited her more.

'I dunno'. Ted just shrugged, like he hadn't a care in the world.

'I don't know what I'll do either...' Rose admitted, 'it's scary isn't it?'

'Yep. It is. But hey, who cares? Wherever I go or whatever I end up doing next, at least I'll have fun figuring myself out along the way. We're exactly where we're supposed to be, right?'

'Right.'

Ted held Rose's hand then, and she smiled too. And just like that, the two of them surrendered. They surrendered to the madness of life, to the uncertainty, to the not-knowing, to the being lost.

'Besides, call me crazy, but I actually kinda, sorta miss Birmingham', Ted joked.

'Wow. Maybe you need to go back to the hospital, it sounds like the doctors missed something wrong with your brain...' Rose replied.

But then, like a Trojan-horse infiltrating the sincerity of the moment, Ted's mind concocted a roguish idea.

'Hey loser, how's about a dip?'

Rose's face dropped, she suddenly began shaking her head frantically.

'No.'

'C'mon.....' he teased back, gesturing towards the liquid-metal looking ocean behind him.

'No way in hell Ted. It's the start of April...it's gonna be freezing...'

'Oh I'm sorry, I didn't realise you were scared.'

'I'm not scared. I'm most certainly not scared. I just don't like swimming in oceans that rival the Polar ice-caps in temperature, so no, I will most definitely not be "taking a dip"'. Rose crossed her arms defiantly and refused to move.

'Nope. It definitely sounds like you're scared to me Rose. What's wrong? Don't wanna ruin your makeup? Aww.'

'Ted, I'm not joking around here. I haven't got my swimming costume or anything...and even if I did I-'

Rose screamed as Ted kicked up a puddle of ice-cold sea water all over the unsuspecting blonde.

'TED!!!'

He began laughing uncontrollably, whilst Rose shivered beside him in drenched clothes.

'Oh you're soooooo in for it now. That does it!'

Ted immediately took off and ran towards the sea with Rose in pursuit, chasing right behind him.

'Catch me if you can, sucker!' he cried joyfully, never looking back.

She no longer bothered trying to pretend to be angry, instead Rose laughed freely as she ran, following Ted, fully-clothed, into the shallow waves of the ocean, drowning her tights and skirt along with her. The two splashed playfully, using their hands and feet to fire water-torpedoes at full force into each other, until they were both completely soaked from head to toe. Not once did they think about the terrifying future, only about the now. And around them, the oceans great heft was thinned out by the gentle lapping of the waves, like Fathers hushing their sons to sleep, after telling them a very, scary story.

THE END.

Printed in Great Britain
by Amazon